BRIDE OF THE RIVER

BRIDE OF THE RIVER

RIVER

LAURA HARRIS

THOMAS Y. CROWELL COMPANY   NEW YORK

c. 2

HR

BRIDE OF THE RIVER

A pampered New Orleans belle steps into the harsh life of the river as the bride of a riverboat man. Her problems include an infatuated brother-in-law, a hostile mother-in-law and the misgivings of the townspeople. Set prior to the CivilWar.

CHAPTER I

IN THE RUTLAND CARRIAGE RATTLING OVER NEW ORLEANS' NEWLY laid cobblestones on "the master street of the world" sat Mary Marie and Papa, their white faces vis-à-vis to the black ones of their servants Mammy Fay and Julee. The coachman, Caesar, had had the good sense to lay back the top of the carriage on this fine October day in 1837.

Actually, Mary Marie didn't need her parasol, but it was a small fashionable new one, neatly hinged to be tipped coquettishly, and so added to the splendid picture of an elegant young lady of fashion being escorted by her parent and servants from their plantation outside New Orleans to a handsome river steamboat, *The Rising Sun*, which would sail at three o'clock.

New Orleans was a city of drays. The street was crammed with drays. Their speed set the pace—sometimes slow, sometimes breathtakingly fast for the rough road. Caesar had to stay in line; to pull out would be dangerous. They might tangle with a load of cotton and get thrown into a struggling heap—all of them.

What a racket the rims of the wheels made on the cobblestones. It made the very drums of her ears ache, conversation all but impossible. Nobody but Julee wanted to talk anyway, certainly not Papa nor Mammy Fay. My! What a relief it would be when she got away.

Two mules, running tandem, swept by, their heavy dray swaying clattering after them. It swung and barely missed a brush with the carriage. A street vendor, his wares in a cloth-covered basket, jumped back—cursed. Mule drivers whooped and swore. Caesar,

1

stoutly braced on his box, the carriage horses' reins tightly held, answered curse for curse. They sped on.

Mary Marie clung to the side of the open carriage and hoped they wouldn't upset and be flung to the cobblestones. Papa made no move to protect her. Mammy Fay put her strong black hand on Julee's knee to help hold her in her seat.

The pace of the vehicles slowed down. A mule brought to a sudden halt beside the open carriage reared, his hooves pawing the air above Mary Marie. She sucked in her breath—those awful sharp, shining shoes—one strike on the head! The driver's whip whistled about the mule's ears and Mary Marie was vaguely aware of frightened screams. The hooves came down—on cobblestones.

Shaking, she turned toward Papa's cold voice, "Can't you keep the French in you controlled? Ladies don't scream!" She hadn't known until then that the screams were her own.

As they approached the boat landing, which curved for miles with the river, Mary Marie suddenly felt small and alone. She wished she had some family going with her on *The Rising Sun*. Papa should try visiting Uncle Philip and Aunt Lucinda at Quercus Grove just once. He'd find out how good it felt to have kinfolk glad to see you. It would warm Papa.

"I wish you would come with me, Papa," she said.

"Why ever should I?" he asked. "Sleep cramped on a shelf, eat with a lot of boors. No thank you."

Mary Marie subsided into silence. Maybe it was better not to urge Papa to come along. He had a way of spoiling things. Maybe it was silly of her to think she could ever get close to him, understand him, be a companion to him, make him a little warm and happy. It wouldn't matter to him if she went far away and he never saw her again. But where could she go if she didn't marry that old Mr. Tazewell, as Papa wanted her to? He didn't care who she married or whether she were happy or not as long as he got rid of her.

She raised her head with an arrogant toss—and there was *The Rising Sun!* Oh! Captain Cleve must be very proud of his new boat. What a beauty! A great gold burst of a sun swung between her tall chimneys, which were crowned with cut filigree oak leaves. She was a splendid side wheeler. On each paddle house in strong reds and yellows were other great bursts of rays, suns newly risen over greener hills than God had ever made. Below the bursts printed in bold black and gold letters on the bluest river was her name—*The Rising Sun.*

Bare black feet shuffled in rhythm across the gangplank.

> *"Up sack! You gone!*
> *Up sack! You gone!*
> *N'Yaulins niggers ain't got no sense.*
> *Up sack! You gone!"*

The boat's mate, black snake whip in hand—just in case—bossed and tallied the work of the Negro gang laden with heavy sacks of coffee.

"Whoa!" Caesar stopped the carriage at the sign of the blue diamond pennant fluttering from a pyramid of cotton bales in front of *The Rising Sun.*

"Drive over to the marquee, Caesar," Papa ordered. "Nobody wants to walk or stand in this blasted sun."

Caesar edged the carriage through the crowd milling before the gangplank. Children screamed, dragged along by flurried mamas and black nurses; men lifted bandboxes to their shoulders to avoid the crush, carpet bags banged knees. Angry glances were cast at the Rutland carriage.

How like Papa, Mary Marie thought, to consider his own comfort even if it jeopardized the safety of others. Impatience with her father welled within her. When he offered her his hand to assist her from the carriage she preoccupied herself with her skirts so she wouldn't have to take it, and stepped down unaided. When she looked at him his lips twitched, his supercilious eyes disdainful, as he turned to Captain Cleve of *The Rising Sun.*

In the shade of a pitched tarpaulin, Captain Cleve finished talking to one of his clerks, who sat at a table checking papers, and turned to the tall young man beside him. He had to reach up to clap a hand on the man's shoulder, "There you are! All fixed up! Glad to have you totin' wood for us, my lad!"

"Thank you sir," said the young man. He wore heavy boots, homespun shirt open on a tanned skin. He looked more like an Indian than a white man except for his hatless curly hair, burned white by the sun. It was something about the proud way he stood that made one conscious of the strong erect body within the coarse loose clothing.

"Good evening, Captain Cleve," said Papa.

"Mr. Rutland! Howdy sir!" cried the captain with outstretched hand. He swept his gray plug hat across the gold-plated buttons of his long-skirted coat, made of the very best blue broadcloth, and bowed deeply to Mary Marie. "Figgered you were comin' this trip when I seen your young 'log cabins' come aboard. Tell me, what you got in them trunks besides clothes?"

Mary Marie came erect from her curtsy to Captain Cleve, laughed brightly, fluttered her eyelashes and said gayly "Secrets!"

She tilted her parasol just enough to cut off the view of her face from the young man who still stood nearby. Self-consciously Mary Marie knew he hadn't taken his eyes off her from the moment he had first seen her.

At this point Captain Cleve asked Papa if he could be of any service to him in the Queen City, Cincinnati. Papa said no, not this trip, but that he hoped that the captain would be solicitous of his daughter's welfare while aboard. This trip she was trying her wings alone, except, of course, for her young servant, Julee.

"An honor, sir," said the captain, swinging his coattails in another bow. "Like to have you folks meet a young friend of mine. Mr. Rutland, sir, meet Levi Blaisdell from Indiana. An' you two young folks who'll be traveling with me, make each other's acquaintance."

"Mister Captain, sir!" The words were gasped by worrying, fussing old Mammy Fay, who had been standing with Julee and Caesar —a respectful distance behind their master and his daughter. Only Mary Marie realized that Mammy Fay objected to the introduction. No one paid any attention to the old Negro.

Papa gave Levi Blaisdell a brief nod, didn't bother even to touch his high silk hat, and ignored the young man's extended hand— which was quickly withdrawn.

Levi turned to Mary Marie, his eyes looked straight into hers, "I'm mightily pleased to make *your* acquaintance."

His voice! Oh God in heaven, his voice! It picked her up and held her quivering in mid-air. Nothing in Papa's library, not even Sir Walter Scott's books, had prepared her for this great upsurge of feeling. She bent her knees in a curtsy and felt at once a fool. She came erect and looked up into his face, "And I . . . I . . . I am pleased to make yours."

4

"Now that's fine," said Captain Cleve. He gave Mary Marie the slightest of winks. "Levi, here, can keep an eye on you when I'm busy. 'Course Levi aims to earn his way loadin' wood for the boat. Most broadhorn men do." Captain Cleve laughed. "Two kinds of men, flatboat men, either they lose everything they make in New Orleans and can't buy a berth, or like this young feller—too stingy. When this young feller earns a dollar, it's got home."

"I've changed my mind, Captain Cleve. You've just lost a wood-man. I'm off to buy a berth," Levi said.

"Might as well take the young lady's bandbox in that case. Show the folks up to my settin' room, Levi. You'll come aboard, Mr. Rut-land, sir? Plenty of folks aboard eatin' dinner, admire to have you sample the 'que-seen' of *The Rising Sun.*"

But Papa said, no thank you and, as he had pressing business in New Orleans to attend to, he would make his adieus; Caesar had got down his mistress' boxes and reported everything was aboard. Papa shook hands with Captain Cleve.

"Master Rutland—!" Mammy Fay stepped before him.

Papa's face, cold—froze.

Mammy Fay slowly turned to Mary Marie and clasped her tightly in long black silk arms and whispered, "Remember all I tell you—!"

"Careful, you're crushing my sleeves, clumsy," said Mary Marie. She wished to goodness Mammy Fay would cry and get it over. That would be easier to endure than her everlasting long suffering patience.

Mammy Fay laid a strong black hand on Julee's shoulder, "You be a good girl, too," she commanded.

Papa made the briefest gesture of embrace to Mary Marie. In farewell he said he hoped she found her uncle and aunt in good health, to give them his kind regards, and, then added, with a smirk, "my blessings, Daughter, on your task of leading Creighton Tazewell in the right direction."

Papa could be *mean.* Marry, marry! was that all a girl could do? And bringing it up in front of strangers! Blast Aunt Lucinda, Mammy Fay, Papa. Blast the lot of them!

"Come along, Julee," Mary Marie ordered. She angled her par-asol to hide her face which felt so hot it must be beet-root red. She bit her lips and fought the tears and turned blindly toward *The Rising Sun.*

5

"I say, you want to watch where you're going," said Levi Blaisdell.

Why, oh why, did she have to stumble right at the gangplank? And how dare this clout hold her elbow to guide her over the rough boards? Why did he have to be a flatboatman, a brigand, a pirate, dressed in clothes no better than those worn by field hands?

"You better put down your pert little umbrella before you poke my eye out, miss."

The insolent wretch! She lowered the parasol and snapped it shut. Her eyes glared at the upper deck of *The Rising Sun*.

"You know, you're as cute as a pair of little red shoes."

She made no answer to that but kept right on up the forecastle companionway hoping to lose him in the mass of passengers struggling up the stairs.

"Bet you're even sweet, when you aren't mad at your gov'nor and black nurse." The voice bent close to her ear, "Who's this Creighton Tazewell your father's talking about?"

"None of your business." Oh! He had provoked words from her when she'd vowed she'd never, never speak to him.

He bent closer, "Got a notion he might be."

"Might be what?"

"My business."

Before Mary Marie could think of a proper retort, he had turned on his heel and left her.

At sailing time, three o'clock that afternoon, on board Captain Cleve's "opulent new craft," Mary Marie stood with Julee on the hurricane deck beneath the boat's fluttering flag, a blazing rising sun. On the staff astern, the American flag with its twenty-seven white stars was run up. The offland breeze rolled the great dark columns of smoke, which rose from two tall smoke stacks, into huge black clouds to hang over the wide river.

"All dat ain't a-goin', please to git asho'," shouted a steward ringing a brass handbell high over his head as he pushed his way through the crowds milling on the decks below.

There was the usual last-minute flurry—a man running across the levee hindered by his heavy carpetbag, risking his life dodging between drays, his wife struggling after, waving her reticule commanding the boat to wait. Bells rang, the stage plank was pulled in, hawsers were freed from levee stanchions, hauled aboard and

6

coiled; all under the swearing, commanding directions of the boat's mate.

The boat shuddered and gathered herself together from the shock of the first turns of her two great side wheels. She slipped away from her berth between two other packets so close one could have stepped from guard rail to guard rail. She backed off, well out into the wide river, bells ordered her to turn her nose upstream, she collected herself again, straightened and gathered strength to carry her load against the current of the mighty river.

A roaring cheer for *The Rising Sun,* loose at last from New Orleans, came from the men massed on the forecastle below. The boat stood proudly up-river, for the northern Queen City, Cincinnati, and way-points. Mary Marie on the upper deck looked down upon these men, firemen, deckhands, and flatboat men—the latter working their passage by wooding the boat.

Common men! One of them, the man called Levi Blaisdell, leaped to the capstan, waved his hat in her direction, laughed, reached into his pocket and held up a coin for her to see before he flipped it over his left shoulder into midstream. The other men turned up their faces, following his glance, and seeing Mary Marie let out another mighty roar.

It was frightening, and how dared he! Call attention to her, a fine lady! "Come Julee," she commanded the young Negro and led the way below.

To get to their stateroom, they had to walk the length of the main salon, for, of course, Captain Cleve had assigned her the best and safest stateroom in the stern of the boat. Mary Marie could remember when boats didn't have staterooms, only a section at the rear of a long deck curtained off for ladies. The most striking thing about Captain Cleve's new boat, though, was how this main deck sloped toward the middle. She had to walk downhill and up again to get to her stateroom. Yes, indeed, Captain Cleve's new boat had style. Anyone with half an eye could see that a new style of steamboat was coming in fashion!

Mary Marie's daintily gloved hand lifted her skirt slightly and exposed the tips of her black-beaded slippers as she swept grandly along the salon. Her costume designed by Mammy Fay with the help of Mr. Godey as a Toilette de Longchamps was not too elegant for travel on so handsome a boat. The extravagant large sleeves of last year were going out, the tops of the sleeves of her

7

green mantle were "middlin' tight," its cape of entirely new form trimmed with black lace. Best of all was her new bonnet bought only recently in New Orleans, the very latest thing from Paris— Peau de Soie—front deep, crown drooping, wide ribbon trimming very full, a bunch of flowers on the left side. Mammy Fay had insisted it looked particularly well with the new pink rinse on Mary Marie's reddish hair. Mammy Fay said Mr. Godey's new fashion book was a great help—Young Miss could have as fashionable a turn-out as any Charleston or New Orleans belle. Young Miss could feel very sure of herself any place, any time.

With complete confidence Mary Marie swept past the empty chairs lined along the walls of the salon. She regretted that the passengers were on deck watching the departure of the boat. It was their loss not to see a young lady of fashion promenade. She paused before a narrow white door on which was lettered in gold the word, "Georgia." A fine Southern state—Georgia—not a horrid Western state like Indiana with its broadhorns carrying stinking hides. No Levi Blaisdells in Georgia!

"Don't stand there, stupid," she snapped at Julee, "Open the door." She stood aside so Julee could reach the door knob.

Inside the box called a stateroom it was close and stuffy. The shuttered door to the guard rail let in very little fresh air. The narrow berths—shelves, Papa called them—were on one side, one above the other. On the opposite side was a crude washstand with wash bowl and pitcher, beneath it was the chamber pot in full view. Above the washstand hung a small mirror, to either side were two straight chairs. There was hardly room for Mary Marie and Julee. Their skirts took up all the space.

Mary Marie sank onto a chair, "Fan me," she gasped.

"Yes Miss," said Julee, " 'cept I don't rightly know can I lay my hands on Old Mr. Palm Leaf. Everything so helter-skelter in this here place."

"Find the *Eau de Botot.* Do something, girl, before I faint."

"You can't faint in here Miss Mary Marie—no place stretch you out. Both these bed shelves full you' trappings, if I puts them on the floor I can't lifts you across them." Julee estimated the floor space. "If I lays you on the floor, got both doors blocked, can't git you no air. You better not faint in here, Miss Mary Marie."

Mary Marie jumped up from her chair, "Well, get these clothes off me before I suffocate."

8

"Yes Miss!"

At last Mary Marie sat again on the chair in her pantalettes and under-bodice and said that was better and the cool washcloth Julee slid over her face, shoulders and arms felt so good.

"Get the boxes and things off my berth, I want to rest."

"Where I put them?"

"Oh, for heaven's sake, how do I know? Put them in the top berth, on the floor, any place. Take a chair right outside the door and stay there, in case I want you. Now, get out!"

A slight river breeze came through the shuttered door. The afternoon must be almost over, soon it would be time to get up and dress for supper. Of course she would be seated with Captain Cleve, her protector.

All dat ain't a-goin', please to git asho'! She was on board, on her way. She wasn't goin' git asho', she—was—goin'—goin' with the pat-pat of the paddle wheels.

CHAPTER II

Mammy Fay's vile temper that morning before the sailing of *The Rising Sun* had been caused by Papa's discovering her smuggled boxes on the wagon. She had come back upstairs mad as an old wet hen, had clucked her tongue and scolded, "You Julee! Not dressed!"

Julee lay sprawled on her narrow slave bed fast asleep. She was Mary Marie's milk sister. Their mothers had come to their time together, so by custom Julee belonged to the white child—first as playmate, later as body servant. She lay almost naked, her quilt on the floor, her shift twisted under her arms. Her smooth round belly was centered with a whorl as pretty as a rare black shell. Mary Marie was jealous of Julee's belly button. When they were children Mammy Fay used to point out that Julee had the better granny knot because she herself had tied it, while a dirty old doctor man had tied an ugly bunch on Mary Marie.

Mammy Fay scolded, "And you, Miss! Dancing around in your bare feet. Onto the chaise."

Mammy Fay tucked a throw around Mary Marie's feet, pulled a dressing gown close about her shoulders and handed her a tiny cup of black, black coffee, strong and bitter to shock a sleepy body awake.

Oh! She just had to escape Mammy Fay's black thumb. She couldn't remember a single night in her entire life that Mammy Fay hadn't slept at her feet. Across the foot of the wide tester bed was Mammy Fay's, where she slept with her old knees drawn up because the slave bed was too short for her long thin body. At times

10

when Mammy Fay declared her bed hog-tied her, Mary Marie would tell her to go sleep elsewhere. She didn't want her in her room anymore. Mammy Fay said, "unn-nh! I stay. I got the right. I promise your mama."

So every morning, when long toots on the old ram's horn blown down in the quarters cracked the day wide open and ordered the field hands to fall out of bed, Mammy Fay would jump at the sound and crack her big toe against the footboard of her too-short bed. Mammy Fay slept in a bundle of clothes. She said it wouldn't do for her to sleep in a shimmy tail before her young Miss. In spite of sharing the same suite all these seventeen years, Mary Marie had never seen any of Mammy Fay's body except her face, hands, and feet.

She took a sip of the hot strong coffee now and felt somewhat better.

"You'll catch the river sickness," Mammy Fay grumbled. "Nobody to watch you—bare feet! You' too young to go to Quercus Grove—alone—on a steamboat."

"There's Julee."

"She young too. She only rattle, rattle her brains about, she don't use them."

"There's Captain Cleve."

Five years ago on that first trip to Quercus Grove, Uncle Philip's plantation up in Mississippi, they had traveled with Captain Cleve. He had taken a fancy to the "Rutland young-un." That first trip had been made because Aunt Lucinda said it was high time someone took a hand in Mary Marie's upbringing. If someone didn't she'd become so queer no man would be willing to marry her. For once Papa agreed with his brother's wife, so periodically there were visits to Quercus Grove. They always went on Captain Cleve's boat even if they had to wait in New Orleans several days.

"How's Master Captain goin' oversee you? He got to run his boat. How he know when some man let his eye roll over you?" Mammy Fay shook her head. "Unn-nh!"

Cornwallis, the parrot perched on the back of Mary Marie's chaise, mimicked Mammy Fay by shaking his whole body, no. He cackled a wicked laugh—and let go a squirt on the Aubusson rug. Mammy Fay scolded and cleaned it up, while Cornwallis weaved up and down the back of the chaise and upbraided Mammy Fay with parrot cat-calls, "What are you doing?"

"Hush you' mouth you—you Cornwallis!"

Mary Marie smiled into the tiny Sèvres light-blue coffee cup.

"Who chaperone you at Quercus Grove?" Mammy Fay demanded.

Mary Marie refilled her fragile cup from the silver coffee pot. "There's a proper mistress at Quercus Grove."

"Her!"

"Careful, Mammy Fay. She's kin." Poor Aunt Lucinda, somewhat beaten, unable to cope with climate, household and children, always complaining, had long ago drifted into an inefficient indolence.

"She not watch and listen. She get sleepy on the chaperone seat, she go to bed. Who protect you?"

Mary Marie poured coffee into the saucer and let Cornwallis drink it. She laughed and said, "Mr. Tazewell is a man of honor. Uncle Philip and Aunt Lucinda vouch for him; he's their neighbor. He wants to marry me. He wouldn't sully my youth." She shrugged her shoulders. "At least not until it is his."

Mammy Fay dropped to her knees beside the chaise. Her black eyes and her mouth were pleading. "Honey, let me go. Make you' papa send me with you. I keep that Master Creighton Tazewell 'way from you. Don't marry him, Sugar. He too old for you. You make you' mama mistake. I watch her lose her pretty happy look. That bride trip broke my heart. The live-long day I lurch, 'long side Caesar on the coach box, figgerin' what could I do. At night I climb down and see her pretty face pressed to the glass I wants to tell her we picks up our skirts and we runs back home to Ole Miss in Charleston. We stops places fit for the hawn-and-tail one. I tell you, it made this old colored Mammy cry to have to go downstairs and tell Mr. High and Haughty she was un-rigged—ready for *him*."

Mary Marie had heard too much, too many times. She thought if she heard any more she would scream. If only she could find some way to be free. She wasn't black but she was as fettered as a slave. What kind of a chance had she? She was good and tired of all these years, listening to Mammy Fay and her tales of past glories and her word pictures for the future. Both held too much Mammy Fay. Mammy Fay had an exaggerated idea of her position. After all she was nothing but a slave, in spite of the tradition that her grandmother was an imported princess of some preten-

12

sions. As proof there was her tall dignified carriage, the assured expression on her face.

But Mary Marie doubted if she wanted Mammy Fay, in her black dress, snowy apron and fichu, always standing behind her for the rest of her life. She longed to go far away from her nurse where she would not have to listen to her eternal, "be a credit to the family." She'd show her, she'd marry Mr. Creighton Tazewell and stay in Mississippi. She'd take Julee but tell Papa he could keep Mammy Fay. Let her run Papa for a while.

"I'll give my hand to Mr. Tazewell," Mary Marie proclaimed.

"I objects."

"You can't stop me. You've no right to say what I shall do." Her grammar had improved. When smaller she had stamped her foot and said, "You're none of the boss to me."

Mammy Fay got to her feet, stood over Mary Marie on the chaise. She held her long strong black palms before the girl. "These hands give me my right. Look at them!" Her voice compelled Mary Marie to look. "These hands tended you' mama in her cradle, they put her in her holy sprinklin' clothes, they togged her into her weddin' finery, they give her body the last wash, the last robing, these hands—look at them." Mammy Fay's voice made Mary Marie's own hand tremble on the coffee cup. "These hands, they give you you' birth greasin', you' first bath, they put you in you' holy sprinklin' clothes, they'll drape you' weddin' finery—they'll—" Mammy Fay couldn't recite the final robing. She said, "These hands give me my right."

"Oh! For heaven's sake, Mammy Fay!" said Mary Marie. "Stop it!"

"You do like I say, I makes you." Mammy Fay's long black hand crept behind her and pushed her full gathered white apron forward in order to slide her hand into the pocket of her black dress where her fingers squeaked dark hidden objects of conjure. Mary Marie goosepimpled as she always did in fear of Mammy Fay's power over her. She must break her spell. If only she could command the old woman to turn out her pocket but she didn't dare, to do so would take more courage than she could summon. Instead she screamed at her, "I'll do as I please, you black devil witch."

Mammy Fay set her face in sterner lines. "You mind you' manners, Missy Ma'am." And turned away.

The girl's whole body quickened, her muscles tightened, her

13

need was so great that she had to strike out. Her hand let fly the brittle coffee cup at Mammy Fay's head.

A shamed hush filled the room until Cornwallis, the parrot, broke it up by screaming, "What are you doing, Marie?"

Just then they heard Julee clashing the water cans outside the door.

Mammy Fay stopped, picked up the broken cup and ordered Julee, who staggered in with the water cans, "Attend!" Mammy Fay, head high, back broomstick-stiff, disappeared through the doorway.

Mary Marie was disgusted with herself and this sheltered life. She looked at the ducks flying over French marshes on the paper screen behind which Julee was clattering her cans. Even the birds had nothing to say—whether they were to be born in nests built among the reeds, against a wall, or in a tree.

"You' bath ready, Miss Mary Marie," Julee called.

Mary Marie sat on the bath stool and let Julee pin her hair high on her head. She took the wet face sponge and half heartedly washed her own face. When Julee told her to stand up so that she could remove her dressing gown and sleep gown, she obeyed absent-mindedly and sat down again on the stool.

Julee sponged her. "My! You' body, it pretty an' cuddly—Oo—OO! You got right 'mount of bumps in all the right places. Reckon a man goin' find you mighty sweet under his hand."

Mary Marie scowled and bit her lip.

"I picks us fresh vervain for us journey." Julee unbuttoned her bodice, reached in and pulled out the deliciously scented herbs, gay colored, eyed and striped, and gave them to Mary Marie who slowly twirled the stem between thumb and finger. Vervain, grown at a doorstep, plucked, worn next to the heart to attract lovers.

"Reckon Matt'll see to it he get hisself down to the boat landin'," Julee said, sponging Mary Marie's back. Julee was mighty happy to be going to Quercus Grove. She was in love with that black buck stable boy, Matt, belonging to Uncle Philip. Julee rubbed real hard with the bath towel. "Things got to come right for Matt and me."

Mary Marie knew she never had felt for a man what Julee felt for Matt. She wasn't ignorant of life and sex which was visible all around her and she had read enough in Papa's library to agree with him that Aunt Lucinda's Sir Walter Scott was "Tosh!" But

14

she couldn't, truly she couldn't, marry Mr. Creighton Tazewell! As for eligible young men, she might as well live on an island as this old plantation where Papa's bad manners to lady neighbors had cut her off from the usual society. It wasn't fair. She'd go off with the first young man she met. She'd show them!

Julee prattled on, "Matt, he worth a sight of money. Maybe a whole thousand dollars, maybe worth more than that new buck you' papa buy. That nigger he too uppity 'bout hisself. Jist 'cos Matt is kin 'herited nigger what's never been stood up on a fancy block in a New Orleans hotel paved fancy with black and white marble, don' mean he ain't a first-class trade for you' papa to make. You gets you' papa to trade Matt for that nigger. He ain't no good. He got hand trouble."

"Hand trouble?"

Julee sighed, "Wanderin' hand trouble. Womans are funny. I wants Matt 'flicted with hand trouble awful bad, but any other— Unn—nh! They make me close myself shut. But this new nigger, he got powerfu' strong hands, powerfu' strong. But he don' love me. Matt loves me and I loves Matt."

"How do you know?"

"Honey, Miss, you knows 'cos everything clicks right in place when you both loves."

Love!

Julee, on her knees, let the wet sponge drip unheeded. "Miss Mary Marie, you fix it 'tween you' papa and Master Quercus Grove Rutland to swap Matt for one of our Rutland Hall niggers so's Matt and me can live together in the holy matrimonies for keeps, 'stead of just layin' together, careless? I *loves* Matt."

Why, the girl was in actual pain, her face screwed up. Open raw emotion was as ugly as a gaping wound. Mary Marie said, "I might try."

Julee put her arms around her mistress' bare legs and bowed her head. "Thank you, Miss, thank you, thank you kin'ly." She raised her black face wet with tears. "I'll never be bad again."

"Get on with my bath, girl," Mary Marie ordered not unkindly.

"Yes, Miss. I knew if I puts it to you rightly you'd help, Miss. Vervain all right to kotch 'em, but you gots to use yer head to hold 'em. Men's a right slippery lot—'specially ones ain't *got* to marry." Julee slowed her towel. She puckered her face. "Matt wants steadyin'. Last time he make big talk. He say even if you born in

15

a stable it don' make you a horse. You better gets Matt where I kin steady him. Reckon Master Creighton Tazewell be down to the boat to meet you?"

"I'm not promised to him."

Papa had given his consent to Mr. Tazewell to pay court to his daughter. Papa found his financial condition satisfactory, his blood lines were sound and he had said "for God's sake try to behave so Mr. Tazewell won't catch on that there'll be no quiet and peace in his house."

Aunt Lucinda had added, "He's considered a catch, an older steady man with a good plantation. And he lost his wife and children from the milk sickness so it's sensible for him to make no delay in marrying a young girl—to start another family."

Julee said, "We tucks vervain in you' bodice, then everything come right 'tween you an' he. 'Spect Master Tazewell if he not 'lowed to pay court at the boat, he wait right in the summer house wavin' his han'-keer-chief."

"Not so tight, Julee, don't lace me in so tight."

"Reckon you marries Master Tazewell, he buy Matt?"

"Oh! Shut up! Matt! Matt! Matt!" Mary Marie flounced out from under Julee's hands. She didn't want Mr. Tazewell. Wandering hand trouble! No! No!

She sank onto the round-skirted stool before the elaborate black and gold dressing table cluttered with dear dead Mama's Florentine tooled leather boxes, cloisonne scent bottles, combs and brushes. A music box had a porcelain lid with a blue enamel band enclosing in gold relief the figures of a man and woman. Mary Marie raised the lid and out of the box came a small volume of sound, a pip squeak, which the legend on the lid claimed to be a Mozart Serenade. She flipped the lid shut. She herself was no more than a figure on a porcelain lid unable even to tinkle, tinkle. Tears rolled down her cheeks. Then pretending to examine her face she quickly wiped them away at the return of a tight-lipped and dignified Mammy Fay who was in no humor to deal gently with her mistress.

"Ouch!"

Another rake with the comb. Mammy Fay *was* in a vile temper.

"Mammy Fay!"

"You' hair snarled."

"You spoiled my hair with your old dye."

16

"You' hair pink," Julee said.

"It's pink all right. You used too much dye in the rinse. Mr. Godey's magazine said to use only enough to be felt, not seen."

"I learn how much. You bleach you' hair ridin' without a hat, you' face all freckles, no skin to you' nose. For shame—!"

"Don't say it, Mammy!" Mary Marie didn't want to be a credit to the family.

"Pink! Pink! Make the boys wink!" giggled Julee.

"Pink! Pink!" screamed Cornwallis and cackled his devilish laugh.

"Julee! Attend!" Mammy Fay laid down the comb. For the second time that morning she left the room in a huff.

Mary Marie pounded her fist on Mama's dressing table making the music box give a muffled squeak. She said, "I've got to get away. I've got to be free."

Papa, dark and of rather slight build, was already eating his breakfast in the dining room when Mary Marie came downstairs. He was impeccably dressed for the twenty-mile drive to escort Mary Marie from Rutland Hall to New Orleans. But the color of his green silk-trimmed coat did not become his complexion which tended to match goat willow leaves, nor did the lines deep hooked in his face lend him an air of happiness.

Mary Marie had to repeat her "Good morning, Papa," before he grumbled "What's good about it?"

An important day—a gala day—she was going away! She wouldn't let Papa's ill temper, or Mammy Fay's fuming, or Julee's chattering rout the new bounce with which she had awakened that morning.

"Mornin' Miss," said Little Ambus, the current fly sweep, a very black ninny in white pants and turkey-red calico slippers, who swung in a swing hung from the ceiling over the table. He was the cutest ninny they had had for a long time. He had a way of rolling his black eyes at her, of licking his bright-red tongue over his lips and having to swallow very fast to keep from drooling at the sight of "biggedy folks" food.

"Good morning, Ambus." Mary Marie gave him a strip of bacon which he pushed into his red mouth all at once, and swung harder than ever to give her his thanks. Mary Marie laughed. She was fond of Little Ambus.

17

She didn't need to look under all the silver lids to know there was the usual breakfast spread: water-ground hominy grits, fried ham, old and smoky bacon, eggs, waffles, biscuits. But there was no one to pull out her chair nor serve her plate. Horatio, the serving man was not in the room, nor Mammy Fay who acted as prime minister below stairs. It was Mammy Fay who saw that the household ran efficiently—there wasn't a Rutland slave who didn't bend low to Mammy Fay just like they did to white folks.

"Mammy Fay! Horatio!" yelled Mary Marie.

"Save your breath," Papa said.

"I want my breakfast."

"Get it yourself."

"Where's Horatio?"

"I've sent him to do more necessary things."

Mary Marie gave Papa, cold and arrogant, glare for glare. With an appearance of unbending poise she helped herself to a generous breakfast.

"It's a good thing you're going to Quercus Grove," said Papa. "God knows I don't think much of your Aunt Lucinda but maybe she can train you sufficiently to be a Mississippi plantation mistress." Papa said it as though it were an impossible achievement even for a backward place like Mississippi.

"I've decided I'm not going to marry Mr. Tazewell."

"Good God, girl, you *have* to marry. You're already seventeen and I want some peace. Presently I'll be no better off than Mr. Baptista with his daughter Kate."

Papa, Spencer Stuart Rutland, the "dear first born" had carried out his father's dream to build Rutland Hall in the manner of the Georges and to live in America as an English country gentleman with blooded horses. That distinguished old man, prosperous and closely connected with the mother country, had remained loyal during the Revolution. When it was over he fled from South Carolina to Louisiana, preferring Spanish rule to the damn Federalists. His rage, when the United States in 1803 purchased Louisiana, burst a blood vessel in his brain and killed him.

Papa, carrying out his father's order, had carved on the tombstone, safely enclosed within a black iron fence beneath a live oak at the edge of the home field the words, *Opposed To The Federal Constitution* and then set himself to fulfill the vision of Rutland

Hall. It had taken Papa ten years to complete his task, witness the decline and death of his mother, scrape together a patrimony for his younger brother, Philip, and god-speed him to his lesser fortune in the new state of Mississippi. Only then did he decide that it was time to find a wife to preside over the balanced and scaled formal brick house at the end of the live-oak alley.

In 1818 he journeyed to Charleston, South Carolina, where he paid court to Marie Isabelle Fee who was of a French Hugenot family of good repute with no particular Federalist bias. Early in 1819 he brought his bride to Rutland Hall together with her generous dowry, slaves, household goods, a casket of jewels, and a fine trousseau. But the bride's best gift was from her mother who gave her Fay, her own personal servant. "Take her, my darling, you'll need her, so far away, so alone."

They must have made quite a procession coming over the long rutted road from South Carolina. Mammy Fay had told the story over and over until Mary Marie almost believed that she had shared the trip herself—even been there when the marriage was arranged. "You' papa," said Mammy Fay, "he come pick a bride same as he pick a horse. He pick and pick 'til he narrow the field to you' mama. Already she been picked by the belle-pickers at Saint Cecelia's ball. She could have married anyone, but her papa favored Master Rutland." Mammy Fay shook her head. "White folks fixed marrying don't work for them any better than black ones. You' mama a lark, she young. You' papa a stiff solemn old bird, he old."

But when overcrowded with questions about Mama and Papa, Mammy Fay would say only, "You marry for love."

According to Mammy Fay, Mary Marie favored her mama in her small size and in other ways, but she was a Rutland too. Part Fee, part Rutland. The confusion about her name proved this.

Papa called her Mary. "It is the name you were christened."

But Mammy Fay called her Marie for her dear departed mama. "You' mama cry and say 'You poor little girl, you Marie, you not Mary.'"

During her tantrum days as a child she had insisted with screams, "I, Mary"—or "I, Marie"—depending upon whom she was trying to plague—Mammy Fay or Papa. It hadn't been easy to be separate pieces lost in a wide world, so with childish effort she tried to bring the pieces together to make a whole by naming herself Mary Marie. But Papa continued to call her Mary, and Mammy Fay, Marie.

Mammy Fay blamed Papa for the "dirty" doctor who gave Mama the childbed fever that killed her. Once Mary Marie heard Mammy Fay whisper, "I pure hate every gut wattled in him." She had meant Papa.

And Papa hated Mammy Fay even if he did depend upon her to perform the plantation duties Mama would have carried out. Over the years, Aunt Lucinda said Mammy Fay had advanced to the position of a black matriarch. To Aunt Lucinda it was beyond belief how Spencer Stuart Rutland allowed Mammy Fay to claim unhindered the mother right to his only child. How could he have had so little concern for matters above stairs?

Not until Mary Marie was six years old and Mammy Fay decided there should be a birthday party, did she succeed in securing Papa's attention.

Mammy Fay said you couldn't begin too early to get a child acquainted, learn to be a little lady, a credit to the family. Mammy Fay was equal to everything but the invitations, proper notes to be carried by Caesar to the neighboring plantation ladies, begging the honor of their children's attendance upon the occasion of Young Miss's birthday. So she put a clean frock on Mary Marie and told her to sit quietly in the big chair in the library. When her papa came in she was to ask him nicely to write the invitations.

When Papa returned she had discovered the only picture book among the dull and musty shelves. It was like Mama's alphabet book in which she had been studying her lessons in French with Mammy Fay. She showed him Voltaire's *Raison Par Alphabet* in which she had been examining a picture of Adam and Eve, wondering what had become of their clothes.

Papa was horrified to hear her recite the alphabet faultlessly in French! And then and there ordered her to come to the library each day and he'd teach her himself. "Now get out—I've got to think."

After Papa had done his thinking he wrote the invitations for her sixth birthday—but Caesar carried back dainty little perfumed notes of "deep regret," so Mary Marie had celebrated her birthday alone.

Mammy Fay said, "It's you' papa's fault, he wasn't nice to the plantation ladies after you' mama die. They come runnin' to divert him, but you' papa brush them off. Plantation ladies don' like that. Ladies can't rest if there's a man loose. It's like they ride in their carriages to a hunt yelling "Loose man! Loose man!" But nobody is able to catch you' papa. He outfox the ladies. When the chase got too close he hide himself in New Orleans where, likely, he take care of hisself. Now the ladies get even with him, they not let their children come to you' birthday party. You quit you' cryin', or you' papa won't bring you a present from New Orleans. You got you' nice gourd seed necklace I made you and the new dress for you' mama's doll.

But Mammy Fay was "flab-gasted" the day when Master Rutland rode up the live-oak alley escorting Caesar who drove a pair of mules pulling a horse box mounted on a wagon bed. In the horse box was a fat brown Shetland pony with four white feet, mane and tail, complete with little saddle. From under the wagon seat Caesar fetched out a box. My, oh my! A kilt of Stuart tartan, a complete outfit including a glengarry which Mammy Fay lost no time putting on the child.

When Mary Marie was mounted, her feet wouldn't reach the stirrups. Papa said the best way to get a good seat was to ride without stirrups anyway, and rode off down the oak alley. She whacked the pony with her riding whip bringing him into sudden action for which she was unprepared. Wham! She came a cropper. She was as mad as blue glazes. She stamped her foot at Caesar and said, "You get that pony, bring him back."

Caesar laughed and led the pony to her.

"Put me on," she ordered. This time she hung on.

Papa was pleased. "It's the best thing that could have happened. Now you won't be afraid. I'll make a horsewoman of you." But even when she became so proficient that she could outshine her father or any man on the place, he would only admit that "with practice, you might become a tolerable rider." Papa could turn honey into gall and vinegar.

But now, in just a few hours, she was getting away from Papa. It was up to her whether it would be for a few weeks or forever.

CHAPTER III

In her berth on *The Rising Sun*, Mary Marie punched the lumpy pillow. It was frightfully hot in the stateroom. She'd like to have Julee fan her, but she couldn't stand any more of that girl. Julee was so smug because she was going to see Matt at Quercus Grove, and all Mary Marie had to look forward to was Mr. Tazewell! It wasn't quite fair of Julee to fall in love, she should have waited for her mistress to do so first.

Mary Marie slipped her fingers beneath her bodice and pulled out the vervain that Julee had given her. She clutched it and commanded it to send her a lover—not a simperer like Creighton Tazewell, nor a western country clout—How dared he! Call the attention of others of his kind to her as he had done with that foolish coin business. She threw the vervain on the floor and instantly wanted it back again. She had half a mind to call Julee, make her come in and hand it to her. Then she leaned far out of the berth, rescued the vervain and restored it to warm safety.

Presently she slept, and was awakened by Julee who said, "They done rung the bell to get dressed for supper. What you wan' put on, Miss Mary Marie?"

Something to startle a westerner if she should happen to pass one when she went out on deck after supper for a breath of fresh air. The best way to avoid attention from a clout was to overwhelm him with her remoteness, her inaccessibility because of their dissimilar stations in life. The evening being warm, she finally decided on her white India muslin redingote over pale blue silk. Mammy Fay would probably have said its heart-shaped neckline was cut too low to wear to supper on a steamboat; it was more suitable for a formal soiree. But Mary Marie liked the way the billows of lace and embroideries tumbled from the crease in her bosom, down the length of the pale-blue silk under-dress to her tiny kid slippers. She liked the proud sweep the split overskirt made when she walked.

Then she examined her face in the small mirror over the washstand. Micheaux' freckle wash had not done as good a job as the label had claimed it would. Mammy Fay said a proper young lady protected her face and hair from the sun, she didn't go riding bareheaded, and for Mary Marie never to permit a gentlemen caller to see her act with such abandon, it wasn't ladylike. "I hate my dyed hair," she repeated rebelliously.

Julee giggled, "Pink! Pink! Make the boys wink!"

"Julee you're not to say that again. For that you can do my hair over," snapped Mary Marie. "You have the knot too tight." She wore her hair in a soft Grecian knot, a new cameo pin tucked in it, high gallery shell combs being out of fashion. On her temples were little soft curls.

"Not the bergamot scent. It is too coarse for the dress. Use frangipane!" The perfume of jasmin—a summer evening, the deep portico, the wide lawns, the sound of dance music within. Sir! It is an honor you do me.

"Fool! Quit! I don't want to reek!"

"No—o—o Miss!" said Julee. "White ladies they can't take perfume the way us colored folks can. Our men got more powerful smellers than white men. Reckon my Matt, he strong nuff to take the musk straight offen the deer. Wish I could get some fresh. Perfume a right good conjure to ketch a man—and vervain. Hopes you have right good luck this evenin' Miss."

"Did you see anyone likely while you sat outside the door?"

"No'm, can't say I did. That one you call western clout, he stuck his head in the ladies' cabin the mostest. Every time he look real hard at me sittin' 'gainst you' door. Can't say I see a 'eligible' on board. Miss Mary Marie can't you like Mr. Tazewell the least bitty bit? Miss Mary Marie if you did, you could get him to buy Matt. Mens do most anything for second wives."

"Matt, Matt, Matt! I'm sick and tired of hearing you whine about Matt."

"Yes'm," Julee snuffled. "But Miss I'se so worried 'bout me an'—."

"Don't! Don't say his name again or I'll scream." Mary Marie pushed Julee aside and flung open the door just in time to get caught in the great rush for seats at the supper table. "Suppah! Suppah!" clanged the steward's handbell along the outside galleries of the boat.

On Captain Cleve's elegant new steamer the old long table stretching the length of the cabin had been done away with. Instead small square tables were fitted together to form a new long one. Between meals they and the dining chairs were pushed to the walls to make a spacious cabin; one might even venture to call it a salon.

"What a crush, Captain Cleve!" laughed Mary Marie when she had at last elbowed her way to the head of the table where he presided.

Captain Cleve bowed to the elegance of her dress, "You are looking charming this evening, Miss Rutland."

"Oh! Thank you, Captain." Mary Marie giggled inside herself and wondered how long Captain Cleve would maintain with her his manner put on to impress his passengers.

For the captain was two persons. One was this gracious host, dressed in the finest of broadcloth and linens, his tongue ready to pay a lady a compliment. He could hold his own with the most learned or take command of his boat, his men, or drive a hard bargain in business. The other captain was the one who liked to retire to his "settin' room" in the bow of his boat, take off his blue broadcloth, gold buttons and braid, his tight squeaky shoes and, in the comfort of a homespun jacket and worn carpet slippers, sit in an old Boston rocker smoking a pipe.

There while his eyes, bright and clear, searched the waters ahead he told you how he once had a little girl, "just about as old as you," who lived with her mother in a little white cottage which faced the river, where some day he would go and sit on the front portico with nothing to do but watch the water, only he'd have to . . . "set by myself, 'less I get me a red setter to keep me company, 'cos there is no little girl nor her mama in that cottage waitin' for me any more."

On that first trip to Quercus Grove five long years ago, the captain had made her both sad and happy by saying she reminded him of his own daughter. On that trip too Mammy Fay had stood behind her chair the entire meal until Captain Cleve told her to skedaddle, he'd see that her Young Miss came to no harm. Thereafter it was taken as a matter of course that Mary Marie always sat with the captain in the seat of honor.

"Allow me, please. . . ."

Mary Marie hadn't noticed that Captain Cleve was holding out her chair, to the right of his at the table. "Oh, I am sorry, Captain. My mind was wool-gathering."

Every place was taken except the one on the captain's left, opposite Mary Marie. In front of each person the waiters were rapidly placing whole flocks of little oval dishes, each with a different bit of something in it—beet root, apple sauce, pumpkin, corn fritters, baked pork and beans, pickles. Platters of hot fried beef and ham steaks, roast and boiled chickens and cold cuts were passed. Down the center of the table were mounds of hot breads, with appropriate dishes of preserves nearby, and butter held firm with ice.

"It is truly an elegant boat, Captain," breathed Mary Marie.

"Finest que-seen on the Miss'sip," said Captain Cleve.

Mary Marie sat a little straighter in her chair and her breath seemed to catch in her throat as she sighted Levi Blaisdell striding purposefully toward them.

"Well, young man! What's kep' you from your feed bag?" Captain Cleve smiled as he invitingly patted the back of the chair to his left.

"Sorry, sir! Had a bit of trouble laying my hands on my duds. Hadn't figured on needing anything but my homespuns this trip."

"Well, I'll be blessed! Slicked down with bear's grease sooner than I'd expected," murmured Captain Cleve.

Levi looked as scrubbed and scalded as though he had been dipped in the barrel of hot water used for dressing chickens. His clean-shaven face indicated a visit to the boat's "tonsorial artist," who kept shop aft of the wheelhouse. His fair, curly hair had been stroked and pomaded into dark flat ringlets over his forehead. He wore a high collar with a gayly flowered neckerchief above his buff-colored waistcoat. Oh! What a divine narrow waist, held tightly by the green claw-hammer coat. Mary Marie felt her face grow warm. She bent her gaze upon the clutter of little "bird-bath" dishes in front of her.

"Set up!" said Captain Cleve. "Reckon you ain't as hungry as you'd be if you'd been totin' wood. But 'low you'll make out a meal 'spite these fancy fixin's. Ain't more'n a spoonful in each dish, not enough to feed a sparrow. When you find one to your likin' ask Dink to bring you more. Eat boy, until your eyeballs say you got enough. Miss Rutland here, she pecks like a bird 'mongst all these little dishes. Can't Dink get you something else?"

"No, thank you." She couldn't say more.

Where, oh where, had all her small talk gone to—those bright little useful quips? She became conscious of the clatter of sixty or seventy spoons cleaning out the little bird-baths, all down the length of the long table. Rows of mouths eating enormously with a chomping sound, a satisfied belch down the table a ways, a sucking sound closer by as someone tried to dislodge a morsel stuck between his teeth.

There was no conversation. Nobody said anything to anybody, not even "pass the jell." A long reach obtained it. The women tasted one dish after another and pushed them away for the next. The men, like all men no doubt, had weighty problems on their minds regarding the state of the universe. But these they would delay until they were free to make man talk in the privacy of the bar.

Mary Marie wished she had stayed home. Whyever had she thought this new boat was elegant! She hated it and everything on it. Most especially she hated the man opposite her who ignored a perfectly good butter knife in the butter dish. Instead he reached in his own knife, and took a great hunk of butter. This he clapped between a split biscuit, and held the knife waving high in the air until practically the whole biscuit had disappeared into his mouth. Then he waggled his knife at Captain Cleve and said through the biscuit, "I've been over her from bow to stern, sir, and I say she's a honey. Never saw a boat with such shear!"

What on earth was shear on a boat? Captain Cleve and the westerner were off—boat, boat, boat! They had forgotten Miss Mary Marie Rutland, that elegant young lady of fashion. It was not for this that Mammy Fay had trained her to sit bedecked in laces and silk damask at the end of her father's Chippendale table and make bright civilized conversation until it was time for her to withdraw and leave the gentlemen with their coffee, toddies, and talk of Cotton.

At last she laid her napkin firmly on the table as a signal she was finished, Captain Cleve sprang to his feet and attended to her chair. Neither Creighton Tazewell nor any other young man of breeding would have permitted an older man to assist her to rise. But this Levi kept right on talking about the merits of *The Rising Sun*. She tried to wither him by playing the part of a fine southern hostess, the meal completed, withdrawing from the gentlemen at table, leaving them to their coarse man talk while she led the ladies to the drawing room to engage in polite conversation.

"See you later on deck," called Levi with a careless salute.

She maintained her pose until she reached the guard rail at the stern of the main deck. Never had she been so furious, she was mad enough to spit in the river! A small voice within her reasoned, why should she be mad? Because Papa was right when he refused to travel on steamboats where he had to endure homespun? Because Levi had told her he would see her on deck instead of simpering, "May I have the honor to attend you on deck for a breath of fresh air?"

Yes after all there was something to be said for a man like Mr. Creighton Tazewell who walked far enough behind so he wouldn't step on your shadow. But actually she wanted her shadow trampled—or did she? Did there have to be reasons for everything you felt or did? Couldn't she just be mad at everyone if she wanted to? Why not?

She heard bells and voices across the water. *The Rising Sun* was passing a boat going down-river. The boat was so loaded with bales of cotton nothing could be seen but her chimneys and pilot house. Cotton was the life of the South, everyone said so. She belonged to the South. She had better smother these new feelings aroused by a westerner. She had better stick to her own kind.

She hit the guard rail a good blow with her fist, "I'll do as I please," she told the cotton boat fiercely.

But she gave an awful jump when she heard a voice beside her; she hadn't realized anyone had joined her at the rail.

"What're you doing? Making 'fightin' words' all by yourself. Takes two to pick a fight they say where I come from." It was Levi. "You just smooth down your pretty little feathers, on account of I'm not going to have fightin' words with you. You can forget your uppity ways with me. I've a notion they're not yours anyway. Reckon they belong to your black mammy. Now you've got a chance, why don't you try to find out what kind of a person you really are. It doesn't set too well when you try to wear somebody else's cloak."

Someone else's cloak. Like a flash the words summed up all her restless feelings. Why yes, certainly, that was the trouble with her. She was smothered by other people's cloaks. Everyone wanted her to be his or her own particular kind of person. No one wanted her to be herself.

"The way I have it figured out, everyone has a right to do what he wants to do. Now take me, I'm a river rat. No power on earth could keep me off the river. Once the river gets in your blood it stays there.

A river rat! If she had thought and thought, she couldn't have found anything meaner to call him. But the way he spoke the words meant he was proud of his lowly profession. A river rat!

"Are all western flatboat men—river rats?" She hoped the way she dilated her nostrils made him understand she remembered full well the horrible stink of their cargoes tied up at the New Orleans levee.

"No, some never get the river into their blood. I have a brother, just a youngster, he doesn't take to the river, he likes the land. Wanted him to come this trip. He didn't want to. Say! I'm not a westerner, you understand. I'm an Ohio River man."

"I thought all flatboat men were westerners. Where is the Ohio?"

"You mean you travel on Captain Cleve's boat and you don't even know where the Ohio is?" Levi shook his head slowly at her. "And I thought you were smart as well as cute. Say, where do you think Cincinnati, the Queen City, is?"

"Oh some place above Greenville, Mississippi, near St. Louis."

Levi sighed deeply at her ignorance and shook his head again. Grinning at her with his fine set of white teeth gritted in mock despair, he put his two great hands on her shoulders and gave her a shake, "You'd better learn some geography."

"Why?" she demanded. She wasn't going to make a scene on the deck of a steamboat and she wasn't going to let this boor think she was the least bit afraid of him. But he was so big!

"Because how'll you know where I am if you don't know the geography of the Ohio and Mississippi Rivers?"

"Sir!" She tossed her head, looked up to scorn him. "That is no concern of mine." Unfortunately her voice played a mean trick on her—the last word was nothing but a gasp. Rage welled up from within her. She twisted her shoulders out of his grasp and turned toward the river. Her eyes filled with tears. She might as well have the whole of the muddy Mississippi in them for all that she could see. She held herself erect. But tried not be so conscious of his long body hunched to lean on the guard rail. She tried not to listen to his voice. That voice which was now talking of love. Love for something called the Ohio River.

"She's a beautiful river, just the size a river ought to be."

(You're a beautiful girl, just the size you ought to be. Oh! To have a gentleman caller whose voice could both make you quiver with pleasure and stab a pain into your middle.)

"The river, the river," the voice went on beside her as though he were whispering, "My love, my love."

"You can row across her in ten or fifteen minutes, in low water you can swim across her. She's never the same. Sometimes she's covered with fog so you can't see her, other times she's lazy under a warm sun. When she's had a good lashing from winds, she's full of frothing white caps; when she's cold, she freezes solid and gives in to no man. Yep, she's like a woman all right—has to be wooed—but oh how I love her, La Belle Rivière."

Mary Marie couldn't think of any answer to this outburst. She wondered how she could get this same kind of attention directed toward herself. It jolted her to realize that she wanted it.

His voice went on as though he didn't know she was there. "Someday I'm going to build me a boat worthy of her." He laughed. "The captain joshes me about being stingy. I'll show him someday. His new boat is better than the first clumsy old tubs. But wait till you see the boat *I'm* going to build!"

Somehow she had to get this man's attention focused on her and instinctively she realized that no ordinary feminine wiles would work with him. It made her really mad to have to reach him where his own interest lay, but she asked meekly, "What is a shear on a steamboat?"

He turned eagerly and explained. But it didn't matter to her in the least that steamboat builders had at last had sense enough to use the cantilever principle, whatever that was, to keep the ends of a boat from dipping; that they used hog chains from stern to the forward part over the hurricane deck supported by heavy stanchions of wood to keep the stern from settling.

"Didn't you notice *anything* different about the main deck?"

He asked the question as though he thought her a complete idiot.

"If you mean it sags in the middle like an old sway-back horse, I did indeed, sir."

"A sway-back horse! Compare a boat to a horse! Holy smoke!"

"A horse is nobler than a boat—you—you—"

"Gosh! You're pretty when you're riled up, Sorrel Top. I wouldn't risk a huckleberry to a persimmon you wouldn't throw something at me if your pretty little hand could pry anything loose off Captain Cleve's boat. You're just like a Mississippi snapping turtle."

"And you—you're a miserable westerner!"

"Aw! Come on Sorrel Top, let's not spat except in fun. We left New Orleans at three this afternoon. This time tomorrow night we'll be at Natchez—the next morning, it's Vicksburg and that evening about six o'clock Captain Cleve tells me he expects to push his landing stage in at Quercus Grove. We haven't got time for you to fly the cathole. I overspoke myself just now. It's going to be an awfully short time before I see your Uncle Philip, your Aunt Lucinda and your cousins all lined up to welcome you at Quercus Grove."

"Do you know my kinfolks?"

"Oh yes, I know them."

"How?"

"Captain Cleve often asks me to do some business for him. I've heard about you but I can't understand why I never saw you there. Reckon we've wasted a lot of time—not meeting before."

She looked down at the kick the wake of the boat made on the water, she listened to the pat-pat of the paddle wheels. Then she lifted her chin and studied the distant low flat banks of the wide muddy Mississippi. The river rolled behind her, hour after hour it would go wearily on—forever. There was no sound of birds, the shores were too distant, the trees stunted.

The river was really a desolate place except when there was life on it. She remembered the excitement when leaving the crowded wharf in New Orleans, the shout of the men when *The Rising Sun* had finally stood off for her up-river trip. The second shout of the men when Levi had flipped his coin over his shoulder into the river. She wondered why he angered her so easily. But it was true what he said; the sight of Quercus Grove would come all too soon.

She turned to Levi and asked, "Why did you throw that coin into the river when we left New Orleans?"

"Don't you know?" he asked in surprise. "Don't you know *anything* about rivers? Don't you live on one?"

"No, I live inland. I only know the little I've learned traveling with Captain Cleve and on my visits to Quercus Grove. I suppose it's dreadful, but I've never paid much attention to the river." She decided not to tell him that she felt about horses the way he felt about the river and steamboats. "Maybe you wouldn't mind teaching me—a little?"

Levi beamed. "That would be a pleasure—a real pleasure."

His voice! Enchantment! Only now did she understand how stones and trees might be made to dance.

"I threw the coin to bring good luck," Levi explained. "You have to wait until you're midstream and throw it over your left shoulder or it doesn't work."

"And do you want to have it work especially this trip?" Mary Marie thought of the vervain in her underbodice.

"Quit being such a skirticoat, rolling your eyes and flirting."

"Mr. Blaisdell! I'd like you to know—" Well maybe she had batted her eyes a little.

"Thunder and potatoes, girl! Don't you realize this new boat of Captain Cleve's goes so fast we'll have our ears pinned back. We haven't time to go through all the fancy rigamarole as if we were dancing a ball-room minuet. Don't you realize we'll be at Quercus Grove on Friday, and this is Wednesday night?"

Mary Marie's recollection of the next thirty-six hours encompassed only bells—steamboat bells—quarrels and kisses. She and Levi together in the evening at a secluded rail of *The Rising Sun,* quarrelling, making up, kissing—and kissing.

She had said to him, "How can you spend so much time studying Captain Cleve's old boat?"

She was annoyed with Levi. He spent hours away from her, going over and over the boat when he himself had declared that two days were all too short a time for them to get acquainted. It was galling to find that he expected to find her waiting for him to finish playing with the boat. It made her even angrier because that was exactly what she did—waited for him—waited for him to amuse himself with *her* when he was ready. And then she had to listen to his harangues about cylinder heads, excess vapor, and cracked driving rods!

"But don't you see," insisted Levi, "fewer boilers would give enough steam and there'd be more room for freight."

"No, I don't," she replied perversely.

"My, but you look cute when you spark and crackle, but aren't you kinda scared you might set fire to yourself?"

"And what difference would it make to you if I did?"

He drawled, "Well, I'd kinda hate to see you get singed."

He leaned over her with a twinkle in his eyes, while a tender smile played across his lips. She felt her own lips part slightly and knew they were waiting for his. She longed for him to lay his mouth on hers.

"Levi! Levi!" she was crying to him for help as he crushed her mouth with his. A current passed between them. She trembled. A warmth rushed up her legs and spread through her until she had to withdraw her mouth from his and bury her head momentarily against his chest. She pressed her firm little breasts to him, closer and closer. She wanted him to fondle her. She longed for him intensely. His hands on her inexperienced body had the effect of suffocating her with a rush of emotion which left her breathless.

So this was what being in love meant. I'm in love, I'm in love. All the unhappy past is gone. I'm in love, she thought wildly, exultantly.

All too soon they stood at the rail of *The Rising Sun* watching for Quercus Grove, its wings widespread in welcome as she remembered it, standing away from the river at the end of a double row of live oaks. Even the end of this blissful trip, however, could not dim their happiness in each other or their confidence in the future.

Mary Marie could hardly wait for the boat to draw near enough for her to see her kinfolk lined up to greet her at the landing. Uncle Philip would be there and Levi would declare himself and ask her uncle's permission to court her and to seek her hand in marriage. For, naturally Levi, in spite of his amorous advances, observed the conventions and would not speak of marriage until permission to do so had been granted by Mary Marie's only available male kin.

CHAPTER IV

A GREAT FEELING OF JOY OVERWHELMED MARY MARIE WHEN she saw Quercus Grove, the house sprawling open, rangy and easy. Papa's and Uncle Philip's houses were as different as the brothers themselves. Papa was erect, classical and formal. Uncle Philip slouched, was easy and careless. And in spite of its high piazzas, his story and a half house gave the effect of being low and rambling. Axe and adze marked its cypress timbers, its wooden pegs and home-forged iron nails showed clearly. It was rough and comfortable.

Mary Marie stood on the forecastle stairway, waving her handkerchief, laughing, exclaiming, while she waited for the landing stage to be pushed to the shore. The water was too shallow for the boat to edge in close enough for the stage to clear the mud.

"Lay me a gangplank," shouted the mate. "Lay me a gangplank!"

It was scarcely in place before a dozen Quercus Grove Rutlands scrambled aboard led by Uncle Philip and his eldest son, Buford, who were welcomed at the head of the stage by Captain Cleve himself.

Mary Marie flung an arm around each of them, almost in tears of joy at seeing them again. Buford, a year or so older than Mary Marie was her closest friend. He was taller than she was by a foot and quick and eager. They shared a passion for good horses and books, and he did much to fill Mary Marie's need for close family ties.

In a moment Mary Marie was smothered with kisses and hugs from the "kithin' kin," so dubbed by a lisping Rutland long ago.

Every slave on the place must have knocked off from work to come down to the shore to meet her and perhaps to see the new *Rising Sun,* or maybe just because they had a good excuse to quit work. They laughed, they called greetings to Negroes on board, they showed off by turning somersaults and cartwheels.

Mary Marie knew Julee was trying to see Matt over the heads of all the Rutlands. It wasn't too easy to single out quickly one favored face from close to a hundred other black ones. The *shape* of the clothing told men from girls, but otherwise they all looked alike, in homespun made by the frump-frump of the loom in the weaving house. "I can't see him, Miss, I can't see Matt," whispered Julee.

"Mr. Rutland, sir, will you join me in a spot of liquid refreshment?" invited Captain Cleve. "And Miss Rutland, will you kindly see that the young folks are served suitable refreshments in the dining salon. Levi, come with me, please."

So, that was the way it was. She was relegated to the role of another child or a black nurse to see that all the little Rutlands were fed floating island aboard *The Rising Sun,* while Levi went off to the bar to drink with grown men.

But something happened over the juleps. It was a very sober Levi without a wicked wink or a cheeky grin, who accepted Uncle Philip's invitation to pay his respects to Aunt Lucinda up at the house, while Captain Cleve laid over to see some necessary repairs on a boiler.

Mary Marie was more than a bit piqued that Levi now paid no more attention to her than to any other man who came to talk business with Uncle Philip. He danced attendance on Aunt Lucinda; he told Hoosier tall tales to open-mouthed little Rutlands; but mostly he talked with Uncle Philip.

"I figure the broadhorn days are about finished. When a steamboat can do in six days what a flatboat does in thirty or forty, you can be sure a flatboater's days are numbered. I plan to get into the steamboat trade, sir, just as quick as I can."

"I understand from Captain Cleve that you're coming up fast the hard way."

"I never thought of it like that, sir. We Blaisdells are used to fending for ourselves. My folks came out from New York state by canal, made their way down to the Ohio River when it was a wilderness."

"Yankee, eh?"

Mary Marie added the new word, which had a hateful sound, to her string of mean things to call him—he was a Yankee, a westerner, a Hoosier, a river rat—that was what he was!

"My father isn't given to being a river man." Levi laughed. "But me! Reckon my first bath was Ohio River mud, the first drop of water I swallowed was half sand. Whatever you're born to be, sir, that's what you've *got* to be. *I'm* a river man."

"What about railroads?" Uncle Philip asked.

"Up our way we had a governor a few years ago who had fancy ideas on that. But sir, railroads cost too much, you've got to lay a roadbed, build carriages, make repairs." Levi shook his head. "No sir! Our future is on the rivers. We don't have to have roads, even, to build a great inland empire. Sir, look from your own window," Levi waved a hand toward a vast Mississippi. "Is that river ever empty of produce? You are on the highway of the world, at one end is the Queen City, at the other is New Orleans. Maybe it's a dream, sir, but why couldn't an ocean-going vessel be built at Rivertown, loaded there, run on steam to New Orleans, and shift to sails for the Atlantic?"

Uncle Philip gave a satisfied grunt. "You're at least ambitious, lad. This country needs young men like you. Things aren't going too well, y'know."

"Sir, both in Cincinnati and New Orleans they think we're through with revulsion of trade."

"Oh yes, business is good again. I wasn't thinking of that."

"I don't understand, sir, if general business is good, and cotton reigns—?"

"There's this talk by hotheaded demagogues. They fan the flame of discord, lead the cause of nullification and disunion."

"Folks up my way think we settled that question when we brought Maine in as a free state to offset Missouri coming in slave."

Uncle Philip shook his head, "Too neat. There's a strong feeling in some parts down here for a southern confederacy. Had a letter the other day which showed me folks were still harping."

"But, sir—"

Mary Marie went up to bed that night a very disgruntled young lady. Why, they had hardly even looked up to answer her "good night."

In addition to a ram's horn, Quercus Grove had potracking guinea fowl to help open the days. Uncle Philip's field hands were still having to work from "kain to kain't," day break to dusk, to get the autumn work done. The horn wakened Mary Marie.

She didn't open her eyes, but turned her head on the bolster and pulled the bedclothes over it. She hoped to shut out the short toots on the horn which followed, but she heard them. Ordinarily she never even heard the old horn, but lately it had been wakening her and she would have to lie there until Julee brought her morning cup of black coffee. She was bored with reliving the same old scenes which yielded no comfort. If she had the gumption of a chicken she'd forget the whole business—and *him* too!"

It had been more than a full month since he had gone away. Why hadn't she let him say goodbye instead of riding off by herself? Maybe now she'd know something one way or the other. It was all so confusing. And she had only herself to blame. If she could have said it was all his fault—! But what could a girl do when a man ignored her for two whole days, showed he preferred talking business with Uncle Philip. She wished he had never walked off *The Rising Sun*'s landing stage with her the day they had arrived at Quercus Grove. It jolly well served him right not to be able to tell her goodbye. He took too much for granted. She had shown him!

She opened her eyes and told a bedpost she wished she hadn't run away from Levi's goodbye. Had he only made western-Yankee advances to her? Had he laughed at his easy conquest? She should have slapped his face instead of answering his first kiss.

Julee and all her superstitions! Julee said if you named bedposts for lovers the first one you looked at when you wakened would be *the one*. Mary Marie had named all four bedposts Levi. But what good had it done?

She jumped out of bed and ran across the room before she remembered that Aunt Lucinda didn't have bell pulls to summon service. Where was Julee with her morning coffee? If she had slipped out to Matt again! She wouldn't allow her very own servant to be a Negro slut, neither would she give her consent for Julee to marry Matt. It wouldn't hurt Julee to learn a little self-control.

Everything was all jumbled up at Quercus Grove. There was

no Mammy Fay to see that the plantation was well run while Uncle Philip was in his counting house, his servant at his side. Aunt Lucinda was too beaten to make sure that the meat cook was at his spit, that the bread cook beat biscuits on a marble slab, that the maker of possets and potions was in the nursery, that feet came running in response to the jingle of a little brass bell. If you wanted anything at Quercus Grove you just yelled for it—or waited until the black powers decided what you wanted and when.

Confound Julee! Why *didn't* she bring her coffee? Julee was picking up slovenly habits at Quercus Grove. It was time they went back to Rutland Hall.

Mary Marie jerked open an armoire and started pulling out her clothes, flinging them on the bed, chairs, floor.

Julee gave her an awful jump when she said, "What dress you look for, Miss?"

"Won't you ever learn to knock?" Mary Marie shrilled.

"I knock Miss, but you so dog and cat with you'-self you don' hear me." Julee set the tray holding a small coffee pot and tiny cup on the night table. She clucked her tongue at the tangled muss of Mary Marie's bed, set to work and soon had it to rights.

"There, honey chile, you hops back into bed. You drinks you' nice coffee 'fore it gets cold." These days nothing could ruffle Julee. She hummed quiet little songs of contentment just like a hen who had found her way into a flower bed. She put the clothes to rights in the armoire.

"Get down my boxes," ordered Mary Marie.

Julee clutched Mary Marie's green velvet riding habit close to her. "What for?"

"To pack. We're going home on the next boat."

"We just got here."

"A whole month isn't just getting here."

"Mr. Tazewell, he be a mighty disappointed man you go home now."

The thought gave Mary Marie pause. If she left she'd have to give Mr. Tazewell her answer. Why did he have to come courting her? She wished he'd stay down on his plantation where he belonged. As soon as he received Aunt Lucinda's invitation he had come "on the double."

Mary Marie had told herself she was glad to see a civilized

southern gentleman after the gaucherie of a western flatboater—Yankee—river rat. But in the evening when Mr. Tazewell stood beside her to turn the music and sing in a thin tenor, "I Have Found Thee," she hated his voice because it didn't pick her up and hold her quivering in mid-air.

Later when he proposed she was furious. He fussed over his stage settings as if he were playing a charade. He invited her to sit on the sofa, "Not on the end, please. Do you mind very much? Please sit in the center. Ah! A portrait of you done just so. Admirable!"

Mary Marie laughed in remembrance. If he had only known! Aunt Lucinda's sofa had its middle springs all untied so that their sharp edges bit her roundest parts. At the time she had a wild impulse to start bouncing on the broken, twanging springs until she caught the meaning of Mr. Tazewell's position and words.

Then he had dropped to one knee before her and said, "Do you think you could accept such a one as I? I hope I haven't startled you—so young."

Why he must be at least forty—maybe more. Why, he's old, like Papa!

"It is best you have time to consider your heart's desire . . ." Her heart's desire, a lot of good it did her to know it. "I doubt if I could find anyone I like better, for I find your character stands fair," vowed Mr. Tazewell. "I will return for your answer."

That other one, the westerner, hadn't even popped the question. He had never said, I love you, will you marry me, I may have startled you, I'll return for my answer. His sheer braggadocio took a good deal for granted. His very exuberance made her respond to his kisses, but she'd be a little fool if she sat and waited for him to return to Quercus Grove. She'd show him; if he wanted to find her he'd have to ride through all that dust to Rutland Hall. She wouldn't be waiting under the lone live-oak tree at the top of the bend in the broad Mississippi where the channel swung all the down-river traffic close to the shore.

"Go to the store room, Julee, get the boxes, start packing while I have my breakfast."

In the dining room the Rutlands were gathered together for a whopping big breakfast. Ceremonious meals were not usual at Quercus Grove, but every Rutland was expected to be ready and in his place by the time Uncle Philip came.

Aunt Lucinda always said that Uncle Philip gurgled as soon as he was awake. He would be dead to the world when she called him and at once there he was, wide awake, merry. His great voice could be heard booming all through the house, whistling and singing. He came into the dining room drawing an imaginary bow on the strings of an imaginary violin, capering the steps of the Fisher's Hornpipe. To the delight of all the waiting Rutlands he bade each "good morning" with a tug at a freshly brushed curl, a tweak of a red-scrubbed ear. He said happiness had to be inhaled with the air of daily life.

When the plates had been served, Mary Marie took a deep breath and said, "Dear Aunt Lucinda, Uncle Philip, I speak from a full heart of the unspeakable comfort and impartial love you have bestowed upon me . . ." Mary Marie thought her prepared speech was going rather well until Uncle Philip fixed a quizzical eye upon her. "Well," she stumbled. "Well, I thank you very much. I just wanted to say I'm having Julee pack my trunks."

"Whatever for?"

"If you'll please hail the next down-river boat . . ."

Then she became terribly conscious of the table full of Rutlands abandoning their grits in astonishment that she could consider terminating her visit after only a few short weeks. Suddenly they all began talking at once.

"You promised to teach me to ride."

"Charades! Who'll lead our side against Papa's side?" This from Buford, who conceded few superiorities to Mary Marie except in the dramatic line.

"My music lessons . . . ?"

"My new doll outfit?"

". . . to dance your pas seul."

"Our backgammon games in the evening, my dear." This was Uncle Philip speaking.

"Is there something wrong, dear?" asked Aunt Lucinda.

Oh no, Aunt Lucinda, there is nothing wrong except everything in the whole wide world has gone kim-kam for me ever since I first saw him. Mary Marie could hardly keep from bursting into tears. She didn't dare trust her voice, she had to shake her head, "no."

"I don't want to impose on you, dear, but I was wondering if you would help me," Aunt Lucinda made vague movements with her hands. "There is so much to see to, so many steps, so hard to get about. (Aunt Lucinda was large with yet another kicking, wriggling Rutland.) I thought, dear, but of course, dear, if you are not happy here with us, dear, we wouldn't want to keep you, though what dear kind Mr. Tazewell will think if you run home, I don't know. He's such a perfect gentleman, he hasn't said anything unseemly has he; but of course Mr. Tazewell wouldn't.

"You probably feel restless because you haven't been able to make up your mind. If you think an absence would make your heart grow fonder . . . but really, dear, I do need you. I don't know what we'd all do without you if you went home now—do we, dears?" Aunt Lucinda appealed to all the Rutlands.

"No!"

Their hearty response warmed Mary Marie through and through.

Back home at Rutland Hall she wouldn't have anything to do but to put a needle slowly in and out of a piece of petit point in a frame, play a few bars on the melodeon, tease Cornwallis, listen to Mammy Fay's chidings, and have Papa make her feel mean. She couldn't stand Rutland Hall, now. It wasn't on the river. If she didn't stay with the river she'd never see *him* again. He wouldn't leave his old river to go look for a girl who lived in the interior. It galled her, but she'd have to wait for him—and what if he didn't come?

". . . so you see, we do need you, dear." Aunt Lucinda must have been talking all the time.

Mary Marie looked around at the eager Rutland faces. She jumped up and ran to her aunt, gave her a hug and a kiss. "If you need me, I'll stay."

"Goody," shouted the Rutlands and sang, "Miss Marie, had a flea on her knee, holy gee!"

"I'll get even with you later. I must tell Julee to unpack."

When she did, Julee said, "They ain't packed."

"Why not?"

"I figger we don' go, so what's the use to pack and unpack?"

There were times when Mary Marie wanted to slap Julee's dark velvety face. Once when she was little she had hit Julee with Papa's cane. Mammy Fay had given her Young Miss a whale of a licking to teach her that great ladies have a responsibility to their servants and do not mistreat them. Now, Mary Marie rep-

40

rimanded Julee with her eyes and wondered if anyone had ever had such a strange bringing up. "I'm only staying because Aunt Lucinda needs me."

"Yas'm," said Julee.

"I won't have you picking up Matt's slovenly ways, either. Yas'm, indeed!"

"Yas'm."

"Julee!"

"Yes, Miss Mary Marie."

"Well, I should say so. Now come along, you and I are going to put this place to rights."

CHAPTER V

Mary Marie surprised even herself by the efficient way she took over the household duties of the plantation. Mammy Fay would have been proud to see how much her charge had absorbed of her own standards of operation.

While Mary Marie went about the plantation business, the thought of Levi accompanied her everywhere. Daily she had to resist the temptation to ride out to the lone live oak on the river bend to watch the boats go by.

If Levi came, he would come round the bend by the oak. She mustn't think *if—when* he came . . .

One day as she stood in the cobbler's shop, checking on the progress of shoes for the coming winter, she was suddenly overwhelmed by the smell of the tanned leather. It reminded her of the cargoes of the western flat-boats in New Orleans where she had first met Levi.

She picked up her skirts and ran from the shoe shed. She ran to the big house.

"Julee!" yelled Mary Marie.

Julee didn't answer, but one of the little Rutlands said, "I saw her going toward the stables."

Matt! Julee just couldn't keep away from Matt.

Mary Marie pounced on a small ninny. From a pocket she produced a biscuit and gave it to him. "Run to the stable and tell Matt to saddle Prince and tell Julee I want her."

Out of sheer gratitude for what she was doing for Aunt Lucinda, Uncle Philip had given her Prince, a beautiful thoroughbred.

When she had changed to her riding habit and was mounted,

she nudged Prince with her knee. "We'll not go near the bend, you hear?"

Cardinals, buntings and meadow larks sang again after the heat of summer. Ivory-billed woodpeckers kept calling—pet, pet, pet. On the sand bar the willows were still green but the cypress trees behind them had turned russet brown. On the ground the Virginia Creeper ran scarlet. Across the land a field hand began a song, *Way—down in de bottom,* another hand joined in, *Whah de cotton so—rotten,* then another and another, until there were dozens of Negro voices across the fields, singing.

Mary Marie halted Prince beneath the lone live oak at the top of the bend in the broad Mississippi. A steamboat was in the channel which swung in close to the shore at this point. "Oh, make him be on it," she prayed. "This time, please come."

She had watched here so often she knew every little eddy of the river. "Levi, my darling, come back to me." Now she was here, she was shameless, letting herself go with yearning.

The steamboat came on, it looked as though the pilot was going to run his boat right up under the tree. She could see him throw the weight of his body to "hard over" his wheel. The boat turned expertly, straightened into the clear stretch.

As the boat passed Mary Marie searched every deck for one face. When she heard the order, "Full steam!" shouted through the trumpet to the firemen below, she knew that another boat from up-river was not going to put in at Quercus Grove to let off any western Yankee. Anger or sorrow, she didn't know which, filled her eyes with tears. She took her hankerchief from where it was tucked amongst the embroideries of her white cambric riding basque. She fought to control herself, she would not give in and shed any more tears.

Then she heard a weird prolonged sound. It came from the river. She uncovered her eyes and looked.

There was a broadhorn! The man on its left sweep was working like mad to help the steering oar at the stern to head in for the channel. On the closed hatch was a tall figure. He wore a loose blouse, full sleeved, open at the throat; his hands held a horn to his lips; this was what had made the strange sound. He had on no waistcoat and, oh, what a fine pair of legs were encased in the tight pants. Oh! It was Levi all right, floating down-river on a flatboat.

43

He waved his horn when he saw her. "Cracky! There's my girl!" he shouted.

He motioned to his fiddler on deck to play a tune. He sang and skipped into a dance on the hatch of his broadhorn. His boatmen swung his boat—and him—in to the shore—to her.

He put his two strong hands on her waist and lifted her from the saddle, clipped her to him, bent his head and laid his mouth on hers. She was exalted, floating, without identity. "My Levi, my Levi," she murmured while his lips searched the far corners of her face.

He waved to his grinning men on the broadhorn, who returned the gesture with a shout. The fiddler played a lively tune on his violin.

Levi turned back to Mary Marie. "What was that you said? Say it again, 'my Levi'!"

"I won't say it again, Mr. Smarty. You're too sure of yourself. What would you have done if I hadn't waited?"

"I knew you'd wait."

"How?"

In answer he sang to the tune of his dance, *"Never saw a girl in all my life, But what she would be a boatman's wife."*

"Oh! Is that so! You and your boat—you're married to a river. You can't even tell a girl you love her."

"Look, Half-pint, do you want to be *told* how I love you or are you willing to let my actions speak?"

"Well—a girl likes to hear it."

"All right! I'm telling you once and for all. Listen! If it's fiddle-faddle you want to hear. You fill my mind. I dream all night of you, all the boats on the river are named for you, they are going to places all named for you, all the signs say your name. I bought two new outfits, the legs of my old ones are too short, the old coat too tight, its collar limpsy. I squander my money, I buy things I don't need, give them away. For the first time in my life, I envy those poetry chaps who make rhymes. I can't. I only dance and sing. That is how it has been—away from you. But when I'm with you—my mind's got home. When my hands, my lips touch you —like this—why try to say anything?"

Mary Marie was well content. She would not dread the days until he returned from New Orleans, for he would have to complete this trip.

44

The men pushed off from the shore, swung the broadhorn into the current. Levi stood on the hatch, the fiddler played, Levi danced and sang,

> *Never saw a girl in all my life*
> *But what she would be a boatman's wife.*

She watched the sweeps flash in and out of the water as the broadhorn floated down-river until at last it disappeared behind a point of willows.

Again she heard the sad weird note of her boatman's horn, and she knew she'd follow it to the ends of the earth.

A boatman's wife, a boatman's wife sang the turning wheels of the carriage in which she rode with Levi, Uncle Philip and Julee toward Rutland Hall several weeks later. The words had given her strength to carry her through Aunt Lucinda's tears, Mr. Tazewell's shock at her rejection of him, Julee's wails of what was to become of her and Matt if Miss married the westerner.

Everyone had been mighty surprised except Uncle Philip, who said Levi had honorably declared his intentions to *him* during his stop-over on his up-river trip. Uncle Philip, acting in the role of the male relative at hand, had asked Levi not to profess his love as yet. He had urged Levi to return to Rivertown and if, after a lapse of time, he were still sincere in seeking Mary Marie's hand in marriage they would then decide upon a procedure of courtship.

"Oh, Uncle Philip! All the wretched uncertainty you made me go through!" Mary Marie cried.

Uncle Philip looked unhappy and said, "But my dear, sometimes young men have passing fancies. I don't want you hurt if I can help it."

Aunt Lucinda, when she had done weeping, said Uncle Philip must take Mary Marie home at once. This was a matter for the girl's father. But Mary Marie felt that Aunt Lucinda didn't want to put herself in the position of catching the brunt of Papa's anger because his daughter had been unsuitably matched while under her chaperonage.

"Why can't I just *marry* him?"

"If you do," Aunt Lucinda was insistent, "you'll regret it the rest of your days. You must go home and have this young man pay his court there. It will help you to know if you truly love him to see him in your own home and with your father."

But even now, jolting along in the carriage over the rough road approaching Rutland Hall, it still seemed a poor idea to be coming home to Papa. Levi and Uncle Philip must think so too, they were so silent. Uncle Philip's kind round face was serious at the prospect of bringing home to his brother a suitor for his only daughter. Levi looked hot and uncomfortable dressed in his best clothes.

Papa's scorn of Levi would be painful. She'd need a strong armor to endure it and break down his resistance. Papa had such awfully strong resistance. Oh! It would be much simpler just to go off with Levi. And then there was Mammy Fay to reckon with. In some ways she dreaded Mammy Fay's devotion more than Papa's scorn. Having Uncle Philip on their side would help, of course, but mostly she'd have to depend upon herself. She was not going to be denied her chance for happiness.

She smiled at Levi. She felt that her very soul stood in her eyes, intoxicated and thrilled. She had only to cling to the fact that Levi was her man, to marry if she pleased. It concerned no one but herself and Levi. She was coming home Papa's daughter, but when she left, she would be Levi's wife! She would! Nobody could stop her!

The carriage took the turning for Rutland Hall and to her surprise Mary Marie felt a home-coming tug.

It was nearing dusk, the "kain't time," when the hands could no longer see to pull fodder. Fodder-pulling time meant a lot of sickness. At the end of day during this season every field hand came to the sick house for a cup of whiskey to ward off the chills and fever brought on by the hot work among the cornstalks. Mammy Fay would be standing in the doorway while the field hands waited in line to dipper from the barrel of whiskey provided by Papa. Mammy Fay trusted only her own expert eye to look for the sick signs among the slaves.

It was Mammy Fay who knew how much blue mass to balance on a knife blade, when to give the ipecac. Any day now she would be doling out the undershirts, breaking out the piles of blankets waiting in the store house. No one would get an extra because Mammy Fay knew down to the last ninny just how many were needed for each cabin.

Mammy Fay would be surprised when Mary Marie told her she had distributed the blankets at Quercus Grove already. She would tell Mammy Fay how well she had managed plantation matters for Aunt Lucinda, how experienced she was to be the mistress of her own home. Of course she wasn't going to live on a plantation. She would live in a city called Rivertown. A boatman's wife wouldn't have many slaves to manage, probably no more than house servants, like New Orleans ladies.

My! Things had changed for her! Wouldn't everyone be surprised, she thought as the carriage rolled down the alley of live oaks.

Mammy Fay must have finished her work at the sick house for there she sat on the bench which long ago she had claimed for her own. She had cushioned it with gray moss and corn shucks and placed it under the china-berry tree near the front of the big house. From this vantage point she could keep a supervisory eye on the front door and the rear, the cook house, the store room —even down the main street of the quarters. There she knitted away on endless socks to cover white legs and black, and mighty little escaped her. No siree! She had a way of pretending to count stitches while from under lowered eyelids she watched what was going on.

So now she didn't trick Mary Marie when she got up from her bench and moved slowly, still knitting, to the rear of the house. Mammy Fay would be but a step behind Horatio when he opened the front door for them. She was. She stood, tall and narrow, her long, bony, strong, black hands clasped on her stiff white apron. She tried to keep her black face impassive at the sight of her Young Miss returned unexpectedly. But, by every mouth quirk and eye crinkle Mary Marie could tell how all her motherly instincts were overjoyed at the sight of her child come home.

"Oh! Mammy Fay! Mammy Fay!" cried Mary Marie. Surely since Mammy Fay loved her she would help her white child marry the man she loved so terribly?

Mammy Fay said, "You return early from you' visit." She gave Levi a long straight look and bowed ever so slightly to him.

"Hello, Mammy Fay," said Uncle Philip.

"Master Philip." Mammy Fay gave him a deep bow.

In spite of her stern exterior, Mary Marie thought, she is churning with questions. But before she asks them, she, the major-domo of Rutland Hall, will see to the reception and arrangements for the comfort of the household's guests. Only when she has directed all the household affairs to her satisfaction will she come to the bedroom for an accounting of the situation.

Mary Marie waited on the stool before her dressing table in the shadowy room darkened early by the moss-hung trees—a child waiting for the bed-time chiding.

"Now! Missy ma'am, what have you done?" Mammy Fay started talking even as she glided in the door.

"Nothing," said Mary Marie. She hated Mammy Fay for making her feel like a naughty child. She hated herself for not being grown up enough to handle Mammy Fay. She would have to do better than this or she'd be in trouble. "I rejected Mr. Tazewell, Mammy Fay."

"*Bien! Bien!* But this young man, who he?"

"Master Levi Blaisdell."

"Who he?"

"A friend of Captain Cleve—Uncle Philip. He's from River-town, Indiana."

"Where's that?"

"Near the Queen City, Cincinnati."

"This Queen City—what it like?"

"New Orleans, only better."

"How better?"

"Levi says . . ."

"Who?"

"Mr. Blaisdell says Fourth Street is as crowded with carriages as New Orleans. Up there they've got wealthy merchants and owners of steamboats. Their public landing covers ten whole acres; they've got a whole thousand feet of water front. He's going to build his own steamboat. Oh Mammy Fay, it's going to be wonderful. I'm so happy."

"*What* you say?"

How could she find the words to make Mammy Fay understand what it was like to be stirred to the very depths of her being, that she was aroused to a point where her whole body was in a great up-surge, her mind a tumult. Her voice longed to cry only, "Levi! Levi! Levi!"

With an effort she made the spasms in her throat behave. With her blood thudding in her ears, she said as calmly as she could, "I'm in love, Mammy Fay. You were right when you told me to marry for love."

48

"How you know? Give the love-sign feelings."

She tried so hard to think of the right thing to say to Mammy Fay. The best she could do was to quote Julee, " 'Cos when you both love everything clicks right into place."

She begged with her eyes, her thoughts, her whole being as hard as she could to make Mammy Fay believe. She tried again to think of something which would force Mammy Fay. Nothing seemed adequate. Yet while she was thinking she felt a change come over Mammy Fay, a slight wavering. Could it be that behind that black impassive face there was some unknown power working in her behalf? Mary Marie watched Mammy Fay closely, alert for a chance to press her point if the old slave's armor showed a weak spot.

At times Mary Marie felt that she didn't know or understand Mammy Fay at all. In childhood there had been goose-bump stories and haunting songs about strange black ways. Black bedtime after black bed-time Mary Marie had watched through the black oblong window the darkened moss swing from the shadowy trees against the stars in the dark sky. Closer at hand, inside the room, rocked the black shadow of Mammy Fay, her lullaby a sorrow song moaned to Lordy Jesus. With dark sobbing and grievous words she told Him the troubles of His trampled people and how poorly, mightily poorly His children were doin' and maybe He'd better, if He was a mind to, send someone down with the Jubilee time which was a long time a-comin', too long a time a-comin'— Lordy Jesus!

Dark ways were Mammy Fay's ways, filled with the dark memory of her people and the bitter taste of a captive race.

Even though she had spent her waking and sleeping hours midst these ways that were dark—they remained alien to her, Mary Marie thought. She looked out the window at the black shadow which was an immense tree—its roots, deep, dark and hidden. A cold wind swayed the black mourning draperies of moss that hung on the tree. Her mind was clutched by a cold fear. She had to push her mind to focus it on Mammy Fay's question.

"What about Julee?"

"She still wants to marry Matt. Levi—Mr. Blaisdell—is willing to buy Matt from Uncle Philip. I could use Matt. He's a good stable boy. I'll need a coachman."

"How many slaves this Master Blaisdell, he own?"

"We-ell, none."

Mammy Fay shook her head and said, "Unn-nh! What kind moneyed man he, if he don't got slaves?"

The state of slavery in Rivertown, Indiana, was confusing to Mary Marie. But she tried to explain it now as best she could to Mammy Fay from what she had heard Levi tell Uncle Philip. "Indiana is a free state, but they aren't fussy in the river counties if folks want slaves. Mr. Blaisdell says we won't have any trouble."

"Lordy Jesus," said Mammy Fay. "Free!—Julee!—Free! Jubilee time! Juba! Juba!"

"She wouldn't be free," said Mary Marie.

"No, no! I don't want Julee to be free. Julee you' body servant all you' life. But Julee to live in a free state. You not sell her, 'low no black snake on her pretty back. I trusts *you*. I wants no shame for my Julee. I wants you happy too, my little white pigeon. Us got to be mighty mighty sure 'bout this Master Blaisdell, Honey. God sure!"

"You'll love him, Mammy Fay, as soon as you know him."

"Us'll see," said Mammy Fay.

There was a rap at the door. It was Horatio who said, "Master Rutland is come. He wants to see you in the library, Miss Mary Marie—right away quick he say."

"Has Papa seen Master Philip?"

"No, Miss Mary Marie."

"Go at once to Master Philip, Horatio, and ask him please to come along down to the library as quickly as he can."

Papa came straight to the point. "What is this I hear, you bringing home a river rat to ask for your hand?"

Julee! Mary Marie had forgotten to caution Julee not to say anything before Papa was dealt with. She was extremely annoyed with herself. She snapped back at Papa, "He's not a river rat. Uncle Philip knows all about him. He comes from fine stock, he's building his own steamboat, or will, just as soon as he gets back, and I want to marry him. I love him, Papa."

"Hah! What can you know about love? A chit of a girl?"

She wanted to scream at him that she knew a darn sight more about it than he did, but it wouldn't do to have a fight with Papa just now. She had too much at stake—Levi. Surely there must be some way to get through to Papa. If only Mama were here to help her.

"I want to be happy, Papa. Don't make me bitter," was all she said.

"Oh my God, Mary. That's what *she* used to say."

"Who, Papa?"

"Your mother. She thought I didn't love her, but I did in my way. She was a gay little thing which was what I liked best in her. Maybe because I was so solemn myself. Had she lived things might have worked out differently."

"I'm sorry, Papa."

"You look like her, Mary."

"But not gay like her?"

Papa twisted his face as if in pain. "No. You've too much of me."

Mary Marie was profoundly shocked. It had never occurred to her that she could be the least little bit like Papa. She had never felt closer to her mother than she did this minute.

Papa was saying, "I don't suppose I've made it any too easy for you to find a suitable husband."

"Oh, but I have Papa. I *have*. Wait until you talk to him. You'll like him, Papa."

"I doubt it."

Uncle Philip rapped on the open door.

"Well, Philip, how are things with you?" Papa asked.

Horatio soon came to say supper was served and should he call the young man.

She let Papa and Uncle Philip precede her to the dining room. She stopped in the drawing room and looked up at Mama's picture in the heavy gold frame. "Don't worry, Mama," she whispered. "I think everything is going to be all right. Mammy Fay told me what you said about Marie not being Mary. I think I know now what you meant. But Mama, I think Papa *did* love you only he couldn't show you. I'm going to show Levi. You'd love my Levi, Mama—he's gay."

Supper was not a happy occasion.

Mary Marie was conscious of many emotions, but principally she was ashamed of herself. No matter how hard she tried, she continued to see Levi as Papa saw him—as she herself had seen him at first.

She remembered her revulsion at the homespun clothes, the broken nails and tousled hair, the unpolished manner. Tonight he was clean and well dressed, he was at ease with the older men and in the elegant surroundings—but somehow Papa made him seem out of place. Somehow wrong.

Levi pierced a piece of ham on his plate. He said, "Mighty fine ham. You folks must have a special seasoning. Better than up home."

"Ah yes!" said Papa. "Long ago we learned the art of gracious living."

"I'd be mighty pleased to know how you cure your hams."

"Ah!" said Papa. "It takes hundreds of years, many generations." And Papa wasn't talking about hogs. "Horatio, do offer Mr. Blaisdell the ham."

Levi didn't seem to know that Papa was insulting him. Or maybe he was too much of a gentleman to show his knowledge.

Later she wanted to tell Levi with her kisses that Papa had been very ill mannered and for him not to mind, but she couldn't because of Mammy Fay who sat on the chaperone seat in the drawing room.

"Can't you get rid of her?" Levi whispered.

Mary Marie shook her head. It was all very strained and uncomfortable.

The brightest spot was when Mammy Fay said to Levi, "Tell me, Master Blaisdell, sir, how is it with you about my Young Miss? I wants to know from the beginning."

"Well, Mammy Fay, there's a funny thing. I've known the Quercus Grove Rutlands for quite a spell, but I never happened to stop by when she was there. I'd heard a lot about her from Captain Cleve. He's pretty gone on her himself and he's got an interest in me. He says when you know two young-uns that are the apples of your own two eyes you want them to like each other. 'Course I didn't pay much attention to him." Levi grinned. "You know yourself, Mammy Fay, that's not the way to pick a wife."

Mammy Fay nodded her head.

"But when I saw her!" Levi caught Mammy Fay's long black hands and squeezed them. "Mammy Fay, she was like a flash of lightning through a gooseberry bush. I was a goner for sure. Been stepping high like a rooster in deep mud ever since. Mammy Fay, she's sweet as a punkin and as pretty and cute as a pair of little red shoes."

Mammy Fay couldn't help but laugh at Levi. But she sobered and said sternly, "You be good to my baby?"

Levi sobered too. He said, "I'll try. Maybe I won't always know how, but I'll never want to be anything else, Mammy Fay."

Mammy Fay withdrew her hands from Levi's; she turned to Mary Marie and said, "He do."

Papa's questions were of a different nature than Mammy Fay's.

Papa and Uncle Philip closeted themselves with Levi in the library. At long last, Papa decided Levi's blood lines, while not as long or as notable as might be wished, might do under the circumstances; his financial condition was not too sound, but he seemed sober and ambitious; and furthermore the lot of them had worn him down to a point where he didn't care too much anymore whom his daughter married. If she wanted to throw herself away on a western clout, she could go ahead and do it.

"You consent, then, Papa?"

The best she could wring from him was that he did not forbid it. He told her not to get so excited and please not to expect him to feel jubilant about it. Bluntly she was to spare him as much fuss as she could for he was not inclined to put up with much in the way of celebration.

"But my wedding, Papa?"

"It'll be a simple ceremony in the library."

"But Aunt Lucinda, and the cousins . . ."

"Good God!" shouted Papa.

"I want them—all of them. I want it to be fun! It won't be fun without them. There's nobody else to make it a party—'cept the 'kithin' kin.' "

"Kithin' kin. Good God! What a way to talk! Isn't it enough that I give my consent, even if I think you are a little fool? I don't deny you my house to stand up in, but you go too far if you expect me—! Go to your kithin' kin! Let them be fools too!"

"You'll come won't you, Papa?"

"No!"

Mary Marie had been glad when Levi and Uncle Philip left. It was too strained and uncomfortable having them around with Papa.

Her last days at Rutland Hall were very sad. Papa drew within his cold, arrogant, self-sufficient armor and there was no way to

53

break through it. There had been just that one brief moment when the memory of Mama had seemed to bring them closer together. Mary Marie was hurt now that Papa would have nothing to do with her marriage. But as usual, Mammy Fay took over.

Mary Marie had expected to do battle with Mammy Fay over Levi. She had never hoped for her aid. It was better not to question Mammy Fay's acceptance of this westerner who surely, when all was said and done, was a far cry from the glories of a Saint Cecelia's ball in Charleston. Nevertheless, it was Mammy Fay who said to Papa, "Master Rutland, she a Fee, she a Rutland. You have you' duty to you' daughter."

Papa without a word went to his strong box and handed Mammy Fay a great deal of gold and said, "Get whatever she needs in New Orleans."

To Mary Marie he said, "Do you want Mammy Fay? She was part of your mother's dowry."

"No, Papa. I couldn't *own* Mammy Fay. But I want you to send her to Quercus Grove for the wedding. Julee is to marry Matt. Mammy Fay should dress us for our weddings. Papa! Won't you come, too?"

"No!" The answer remained the same.

Mary Marie was glad when she finally got all of her things packed and loaded into the wagons to be taken into New Orleans.

"Papa, won't you even come into New Orleans?"

Papa said, "No, I have no business to transact there."

In New Orleans her hurt followed her everywhere all the while she considered, with Mammy Fay and Julee, trousseau fabrics and fripperies. "*Amo, amas, amat*, what do the words mean, Papa?" she had once asked during a lesson. "Do the plural," Papa had ordered. "*Amamus, amatis, amant*." Papa thought he knew how to conjugate love, but he didn't. Gradually her hurt lessened to a small cold knot.

CHAPTER VI

Aᴛ QUERCUS GROVE, MARY MARIE FLOATED ON A RIVER OF HAPPINESS
—of loving and being loved by everyone from Uncle Philip and
Aunt Lucinda down to the lowliest slave. She was going to be
married.

Uncle Philip said she and Julee acted like a pair of flying larks.

Matters for Julee had come right as last. When Levi had offered
to buy Matt for Mary Marie, Uncle Philip had said, "No, indeed.
My wife and I are deeply indebted to our niece, we want her to
accept Matt as a gift from us."

Julee was all wound up these days. She talked the language of
signs, good-luck signs, bad-luck signs. "You wants to be careful,
Miss, what day you picks for us to get married. Monday a bad day
all 'round. Tuesday, not bad, our mens be good and live long.
Seems like mebbe Wednesday the best day, our mens good, make
us happy but we gots some trouble."

"What about Thursday or Friday?"

Julee shook her head and would only say, "Them days—bad.
Saturday and Sunday bring us no luck. You better picks Wednesday, Miss."

Mammy Fay arrived with a whole boat load of boxes. When
she unpacked them everyone stood around and oh-ed and ah-ed
at the creations she had made with the help of *The Lady's Book.*
There was one of gold-colored silk trimmed with white-point lace
and buff crepe pleatings, girdled with long tassels. To be worn
with it was a white cashmere cloak trimmed with red ermine.
Young Miss was to wear white and red ostrich feathers in her
hair.

"But my hair is too red."

Mammy Fay commanded, "Wear the feathers."

But the costume that everyone said was the best was the lavender silk, brocaded with silver snowdrops drooping in clusters. Several little metal hands, hung on fine chains attached at the waist, held up the skirt a trifle to show flounces of underskirts just short enough to expose a dainty foot encased in a silk gaiter the same shade as the dress.

"Yes, they're handsome gowns," Aunt Lucinda said. "I doubt if Queen Victoria, herself, had any more beautiful for her eighteenth birthday. But I wonder, dear Mary Marie, do you suppose this trousseau will be quite suitable for Rivertown?"

Mammy Fay defended her selections, "Master Levi, he say it near the Queen City and it like New Orleans."

Aunt Lucinda said, "Well, maybe so."

It was a lovely wedding in the early spring of '38.

They decorated the house lavishly, the broad hall with magnolia leaves, cherokee roses, and lighted candles. The piazzas were crowded with slaves in their Sunday clothes. All the young Rutland faces were scoured raw and red, their hair wet and slick. Aunt Lucinda kept her sobs in a quiet key. Uncle Philip, acting for Papa, handed Mary Marie over to the minister, who ceremoniously maneuvered his way through the lovely service.

Levi had said he didn't care what kind of tomfoolery she put him through just so she felt she was marrying him for keeps. He would have been glad to jump over a broomstick if it held the rightful meaning. When he fingered the brocade of her wedding dress he reckoned Mammy Fay had paid all of forty bushels of corn per yard for it; and as far as he was concerned his bride could have stood up in calico.

Just the same he had fixed himself up extra special. His blue broadcloth had cost more than the brocade, sixty bushels of corn a yard. His waistcoat was light buff; his stock, above a ruffled shirt front, black satin; his striped narrow pants set off his fine long legs. He was her Levi. Papa had been wrong in his prediction that when she stood up in front of the minister and the family she would be ashamed of him. She wished Papa were there so he could see for himself what a fine couple they made.

As soon as the minister had pronounced them man and wife,

before God and all the relations, they stood aside. Then Matt and Julee took their places, hand in hand, before the minister.

They weren't dressed in homespun from the plantation looms. They were dressed in outfits of new city cloth bought by Mammy Fay with Papa's money. When Levi saw Julee's dress he told the beaming Matt he'd have to keep his eye on her aboard *The Rising Sun* or she might be mistaken for a monster checkerboard in her red and black calico, and the men might start playing across her.

Then after the minister had heard all the promises, Julee threw her arms around Mary Marie and said, "Us got our mens."

Out under the live oak trees there were long tables spread with a fine wedding feast of meats, cakes and sweets for Matt and Julee and all the Negroes of the plantation. Preparations had been going on for weeks; oxen, pigs, turkeys, chickens, ducks—all fed to plump sleekness in anticipation of the great day. There was one long table loaded with nothing but sweet cakes and trifles. Two "waitmans" went for the barrels Uncle Philip provided—one for the men, one for the girls. Aunt Lucinda said she didn't want the girls drinking whiskey straight, so sugar and water had been added to one of the barrels.

"But us young gals always sneak the whiskey, Miss, not the toddy," Julee said. "It's a tearin'-down wedding better 'n 'spected. It's big doin's they give us. Master and Mistus Rutland stomped down fine folks. Give us a head weddin'. How you Mistus Bride?" Julee was already a little drunk.

To the sound of Julee's and Matt's merrymaking with fiddle, banjo and bones the Rutland family formed a procession to escort Mary Marie and Levi to their wedding feast in the dining room.

When Uncle Philip stood with his raised glass the lump which had been steadily growing larger in Mary Marie's throat all but strangled her. She thought she could have kept back the tears if it hadn't been for little black Dabney in the fly swing. A strange longing filled her. She wanted to see little black Ambus in his swing over Papa's table. Papa!

Papa would now be sitting alone at his long, bare, polished table, refusing the servings offered by Horatio, unmindful of little black Ambus grown careless with drooping feathers. She had to blink very fast to keep her tears from edging over onto her cheeks. She told herself she was a little fool to feel bound to Papa. It was best that she was going far away from him. It would serve him right if he got good and lonely. *The Rising Sun* would come any minute to carry her a thousand miles away from Papa.

When someone spied the smoke stack of *The Rising Sun* they made a gay procession to the shore. Prince, decorated with ribbons and flowers and led by a proud stable boy, headed the cavalcade. Next came the carriage festooned with ropes of green studded with white cherokee roses. On the box was a very proud Matt, beside him a very happy Julee. In the carriage, its top laid back, sat Mary Marie with her handsome Levi laughing at the crowd of field hands in their Sunday clothes trotting towards the river. Behind them rolled a Dearborn filled to overflowing with laughing, shouting, singing Rutlands. Then came the wagons loaded with the trunks and boxes, holding the truly superb trousseau and dowry. Mammy Fay had managed to do right well for her children.

Mammy Fay had remained impassive the entire wedding day; no one could guess what went on behind the utter blankness of her face. Mammy Fay had said she didn't care to go to the boat; she'd make her farewells in the bedroom where she had helped her two children, one white, one black, dress for their journey. Mary Marie had cried on Mammy Fay's white fichu and laughed at what a fool she was making of herself. Julee hadn't cried when Mammy Fay held her in long black arms, lecturing her affectionately, "You mind you' manners in that free place you goin'. You be good girl."

The crowd sang, whooped, and hollered while they waited for *The Rising Sun* to put in to Quercus Grove.

Captain Cleve too did handsomely by his favorites, Levi and Mary Marie. He had a barrel of whiskey rolled off the gangplank and set up on the river bank for Matt's and Julee's friends. The Rutlands were invited aboard to partake of punch and cakes served in the salon.

"All dat ain't a-goin', please to git asho'."

It was time to kiss them all goodbye.

"Don't cry Half-Pint," said Levi beside her at the rear guard rail. "I'll make you happy."

"Will you?" she sobbed, waving a wet handkerchief at the black speck which was Quercus Grove.

58

"Half-Pint I'll make good on my promise. When you come back I'll ride you right up to Quercus Grove's front gate—on our very own steamboat. So what're you crying for?"

She couldn't tell him how she had always wanted something without knowing what it was and she was so scared that riding a steamboat up to Quercus Grove might not be it. So she said, "I'm crying for Mammy Fay."

"Why?"

"Oh! She's been devoted so many years, has worked so hard to make me a credit to the family."

"I'm glad you didn't want me to buy *her*."

"*Buy* Mammy Fay. Nobody could *buy* Mammy Fay."

"She's a slave isn't she?"

"No." She couldn't think of Mammy Fay as a slave.

"Just the same I'm glad we aren't taking her to Rivertown, don't know what folks would make of her. Which reminds me, Rivertown won't cotton to your name, Half-Pint."

"What's the matter with my name?"

"I don't know—Mary Marie sounds funny."

"Does it?" asked Mary Marie.

"Uh-huh. How'd you come to get it?"

She told him the story as Mammy Fay had told it to her, "So there was my poor little French Mama, Marie Isabelle, dying so far away from her kin in South Carolina and there was Tory Papa. So Papa wrote, Mary Isabelle Rutland."

"How did you get the Mary Marie?"

"I'm two persons. One of me is Papa's Mary, the other Mama's Marie. Mammy Fay says Mama, after Papa left the room, held me close and said, 'don't try too hard, Marie, to be Mary.'"

"I don't like it, Half-Pint. It's too mixed up. You forget this Papa, Mama, Mammy Fay business. You're married to me now—a new life! I'm giving you a whole new name—Molly Blaisdell. How do you like the sound of that?"

"Oh Levi! I *love* it."

"Spell it with a y or it's too high-faluting. But we haven't thrown our good-luck coin." He took a coin from his pocket and flipped it far out into the wide, wide river. "For us, Molly. Good luck to you, Molly Blaisdell. Come on."

In their stateroom, the bridal chamber, she asked Levi to step outside and see if he could find Julee to come to her. Levi asked, "What for?" Mary Marie said she needed her.

For answer, Levi kissed her and took off her hat. He twirled it around his big finger and gave a joyous laugh. "Looks for all the world like a scuttle, Half-Pint." He tossed it up onto a berth. He put his big thumbs together in front of her waist, stretched his fingers. "By golly, I can make them reach clear round." He swung her off the floor and did a few steps of his dance, *Never saw a girl in all my life but what she would be a boatman's wife.*

Her body began to tremble.

"What is it?" he whispered.

Her breath caught in a half sob, a shuddering sigh.

His hands began to slide over the soft silk of her dress to soothe her, smooth her, they lingered over the curves of her breasts until her entire body felt all curves melting into one. He held her closer within the circle of his arm while his fingers cleverly undid the buttons and pushed the silk aside. His lips felt tender and soft upon her fine skin. She let out a little moan. "Levi! Levi!" She was crying to him to do something—to do something—anything —to help.

He gave a loving, teasing laugh. "Shall I call Julee?"

She had no need of Julee.

CHAPTER VII

THE NEXT MORNING AT THE STERN GUARD-RAIL OF *The Rising Sun* she watched the South slip away behind the wake of the boat.

Molly Blaisdell! She said the name over and over to herself. A new name—a new life!

She hadn't known what being loved meant. She had intended to be coy and make her man miserable while she enjoyed teasing him. Then he had removed her hat, had been so droll when he called it a scuttle, had shown such delight in the tiny size of her waist, had held her so close in their dance. And when she realized how much he loved her she was ashamed that she had thought to tease him. You didn't tease the one who put you on a cloud and pinned stars in your hair.

This morning, the first one of her married life, she wanted nothing, except to put her Molly hand frankly in her Levi's and go with him, not run away with roguish glances over her shoulder as Mary Marie would have done. Molly Blaisdell, Mrs. Levi Blaisdell, she told the broad Mississippi, was on her wedding journey to Rivertown, Indiana.

"Tell me about Rivertown, Levi."

"Oh! I guess there's not much to tell. It's a nice town, Molly."

"What makes it nice?"

"It's got a good location. River channel runs in close to town, boats of any class that're able to run other places can land there. That's awfully important to a river town, Molly."

"Is the landing big like the Queen City?"

Levi hitched about a bit. "It's a first-rate town Molly, a sight

61

better than most but maybe I overspoke myself. Maybe you'll be disappointed because I puffed it up too much."

"Oh!"

"It's a bully town though, Molly. It has a pretty setting on high bottom land so's there's not much danger from floods. There's plenty of timber on the hills behind it. It's healthy because in wet seasons the water drains off. It's grown fast. There're folks there who heard the cracks of the Indians shooting. Ole Miz Davidson saw the *New Orleans,* the first steamboat on the Ohio, thought it was a sawmill—never dreamed it could be a steamboat.

"Yes siree, those were the days, but so are ours, Molly. I'd rather be alive now than any time I know of—just when steamboats are really getting started. We've got a thousand miles of river winding through as good soil and climate as anywhere in the world, I reckon. Its tributaries drain a land of milk and honey. God's done so much for us there, we don't have to do much for ourselves. We've got everything. All we've got to do is use it. Pa would still like to emigrate further west, but Ma's against it. Ma says she's traipsed as far as she's going with her kettle of fire."

"What does she mean?"

"Ma sets great store by her fire. She's never let that fire go out since she took the coals from her hearth back east."

"Good gracious—what for? How did she carry it?"

"In a kettle. She says it stays right where it is, she won't tote her fire further west. She won't leave Cory, either."

"Cory?"

"Guess I didn't mention Cory before. She was the girl born after Gaithe and me. Ma was always more taken up with Cory than us boys."

"What happened to her?"

"The cholera carried her off a few years back. Cholera's an ugly scarey thing. Ma's never gotten over Cory."

Suddenly the boat sheered to the right and Levi raised his head to peer at the shore. "Looks like Captain Cleve's got a hail over on the Tennessee side," he said. He pointed to a tangle of brushwood, greenbriers and cane on the distant shore.

Yes, there was a man waving something white. Not a house was to be seen along the bank, only an unbroken line of forest, not even a hole in the green to show where a path might be. "This will be a tough landing even for Scoot," Levi said. "I'm going forward, Molly, want to see him do it."

Not for nothing was Captain Cleve's pilot called Scoot; he could scoot in to shore on the lowest water. *The Rising Sun* rounded to now, bells clanged angrily, paddle wheels obeyed. The boat started in, engines stopped, she glided in. With fancy double-cussing the mate got his landing stage down into the Mississippi River mud.

"Lay me a gangplank," he shouted. You could tell he was not pleased at having to board a family of emigrants.

An old lady who must be the grandmother sat in a rocking chair and refused to get out of it. She grasped the seat tightly with both hands, twisted her feet around the legs of the chair and hung on for dear life.

"Pick her up, chair and all," shouted the mate. "Git her aboard. Keep movin' there. Git her aboard."

The emigrant grandmother in her linsey-woolsey and slatted sunbonnet sat in her chair on deck hour after hour. She sat and rocked and wouldn't talk to the curious passengers who made trips to see her. As if she were in a traveling menagerie, Levi said; folks ought to be ashamed of themselves acting so. If Molly went near her she was careful not to look at the old lady.

She was surprised one time when she realized the old lady was calling her, "Honey! Oh Honey!"

"Yes?"

"You're mighty pretty, Miss."

"Why, thank you."

"Take that chair," she pointed a long bony finger. "Set up, Honey. I want to talk to you. Heer'ed you is a bride. What's your new name, Honey?"

"Molly Blaisdell." It made her feel shy to say it to anyone for the first time.

"You got a good man?"

"Oh yes! Levi is wonderful."

The old lady shook her slat-sunbonneted head. "After great heat cometh cold. Certes you'll know what you got after you've summered and wintered him. I wish you well."

"Thank you," said Molly and started up from her chair.

"Nay, set," the old lady said, "with Deborah Goodin. Aunt Debby to neighbor and kin. I'm bereft out of my remembrance. I'd be under a thousand compliments to you if you'd seek out some words in my Bible with your young eyes."

"Maybe I can't. I don't know the Bible very well. What is it you want?"

"I been settin' here thinkin' 'bout the dogwood trees what stood nigh our clearin' back in the Caroliny mountains. Reckon they're all a-bloom 'bout now. A purtier sight you'll never see than them dogwood trees, fillin' the gully like snow, set off by pink rifts maked by the redbud trees. God noted them in nature, one 'gainst t'other."

"I don't understand."

"Don't you Honey? I been heedin' you. I thinks to myself, she's got the rightful looks to mind the sign."

Molly felt uncomfortable under Aunt Debbie's earnest gaze. The old woman sounded so queer. Molly wished she could escape, but yet there was something so gentle, gracious and courteous about Aunt Debbie that she didn't want to be unkind or rude to her.

"It was Judas, don't you remember, Honey? He betrayed our Lord for thirty pieces of silver. They made the holy cross from the dogwood tree and the Lord said nevermore would He let it grow straight. You look at the next one and you'll see. Even its petals shape a cross. And our Lord named the redbud tree Judas, and set it 'long side the Holy-Cross tree as a sign. Once a year He flowers them together to remind us weak humans we're not to betray Him but mind His teachings. You need to remember that Honey whar you're goin'. Whar your man journey you?"

"To Indiana."

"I don't rightly know whar 'tis. But you mind the dogwood and the redbud trees every spring and think on what I tell you."

"Thank you, Aunt Debbie. Where are you going?"

"They're goin' to set me down in Missoury. I didn't want to come. I've done my share of traipsin' hither an' yon and it's my downright conclusion that folks are mistaken to think that traipsin' will cure their troubles. They forget to figger mebbe the trouble is right in their own-selves. They can't leave their past anymore than you can your ole hound dog what's determined to go along. You can scold him, beat him, stone him, and just when you stop for a moment to ease up—in less time than it takes to swing a cat—the

64

durn, sneakin' thing's caught up with you again. You might as well let him come along with you in the first place, you might even have pleasured yourself with his company 'stead of feelin' mean and ornery. Did you find it Honey?"

"What?"

"The place in the Bible about the cross."

"Not this time, but I'll try again sometime."

"Wish you would, Honey," the old lady said. "I once know'd a body, I don't rightly remember who, but she said it was in the Bible. She said she could lay her finger right on it, so it must be there, but I ain't found it yet. Be a sight of comfort to me if I could."

The next evening *The Rising Sun* headed in for a hole in the willows which Levi said was Missouri.

Molly went to Aunt Deborah Goodin to tell her goodbye, but Aunt Debbie said, "I gave you my sign, for my bones tell me there's trouble ahead. I don't never say farewell if I can helpen."

The water was too shallow for even Scoot to get in close enough to push a landing stage onto the Missouri shore. The emigrants had to be set down in a johnboat. Their few household goods were quickly loaded, rowed in and set on the shore, and the boat returned for the family. They all took their places but Aunt Debbie. She clung as before to her old high-backed, rush-bottomed, rocking chair. The deck hands picked her up in her chair. It was pathetic to see her lowered into the rowboat like a bale of cotton to be set down on shore.

Molly watched as long as she could. The family struggled up a path which led through the willows to a few cabins on the low river bank, leaving Aunt Debbie in her rocking chair in the dusk on the lonely shore.

That night safe in Levi's arms, Molly said, "Tell me about our house, Levi. Is it brick?"

"No."

"Is it like Quercus Grove?"

"No, it's more pioneer."

"You mean like in Missouri?"

"Oh no!"

Then Levi said he was only teasing her. He had taken over a couple of cabins that had a dog trot between. They were situated mighty pretty, on the river bank. He had enclosed the dog trot, made as good a broad hall as at Quercus Grove. They could build wings on when and as they needed them—which he thought would be soon seeing as how they seemed suited to each other.

"Oh you!" Molly giggled. Levi was a tease. She wasn't going to believe one word he told her about their house. Of course he had provided a nice one. Rivertown wasn't a pioneer place. It was near the Queen City, Levi himself had said so.

She saw herself looking mighty handsome, paying calls with Matt on the box. She must speak to Levi about a carriage and pair. White horses would be striking, and she could wear her bright-red dress which did not dim her red hair but made it glow more warmly.

By the time *The Rising Sun* reached the confluence of the Ohio and the Mississippi she had become the queen of Rivertown, the perfectly fascinating bride Levi Blaisdell had brought from the South, who overnight had become the leader of the young society set and whose entertainment was unlike anything Rivertown had ever seen before. Julee would have to double between cook-house and parlor until she could see about additional service. Levi had her a trifle confused about Hoosier housekeeping—that was the man of it. There wasn't a one, Aunt Lucinda said, who ever understood how women managed to run things with the help they had.

From the top deck, where she stood with Levi, she waved to Julee below with Matt on the forecastle—they too were anxious to catch their first glimpse of La Belle Rivière. Indeed she would not be ashamed to show them off in Rivertown. They were as handsome a pair of servants as could be found in the whole South!

She turned to Levi as he pointed out the unfolding landscape while *The Rising Sun* carried them northward.

"See, Half-Pint. That's still Missouri over there, where the big storm cloud is. Looks like we're in for a humdinger. Hope it holds off for a spell. I'd like for you to enjoy the Ohio a while first." Levi swung his pointing finger, "Up there between the Mississippi and the Ohio—that's Illinois. This side of the Ohio is Kentucky."

"Where's Indiana?"

"Only a little ways up. But that's our river, Molly, our very own Ohio. Look at her. See how clear she is."

It was true that the Ohio was bright, clear water in contrast to the muddy Mississippi, but its banks were just as low and flat, its trees as stunted.

The storm thickened with great black clouds rolling in from Missouri; one came in higher than the rest, edged with silver as sharp as a blade of steel. The clouds closed in and the sky grew darker. Over head there came a stirring sound.

"Geese!" Levi shouted. "It's the geese!"

They flew over with an exciting, terrifying swish of sweeping wings.

Honk! Honk!

Thousands of them, each flying to see past the shoulder of the one before him, forming a great V. Their line of flight shifted and changed as the hindmost became dissatisfied and fought for position, changed sides or moved up to take the place of a tired comrade dropping behind. On and on they came, always their high-pitched honk, honk, filling the air. When they reached the dividing waters of the Ohio and Mississippi they broke their neat formation and became a wheeling, milling confused mass without a leader, until a gander stronger than the other birds pulled out of the whirling mass and headed due north through Illinois. One by one the birds took up their position behind him, and again made their formation and soon became a dark point on the northern sky.

"Geese know only two points of the compass," Levi explained. "North and South."

North and South.

Molly wondered how they differed. Until now she had had no doubts but that Rivertown would be enchanted with Southern Mary-Marie-Molly, and Levi's enthusiasm had convinced her that Rivertown on the Ohio was the exact center of a vast inland empire which was the United States. But when she saw Cairo at the Junction of the Ohio and the Mississippi, the sight filled her with misgivings. Only a few inhabitants, wretched, thin and yellow, emerged from the few buildings huddled among the stunted trees on a neck of marshy, flat land, a breeding place for fever, ague and death.

She thought of her trunks filled with pretty clothes, her "moveables" so carefully hampered and crated, the gold girandoles, the nest of delicate japanned tables and the thin, fragile china. She drew in her breath and kept her words behind clenched teeth.

Mary-Marie-Molly, what makes you think Rivertown's going to like you or you it?

Levi was there, but she stood alone in the awful present. Behind her lay her past—before, her future. And she grew frightened for what did one do with so short a present when all else was too awesome to contemplate. Her past was with Papa—serve him right that she had left him to go far, far away with a stranger. For now this man beside her was indeed a stranger; this was not the bearer of divine happiness—ecstasy—who brought a miracle, a shower of gold from the skies. This was a stranger who was forcing her into the unknown, frightening future.

There came a clap of thunder and the moment had become the past and she trembled at the future which was already present. And she groped for Aunt Debbie's words, but a flash of lightning blinded her to their meaning.

"Better not stay on deck," said Levi.

"A last look—at the Mississippi."

But it was for herself she wept. She wept for her unhappy childhood, held in the trap of Papa's gloom and bound by Mammy Fay's restrictions. *The Rising Sun,* cutting through the chop kicked up by the storm, might carry her far away, but the past would go with her into the future.

CHAPTER VIII

Levi's loving that night and the next morning wiped clean her black thoughts upon leaving the Mississippi. As on her bridal night, her whole being responded to his tender little words, his loving seeking mouth and hands. She was stirred to the very depths of her being and ached for Levi's body to clash with hers until she was swept onward to yearn over him and to know she was the satisfied center of his world.

But this morning—!

This morning there had been a roughness and suddenness to his loving, and her small world rocked on its axis. When he had touched her there was a difference in his too hasty hands and harsh lips, and she was left baffled and unsatisfied. She was unnerved almost to the point of hysteria, but her indignation that Levi could treat her so—she who was as daintily lovely and fragile as the little rosebuds and heart's ease embroidered on her silk dressing gown—restrained her. She was angry with Levi, but she was also angry with herself because she wanted him to notice her discontent, but would have died rather than admit it. Levi had abandoned her. She hated him.

He sprang up, swelled out his chest and postured himself like a triumphant satyr.

"Gosh all hemlock, it's good to get back where I belong. Up here I know I can swim like an eel," he grinned down at her, disheveled, tossed about.

He reached for his shirt and pants. "Come on Half-Pint, get up. Top deck, there's an Ohio River spring." He banged out the door.

She waited for him to come back to her, but he didn't. When she was finally dressed and came on deck, she couldn't find him anywhere.

It was Captain Cleve who pointed out to her how pleasantly warm the spring sunshine was, how the water of the Ohio was clear as Levi had said it would be, how it flowed through beautiful country, the Kentucky side handsomer than the Indiana, how the wild forests reached from the tops of the knobs down to the water's edge, how occasionally great cliffs appeared, straight up and down rocks. How did she think she'd like to live in a house like that one in the clearing surrounded by dogwood and redbud trees in bloom?

She nodded her head. What a green meadow! Oh! Wouldn't it feel wonderful to be riding Prince again at a good gallop (poor Prince who had been shut up so long below decks), to follow a back country road. She strained her eyes to see one.

"I can't see the roads, Captain Cleve."

"Good reason, there aren't any."

"No roads?"

"The river is the road."

She couldn't ride Prince on the river. "But the interior, doesn't anyone go inland?"

"Farmers have wagon trails into the back country; they have to get their produce down to the river for shipping. But see here, Honey, you stick close to town, don't go ridin' 'round."

"Why not? Matt is an able groom."

"Reckon Rivertown ladies wouldn't take kindly to your ridin' 'round just for fun. If you got to go somewheres and that's the only way to get there, then a lady might put herself on a horse."

"They take their pleasure airing in carriages, then?"

"They do up to the Queen City but I don't recollect ever seein' one in Rivertown."

"But, Captain Cleve, how do the ladies get about?"

He crinkled his eyes at her, "The way God meant 'em to, I reckon—shank's mare."

"Oh!"

"See here, Honey. There's something I been figgerin' on tryin' to say to you. I don't rightly know how to put it."

"Yes, Captain Cleve?"

"Well, Honey, it's this-a-way. You're goin' to find things different

70

up here. Outward things. You'll catch on to 'em quick enough. Still it might help you to remember that folks are pretty much the same all over. I go up and down these rivers and I've come to the conclusion there're just so many kinds of folks, some are good and some are bad. You'll find 'em wherever you go, so don't get to thinkin' Rivertown's different." He smiled at her, "Like as not, you'll get a few knocks. We're comin' up for our last woodin' 'fore Rivertown. 'Fore we get there I want to say if there's ought I can do for you anytime, let me know. I feel kinda responsible for you."

She laid her hand on Captain Cleve's blue broadcloth sleeve. "Thank you, Captain Cleve."

They were silent while Scoot, the pilot, edged *The Rising Sun* in as close as he could to the woodyard landing.

The tall, skinny wood cutters leaning against the door jambs of their huts, built on piles, had the usual peculiar complexion which came from the "river sickness." The mate yelled his usual, "lay me a gangplank." But the plank proved to be too short and it was easy to see why the apprentice who was supposed to arrange for the wooding was called "a mud clerk."

Captain Cleve raised his speaking trumpet and shouted down, "Tell 'em if the water keeps droppin', they'll have to flat the wood mid-stream for the down trip."

"Is the river low?" asked Molly.

"Lower 'n tarnation. See that big sycamore up the bank, by rights this time of year water ought to be up to it. Water's droppin' fast. Too fast! Infernal mud makes fueling slow. At this rate we'll be hangin' up on sand bars."

Molly watched the men, white men, some German and Irish and the western American flatboat men like Levi, working their way up-river by wooding *The Rising Sun*. Here indeed was a difference between the North and South—white men doing black men's work.

"Good boy!" exclaimed Captain Cleve.

"Who?" she asked.

"Levi! Said he was muscle bound. Wanted to limber up, did I mind?"

No! But it was true. There was Levi, again a westerner, a clout in rough clothes, wading through the mud to toss what looked like a young tree onto his shoulder. And after they were done he

71

shouted coarsely with the rest for the "old white pitcher." He laughed, whooped and took his turn when the bartender sent the desired whiskey-filled crockery below.

Why, they behaved just like Rutland Hall slaves, lining up after a day in the fields. And Levi was one of them! The sight made her feel ill.

"Forgive me, Captain, I'm going in. I don't feel very well." The bride hurried along to the bridal stateroom and threw herself onto the bridal berth.

How could he do such a thing to her—on her wedding journey! Oh! Oh! What had she let herself in for? How could that man swigging from a common pitcher be the same one in whose arms she had lain last night and every night? She turned her hot face into the pillow. Oh! The shame of it—in bed this morning. What kind of person *was* she? She bit the pillow—she had sort of liked it, or might have. But of course she didn't really. She doubted if ladies did.

If that was the way a western clout behaved, she wanted no more of him. But she was married to him. She was about to arrive in some outlandish place called Rivertown, where ladies didn't ride horseback or take airings in carriages. What was she to do? In a matter of a few hours she would be received by her new kin, the Blaisdells. Tears were not an asset; she must look her very best when they came aboard to meet her and partake of Captain Cleve's refreshments.

The door of the cabin burst open.

It was Levi, dirty in his homespuns, hot and exhilarated by his homecoming, the physical work he loved, and the "old white pitcher."

Molly jumped from the bed and faced him haughtily, her eyes futilely demanding an apology for something far now from his thoughts.

"You're pretty enough to eat, Molly. My, but I love you," he held her close and as quickly released her. "Durned if I don't feel like 'the leapin' trout' of the water again. I'd begun to choke to death like a cat fish on a sand bank. How can you stay in this stuffy old cabin-hole?"

She wished she was big enough to beat him into doll rags. He hadn't truly looked at her or sensed her anger. She turned to the washstand and poured some water into the washbowl. Suddenly she had no control over her hands. She hurled the water pitcher at Levi, not caring if she killed him; but she gasped with sudden fear when the pitcher crashed on the cabin floor. What if her aim and strength had been better and the pitcher had broken his head? If anything were to happen to him she couldn't stand it. She didn't care what he was, he was her Levi.

He looked at the broken pitcher and the water on the floor. "Looks like you've kicked up a right-smart plug muss in here."

"Get out!"

Levi went out and closed the door only to open it again, to show his face with a big grin on it. "Sweet as punkin, that's you, Sorrel Top. See you top deck."

By the time she joined him she had regained her equilibrium. She need have no silly fears about Levi, his family, his Rivertown. Deborah Goodin, the old pioneer woman, bereft of her rightful remembrance, confused in her dotage, rapping out meaningless prophecies and muttering the warnings of old age, had upset her. She, Mary Marie Rutland Molly Blaisdell had nothing to fear; she would quit being silly, everything would be all right—it had to be!

She was a bride being brought home by her bridegroom rigged out in her wedding finery. Levi gave her appearance a proud glance, for Julee had gowned her with extra care.

"Suck in you' middle, Miss, us been relaxin' too much," Julee had giggled as she had pulled the lacings tighter and tighter.

Then Levi said, "Watch now. After we round this bend you'll see Rivertown, Molly Blaisdell."

That was the key to the future, she'd begin a new life in this new place. Those other selves she'd push down, down, down until they were drowned. She'd be no one but Molly Blaisdell. She rested her gloved hand lightly on one of the white wooden floats, a life preserver, hung on the guard rail of *The Rising Sun*. In black letters on the float was painted, *In God We Trust*. "Levi," she said, "I'll shut my eyes, and you tell me when to look."

His hand closed over hers. "I'm sorry I made you mad," he said gently.

She smiled trustingly up at him and was content. She heard the pat-pat of the paddle wheels, the swish of the water, the creak of the boat's wooden structure as *The Rising Sun* strained against the mighty current, and she felt strong.

"Look!"

73

Rivertown was set down in the scenery where the river flowed in graceful loveliness through the hills now a mighty flood of spring color, bronze reds, soft greens, yellows, pinks, grays, and silver-white amongst the dark greens of pine and fir. The rose-red close-set blossoms of the Judas trees poured over the slopes like wine staining the medallioned white cloth of the dogwood trees. Nature had fashioned a landing beneath the first rise and, once up the bank in the shadow of the more rugged hills, she had left ample room for a town plotted in neat rectangles. There was space for the streets of trade and the more shaded streets for houses with porticoes, gardens, orchards and barns.

Front Street, the most important street, faced the town's roadway to the outside world—the river. In and about this area was the true core of the town's being: THE Public Landing, inadequately timber cribbed, badly graded, unplanked, seasonally rutted in mud or dust; the all-important warehouses of produce to be shipped, the two distilleries, the fanning and flour mill, two cotton mills, cabinet shops, tanning yards, brick yards and iron foundries.

Levi bragged, "In the revulsion of trade not a single business failed."

"It's a pretty town, too, Levi."

"Yup, she's pretty. I got to go below, find Matt, see to your plunder."

"But meeting the family—don't leave me alone!"

"Well," drawled Levi, "not likely anybody'll be down to the landing, except maybe Gaithe." Levi grinned. "He's probably been hanging around watching every boat for days."

"But the kin will come aboard to welcome me, have some of Captain Cleve's refreshments?"

Levi gave a short laugh, "You'll soon learn, Molly, folks up in these parts don't spend much time dawdling."

"But Captain Cleve—"

"Is a shrewd business man. When he's south, he plays southern hospitality; when he's north, he's as Yankee as a wooden nutmeg. Folks up here don't mix business with pleasure. There won't be any party on board. You be a good girl now and wait here. I'll send Julee."

Be a good girl! Molly bit her lip. Levi had a special knack today for making her blow first hot and then cold. She was angry with

74

him again. Why should she be a good girl? If there wasn't to be a welcoming party, she'd get off the boat when she pleased.

When Julee came, she said, "Come, Julee. Attend!"

She pressed and elbowed her way haughtily down the main companionway and out onto the gangplank. She faltered only when the mud clerk said, "Careful, Ma'am, there's a mite of mud. Water's low."

She was looking for a place to set her dainty boot and so was not prepared for the avalanche of human flesh which all but knocked her down. Clumsy clout! Her eyes took in the rough rawhide shoes, the homespuns, and when they reached the face she was looking up at a younger Levi.

She smiled, "You must be Gaithe!"

"Yes, Ma'am," he snatched his hat from his head and succeeded in looking mighty flustered. But his admiring Blaisdell eyes still took in all the carefully arranged pleats, flounces and edgings. "You're Molly."

"Yes, I'm Molly."

"Where's Levi?"

"On board."

He started past her.

"Don't you want to help me, Gaithe?" Her eyes followed his, discomfited by the usual riff-raff of men beyond the mud, lounging along the solid wood crib of the landing. Long, lean men, spare but wiry frames, homespun open on unusually long, scrawny, molted-turkey necks with Adam's apples jumping up and down in gleeful agitation at poor Gaithe's plight.

One, in a bright red shirt, who looked more like the kind of human being she might have seen before, called, "Mind your manners, lad. Help the lady."

"Old channel cats, don't mind them," Gaithe said, helping her to jump across the mud.

The feel of his clammy cold hand through her glove told her better than anything else how these river rats were making Gaithe suffer. He was a sensitive lad.

"Gaithe," she said, "I'd be more comfortable if you'd show me to the carriage. Come Julee!"

"She yours?" Gaithe's eyes opened in astonishment as he jerked a thumb in Julee's direction.

"Oh yes."

75

"Reckon Ma didn't figger on *her*."

"Didn't Levi tell her I would bring two servants, a riding horse, a proper dowry?"

"Aw, shucks! Reckon he told her when I wasn't around." Gaithe's eyes avoided hers.

"The carriage, please Gaithe," she reminded him.

Gaithe shifted his weight on his feet. "Haven't got one, got workin' horses and carts—open—but no carry-all. There's a coolin' board on the bank," he suggested hopefully.

"What's a cooling board?"

"Just a board between a couple of tree stumps, where you can set a spell to cool off."

"Come, Julee, we'll *set*."

"I'll go help Levi," Gaithe said, "so's you won't have to wait so long." It was evident that Gaithe wanted to be free of the embarrassment of escorting Levi's bride in front of the town loafers.

Followed by Julee, Molly picked her way unassisted through the mud, threaded her way among the deck hands rushing off the freight consigned to Rivertown, past the merchants transacting business with Captain Cleve and his clerk, and the woodmen yelling for the "ole white pitcher." Stiff-backed, head high, she climbed the steep pitch of Rivertown's Public Landing past the lounging loafers who silently took her apart and put her together again in their curiosity about a petticoat newly arrived in town.

Then the two brides in their finery gingerly sat upon the rough puncheon cooling board.

In silence the loafers returned to their whittling. From one pocket a man would take a small piece of wood, attack it with a toad-stabber knife, whittle, slip it into the opposite pocket and reach for a fresh piece of wood. Without letup, on and on they whittled.

Julee whimpered, "Us don' like it here."

At last they saw Matt leading Prince, blind-folded, off the gangplank. Levi followed and came up the path.

When the loafers saw him their knives slowed, stopped altogether. Knives snapped shut and were slipped into sagging pockets. To a man, they snapped to attention like fusiliers, and let out a mighty roar. It took her a second to realize the roar was for Levi. They thumped him on his back, patted his clothes, made rude remarks.

"Oh, they're a bad lot, Miss. It's not the same. Us scared. Us wants back on the boat with the captain man." Julee was trembling.

"You can't."

"Oh Lordy, Lordy. It's not the same, Miss. How us make out?"

"Julee, be quiet. Captain Cleve is coming to say goodbye."

"Well, young lady!" The captain was hearty. "That's quite a welcome the lads are giving your bridegroom. Levi's friends think a sight of him."

"His friends?" She felt weak.

"Cal Preble there, giving him a good pummel, is his best friend so to speak. Remember 'em all as lads—good lads, too."

The captain must be mistaken. These men couldn't be Levi's friends. Cal Preble, mauling Levi as if he were a long-lost brother returned, was the man in the red shirt—the only one of the lot who didn't look like a bandit of the outlaw years on the Natchez Trace. She wanted to take Julee by the hand and run back on board *The Rising Sun.*

Captain Cleve said, "I'm looking forward to seeing you with greater frequency. I put in here every trip, be a pleasure to have you come aboard. Anything I can do for you, I'll be glad to help."

"Thank you, Captain Cleve."

"If you ever need any noses punched, I'll punch 'em for you. I feel kinda responsible for you."

She threw her arms around him. She kissed the funny little round man all done up in blue broadcloth, gold lace and fancy buttons. She wasn't alone after all. If she didn't want to stay in Rivertown all she had to do was to get on *The Rising Sun* and Captain Cleve would take her back home; she had been an old silly to think there wasn't a way to return. She wiped the tears from her eyes when the boat jangled her bells and pulled away from Rivertown.

Levi freed by his friends said, "Ma's had time to wipe up any spots and change her apron. Gaithe said Selena Cranch ran to tell her we'd come." He took her arm.

"Levi, do I have to walk?"

"Reckon you do. You aren't crippled, are you?"

"I can't possibly walk in these shoes," she wailed. "I'll have to ride. Matt! Let me mount Prince."

So this was the way a new wife was welcomed to Rivertown, no proper reception by the kinfolks, not even a carriage sent for her to ride in. She was a very angry bride in her bright green silk deeply fringed with black. Her side curls bobbed indignantly from under her scuttle hat. Her hair, rinsed by Mammy Fay to what she hoped was a tint of pink to be felt and not seen, had turned out to be only a shade lighter than Prince's sleek sorrel coat.

She was too good a horsewoman to be actually uncomfortable because she couldn't sit properly in her saddle—she had to sit sideways and dangle her feet—but she was madder than blue blazes. What a bridal procession! Durn! Beside her walked her bridegroom, more than a bit warm, crumpled, and wilted from his exertions with her luggage and his over-welcoming friends, while on the other side, like a faithful dog, loped Gaithe.

Men in warehouse doorways and store windows nodding "Howdy" to Levi, curtains stirring at windows of houses built wall to wall flush to the street, brought home to her the incongruity of her position. She kept her eyes forward on her stable groom Matt, a fine specimen of ebony flesh, and her body servant, Julee, the black bride in her red and black checkerboard dress.

"You aren't seeing much of the town, Molly," Levi said. "Ma sent word I was to bring you home the back way—she thinks it unlawful for town folks to look on the bride before her in-fare."

"What on earth is an in-fare?" Molly interrupted.

"Oh, that's when you have all your friends and neighbors in after a wedding and they meet the bride and groom and eat for hours. Women set store by the in-fare. The men-folks are more interested in the belling. You sure you got things set, Gaithe?"

"You got no call to worry, Levi," Gaithe replied. "The boys are goin' to give the best bellin' the town's ever had."

Molly's blank face showed her confusion. She felt almost as if she were in a foreign country.

"Don't you know about bellin's either?" Gaithe asked.

Molly shook her head.

"You better tell her, Levi. It might be scarey if she doesn't know."

"I'll tell her when the time comes."

They had passed along tree-shaded streets until they arrived at a thin, narrow, two-story frame house without a welcoming portico. A one-room wide house, each room behind the other—a

78

shot-gun house. But inside that house waited a mother's welcoming arms—and that was all that mattered.

"Ma's lilacs are in bloom. She sets great store by her lilacs. Fetched them with her all the way from York state along with her fire. Ma's got more sentiment than you'd first realize. Apple trees are about ready to give their spring snow storm. Well, here we are."

Levi held her to him a moment when he lifted her down and said, "You'll like it." He was proud that he was giving her a sugar plum. "You might as well start right off being one of the family. About the only time the front door is ever opened is when Ma scrubs the stone step," he said as he led the way to a side door.

"Ma!" Levi called from what must be a small back sitting room.

"In here, Son."

"Wait here, Julee," Molly said.

Hester Blaisdell stood in her parlor, a supernumerary room, furnished with austerity, a room in which one would not be tempted to do anything untoward. No dust particles danced and climbed the band of afternoon sunlight coming through the square-paned windows neatly framed in white curtains held back in prim loops. The wide floor boards' repeated waxings showed no footprints and yet the few scatter hooked rugs were too far apart to step from one to another. The horsehair sofa looked hard and slippery; the keys of the harpsichord untouched.

Hester Blaisdell stood uncommonly tall beside a small table in the exact center of the room. On the table was a single brass candlestick and the Big Book, unmistakably the Bible.

"Well, Son!"

"Well, Ma!"

There was no gesture of welcome or embrace between them.

"Well, Son?"

"Well, Ma, here she is. This is Molly, your new daughter. Where's Pa?"

"He went along with Salena to meet you. You must have missed him."

Hester's eyes questioned. Molly answered with questions in hers. Both women were trying to see what felicity one might find in the other. Hester slowly closed her eyes and bowed her head. She said, "You are welcome to our home, Molly."

Molly curtsied a thank you, ma'am. She saw Hester's hands un-clasp and clasp again against the white apron covering the dark plum-colored merino dress. Molly wondered what mother's memories these clasped hands held. It was hard to imagine that they were hands that fitted soft little shoes, merry hands with the knack of untying apron strings tied in jest to a chair, hands to wipe either the sweet, sad tears of separation or the joyous tears of reunion. They were not hands to clasp the heart longing for a mother's love.

A wave of complete misery washed over Molly, dragging her down and down until the sound of the sitting-room door opening and closing and Gaithe's voice brought her back to the surface.

"Oh hello," Gaithe said, "what does she call you? What's your name?"

"Julee, sir."

With sudden alarm Hester Blaisdell asked, "Who's that?"

But surely she must have peeped at their arrival. What kind of a woman was she if she had waited with bowed head by the Bible and lone candlestick? Molly wondered with despair if she had exchanged a black matriarch, Mammy Fay, for a white one.

CHAPTER IX

Ma was surprised and ill pleased at the extent of Molly's dowry. Apparently she had expected Molly to come amply provided with a bit more than the required six sheets, six pillow cases and two tablecloths to set up housekeeping, but she was in no way prepared to provide for two slaves in her household.

"She didn't even want me to come up to freshen you after you' journey," said Julee, when she and Molly were alone in the spare bedroom. "Her nine years older than God. I knows you don' believe in all the signs, Miss, and I can't rightly name it, but when it not natural it's a sign. Her makes the goose bumps jump up all over me. I don' like it here, Miss. I wants to go home." Julee's dark velvety face quivered, crumpled. She threw herself, weeping, upon Molly.

"Hush, Julee. Don't let them hear you."

"Her house no good. Old rottendy house! No more style than a corn crib. Us gots no place to sleep. Oh Miss, what become me an' Matt? Us go home. Take us home. Us run back to the captain man's boat."

Julee finally had to admit that the boat was gone; she had seen it stand off from shore. The white bride comforted and scolded the black bride, "If you don't behave I'll get right in behind you with a switch. She's kin, now. What would Mammy Fay think of you behaving like this?"

"Mammy Fay say she act too biggedy, too whoopity." Julee giggled a little between sobs. "Reckon I won't let her out-whack me, nuther."

81

"All right, now," said Molly. "But see you mind your manners. Try to be useful." An up-hill business.

Downstairs later on Hester Blaisdell told the brides she didn't want any help with the supper. Julee should go sit outside on the back stoop—Levi was showing Matt where to put "that horse" —and Molly was to sit in the parlor with Mr. Blaisdell until supper was ready. The end of winter was a poor time of year for vittles, but she guessed they'd manage to make out. The way Hester said it made Molly feel she should have married Levi at another season of the year in order to accommodate his mother's pantry.

Ira Blaisdell was as sweet as his wife was sour.

"Let us have a look at you, now," he asked Molly after pumping her hand. He stood her off, his hands holding her lightly by the shoulders. Then he raised his chin and took a long look down his nose in a kind of mimicry. He bunched his chin, puckered his mouth in disapproval and shook his head, his eyes remaining merry all the while. He was really quite funny play-acting disfavor.

"Can you make a puddin' and a shirt?"

She shook a doleful head.

"Want to learn?"

"I don't know, sir."

"Bully for you! An honest answer. Now most young ladies would have said a lot of simpering twaddle. Maybe you're a mite different than what Miz Blaisdell and I had expected Levi to bring home to us for a daughter, but when all is said and done reckon it's Levi's affair. After a while you'll know who's to be general and who's adjutant in the war of marriage. Once you get that settled you'll go along right peaceful." Already it had been borne in upon Molly who was general in Ira's and Hester's marriage.

Hester called them to the table where they "made out a meal" of a platter of fried ham and eggs, fried potatoes, dried corn, great bowls of many kinds of preserves and pickles. "Ma's got a way with pickles. Always stay green as grass."

When Levi asked for pickled peaches Ma said she didn't have any to spare. She was saving them for the in-fare. Then turning to Molly she added, "I'm sorry I won't be able to do as well as I'd like to for your in-fare. If it were only June—strawberries—fresh things!"

Hester rose from the table and picked up her plate. She jerked her head in the direction of the back stoop where Julee and Matt sat, "Suppose they've got to be fed."

No one said anything.

"How do I feed *them?*"

Poor Julee! Poor Matt! Molly said, "If you'll tell me what they may have, I'll fix their plates. They can eat out there."

"Where they goin' to sleep?" asked Gaithe. The ugly question was out in the open at last.

The Blaisdell house was small. There was just the spare room for the bridal pair, Ira's and Hester's room, and the cubbyhole over the kitchen, "the boys' room."

They all looked at Ma Blaisdell, grim and silent. Her gaze at her husband demanded that he do something.

He moved uncomfortably on his chair. "Haven't you a spare tick we could stuff, let 'em knock down on the kitchen floor?"

Hester looked at her scoured white hard ash floor and said, "Not in *my* kitchen."

Mary Marie said, "Perhaps some neighbor would be glad to have them share quarters with some of their own servants."

Gaithe said, "Nobody's got help."

"Are there no Negroes in Rivertown?"

They all shook their heads at her.

"Who does the work?"

"Folks," said Gaithe.

Ira said, "Slaves are brought across the river sometimes, hired out by their owners who see to it they go back at night so's they don't run away."

"What about free Negroes? Aren't there any? Rutland Negroes don't run away."

"No," Ira said. "State's actually got a law against them immigrating here. 'Course along the river most folks got sympathy with the South. The blacks themselves want to push on, scared to stay here."

Another uncomfortable silence filled the room. Molly kept saying to herself, as she had to Julee, "Mind your manners, they're new kin."

She turned to Levi. Surely he had some solution for this unpleasantness; he had raised no objection to her bringing Matt and Julee. And he'd better not squirm in his chair like his Pa. She'd hate him if he did.

Levi said, "Bed them down in the stable."

Molly glared at him, "Matt might not mind, but I can't let Julee. She'll have to sleep in the house."

"Indeed!" Hester plunked a supper plate she had been holding down on the table.

"Julee has never slept in slave quarters. She has always been with me," Molly felt her face flush, "until now."

The discussion continued for what seemed hours, with no help from the menfolk. All Molly's suggestions were rejected with disdain by Hester.

Finally Ira cut in to everyone's great relief. "While you folks've been gabbing I've been trying to think how we might get off this snag we're hung up on. I've hit on a way. Come on, boys, we've a job to do out in the woodshed."

When they had done fixing up the woodshed as sleeping quarters, Ira said, "Pshaw! Don't know why I was so shortheaded such a long spell. Reckon you folks got me so lost in your argufying objections I couldn't think."

Molly herself would have preferred the comforts of the woodshed to Hester's spare room, the room held in reserve and sparing of any luxury or lavishness—even denying the need of bodily indulgences. The room held only the simplest necessities, a chair, a stool, a chest, a bed—uncanopied—and the plain cream, unadorned queen's ware in the washstand. Here was no aura of romance, no seductive atmosphere in which to surrender. Hester's spirit seeped in through all the cracks and looked askance at the conjugal bed.

It had been a long hard day, badly begun with Levi, and it ended the same way. As in the morning her physical union with Levi was incomplete. She was too tired, too overwrought, too Hester-ed. Then Levi at once fell asleep, his arm a great weight flung across her. She moved from beneath it, but Levi did not pull her back to smooth away her frustration.

She was alone with her wakefulness.

The bed, barren of satisfaction, became an offense. She had to leave it.

Her feet found her slippers, her hands the bride's robe embroidered in rosebuds and heart's ease. In the small cramped room in Hester's spare narrow house, her heart emptied to dryness. She felt that Hester and her house would entangle another sinister thread in her mingle-mangled life if she didn't get out of it at once

She caught up her dark cloak. In a finger play of shadows out in the hall she listened, but heard nothing. Her hand found the rail, her feet the stairs—steep, narrow, and straight down. Her eyes followed a slight beam of light, a thin radiance, through the parlor, the sitting room, to the big kitchen room where, on the table, a candle burned low in its socket.

She stood spellbound.

There, in the flow of light from the candle, on the brick hearth —the very altar of the house—she found Hester upon her knees. Polished brass and copper pots, arranged on the chimney breast, reflected a pattern of light and embroidered in gold the dull merino dress. Hester's face held an absorbed, inscrutable expression while she painstakingly selected certain coals from the glowing fire and banked them in the three-legged iron pot for the safe-keeping of her perpetual fire. The same fire she had brought all the way from New York state so many years ago and never allowed to go out. Smoke, like incense rising from an altar of brick, curled through the perforated iron lid covering the fire which Hester kept ever alive.

She put the pot to one side now and, as though compelled by some ancient law, brushed every ash from the hearth and then cleansed it with water. Hester's scrubbing of her floor was more than a fussy neatness, it was some kind of ritual. The mask of her face while she performed these acts filled Molly with terror and made her spine creep coldly. This was much worse than the dark doings of Mammy Fay who, after all, *loved* her.

Trembling overcame the girl.

Escape! Escape! She must escape. She must get away from Hester's spell, her house and everything in it. She must get to Julee—the known, familiar Julee—and be assured that this was only a dream. She backed into the deeper shadows of the sitting room and thanked God the side-door latch moved without noise beneath her shaking fingers.

Once safely outside the house, she drew a deep breath and stood for a moment to get her bearings to the back stoop and the path leading to comforting Julee in the woodshed.

But *something* was there close beside the house. She felt a presence even before a tall figure moved toward her. Her knees turned to jelly. She took in her breath for a mighty scream. Before it came, a voice said, "Molly, it's me! Don't be scared. Don't yell."

"Oh, Gaithe! I am scared." She fell against his long body with relief. His arms, strong as Levi's, came about her, held her safe.

"I won't let them hurt you."

After a moment she gently freed herself. "Won't let who hurt me, Gaithe?" she whispered.

"Why, the bellers. Didn't Levi tell you about it yet?"

"No, Gaithe. What do they do?"

"The men and boys come around with bells, kettles and things to serenade the bride and groom on their wedding night. If they like the couple they don't treat them mean. They were mad when old man Griffin married the Hastings girl. They kidnapped her and wouldn't let him have her 'til they were a-mind to. Don't be afraid, though. Levi's got friends."

"Oh, they couldn't kidnap me. Levi wouldn't let them."

"Maybe he couldn't help it."

"But Ma . . . they wouldn't dare! Nobody could get rough with your mother here."

"Take more than Ma to stop that crowd once they got going. Grapevine word's been passed around downtown it'll be tonight. Bound to be a big affair. Levi's well liked."

This was too much for Molly in her highly emotional state. She was close to tears. "No, Gaithe, no!"

"You can't stop it, Molly. Nobody can. They won't get rough if nobody holds out on them."

"Oh Gaithe, I'm scared. I feel hunted!"

"Well, we'd better get inside the house. I think I hear them coming."

"No! I'll not be belled by a bunch of rabble rousers."

"We better get outside the fence then. They'll be here in a minute.

They came in hushed silence, a gang of hoodlums carrying weapons of din. They moved in until they were massed shoulder to shoulder in front of the Blaisdell house, at least a hundred of them. Not a sound did they make, just a jostling. The dark figure of a leader could be seen against Hester's white front door. A light flared from one of those new friction matches.

"That's Cal Preble," whispered Gaithe. "He's leading. Hope they don't notice us standing here so quiet."

"I can't stand this," Molly whispered tensely, "I know what I'll do—I'll bell myself!"

"Hide behind me close to the tree 'til the crowd gets big," Gaithe said, "then beat with this spoon on the pail so's they'll think you're one of them." Gaithe handed her the brass pail and spoon he had been carrying in anticipation of the festivities.

Then Levi's best friend gave the signal for all bedlam to break loose. Horns blared, cow bells clanged, skillets and kettles dinned, sleigh bells jingled, military drums beat and rolled, firecrackers burst on Hester's scrubbed front-door step. Most frightening of all were the yells and war cries let loose by the hoarse throats of a hundred tough Hoosiers.

"Beat, Molly, beat!" whispered Gaithe, " 'fore they catch on."

She beat with all her might, and each time she whacked the pail it was one Hoosier clout she beat—or Hester herself.

The noise quieted a bit, and she grew afraid at their shouts, "'Bring out the bride!" "Show us the gal!" "Where's the groom?" until they became angry and changed to a nasty chant, "We *want* the gal." "We *want* the groom."

"We're in a real pickle," whispered Gaithe. "They're getting mean."

The front door opened. Levi, in his rough homespuns, stood there with a candle in his hand.

"Show us the gal!"

Levi raised a hand to silence them. "Well boys, this is a mighty fine honor you pay me. I can't remember when Rivertown ever gave a better belling. I've done my share in this kind of play party, but can't say I ever was smart enough to think up . . ."

"He's stalling," whispered Gaithe. "Oh, Molly, we've done wrong. They'll get ugly, no telling what they'll do. They won't stand for not seeing you."

". . . some of the noise makers you fellows have. Now take Jim, here, whoever . . ." Levi was trying to hold them with palaver.

"We *want* the girl!" "We'll *take you*." A firecracker exploded on the step at Levi's feet.

The crowd surged forward. Levi braced his legs far apart. He was magnificent to see. But one against a hundred!

Gaithe gasped, "They'll take him."

"Oh no, they won't," cried Molly. "Open the way!" She poked sharp elbows where they would do the most good; she lost her hood; her hair tumbled; she pounded the brass pail with all her might.

"I'll be dad-burned! A-bellin' herself!" She heard someone say.

The crowd roared, fell back to make an aisle for her and beat a mightier din. She walked slowly, her chin high, toward Levi. She expected every minute to have them take her and carry her off goodness only knew where. She was terribly scared but she wouldn't let them know it. Steadily she walked toward Levi's big grin.

Out of the corner of his mouth he said, "Good God, Molly, where've you been? You came just in time. What were you doing out there?"

"Treat!" shouted the crowd.

"Down to Berman's, boys. He's all set up for you," yelled Levi. "Come inside, Molly."

In the parlor, by the Bible table, waited Hester.

She fixed a stern eye upon Gaithe and ordered, "Young man, I'll settle with you later. Go up to your bed."

Gaithe, guilt written large upon his face, silently obeyed.

"Now, young lady, there can be no acceptable explanation of your conduct—this belling of yourself—not properly clothed. I can see your bed gown underneath your cloak. For Shame! Your place is with your husband. Why weren't you there?"

Molly murmured, "I couldn't sleep. I got to worrying about Julee, that she might be lonesome, scared."

"Do you expect me to believe that you would go out in the middle of the night to slaves in the woodshed? No, I can believe but one thing. Weren't you seeking out my boy Gaithe?"

Frightened and helpless, Molly turned to Levi.

"Oh come, Ma, you don't believe Molly went out to meet Gaithe. Like she says, she got to worrying about Julee and didn't think . . ."

"She must learn to think. The entire town now has confirmed what I'm sure they suspected this afternoon when she rode through the town on that—that stallion—like a Jezebel!"

Molly's chin rose, "I wish I had been Godiva so that no one would have looked on my disgrace at being so ill received in my new home."

"I'll have none of your back-talk, young lady."

When they were once again in the spare bed in the spare room, Levi said, "Quit churning. Don't mind Ma. Ma's over particular; she gets notions. I know you weren't up to anything with Gaithe. He's only a young-un anyway, and—my brother! No!" Levi laughed, then sobered. "But let me tell you something. That would be one thing that would make me pack up and get out. Burst me to flinderjigs! Ma's out of her mind if she thinks you and Gaithe—Ma gets the gol-derndest notions. Sometimes I wonder if she'll stay in her right mind. Don't you pay any attention to her; you just learn to step *around* Ma."

Levi patted her tenderly, "You did all right, Punkin. This belling of yourself showed the boys you've got the spunk to be a boatman's wife. They've been a mite worried for me, thought maybe I'd brought home a mealy-mouthed egg sucker. Now they know better. They'll feel right at home with you. I'm downright proud of you, Sorrel Top! You should've seen yourself, no bigger than a minute holding that whole crowd in the palm of your little hand. Gosh-a-mighty, Molly, you were great! I couldn't have held them much longer—they were going to take me. Christ-a-mighty, me, a leaping trout, almost hooked at my own belling!"

Molly went to sleep that night, confident and happy.

CHAPTER X

İT WAS JULEE WHO AWAKENED MOLLY HER FIRST MORNING IN RIVER-town. Levi had left without her hearing him.

"I brought you you' coffee, Miss Mary Marie, 'cause I didn't know how you could let me know when you wants it. Old rottendy house, got no bell pulls."

"Thank you, Julee."

"Her mad. Her say her not have a lazy slip of a daughter-*in*-law what wants a silver coffee pots fetched to her in bed. I tells her you gots to have you' coffee to open you' eye. She say makin' fire and gettin' breakfast for you' man opens you' eye quick 'nuff. I wants to make fresh coffee but she says take what am there on the hearth. It's no good."

Julee had been brave indeed to face the forbidding Hester on her hearth, her throne, and to demand of her majesty freshly brewed coffee for a stay-a-bed mistress.

"Did you and Matt get fed?"

"Umph! Reckon you might calls it that. She push cold bread out onto the steps. Us don' like it here. Master Levi explain 'bout the bellin', but still us don' like it here. Lordy Jesus, Matt and us 'bout had the livin' daylights scared plumb out of us. Matt say us sur-roun-*ded*, they come to ketch us an' put bells 'roun' our necks, make bell niggers outten us, so's us tinkle, tinkle our whereabouts and what us do. Master Levi say nobody do no such thing, this am a *free* country where us can come and go, but just the same, Miss Mary Marie, us don' like it here."

It came over Molly that this was an important moment of her

90

life. With clearness she saw herself suspended between two worlds, the one lavishly and luxuriously furnished with daydreams of a glamorous future which made her restless, petulant and tired; the other world, quiet, bare and clean with the fresh cool breeze of reality blowing in upon her which refreshed, cheered and invigorated.

In that brief moment, reality made a bid and won. She said, "Now Julee, things aren't quite the same up here as they are down home. Captain Cleve explained it to me, he said, 'Some folks are taught one way and some are taught another, and folks do the way they've been taught.'"

"Then why don' she want you to have you' coffee to open you' eye, 'cos that the ways you been taught?"

Julee had a point there, Molly thought, but she spoke sternly, "Watch your tongue, Julee. We're company kin, here, like Quercus Grove. Remember how we helped there? We'll do the same here."

"It's not the same, here," wailed Julee.

Household matters were indeed different in Rivertown. Nevertheless Molly was determined to show Levi's mother that she was already a good daughter, ready to help; she'd make a fresh start. She drew a deep breath and inhaled the sweet odor of the northern lilacs coming through the open window.

Downstairs, when she offered her services in preparation for the in-fare, Hester said Salena Cranch was all the help she wanted. Hester would not permit her son's wife to help her. She did not bid the young woman run down to the cellar for the big yellow crock of eggs, nor take the best china from the top shelf, nor did she offer to lay the white tablecloth together, like mother and daughter. These duties were reserved for the neighbor girl, Salena Cranch.

Instead Hester addressed Molly coldly, "If you really want to help, kindly stay out of my way." Nor would she allow Julee to assist in her kitchen.

Perhaps, Molly thought, she could gather flowers and arrange them in the austere rooms to bring an air of festivity and fun to the in-fare. There were no Cherokee roses nor magnolias as in Quercus Grove, but the perfume of Hester's lilacs was as delightful and seductive as jasmine. "Your lilacs are lovely," Molly said. "May I cut and arrange them for you?"

"Cut the lilacs! I don't cut my lilacs; they bloom on the old wood. Where would next year's bloom come from if I cut them?"

"But there are so many—"

"Because I've never cut them." Hester reached for the egg whisk and laid it into the egg whites on the great white stone platter.

"Oh! I didn't know. There are other flowers, perhaps?"

"Flowers in the house make a muss," Hester sniffed.

"Oh!" When she got into her own house the first thing Molly promised herself she would do would be to fill it with flowers. She'd have flowers in her house always—a whole "plug-muss" of flowers. Aloud she said, "I wish Levi were here to take me to see my house."

"Hoping the first thing for your husband to do things for you is not the way to begin marriage." Hester paused in her beating. "I hope my son has not married a girl who requires the fiddle to sweeten her. Levi has business to attend to." She sprinkled a few tablespoons of sugar over the egg whites and beat again.

"Oh! I know," said Molly, "he must get his flatboats ready to take the May butter. If I'd known I couldn't help you with the party, I'd have had Levi show Matt, Julee and me to our house. But I want him to take me there the first time I see it. Prince needs exercise after being shut up on the boat. Would it be all right if I rode him a little?"

"Certainly not," exploded Hester. "What kind of picture do you think you made yesterday, sitting on that horse—that stallion?" She laid the whisk on the platter of peaked egg whites, turned and faced her daughter-in-law.

"You're not making it easy for me, Molly. Ever since you set foot off Captain Cleve's gangplank you've disgraced us before the whole town by your behavior." Hester plainly wished Molly had never come off the boat. "If I could, this morning I would have tied every tongue in Rivertown after what happened last night. The best I can hope for is that you will be regarded as a child-bride playing a foolish prank with my boy Gaithe." Hester's attitude showed she herself didn't believe this for one minute. "So, young lady, you are to remain in this house until the in-fare. By taking a firm hand I may be able to overcome some of the damage you have done. Now I wish you would kindly leave me alone." She returned to the egg whites which had toppled, losing their glistening peaks.

Molly stood irresolute. She didn't want to fight with Hester.

She wanted to be loved and coddled by a mother. But her great need was answered by the clickety-click of Hester's wire whisk striking the cold stone platter as she beat the egg whites again to glistening peaks of perfection. At that moment Hester destroyed the tender growth of affection that might have developed in Molly's heart. She had made a sincere effort at reconciliation, and her honest desire to be helpful and daughterly had been rejected with such coldness that the new feeling within her—a real capacity for loving—withered away, and the old hard knob of childish resentment, perplexity and despair was all that was left.

In the parlor Molly silently fingered the keys of the harpsichord, and told herself that the trouble lay not only with Hester but Levi himself was difficult. Still she didn't want to fight with her husband. She wanted him to lift her onto a cloud and float with her while he pinned stars in her hair—forever. Instead he made her blow hot and cold until she wondered if she might have the fever and chills of an illness.

The hours dragged on. There was nothing to read in the house but the hymnal, *Pilgrim's Progress,* an almanac, primers—and of course the *Bible,* irrevocably Hester's, on the center table.

Hester kept right dead ahead with the in-fare work from start to finish. She looked ill by the time she declared she was ready for the guests. They could come any minute they wanted to but, they would have to "eat twice." This statement puzzled Molly until Salena, her work finished, came into the parlor and chatted with her, explaining that Hester meant there wasn't room for all the people at once at the tables set up in the kitchen and sitting room.

"Miz Blaisdell was put right to it to know where to draw the line on the invitations she sent 'round. I tell you everybody was watching to see where Gaithe and I was dropping by to ask folks." Salena's dark lively eyes pleasured as she remembered the importance of her errand.

Salena's eyes were her most arresting feature; they showed her lively interest in everything and made a person feel she was downright glad to see him.

"Your wedding dress is awful pretty, Molly. My! It must be wonderful to be so beautiful. I heard the Mister tell *her* you couldn't help it if the Lord made you look the way a woman ought to look. But she said that didn't give a body any right to enlarge upon the Lord's work." Salena sighed. "Reckon any blowing up of me wouldn't look so good. Reckon Gaithe's never going to notice I'm grown up."

"Do you like Gaithe?"

A faint tender smile played around Salena's parted lips. She said softly, "Do I like maple molasses?"

"How old are you, Salena?" It was hard to tell the girl's age, she was tall and thin but not slattern, her dark eyes were mysterious at times, her hair grew in great dark wings, a widow's peak, and ripened the olive-tinged oval of her face to a false maturity.

Salena said she was fifteen. "But I'm old for my age because I took on a woman's work early. Ma's passing on the way she did left me working the ashhopper for Pa."

"I'm anxious to meet your father, Salena. He's coming to my in-fare isn't he?"

"No'm. Pa's funny. Right now he's so out of whack he won't come to your party."

"You mean he's ill?"

"Lawsy no, Pa's never what you might call sick; he's real well in his body but he's got kinda low with religion. He's downright discouraged lately. I can't remember when I've seen Pa so low."

"What brought on his trouble, Salena? Was it your mother's death that did it?"

"Oh no'm. It started a-fore that. Pa says it all started that day he wuz just a-settin', not doin' a gol-derned thing when all of a sudden it wuz like a grain of sand stuck 'tween his teeth, and it come to him it wuz mighty confusin' to live where they made up a new religion every day. Pa says he'd no more'n get redd of his grain of sand than his nose started twitchin'. Pa says he knowed right off, 'thout being told, it was religion he smelled. Pa says fresh religion has a real sweet pleasant smell but after it sets 'round for a spell it goes sour and stale—it stinks. Pa's smart, he don't let on to folks what he's lookin' for. I don't neither 'cos Pa's got to have work 'mongst church folks."

"Are there many churches and church people in Rivertown?"

"Oh my yes," said Salena. "Some are high-sailin' and high-falutin, mighty sure folks, holdin' steady, others go hoppity-skip-and-a-jump peckin' here and there 'mongst the graces, hopin' they'll find perfekshun. T'others ain't got the strength to hold on, so kerflummux, they backslide and first thing you know they're back on their anxious seats. Pa says church folks work almighty hard in the Lord's vineyards, they wrastle themselves into a good stinkin' sweat. Pa says when you stand close to the rostrum and all the folks are settin' on their anxious seats is when you can smell religion the strongest. Pa says he hopes some day he'll be able to see religion. He's heer'd so much about it, even smelt it but nary caught sight of it, says Pa. That's why he's a carpenter."

"Why, Salena? I don't understand."

"Well, Pa says he's about give up looking for religion in churches. Pa's notion now is mebbe it is a shy little feller what's hidin' in a little ole forgotten cubbyhole, somewhere's about in somebody's house all unbeknownst to the folks what live there. So Pa figgers sooner or later every house in town's goin' have a repair job for him, he's real neat-handed, so Pa reckons if he don't backslide in his purpose, some day he's goin' to catch sight of religion. Pa thinks if he could see it mebbe he could see what ailed it, mebbe something could be done to keep it sweet smellin'."

"Do you look for religion, too, Salena?"

"My goodness, no. I don't want to get out of whack. Ma allus said a family couldn't afford more'n one mind twistin' itself on matters beyond understandin' so Pa does my twistin' for me. I don' calculate on rummagin' for religion with him. I got my own work cut out."

"Such as?"

"Well I'm right took up, tryin' to be both a child and a woman."

Molly laughed.

Salena laughed too. "Heer'd the ladies say that behind my back. Still they been good to me. Reckon Miz Blaisdell's been the best. She learned me right off how to catch emptins."

"What are they? They sound unpleasant."

"They are if you don't catch 'em the right minute. Pee-yu! If you don't you got to git right out of your house while your bread's bakin'. Miz Blaisdell says now she wouldn't be able to tell one of my loaves from one of hers if they was settin' right alongside each other. Miz Blaisdell sets store by a sweet loaf of bread. How's yours?"

Molly did not dare to confess she had never even *seen* a loaf of bread baked. Cold bread was—well it was cold bread, why set such store by it? They never did back home. However she said, "I'm sure any loaf of mine wouldn't be as good as yours."

"Reckon Miz Blaisdell will show you quick enough."

"I'd rather you did, Salena."

"Proud to," she added ever so shyly, "if you want I should, Molly."

"My first friend in Rivertown, Salena."

"Aw shucks! You'll soon know lots of folks."

"But you'll still be my first friend. I wish the party would start."

Salena said, "This in-fare's not likely to be chockful of fun and frolic, Molly. Some are, when there's kin to in-gather, they go on for three, four days. This one's jest to let folks look you over to see what Levi ketched. They all say he's quite a ketch and you must have been smart to do it. Their other mighty interest is to calculate how you and Miz Blaisdell 'll make out. The winter's been kinda dull and folks hanker for a novelty. There won't be an empty seat in church come Sunday. Preacher Staap'll be right grateful to you for perking up his congregation. What will you wear, Molly?"

"Maybe I won't go at all." That would show Hester she meant to carry her end of the fight.

"Not go?" The crack in Salena's voice made Molly understand how momentous it was for a bride in Rivertown to attend church with her bridegroom the first Sunday after her marriage. "Why Molly what you wear next Sunday is as important as your wedding dress which sure is scrumptious but you'd better wear the right dress to church come Sunday."

And right then Molly got an idea, but she hadn't really developed it before Salena announced, "Here comes the first of the invites, Ole Miz Davidson. She's the be-first and the be-last at any doings. She thinks she's got the right 'cos she's been in this country longer than anybody else. I tell you she's seen a thing or two, spunked right up to a great Indian once and her not weighing more than a hundred and ten pounds and him more than two hundred, and six feet tall, and all he did was to back off and laugh at her. She'll tell you about it. But the thing that makes her real prideful is that she's the only one left hereabouts who saw the first steamboat come down the river. Lawsy me if she hasn't got a bran'-new crimped cap and a pink ribbon. Look at her—a *pink ribbon!*"

Ole Miz Davidson came along Poplar Street waving the hogs and cows out of her way with a heavy, knotted, hickory stick. In contrast to the bobbing gay ribbon, her dress was rusty black. Her face was walnut brown, furrowed, ridged and puckered to her bunch of a mouth. One wondered whether laughing or carping had whittled her face into a hulled black walnut, her mouth to a stem end. Her age had come to a standstill on the western side of life, but it was hard to tell exactly where.

"Heer'd you already raised an awful shindy." Ole Miz Davidson clucked in glee. "Folks' curiosity's been tickled a right smart 'bout what kind of a girl would catch Levi. Sure as I'm a livin' woman things in these parts have stood mighty dull, nothin' to do 'cept make your own shadow. Time was, when every day something cropped up to cause a body's heart to go a sort of pittinpattin, but I'll be durned if I don't think mine's rottin' inside me from lack of spiritin' up. And whilst I wouldn't for the universal world have you get into scrapes, still and all, it's mighty interestin' to have something goin' on. Heer'd Miz Blaisdell was more than a little put out over them slaves you fetched. Heer'd you had a good family jar straight off, ought to make you feel right to home. Well, 'low I better be a-sort of a-movin' along seeing as how others are lined up, wantin' to howdy the bride."

Other curious old women in rusty black took Ole Miz Davidson's place. Their leather-skinned men folk followed, their black coats turned green at the seams, crooked at the elbows, stooped in the shoulders, their eyes crowfooted from searching the sky for weather signs. Giving off an aroma of hams cured in salt and brown sugar smoked with hickory chips and fried, they made awkward handshakes and excused themselves to "make room for the ladies."

The ladies cackling with happy squawks, like geese who have found a hole in the grain-field fence, chatted about their domestic duties, disease and dirt. "He's ailin'" was frequently heard. There was talk of bleeding and leeching, of loose bowels and bowels tightened up—no one seemed to enjoy better health than "just tolerable." There were remedies for this and that and how babies, when asleep in their cribs looked might sweet but how they were a nuisance in the arm while churning, ironing or standing over the hot fire. It was a far cry from Mammy Fay's word pictures of Charleston's row of belle-pickers at Saint Cecelia's ball and yet Molly felt herself picked—yes, picked to pieces!

It wasn't much better when the younger guests arrived. Levi's friends who had been among the bellers were now under the control of their women folk; but in spite of their hair slicked down they remained Hoosier in scale, tall and spare, bold and fearless. Their big red roughened hands, at a loss when deprived of their whittling, fumbled and finally hooked thumbs safely in their pockets. These friends of Levi's took his hand in a mighty grip and did not squeeze less heartily when they wrung his bride's, causing Molly to all but faint from the pain. Then having done their social duty under the prudish eyes of their women, they bolted for the out-of-doors, sweeping Levi along with them. Once free they cracked jokes, told tales, made brags and bets and quizzed Levi about marrying. The bride heard Levi let out one of his guffaws. If he was making jokes about her and marrying she would kill him!

Then she heard Salena Cranch whisper, "It's about as quiet and solemn as a church meeting, the ladies haven't found out yet you're not near as stuck up as they think."

This jolted her back to reality and the smile of Mrs. Calvin Preble. Mrs. Preble said, "I hope we'll be friends, seeing Cal and Levi are thicker'n thieves. I reckon we could start off by first-naming. I'd be downright proud to have you call me Minnie."

Minnie Preble was slender, tall and fair. The bony structure of her face was good. Her profile was as finely cut as the cameo she wore at the neck of her blue cashmere. Her hair, the color of ripe corn, was parted in the middle and wound in smooth satin bands around her head, concealing her ears.

"Cal told me 'bout your bellin' yourself. That kind of thing sets fine with the men. I just want to say I aim to be your friend."

"Thank you, Mrs. Preble."

"*Minnie*—can't you first-name me, Molly?"

"Thank you, Minnie. I'll be ever so grateful to have you for a friend. We'll have so much to talk about. Who is your favorite author?"

"Well, Molly," drawled Minnie, "reckon you might say it's More Anon, that's an author who writes every week in the *Messenger*." For the life of her Molly couldn't tell from the twinkle in Minnie's sweet eyes and the tiny quirks at the corners of her gentle mouth if she were teasing her or not.

Salena interrupted, "Miz Blaisdell says it's time for you weddeners to set up."

Few women were at the first sitting; they were helping Miz

Blaisdell attend the tables. "As for hiring help, you might as well try to hire the governor!" said Minnie.

The bride and groom sat at one end of the long table and at the other end, as their special attendants, sat Cal and Minnie Preble. In between and at the smaller tables sat the old women and men guests.

Reverend Staap, his hand raised, asked a blessing on the young folks, newly joined in marriage, according to the divine appointment in the garden of Eden, that the good Lord might see fit to let them be fruitful and multiply and replenish the earth, and become an honor and a blessing in their day and generation, and to let them live to a godly old age and see their children's children to the third and fourth generation. The bride felt herself verging on a doddering old age by the time the preacher allowed them to get at Ma's food.

With distaste Molly looked upon Hester's in-fare feast. Chicken pot-pie was the main dish, this being a great favorite in the community. There were many fried meats. And the vegetables were invariably pickled in salt, vinegar and something else. There were "sasses" and "presarves." With deadly obliviousness to the ringing of bowls, thumped on the table by the Hoosier ladies, the clattering of knives, the rattling of plates, the Hoosier men attacked Hester's food from which all distinctive taste was lacking.

Molly was tired, nervous and high strung. Great waves of nostalgia broke over her, making her feel ill. She loathed Rivertown and everyone in it. She would return to civilized living in her father's house. But now, as the bride, she must cut the first cake for the uncouth at the table. It was a pound cake like a monument, and about as hard—but a triumph nevertheless to the woman who had baked it.

Hester saw to it that generous wedges of the best cakes were sent to Mr. Folsom, editor of the *Messenger.*

"If she don't," Salena said, "he won't give you and Levi an item in his Hymeneal Column, and Miz Blaisdell would be 'shamed to death if he didn't speak of Levi's bride as An Amiable Miss and lock you in the arms of love and wish long life, happiness and prosperity to attend you. That's what you get for a piece of cake."

Molly knew that it was unreasonable of her to let a simple thing like Hester sending a piece of cake to the editor of the local paper make her so blue-blazing mad. But it did, and she knew then that come Sunday she would give these Rivertowners, whose tongues were hinged in the middle, something to talk about. Nothing she did here was *comme il faut* anyway, so why bother to try to please them?

On Sunday morning she was a long time at her toilette.

Levi shouted up the stairs, "Ma says they'll start walking ahead real slow, and you better hurry, Molly. We mustn't be late—our first Sunday."

"Tell them we'll catch up," she shouted back. To Julee she said, "How do I look?"

"Miss Mary Marie, I 'fraid you' gettin' you'self in trouble. I don' know if you do proper like Mammy Fay want you to. She say you' nice quiet dark blue with the touches of white is you' church gown. Mammy Fay, she say this here gown you gots on is you' musical soiree. You wants to sink you'self completely with these here folks?"

"They'll not out-whack me!"

"No'm."

"Julee! Quit speaking slovenly."

"Yas'm. I mean yes—Miss—Oh, oh! I don' know what name to speak you, Miss." Julee was close to tears. "I cluttered."

So am I but I'll be darned if I let anyone find it out, thought Molly. She swept out of the spare bedroom and down the narrow stairs to join her bridegroom for their first Sunday in church since their marriage.

Levi looked at her and said, "Jumpin' Jehosophat, Molly, is that a church-going rig?"

She turned slowly, for his inspection, in the handsomest gown of her trousseau—the breathtaking lavender brocade.

"It sure sets off your color and your hair, Punkin. You look mighty pretty. Too pretty for church. And did you spill a *bottle* of perfume? Cal Preble's Minnie said the women weren't going to like you if you lord it over them more'n just enough. If you're a mite fed up with Ma telling you what's what, Minnie would be right pleased to show you the ropes."

"Fiddle-de-dee! I'm sorry if you don't like my gown."

"Sure, I like it, Sorrel Top. It's just—."

"There isn't time to change. Come along. You don't know anything about ladies' clothes in any case. We'll be late if we don't hurry and your ma won't like that."

100

They *were* late. The second hymn was being announced. Molly pressed her fingers on Levi's arm to make him wait for the opening bars. When she heard them she opened her mouth wide and led the singing, *Why should I fear the darkest hour.* Proud and defiant and with an unholy satisfaction she walked up the aisle of the church on the arm of her brand-new husband.

The congregation's singing, begun sprightly by the women accompanied by the men's self-conscious tum, te, tum, almost died of astonishment at the sound of the loud new voice as Molly walked up the aisle. The women slowly turned and, at the sight of the lavendar brocade with the little silver hands on little silver chains coquettishly holding up a flounce to expose an exquisitely turned ankle in lavendar gaiter, their jaws dropped and their mouths remained open. They were flabbergasted at the temerity of Levi Blaisdell's bride.

She saw Ole Miz Davidson's pink cap ribbon bobbing in pleasure. She caught a glimpse of Minnie Preble's face, sensitive, flushed, dismayed. She stopped singing, suddenly frightened by the effect of her act. Only Minnie's quavering treble continued to sing the hymn until the congregation, not recovered from its astonishment, but aware of its obligations, joined her in the closing bars.

Hester, rigid in churchly black, froze, her face sentenced her daughter-in-law's behavior. And although Molly was in a pew with Hester she did not enjoy her revenge. Instead she felt disobedient, peevish, and sullen before her mother-in-law's cold unspoken judgement. She heard not a single word of the sermon. She did not know whether Reverend Staap preached of wallowing in the devil's swill tub or walking upright along the paths of rectitude. Gradually she stopped "churning," and saw herself through Minnie Preble's eyes. Minnie was filled with Christian love, but sorrowed at such childish willful misdemeanor. During the closing hymn Molly stood silent and anxiously scanned the faces of the congregation which now were composed again in proper piety.

Cold Sunday dinner at Hester's was a glum affair.

Hester said, "Either you are a very bad child who should be spanked and put in a trundle bed, or you are an out-and-out doxie. I have room for neither in my house."

"Very well, I'll leave." She sprang up from the table.

By the time Levi followed her to the spare room she had it in a cyclone of confusion, a regular twister of silks, satin, and linens hurtling through the air. He fought his way through them to the center of this violent storm and seized her firmly by the wrists. "What are you doing, Sorrel Top?"

"I'm going home. You can't stop me. I hate this place and everyone in it. You hear me. I've arrived, I've been examined—feted and churched—and now I'm leaving. I'm going back where I belong. I'm getting out of here. Let me go, I tell you. You hear me? Let me go!"

He dropped her wrists. "Sure, Honey, you go right ahead."

Hesitantly she gathered her dresses together on the wide spare bed and began smoothing them to fold. She had just gotten them in some kind of order when Levi dropped a great tangle of his shirts, underdrawers, socks, waistcoats, neckerchieves, and nightshirts in their midst.

Anger swelled within her again, but before she got her tongue to say anything, Levi ordered, "Pack 'em up."

"Pack *your* things?"

"Sure Half-Pint. If you want to run home to Papa and your old black nurse, I'll see that you get there. I'll go with you."

CHAPTER XI

When Levi had dumped his clothing in among her laces and flounces, he had shown Molly that she couldn't leave him—run home to Papa and Mammy Fay. Now, she and Levi were as entangled as their clothes had been, tossed together on Hester's spare-room bed. His crude longies in grotesque posture covering her soft feminine things had looked so droll, and his grin so engagingly silly, that she had burst out laughing and let humor melt her anger.

Then, woman-like, she had cried and told Levi she was sorry she'd made such a scene at church. What with laughing and crying and Levi's tender kisses, she finally became calm with the exhaustion of an emotional crisis safely passed. That night she was happy again with Levi and went to sleep sighing contentedly.

This morning she wakened answering Levi's kiss for kiss—eager for her new life to begin. "Show me the town—my house!" she demanded.

Main Cross was the street of shops—of grocers, the tailors, mantua makers and milliners, the makers of boots and shoes, the apothecary, the tonsor, the silversmiths and gunsmiths, the butchers, the saddlers, and the print shop of the *Messenger*, that compendium of world and river news.

In front of the first floors of the shops, galleries or wooden arcades formed continuous passages providing protection for the head and dry comfort for the feet. Some had herringboned brick walks, while others had oak planking, but all were raised sufficiently above street level to discourage horses, cows and hogs from charging up the wooden steps which led to them. The street was high-crowned and deep-ditched on both sides to drain off the surface water when a heavy rain swirled it up to the planks bridging the ditches. Good drainage was almighty important to ward off river sickness and the townspeople of Rivertown were healthier than the residents of most river towns.

Every property backed onto an alley and here, when needed, were the carpenters, painters, glazers, and blacksmiths, the builders of cisterns and privies.

Then there was High Street, the best residential street in town. When Molly saw High Street's brick houses, small but of pleasing classical lines, secure from hogs, cows and horses, behind neat white picket fences or even an occasional ornate black-iron grill, she said, "Why Levi, they're attractive. They're every bit as nice as some small houses in New Orleans. You silly goose, with your log-cabin talk—you had me scared. I'll be quite happy in one of *these* houses."

Levi stuck his thumbs in his waistband and gave his britches a hitch. "Well, as I told you, Molly, there isn't a house to rent and I don't want to put money into building just now. I want to get my steamboat built first. The log cabins are sound enough. Even if they weren't, they'd have to do because they're the only thing left on the water front that's worth shucks."

"But Levi, High Street is better. We don't want to live on Front Street."

"Oh yes, we do; a riverman wants his house on the river bank." Levi's words were a decree, leaving nothing for her inferior wifely judgement to decide. "We turn here."

Levi guided her past Berman's Hotel and Saloon, a house (as attested by the sign) worthy of public patronage, where quarreling and immoral conduct was not allowed and the best of Cognac, West Indies Rum, Holland Gin, Beer, Cider, and Rectified Whiskey were always available.

"Gus Berman's a good man," declared Levi.

Beyond Berman's up-river Front Street climbed to higher ground, where the houses were usually safe from floods. The first settlers, who had come down the river by pirogue, keelboat and broadhorn, had built their crude cabins here—later to be replaced by "wall houses." These were houses flush with the sidewalk, their gables toward the street, one room wide, one room behind another. The continuous wall of houses was broken now and then by narrow gates to narrow, herringboned brick paths leading to dark doorways and beyond to patches of grass and deep narrow gardens.

Across the roadway from the wall houses was the wide river bank, the town's commons. Levi said some Front Street folks were awful mad because the Town Council recently had passed a law that folks had to swill their hogs in their alleys; they couldn't do it out on the river bank any more. Front Street was getting mighty tony.

In front of the last wall house, Minnie Preble was down on her knees scrubbing her door step, a wooden slab of ash as clean and blond as her hair. She struggled to her feet, rubbed her rough red hands dry on her apron and said, "Good mornin', folks, reckon you're headed for your new home. I tell you, Molly, it's going to be mighty nice to have you for a neighbor. I've been kinda lonesome with those cabins empty—nothin' beyond but the forest."

"Doesn't anyone live beyond the cabins?" Molly asked. She was to see for herself in a moment.

The sidewalk ended. Front Street petered out into a crooked path winding through the big trees along the river bank. Molly pulled her skirts more closely about her, watched with care where she set her dainty little shoes.

"There they are!" trumpeted Levi.

Oh, no!

Guardless, unsheltered, exposed, at the edge of a gully cutting deeply to the river, on a high bank cleared of all trees, perched a couple of log cabins. Once the crude shelter of the earliest pioneers opening up the way west, they were abandoned now, forsaken, no longer needed.

Across the gully and beyond lay the forest. Black walnut, hackberry and sycamores had their high heads tipped with fresh spring colors, but through their lower nakedness could be seen the tangle of the impenetrable forest. Huge trees torn from the earth, their roots raw, ugly, had toppled over the lower bushes, briars and thorn. And over all climbed and twisted the creepers and wild grape, wrapping and interlacing the whole as in a giant net.

Molly ached for the red earth of Louisiana land, stretching flat and open for miles, in contrast to the menace of this deep gully

105

and the strange entangling forest. She too felt caught in a net, a net of conflicting emotions. She gave a someone-is-walking-over-my-grave kind of shiver.

"You cold?" asked Levi.

How could she be cold in this warm spring air? She wanted to cry out, I'm frightened—it's not just the forest, it's not any one thing, it's everything, it's a queer time, a bad time. Oh Levi! Talk to me about it. About what? Oh! I don't know what it is but there is—*something*. She said aloud, "No, I'm not cold. It's the forest. It's too lonesome to live here!"

"Lonesome! Aw, no, Half-Pint, it's not lonesome. You've got the river. Nobody can be lonesome with the river before their door."

"But the forest! The gully—!"

"Looks almighty pretty to me—filled with Judas and dogwood trees. Don't look at the forest if it bothers you. Look at the river. As for the gully, it eases down to a good inlet where I can build my flatboats. I'll make a roadway so the loads of produce can be hauled down. Might even build my steamboat down there. Lonesome! You won't be lonesome. There'll be too much going on right on your door-step. Wait and see."

So the moment when she might have tried to convey to Levi her uncertainties passed. Levi, always so secure and sure of himself, probably wouldn't have known what she was talking about anyway. Indeed, neither would she.

Yet the disappointment she had felt at the sight of the crude shelter her groom was providing was more than offset by her escape from Hester's household. She would have been pleased to push a cow out of its stable in order to be in a place of her own—free of Hester. But it was with a sinking heart that she thought of her trousseau, her dowry hamstrung, hors-de-combat in these rough log cabins.

As it turned out the house wasn't bad. The dog-trot between the two cabins had been enclosed and made a wide gracious hall with front and back doors giving onto pillared long piazzas. Ira said it reminded him of an old-fashioned house-raising, when Levi's friends started to fix up the house. Snap—a couple of wings were framed, roofed and floored. Slap—as fast as closing a shutter clapboards were nailed on the outside of the logs, while on the inside matched boards panelled the walls. When Molly asked why he did not put the new rooms behind the others, Levi answered he wanted to be able to see the river from every room. So there was the house, all eighty-five feet of it, facing the river.

"A woman-killer," Rivertown ladies declared when they saw it, but added, yellow-eyed, "Reckon it won't bother *her* none, she's got them slaves."

The bride watched the house grow before her eyes like Jack watching his beanstalk. As she watched Levi's warmhearted friends work, there quickened in her a sense of possession. The realization leaped within her that this was *her* house. She became eager, alive, and filled with expectations. The men down from their ladders refreshing themselves at the barrel must have sensed the change in her; they increased their horse-play and attention to her. It was a gay, happy, busy time.

Then came the women along the river bank footpath, each carrying a basket covered with a snowy cloth.

"Why have they come?" Molly asked. "I didn't invite them."

Hester said, "It's customary," and sniffed. "Reckon they want to make sure their men get fed."

Ira said, "Scissors and potatoes! They know well enough, Miz Blaisdell, you'd provide ample for Levi's friends." He sent a warm beam in his new daughter-in-law's direction, "Even if our little Miss South can't."

"Little Miss South!" Hester snorted.

Ira said, "The trouble with you women is you can't bear to stay away, leave the men alone. You have to turn everything into a female picnic."

"And a good thing, too!" snapped Hester.

With Hester and the women on the job, there was no more foolishness. Now the men, their quips and pranks crushed beneath their women's disapproving eyes, went to the whiskey barrel to dipper fresh brawn only in order to have done with the task as quickly as possible.

Finally the job was done, and the women re-packed their baskets and led their men back along the footpath of rigid rules. With relief the bride turned to the privacy of her walls, where she would "summer and winter" Levi. But she was to learn that in Rivertown's social order, privacy was an unknown quantity.

It was Hoosier custom not to bother to knock, but to open a neighbor's door and come in. It got so Molly never knew what old crone she'd find sitting in her parlor ogling her fripperies. She threw the latch on the door only to hear from Hester that it was being talked all over town that she was inhospitable—after everyone had been so kind to help with the house. The helper became the possessor, claiming certain rights.

Hester came daily with baskets of prepared food, including great loaves of cold bread. The daughter-in-law tried to convey thanks but they were ill received. "Return the utensils more promptly, please. I'm not as well supplied as a plantation."

Molly tried treating Hester as a guest, inviting her into the best room. Hester refused to sit, but ran a sharp eye around to see what had been accomplished from the day before and to what use, if any, the bride had put her mother-in-law's cast-offs. As soon as Hester had gone, Molly vented her rage by throwing the cold bread into the gully but grudgingly ordered the other food to be placed on the table for Levi. Indeed she was grateful since neither she nor Julee knew how to cook.

Nevertheless she grumbled to Levi, "You'd think I didn't know enough to feed you. Tell your mother to quit bringing food."

"Why does it bother you? I'd think you'd be obliged instead of mad."

"But a wife wants to run her own house, decide things like what she'll have for dinner, supper. And while you're about it, tell her to quit bringing her cast-offs."

Levi said, "What's wrong with using some of Ma's things for a spell? They look all right to me."

"I want my own—new ones." Molly wailed. "I want to choose my own potato-masher, my own rolling-pin."

"Well, money doesn't grow on northern sycamore trees, Molly. Takes a lot of money to build a boat. Reckon you can make out with Ma's cast-offs for a spell. You go ahead and fix up your house."

Molly snapped, "You haven't done a thing to help fix the house— I can't do everything."

"I'm sorry, honey, but I've got to finish that flat and be off with the May butter."

"Levi, take me with you! Don't leave me here!"

"You can't go on a flatboat, Molly. As for help fixing up the house, get Gaithe—he won't help me. Just when I need him worse'n tarnation he turns stubborner than a mud-cat. Something's come over Gaithe. Used to be a regular little rip-staver, always trying to ape me—but here lately—" Levi shook his head. "Every spring since he was a little tad he's begged to turn a flatboat with me. It's chancy, but I reckon I might let him take a go at this one seeing he's so mopish. I'll holler when I'm ready so's you can come see the kind of a trained alligator horse you took for a husband." Then with the broad of his hand he gave her a playful smack across her bottom and was out the door.

Molly wondered how that big flatboat of heavy white oak timber, eighteen feet wide, ninety feet long, about the size of their house but built upside down on skids out over the water, could be turned. Levi said, "Myself and one other can do it." That must be just another of his big tall tales. It would take all the oxen, horses, and men Levi could muster to turn it. Two men couldn't do this alone even if one of them was Levi himself who claimed to be an alligator horse from Roaring River.

Levi apparently didn't know what was the matter with his brother—but Molly did. Gaithe had worked right along with the others on the house, but had said with disgust he didn't see why Levi bothered to have a house on shore and suggested he might as well take Molly to live on a dirty old flatboat if he couldn't do any better for her than give her a couple of cabins with a dog-trot hall. There was a doglike devotion in Gaithe's eyes whenever he was with Molly, and her slightest wish was his law. Well, Molly sighed, it was Levi who told her to get Gaithe to help her, so she started off to the kitchen to send Matt with a message for him.

At home the kitchen was the cook house, a separate brick building connected to the dining room by the whistle-way, the runway down which Horatio whistled when Papa was ready for the next course to be legged in to him under its silver cover. She had fought with Levi over the kitchen, which he insisted had to be right in the house. "Come winter, you'll understand, Molly. Don't fuss— this room has to be kitchen, dining, and sitting room—maybe sleeping—it gets durned cold."

Levi had a way of stating his opinion very strongly and there was no point in trying to argue with him or persuade him to the contrary. It wasn't that he was stiff-necked or hidebound like Hester, neither did his stubbornness seem to spring from any selfishness. He just said that the kitchen was to be in the house and would not consider any other arrangement.

Molly, knowing she had lost, told Matt to whitewash the walls, sand and polish the wide floor boards, scrub down with lye the old crude pioneer cast-offs—an old wooden settle with head-high to heel-low back designed to keep off drafts from neck and feet, an open dresser, sink bench, trestle table and spindle chairs.

Matt grumbled, "Takes a sight of elbow grease to rub-wax these old rottendy things the way you want them, Miss Molly."

Julee said, "Big Boy, it takes just as much sweat to shine old rottendy brass and pewter. God-to-Jesus, us don't know what Mammy Fay and your papa do if they know their young miss live like cabin folks. Mammy Fay not like us doin' kitchen work, us a lady's maid, us is." Julee dipped water from the black kettle on the hearth and set a dishpan in the wash bench. She sighed, "Reckon our folks miss us?"

Matt made a bitter sound, meant for a laugh. "If you wants to know how much, Julee girl, you sticks you' finger in you' dish water, then pull it out and look at the hole."

Julee did, and in astonishment looked at the negative result. She whispered, "Reckon you' right, Matt—oh—oh—"

"Julee!" Molly spoke sharply because she felt her own tears so near. "No more crying."

"Honey, Julee," Matt said, "like I told you, us our own folks now."

"Matt! Run find Mr. Gaithe and tell him I need help." They'd all be crying if Molly didn't watch out. The mistress bride not only had to control herself, but she had to control the servant bride and groom as well. So it was a relief to discover that while they'd been talking Salena Cranch had come for a visit.

"I brought you a loaf, Molly."

"Thank you, Salena." Good heavens, another loaf of cold bread.

"Oh, it's nothing, Molly. I came to help. I figger maybe you need a master hand on account of I don't think you and Julee know much about housekeeping. Molly, what on earth are those gimcracks used for?"

Molly showed Salena how the gilded brackets were to be fastened to the wall, and how on them she would put the beautiful Chinese figurines. "Well, I never!" Salena declared. The brackets looked like pure gold.

"Molly," Salena hesitated, braced herself and took the plunge. "Molly, I'd just admire to see the little silver pot and teeny cup folks say you use whilst still in bed."

110

Molly took them from a cupboard and set them on a black and gold table. Salena shook her head at the wonder of them. "More like play-toys." She let out a big sigh. "Seems like I never had play dishes. Reckon I went from pull-toy stage right into washing full-size plates."

"Julee!" Molly called. "Make some coffee. Miss Salena and I are going to play-party."

"Gosh, Molly!" Salena patted her hair, looked down at her dull brown dress. "Reckon I ain't much fixed."

"You're fine, Salena."

"Molly—Molly, would you mind if I learn manners off you?"

"Dear Salena!"

"Well, I just thought with you in the family, mebbe Gaithe might take to measuring any girl by you. I wish I had pretty hair and clothes. Wouldn't do any good, though, I'm like a plank."

Salena was quite right, for of course she was only a gangling girl, more like a younger sister, making a nuisance of herself to Gaithe, who already worshipped his brother's young bride with all the ardor of his boyish heart.

"I hate my clothes. Is that wicked, Molly? They're all cut-me-downs—mostly Miz Blaisdell's. Don't reckon you'd like them either."

Molly was quite certain she wouldn't. It might be fun to see what Salena, with her height, her black eyes, her skin like a white camellia, would look like if she were fixed up differently.

"I'll show you how to do your hair, brighten your clothes. Let's pretend you're my young sister; we've both been cheated of a sister," she said.

"Oh Molly! Would you? We would be sisters if Gaithe—Molly, he treats me like I was *his* sister. He doesn't even *look* at me."

Julee brought the coffee and Molly insisted that Salena pour so she could handle the pot.

"Gosh-a-mighty," Salena said, seated at the little black and gold lacquer table on which Julee had set the gleaming tray holding the wondrous pot, creamer, sugar and little fragile cups. "Gosh! Do you really have this whilst you're in bed, Molly? Gosh!"

Levi came in to say they'd soon be ready to turn the flat and maybe a boatman's wife might like to see how it was done. Molly said she was waiting for Gaithe.

"Darn fool young-un," said Levi.

"Who's a darn fool young-un?" shouted Gaithe from the doorway.

"You are!" teased Levi.

"Well you, you're nothing but a river rat expecting Molly to live in a house like this."

"What would you get her, you little rip-staver?"

Gaithe flushed, "Molly deserves better than you give her. You'd let her live with the hogs!" Gaithe's voice cracked on a high key.

"Why you little—I've half a mind to run you up Salt River."

"Come on! You think you're a ringtail roarer," shouted Gaithe. "Try and do it."

Levi roared, "Why I can lick your weight in wild cats." He charged.

Molly expected Gaithe to be picked up and thrown out her front door. But Levi pulled himself up short. The brothers, angry, stood chest to chest, their legs spread, at the ready. They resembled each other so closely. In a fight Gaithe would be fast and slippery, Levi would close in with his greater weight and wrestle like a bear. Gaithe might get hurt. Molly held her lower lip between her teeth, waiting.

With relief, she watched Levi's anger melt into affection for this replica of himself, so young, comely and straight.

Levi unclenched his fist and dropped a brotherly hand on Gaithe's shoulder. "What's come over you?"

Gaithe jerked himself from under Levi's restraining hand and bolted out the door.

Levi called after him. "We're finished caulkin' that flat. Want to turn her with me?"

Gaithe shouted back over his shoulder, "You're damn right I'll turn her, and land you on your big back side to boot!"

"The hell you will, you little pip-squeak," yelled Levi and plunged after Gaithe.

Then, to fill the painful stillness the brothers had left behind them, Molly said, "I think red would become you, Salena."

"Gaithe won't notice red or any other color on me—now." Maybe Levi refused to recognize what ailed Gaithe, but Salena had given up the pretense. She was as dull and listless as Hester's cast-off brown dress which she wore.

112

Levi's bellow "Oo-oo-oo-ee! Oo-oo-oo-ee!" took the girls to the river bank where they looked down on a scene of great activity.

The monstrous flat, now caulked, was still upside down on skids built out over the water. The men who were helping Levi were running here and there checking this and that. Then armed with huge sledge hammers they took up positions at each skid and waited for Levi's "Go!" and as one man they dropped their hammers and knocked the skids out from under the flatboat.

One mighty splash! And the boat was floating off shore, still wrong side up. The men quickly pulled the flatboat in close to the shore, where they loaded it up with stones, gathered for the purpose in funny high two-wheeled carts. Some of the men, sloshing around in water groin high, handed the rocks up to men on the boat. All worked together efficiently and harmoniously. When the flatboat was loaded to Levi's satisfaction, two johnboats towed it to midstream. The rocks were carefully adjusted again, and when Levi gave the word the johnboats faced the flat cross-wise of the current with the rocks on the up-river side.

"Now they turn it," cried Salena. "Levi's never let Gaithe do this before. It's dangerous."

Levi and Gaithe took up positions, each on a down-river corner of the flat. The men on board started throwing the rocks to the down-stream side of the flat as fast as they could. The weight of the rocks and the current together started the flat to turning. Quick as cats the men jumped to safety in the johnboats—all but Levi and Gaithe!

"Jump!" shouted Molly.

"Shut up!" said Salena.

Oh, my God! The flat was turning, they would be thrown under it into the water and crushed to death as it came down. Molly held her breath. Levi and Gaithe could never get clear of the monstrous thing, they'd both be killed before her very eyes.

But instead of being thrown, each sprinted up his end of the flat. There was a moment when the flat stood perpendicular to the water. In that split-second the brothers leaped into the air. They were magnificent to see—two winged Mercuries poised mid-air while the flat turned. They landed simultaneously on the gunwale of the boat, now right side up, and shouted, "Ho, ho!"

Her fear that Levi would be smashed by the turning flat changed

113

to anger at his cocksure daring. She didn't know whether this was the right way to turn a flatboat or simply a way that Levi had cooked up to show off his exuberant wild spirits. But she was glad Gaithe had done so well. Maybe now Levi would give him a little of the respect the maturing boy needed so badly.

CHAPTER XII

NOW THAT THE FLATBOAT WAS COMPLETED, LEVI ANXIOUSLY watched the stage of the river and each night recorded his observations in his log book (the sight of which Molly grew to hate) and speculated on the chances of a sudden fresh rain raising the water. But no rain came and under the pressure of the falling water he worked feverishly loading his boat.

During these weeks Molly's life was far from her idea of what the life of a young bride should be. Levi worked outside from morning till night, like a common laborer, and when he was in the house he continually whittled away at those everlasting boatpins, making a mess of shavings and paying very little heed to her.

One evening she sat looking beautiful and chic in one of her prettiest trousseau dresses; but Levi, ignoring her as though she were a piece of furniture, concentrated on his usual evening occupation. Suddenly words burst from her.

"Stop whittling!" she screamed.

Levi jumped in surprise at her peahen screech. Patiently he tried to explain how many boatpins were needed to make a flatboat and why all boatmen spent their leisure time whittling. But Molly hardly listened.

Jumping to her feet with a disgusted glance at the rough, work-clothed man she had married, she shouted for Julee.

"Tell Matt to build up the fire in here, fill the kettles, bring in a wash tub."

"You going to take a bath?" asked Levi.

"I'm not, but *you* are!" snapped Molly.

"Why in tarnation should I take a bath *tonight?*"

"'Because you need one. And another thing, I want *you,* not Gaithe, to make and drive my pegs for me. Your mother doesn't understand why I can't get my house in order. I can't because there's no place to put anything, no place to hang anything, no shelves to hold anything, no armoires for my clothes, no presses, not even a few pegs. Oh, no! I can't even have a few pegs put up to hang my bonnets on because you have to whittle boatpins!"

Molly stopped her tirade momentarily while Matt filled the kettles, built the fire up under them, swept the hearth at her command and returned once again to place the wash tub to her complete satisfaction. When Matt had yes-Miss-Molly-ed her sufficiently she let him go and resumed scolding Levi where she'd left off.

"Boatpins you're too lazy to pull and bring back."

"A man can make new pegs faster than he can pull out old ones," Levi said. He added wistfully, "A flatboat's a boat that never comes back. If we can't sell them for lumber in New Orleans, we cut them loose and let them drift. Reckon there's many a lonesome hatch of mine bobbing around on the Gulf Stream remembering the tunes of Jim's fiddle and the fun we had aboard her."

It was as though the great sweeps of a flatboat had carried Levi away from his bride—carried him out on a deep smooth current where he heard the slap of the water without her.

"You're such a smart man," she hit back at him, "I should think you'd have figured some way to bring them back by now."

"You'd better stick to woman's business, Sorrel Top. Why don't you and Julee try to right your kitchen? If you don't know how, Ma'll show you."

"Oh! That's what I'm trying to tell you. I *have* tried. I can't put anything away because there is no place to *put anything!*"

Molly was so homesick she thought she couldn't stand it. She longed to see the neatly ordered store rooms of Rutland Hall with their gaily painted tin bins (here everything was wooden) holding many sweet goodies. How could she ever hang her gilded bracket on this crude board wall, and display her fragile Chinese figurines?

"I want you to take a bath!" she spit at Levi.

"What if I don't want a bath?" he drawled, taking a bead on a boatpin to see if the head lay true to be driven deep by one hard whack of the hammer.

116

"You will!" She went to the kettle hanging on the crane and clumsily dippered hot water into the wooden wash tub and then added cold water from a bucket. "Wooden, everything in this forsaken country is wooden," she muttered.

Levi, still amused at her spitfire ways, slowly came to his feet, tossed his boatpin aside and came toward her with a gleeful expression on his face.

"Who's to have the bath, Half-Pint?"

Before she grasped his intent he had caught her and was busy undoing the buttons of her bodice. She flailed her arms and legs wildly, but Levi expertly captured her twisting, turning limbs in his own arms and legs and gently peeled down her clothes. Then with a quick surprising movement, he doubled her up and set her naked in the wash tub.

"It's wooden," she wailed. "Even the bath tub is wooden. I hate it. I hate you."

When she was finished, Levi wrapped her tenderly in a shawl by the fire where she sniffled quietly while he bathed. Afterwards he held her high up in his arms like a baby. "Do you hate me?" whispered Levi. "You don't, you know. You're my girl."

He didn't wait for her answer but carried her across the wide dog-trot hall. She found he was right. She was his girl.

One evening, waiting for Levi to come to a late supper, Molly sat on the cooling bench he had made her out on the river bank. It was just like Levi to find time to knock together a cooling bench which she did not want instead of the pegs and shelves in the house which she needed desperately, and to spend endless time rummaging through his work sheds looking for pink conch shells of all things.

He said, "Thunder and scissors, you've got to have a cooling board or you're not a boatman's wife and how'll folks know it's a boatman's house if there aren't shells along the path to tell them? I've been collecting and saving shells for a long while."

Yes, Levi was a river man through and through.

He came up the gully path now, unshirted, dirt caked and sweaty. She sniffed and said, "I suppose it's expecting too much to ask you to take a bath before sitting down to table."

"Won't be in for supper. We're pushing off, Half-Pint."

"Not now!"

"Yup! Water's still dropping. Haven't a minute to lose. Hope to make the Falls by morning."

"Your supper?"

"Ma's vittled the boat just fine."

"Your log book?"

"It's on board. No, Honey, I must say goodbye, push off."

"No! Not like this, out here on the river bank. Come inside," she begged.

"Half-Pint, you're as cute as a pair of little red shoes and sweet as punkin and I wouldn't trust you as far as I could throw a cat once you got me inside."

She threw her arm around his neck, "No! You are not going. No! No!" She whispered and begged. His arms closed around her. "Take me inside," she pled now unheedful of the sweaty dirt, only knowing she could not let him go.

For answer he took her lips between his own for one long hard minute of eternity. Then he left her on the cooling board to find self-balance again—alone.

By the time she had recovered, the flatboat lines had been hauled aboard, the boat had been poled away from the shore. Now one broadhorn sweep and the steering oar was in action carrying the flatboat to the deepest current. Midstream the men sang, *Some rows up, but we rows down, all the way to Shawnee town, Pull away—pull away.*

Darn him! How could he dance on the hatch, wave to her, flip a coin over his shoulder? He had had the strength to resist her—her! How could he bear to go off and leave her?

It was a shock to realize that he could. There had been moments when she felt that he belonged to her completely. But now, after he had thrust her aside she was aware of something else. Something hard, unbreakable, unconquerable about Levi. This river was an obsession with him.

She ran her tongue over her bruised lips.

That night Molly was unbearably lonely; for the first time in her life she slept in a room alone—no Mammy Fay on guard across the foot of her bed, no sleepy-head Julee nearby, no strong Levi to hold her safe.

Later she tried having Julee come in from the cabin across the yard, but Julee made such childish pouts and did her work next day so badly that she sent her back to Matt at night in order to have her happy by day. Yes, Molly felt as if every person had gone away and left her, and now she was alone in this strange house set close to the deep gully and the black trees of the forest. High whispers crept in upon her, chilling her, filling her with cold panic.

Was this what it meant to be a boatman's wife? To be alone in a room filled with fear. To be alone in all the world with the same old lonesomeness.

She had thought that by putting hundreds of miles of river, the great Mississippi, the Ohio, between her and her unhappy childhood she would never again suffer this fearful bound feeling. Nor did she—when Levi loved her into the freedom of nothingness. He must not leave her again. She would not be left waiting up on the hill for his return.

Yet a boatman's wife was expected to keep her house in order against the return of her boatman. For fun and frolic in his absence, there was the Thursday Circle.

At the Circle the conversation ran on and on about babies, sickness, and the great need for rain. Not for twenty years had it been so dry and no one had known summer complaint to set in on them so early; they'd no more than got their blood cleaned out from winter's troubles before the next sickly season was on them. Neighbor commiserated with neighbor—they felt none too good, in fact they were poorly, right poorly.

While the rest were droning along in this fashion old Miz Davidson hitched her chair around toward Molly and whispered, "They enjoy poor health."

Old Miz Davidson considered Molly as her private property since she was the one who had defended her conduct that first Sunday in church. "I sez to them, I sez, why should the devil be the one to have all the good tunes. She's done nothing wrong, making a light foot down the aisle, looking uncommon pretty, and singing mighty sweet."

At home Molly busied herself trying to help Julee get the hang of operating Buck's New Patent Stove she had bought from Johnny Briggs down on Main Cross.

"Now, Julee, you are to learn to cook."

"Us a lady's maid." Julee flared her nostrils wide.

"A cook too, Julee. Now here's a cook book."

"How you learn to cook off a book?" Julee's red lips curled with scorn. The terms and directions in the cook book made no sense to her. "If they mean fry why don' they say fry?"

Molly studied the book, asked questions of Salena and Minnie Preble, stood over Julee and read her the directions though the Negro insisted, "You got to have the feel for it, books don' give the feel, besides, you got rec'nize a certain look to the mess in the pan and you got to taste it too."

Yet between Julee's tasting and feeling and Molly's newly acquired book knowledge the two brides finally got the hang of cooking on the new stove and had blessed relief from the open fire in the hot weather. For summer heat had arrived the end of May and was growing even worse in June.

That summer Minnie Preble proved herself a real friend in addition to being an invaluable help to the inexperienced bride. Then too Molly developed a happy and affectionate relationship with her father-in-law. Ira would come by to lend a hand in the house or garden and stay on to chat by the hour.

One day when Ira and Gaithe were putting up some shelves for Molly, and Salena had dropped in as she frequently did they got to talking about the river as opposed to the prairie. Molly was determined to get her husband away from the river by hook or crook.

"Why is Levi so crazy about the river?" she appealed to his father. Surely Ira must have understanding of his son's madness.

The older man examined a piece of planed wood while he deliberated. These Hoosiers not only thought twice before they spoke, but often as many as three or four times. At last, having found the answer, Ira said, "Now there's a downright peculiar thing, Molly. His ma and me were as surprised as the next one, because neither of us give a hoot about the river. At first his ma was as confounded as the old hen that hatched the duckling and she tried mighty hard to keep her chappie on land. Finally she gave in and pretended she didn't notice. Mebbe she realized she was up against a piece of her own substance in Levi. Mebbe you've noticed that Miz Blaisdell can boss us all except Levi. She's never shackled him.

"I realize now I might as well have pushed on to the West. In the end I doubt if it would have made a mite of difference to Miz Blaisdell. Reckon prairie land wouldn't have disgruntled her more

120

than any other since she'd made up her mind none of it was to her liking. She was pure fed up with traipsin', so she said; but shucks, we'd got through the rough, tough part of the journey and only just reached the western country. Could have pushed right on with the going easy.

"But Miz Blaisdel set her fire kettle down and that was that. Never could rightly understand why, don't to this day. When I was a-sparkin' her she took a lively enough interest in going all the way to the prairie country, but we'd come no more than a half-dozen sleeps, when she lost her day-dreamin' spirit, and when we got here there was no budgin' her and her fire kettle, so what could a body do?" He looked at Gaithe and the two girls helplessly and added with regret, "Still and all, I wish I'd had a look around. There's a sight to see what with this and that.'

"I take after Pa," Gaithe said. "I hanker to see what's beyond. Guess maybe women are different; us boys don't take after Ma. Sis, being a girl, might have favored Ma."

Salena's towel slowed on a fragile dish. Salena needed to play-party, brighten her clothes, soften her hair, but her big dark eyes saw things Molly didn't see and reflected an inner sureness Molly didn't have. "*I* would go west," she said softly.

"Hah! Takes grown men and women to go west," said Gaithe.

"I'm a woman," Salena said.

"You're a green apple nubbin!" Gaithe laughed the way Cousin Buford had laughed at his younger sisters. Salena answered with a secret little smile.

Meanwhile Ira kept up a rambling conversation with himself. "Always figured though some day I'd pull up stakes and push on. But after I got that trouble in my groin from lifting too heavy a load, I was no good for doin' real heavy work. Had to settle for a saw and hammer and call myself a carpenter."

"And a very good one, sir," Molly said.

"Pshaw!" Ira tested a brace for the shelf. "Reckon it'll hold." He laid down his hammer. His manner grew confidential. "I'd just as soon none of you'd say anything about this to Miz Blaisdell." He paused and pushed the hammer a little way along the shelf. Then he squared his shoulders and looked from one to the other. "I been thinkin' lately. I been hearin' and readin' how folks is movin' west —*overland*. Why I heard up to Centerville families was going through several hundred a month. This country's started waggin' right behind horses, oxen and mules' tails. You're goin' to see more and more wagons hittin' the trail straight across country."

"Then what, Pa?"

Ira glanced round at each of them, Gaithe, Salena, and Molly, and then having decided they could be trusted, said, "Well, they say Indianapolis is one movin' mass of wagons, cattle, horses, hogs, sheep, men, women and children, all pushing on through to the West. And looky-here, if they didn't keep draining themselves off, why the whole country from the lakes to the Mississippi would be so jammed-packed full of folks there wouldn't be room to swing a cat. So I been thinkin'."

"What, Pa? For gosh sake, what?" urged Gaithe.

"It's like I say, this is going to be a mighty great country once she gets enough folks to fill her up from here to there, and I'd still like to have a hand in her making."

"Then you mean you'll go, Pa?"

Ira shook his head, "No, Son, I leave that to the young squirts like you."

"Ma won't let me."

"That's something you have to decide for yourself. Your ma will keep you if she can. Your ma's shackled herself in some kind of bondage none of us can understand, but that don't mean, Son, that you got to let her bind you. It's taken me half a life time to learn that. But I know now I'm going to do what I always aimed to do—help open up this country."

"But Pa, if you don't go how'd you aim to help?"

"Wagon wheels!" You could tell by Ira's eyes he expected the magnitude of his idea to stun them. "Ira Blaisdell—Wainwright! Wagon wheels made true and strong so's folks can depend on them. Wagon wheels turning to carry folks west to settle a great country." He narrowed his eyes as though he were looking into a vast distance until they glittered with excitement and he grew heady with what he saw lay up ahead. "My wagon wheels will keep turnin' 'till they're fetched up by the Pacific."

"But why west instead of south?" asked Molly, who had been toying with the idea of getting Levi to be a southern planter, though she did not know what he'd use for money to get the land and buildings, not to mention stocking it and buying the necessary slaves.

122

"Folks won't go south, Molly. Everyone's headed west, far as Ioway, where the land is cheap and the soil is good. Mebbe some will go even beyond. What they want to go south for? Any land they could buy would be all worn out, not give a piddlin' crop. 'Less a body's got a lot of money he can't afford to go south. Slaves cost too much to stock a work farm and no immigrating Irish or German will go down there to work in competition with slave labor. He'll work like a slave, even harder, but he didn't come to America to labor alongside one. I got a notion land in the South pretty soon won't be worth much, but even then nobody will go there."

"Why not?" demanded Molly.

"Got a notion nobody'll want to. I don't argue the right or wrong of slavery. I'll leave that to the women who already got up a good head of steam over it. By the way don't rile Miz Blaisdell on it. She's got all the ear-marks of getting her mind set. I notice lately she's been roaring like a female lion on the evils of it and lookin' for somebody to blame for it. But that's something else, we're talking about the West. No matter which way you look at the question of what a young man like Gaithe ought to do, it's plain enough he should point his toes west."

Gaithe, who had recently taken to shaving regularly just like a man, well, at least once or twice a week, spraddled his legs man-style and tipped his chair back against the wall. "When the time comes I'm going, I'm not going to let Ma keep me any more than she can Levi, but I reckon I'll wait up a spell."

His eyes circled the room until they at last rested upon Molly and his face flushed from embarrassment and confusion under her scrutiny. The fool! The young fool! He was going to hang around because of her.

When situations such as this showed Molly the possible complications arising from Gaithe's infatuation she suffered real pangs of conscience. For her subjugation of the boy was not entirely innocent.

Bored and frustrated by the variance of her life from the one she had foreseen in day dreams at Quercus Grove and on Captain Cleve's boat; with Levi away so long, and busy Minnie Preble her only real friend in this alien town; she frankly enjoyed the excitement and feeling of power that Gaithe's attentions gave her. Also, she enjoyed plaguing Hester, who could see no good in her no matter what she did and she was annoyed with Levi for being so calm about Gaithe's obvious devotion to her.

She often invited Gaithe to join her for coffee at the end of the day. He would arrive sparkling clean, his hair slicked down smelling strongly of Old West Indian Bay Water. He had gradually lost some of his awkward gangliness and even gained a wee bit of self assurance.

One afternoon, at the end of a particularly sultry and tedious day, the situation threatened to get completely out of hand. Molly and Gaithe had had coffee, she had read poetry aloud, and now she gaily commanded him to bring out the music box. At this he looked at her with a kind of agony, much like a dog who must obey his mistress in performing painful tricks.

"Come, come, we must be gay. The poetry has made you too sad." Actually it was Molly herself who had grown sad.

Reluctantly he stood up, tried to smooth his clothes, his eyes unable to look at her; her red hair, her green dress, her cunning little foot narrowed in red velvet shoe tracing a coupee of the minuet. She hummed a little tune, rapped out its time with her fan on the edge of the black and gold japanned coffee table, and further marked time with her pretty little head, causing the shining curls on her temples to dance.

Gaithe made a lunge for the music box and brought it forward, wound it with shaking hands and set it on the table before her. She stretched her hand toward him and said, "Ah, Mozart! Let us dance!"

In misery he ran his hands over his pants and braced himself for the actual physical contact of taking Molly's hand in his. She leaned closer to him, wafted the fragrance of her perfumed person toward him, caressed with her eyes his tormented face.

His long arms came about her, pulled her against his trembling body. "Molly! Molly!" he cried.

For a moment she lay against him, wishing with all her heart that he were Levi. Yet this need to be loved and to love on a childish level was not satisfied by Levi. He had cast her in the role of a boatman's wife and expected a more mature performance from her than she was able to deliver all the time. She felt so young, so ill-prepared to grapple with this new life. And now Gaithe, unwilling to leave their relationship on a childish play-party level, was going to ruin their beautiful semi-romantic afternoons.

She pulled herself abruptly from his arms. "Don't Gaithe! Don't!"

He released her abruptly, almost with relief, and stumbled pale faced, from the house.

Hester appeared an hour or so later. "I don't like the way social amenities are being conducted around here," she stated flatly.

Mrs. Blaisdell was such a strong person, so sure of her position that she terrified her daughter-in-law. To combat her, Molly assumed a pose of arrogant defiance.

She widened her eyes now in a manner which she hoped was annoying to Hester. "What social amenities?"

"You know very well what I mean."

"But I don't. Your ideas of what's proper and mine don't agree."

"You know that you are deliberately leading Gaithe on. A fine how-do-you-do! To flirt and carry on with your husband's own brother! For shame!"

"I am no more than kind and courteous to Gaithe. I only want to help him. The poor boy is unhappy, diffident, and sensitive."

"There's plenty of danger lurking when a boy and a girl waste their time together."

"It's not a waste of time to be civilized. My father. . . ."

"I am pleased that you show respect for your father, but I beg of you, spare me another lecture on his superiority. I am warning you, Molly, if you persist in leading Gaithe on you are laying up trouble for the days ahead and you'll hurt my boy."

"What do you want me to do?"

"Quit seeing Gaithe, quit asking him to run errands for you, quit asking him to escort you places. He's your husband's brother. Quit!"

Quit! Quit! Quit!

Molly followed Hester's command—not to please Hester, but because she was frightened to find herself in a situation she didn't know how to handle. As long as Gaithe had kept her up on a pedestal, she was free to dream that she was as fragile as the dainty cup in her hand, something to be cherished and handled with care. But she wanted no Gaithe forcing himself upon her.

So now when he came to the cabin she busied herself with mundane household tasks, or she had an errand down on Main Cross, or she insisted she must go at once to Minnie Preble's for advice on some household matter. The results were alarming.

Gaithe grew moody and restless, had sudden outbursts of belligerency followed by spells of dark brooding. What Hester may have said to him, Molly did not know but she could guess the words: Sin, Crime, and Vice, quickening in him a sense of guilt and weighing him with a burden he had never known before.

CHAPTER XIII

As the days passed Molly thought of ways of persuading Levi to leave the river and go to the wonderful western country where good land could be had for almost nothing. The money he was saving for his steamboat should be enough. She dreamed of a utopian plantation which would be a mixture of Rutland Hall and Quercus Grove, with only the best features of each.

In the meantime, she was faced with having to exist in Rivertown, where life was even drearier than usual that summer.

No rain fell and the river kept dropping. Ordinarily Molly could lift her eyes anytime and see a steamboat. Now fewer and fewer boats came by.

Then one day she saw *The Rising Sun!*

Julee couldn't hurry fast enough to get another dress on her, and Molly's feet wouldn't carry her fast enough down to the landing, which now was the yellow earth of the river bottom, dried and cracked in zig-zag lines, so low had the water fallen. A sorry place for a fine steamboat to push out her landing stage!

"Oh Captain Cleve! Captain Cleve!" What a blessed relief it was to see the familiar rotund man, whose friendship had given her a sense of security even as a little girl. His arrival banished the hateful loneliness of the long weeks past. His words of greeting were so welcome yet saddening too.

"Was hopin' you'd come down so's I wouldn't have to take time to look you up. Been hung up for hours on the bar at North Bend. Got to get on down in a hurry. Only put in here to see how you're makin' out. 'Less there's a freshet I won't get back up here for quite a spell. Levi come home all right?"

127

"No, Captain Cleve. Might he be having trouble?"

"If this keeps up, he'll have to walk. Ain't you noticed, Honey, all the boats are down-boats—nothin' comin' up?"

"Oh! But he's been gone so long!"

"That's bein' a boatman's wife."

"Oh, Captain Cleve! It's too lonely."

"I can hear *her* sayin' those self-same words." He took a deep breath. "Guess it's kinda hard on the women who marry river men."

"We're going to leave the river—go west."

Captain Cleve shot her a startled glance. "This a notion of yours or Levi's?" In answer to the gleam in her eye, Captain Cleve said, "I don't know, Honey, maybe you hadn't ought to try. You're takin' an awful chance when you pester a man to go against his leanin's and longin's. Might as well try to put down his carnal passions as to get a man to leave his trollop of a river once she's baited and hooked him." He patted her shoulder, "He'll be along soon and you'll be scolding him for bein' around under foot."

"Whittling!"

One word of invitation from Captain Cleve and she would have stayed on deck instead of waiting on the baked yellow shore to watch *The Rising Sun* stand off down-river, heading for the Mississippi, broad and deep, steaming down to Quercus Grove where the sloe trees were white with bloom and the children played "Chickamy, Chickamy, Craney Crow" ending with the shrill scream "What o'clock, Old Witch?"

The tears fell down her cheeks so that she no longer saw *The Rising Sun*, but she did hear the soundings of the leadsman, Turkey Neck, who measured the depth of water by dropping the leadline and the chant of his findings to the pilot, "Layin' lead, layin' lead."

Time and time again he heaved the lead and let the line slip through his hands only to call again and again nothing higher than "F'r-rrr fee-ee-t." Turkey Neck couldn't give the pilot more water than that shown by the white piece of flannel woven into the rope at the four-foot mark.

So she knew Captain Cleve spoke the truth when he said there would be no up-river boats. She wiped her eyes for a last look at *The Rising Sun* which, having felt her way between the sand bars, now went into her crossing at the lower bend and slipped out of sight.

For a time boats of shallower draft than *The Rising Sun* came by. But she could hear their pilots swear and angrily clang the boat's bells as the leadsmen chanted of less and less water. Great sandbars, brittle and yellow, came out to glisten and dazzle in the bright sun and to send up shimmering waves of heat to make the eye-balls ache. The shallow pools among the sands dried up and Matt had to go farther and farther to reach water to haul for the shriveled, dried-up plants.

Molly, too, became dry and feverish as the hot days drew on. She sat on the cooling bench by the hour, watching. One day she watched all day and not a boat came on the dwindling, ugly yellowish stream. Her only means of going home was cut off. She realized now, that back in her mind there had always been the thought, "I don't *have* to stay. I can go back whenever I want to."

But the river had betrayed her; it held her a prisoner. She was trapped by the chance circumstance of meeting a boatman and becoming his wife. *Never saw a girl!* The words from that song drummed in her poor aching head until she hated them.

Ira said not to worry about Levi. He would boat as far as he could and walk back the rest of the way. In the old days the flatboat men always walked home from New Orleans—came over the Tennessee Path, got so they called it the "Bloody Way."

Tormented by sleepless nights, and a sense of guilt that her feelings about being a riverman's wife might have hurt Levi's pride, she visualized all sorts of disasters befalling him. He had broken a leg and couldn't move, and no one came along that lonely path. He had fallen on his open knife and lay bleeding to death. Bandits ambushed him, robbed and bound him; a poisonous snake crawled down a tree and bit him. Worst of all, he might not be trying to get home at all, just staying in New Orleans pleasuring himself, spending his money in one of those little low French houses which Julee said were papered with crimson oiled calico same as a couch, with bottles of good old wine and segars, both ladies' and gent-men's. Julee knew all about those places, 'cos that Betsy, Master Rutland brought from New Orleans, had been hired out to one of them.

At night Molly pitched and tossed and had dreams which wakened her terrified, unable to remember what she had dreamt. In the daytime everything irritated her.

The cicadas! Julee called them zizz-bugs because of their incessant singing of the sun high in the trees.

The old dog-trot hall was the coolest place in the afternoon and it was here that Molly brought a quilt and pillow, but she didn't really sleep. Her mind was only a little duller, for now she had sunk into the apathy of the ill—no longer caring what became of her.

And one afternoon, when she heard a thud on the piazza, she didn't bother to open her eyes to see who opened the door. It didn't matter in the least who might come in and find her.

"Where's my girl? Punkin'! Half-Pint!" It was Levi's bull roar.

He petted and cuddled her and kissed all the little places he found dear, all the little hollows of face, neck and arms. But her tears still flowed.

"Darling Molly, please. I'm back, see!"

She couldn't even look, she only burrowed more deeply into the rough homespun and sobbed afresh. She heard the concern and alarm in Levi's voice, "Honey, *please*," but was powerless to stop the flow now that she had finally started to cry after holding back the tears for so long. Levi unwound her arms and laid her on the quilt.

When he returned from bumping about on the piazza, he said, "I brought you something, Half-Pint." But by then she was too exhausted to care if he'd brought her the jewels from King Solomon's mines.

"Sweet, I brought you a present. Look!" She only moaned and rolled her head.

Levi slipped his arms beneath her, raised her as if she were a beloved invalid. "Sweet, open your eyes."

She managed to pry apart her swollen lids and gasped at what she saw, and cried again and chattered, "A ti-ti-tin ba-ba-bath tub, a ti-tin ba-bath tub! Oh Levi!"

It was a beautiful sight. All of five feet from rim to rim, it was shaped like a straw field hat upside down. The crown was the tub with one side of the brim turned down so that, when you sat in it, your feet hung over onto the floor. The opposite brim made a flat seat on which you could sit while wiggling your toes in the water.

"Oh Levi! Tin! See how shiny black it is! Look at the pure gold scrolls. The flowers! Look at the flowers, Levi! Roses! They're Cherokee roses, my love. Wisteria, violets, ferns. Oh Levi! My Levi! You brought me a beautiful tin tub!"

"Yep. I got it here. There were times when I was tempted to leave it with somebody to pick up later."

"Levi! How did you come?"

"Boat to the mouth of the Tennessee, trailed in the rest of the way. Tub may have a scratch here and there."

"You *carried* that tub?"

"Sure! Rigged me up a kind of pack rack to rest the main part of the tub in. I met some fellows on the trail who said I looked like I was about to fly. And I tell you I wish that tub had *been* wings."

"Oh Levi, you carried it all that way for me. Oh, Levi!"

"Brought you something else, too. In my plunder."

In the very middle of his bundle, along with his most precious possession, his log book, was nestled a pair of red shoes. He kissed her insteps when he put them on her.

"Reckon they're a mite tight. I told 'em you had the littlest feet."

"I won't wear them so I can keep them always."

"It's been a long time, Molly."

"Oh, Levi."

Once again she floated on a cloud while Levi pinned stars in her hair.

Soon afterwards she watched him write in his river journal: "July 17, 1838. Reached home by trail. Ohio navigation closed above Tennessee River. Molly well." She turned away. Julee had been right when she said that words in a book didn't give the "feel."

To hide and control her feelings she burst importantly into housewifely duties. She opened the door and kicked her husband's plunder out onto the piazza; she shouted to her servants that the master was home, to build up the fire in the new patent stove, and make the *poulet farci en cocotte.*

Now at last she had her reward for the long hours spent over the cookstove with Julee. Because Levi spooned the last bit of sauce and, with a wink at her, picked up his plate and ran his tongue around it.

"Good!" He leaned back in his chair and heaved a deep sigh of satisfaction. "Good to be home, too. Rest up a spell."

July passed without rain and the dry season was upon them without there ever having been a wet one. The river dropped to eighteen inches, permitting people to walk across to Kentucky, which many did just to brag about having done so.

In low-water times rivermen hadn't enough to do. Levi sat on the piazza with Cal Preble, Sam Higbet, other rivermen, whittling endless boatpins, spinning yarns, and always ready to eat and drink. They had a passion for telling tall tales of earlier, livelier days, which to Molly's ears all sounded alike—just so much Hoosier brag.

Boatpinning would stop only long enough to point a whittle knife for emphasis or to swing a bousing can to ease a parched throat. The piazza was a-litter, and shavings even clung to Molly's clothes. She grew tired of hearing tales about Colonel Plug, Jim Girty, Mike Fink, the Harpes and goodness only knew how many other bullies. There were too many of these river-rats too much underfoot. Too many shouts of here-fetch-Matt! Julee! Molly!

One day Sam Higbet, a great favorite with the rivermen and one of Rivertown's few bachelors, sat slightly apart on the piazza step. With a stick he drew two parallel lines on the hard-baked yellow earth below the piazza steps and considered them for some time. When this drew comment from his friends, he said, "Heard they're going ahead with that railroad from Adams to Indianapolis."

No one said anything. Hoosiers were a slow-spoken lot when matters of importance came up.

Sam drew more lines ladderlike to the first two on the sand and absorbed solace from them. "Reckon they won't do it."

The rivermen's lips cracked in derision that anyone should think the railroad would be built.

Sam said, "Plumb crazy! Legislators are. They got a plan what calls for fifteen million dollars. Crazy! They can't muster fifty thousand dollars yearly assessment. And they talk about going into the railroad business—in partnership with private enterprise."

The rivermen roped their mouths tighter and shook their heads. They'd never stand for any such nonsense.

"No, sir-ee, we don't want the government edging in on our business. What'd we fight two wars for 'cept to be free. And we want to keep this country free—by jeems!"

The men's nods made it unanimous.

Cal Preble said, "They're crazier than a hoot owl if they think they could get up that hill back of Adams."

Sam answered by drawing the outline of a hill to block his railroad track.

132

"It would be pleasant to go for an airing on a railroad car," said Molly.

The men laughed. "Airing! A female junket on a railroad! Ho! Ho! What do you know about railroads, Molly?"

"I know about them. My Aunt Lucinda is distant kin of the Polks of North Carolina and they wrote about how pleasant it is for ladies and gentlemen to take a railroad car airing."

Levi said, "Mebbe they can do that down south, but up north a railroad is strictly business."

Sam Higbet said, "It'll hurt river business though if they ever get going with railroads; they'll steal business along with them."

Levi said, "Naw, and even if they did, except for off years, they could *have* a few piddling loads."

Cal Preble, whose Minnie at times scraped the bottom of the barrel to feed their clutter of young-uns, said there were too many off years for his taste.

"Look at us, all good rivermen, nothing to do but sit on our back sides. The country's only gettin' out of its last revulsion of trade, and what happens? Dad burn it! Look at it! Lowest water a body's ever seen. Even a baby could wade right across to Kaintuck. My own young'un Dan'l." His voice broke.

In embarrassment for Cal because he had shown his feelings, the men gazed at the sad sight of their noble river dwindled to no more than a stinking branch meandering through the sand bars.

"Why do any of you bother with an old river like this? You're all a bunch of imbeciles blinded with sand not to see your old river's got you licked." Molly sounded bitter and contemptuous.

They turned startled faces to her, but she didn't care. She was tired of the heat of the sun, western rivermen, the river smells and the sting of grit in her nose.

Time slowed down in the still hot air while these Hoosiers studied out the full meaning of her words. Their quiet rendered her stupid and she allowed all her little irritations to ripen under the heat waves into a determined resolve to make Levi give up the river. The men, eyes averted from each other and in shocked silence, watched Sam Higbet's stick criss-cross his outline of a railroad blocked by the steep hill at Adams.

At last Cal Preble's drawl brought relief, "Reckon it's onto time to get down home 'fore I catch it from Min."

Embarrassed and shamefaced for Levi the men pocketed knives

and boatpins and sidled one by one down the steps—each to ponder on poor Levi's plight—a riverman with a wife who denounced the river.

Only Sam Higbet lingered on a bit. Finally he heaved himself up and said, "Reckon a railroad might not be so bad when you get out where there's no water."

He hooked his thumbs in his belt and ambled off.

"Dang loon!" Levi said to Sam's back. "Railroad talk! And see here, Molly, you mustn't talk against the river."

"Why not? Can't I have any ideas of my own?"

"You daren't talk against the thing you depend on." Levi spoke as though the river was an evil spirit which must be kept appeased.

His tone so scared her that she ripped out, "That river isn't *anything*. Why if a good wind came along right now it would blow away. It's nothing but sand. Sand! Sand! Look at it, Levi, it's not a river, it's a *desert*. Oh, Levi! Levi! Let's leave this miserable place."

"Jumpin' Jehosophat! What's got into you, Molly? Miserable place! Finest place on the river."

"I'm only trying to pound a little horse sense into you. You won't even listen to your own father when he explains how the future lies in the West."

Levi calmly went on whittling a boatpin and drawled, "Look here, Punkin, there is no sense in your speechifying about something you don't know anymore about than a durn mudcat. You'd best understand first as last, Molly, that you might just as well try to make an eel walk on his tail as to make me leave the river. Nobody remembers the water this low; reckon it doesn't happen more than once in forty or fifty years. Sure there're poor years now and again with the river, but the good ones more than offset the bad. You'll learn to roll with the river, Molly. *Now!* When in tarnation do we eat?"

The hot weather lasted right on through September. The crops failed. Not even Gaithe, who loved the earth, tried to keep the garden alive. Not enough water could be hauled from the sluggish river to satisfy the thirsty ground. There was no "green sass" to freshen the juiceless fare and the women fretted that there was nothing to put down, to lay by against the hard winter ahead, and folks grew leaner under their thin layers of dry brown skin.

Not until October was there an encouraging "raise" to the river, and the grumblers admitted the fall rains must have started up on the watershed of the Pennsylvania and Ohio hills and it wouldn't be long before they'd be wishing for the rain to stop. Small boats appeared on the river, and the most insignificant were cause for whooping and hollering. The knowledgeable old-timers, who listened to the soundings called by the leadsmen to the anxious pilots, said the whole of navigation would be open in no time at all. Soon there'd be enough water for the big boats to come up from below.

Molly listened as anxiously as the pilots to the sustained chant of the leadsmen passing the word of the depth of the water. For only when it was deep enough for the big boats would she be in touch again with home and know that she could return if she wanted to. Levi complimented her on learning the meaning of the chants, and would have been surprised had he known why they had become important to her. She memorized the markings of the lead line, which Levi said a leadsman could recognize by feel even when the night was as dark as the inside of a cow.

There was one leadsman, whom Molly wanted to hear above all others, and that was Turkey Neck on *The Rising Sun*. Captain Cleve said Turkey Neck could hang onto his words long enough for a pilot to hear directly without having to get the word passed along by relays. It was as if Turkey Neck's words hung all the way down the longest neck God ever made. Molly knew she'd recognize his voice long before she could see *The Rising Sun*.

But she waited and waited, long dreary, weary months. Months in which she grew thin and white, her hair dull without the pretty pink rinse—there was no water now even for hair-washing. Goldenrod, aster and purple iron weed had faded weeks before she heard Turkey Neck answer the mellow bell on *The Rising Sun* with, "Fir-r-rst ca-l-l-l," and the roadway to her familiar world was open once again.

At last she was no longer a prisoner of sand; once again she could leave whenever she wished.

CHAPTER XIV

"WHY DIDN'T YOU TELL ME?" THE MISTRESS SCOLDED.

" 'Cos, Miss Molly, I got cotched fustest an' us thinks mebbe you not like that." Julee's face crinkled in puckers of amusement. "Don' you fret, you get cotched; reckon I just quicker woman than you."

Molly wondered then why she hadn't noticed that Julee, in spite of lean rations, had a watermelon-sized belly under her apron.

"Yes'm I'se right good in my health, but I not so good in my mind. Matt, he say not tell you nothing, us got to make out by us own selves. He say he can take a baby same like a colt, he figger out they come the same way an' he brag he know all about horses. But I don' want a horse knot bunched on no baby o' mine. I wants a pretty granny-woman belly button. Matt he say, 'Gal you got no more chance to git a granny-tendin' than a hen to git teeth,' but I tells Matt you the sweetest bestest thing in the world. I say us milk sisters an' you love me an' I love you better than honey and white biscuits an' if I asks you, you gets a good granny to make the knot. You not mean-minded 'cos I got cotched fustest, is you?"

This was indeed distressful news, since Molly did not know how to deal with such a situation in Rivertown. At Rutland Hall Mammy Fay officiated at all the birthings and at Quercus Grove Aunt Betsy took all the babies. There was no one here.

When Molly told Levi about Julee and how she wanted to send for Mammy Fay, Levi only laughed at her and said he wasn't laying out money to fetch Mammy Fay from the South to granny Julee. Not even the argument that a little black baby was valuable property moved Levi. He said plenty of babies got born all the time in Rivertown without all this fuss and feathers.

"But Levi, I don't know what to do!" Molly could stand over Julee and make her clean her cabin even down to the last swing pot filled with fresh water over the hottest fire, but who would attend her when the baby came?

Levi said to ask Ma.

"*You* ask her."

But Levi said Ma wouldn't think it was proper for him to speak to her about bringing a black wench to childbed. And then he added, "Just be sure whatever you do it doesn't cost anything."

Hester said, "Surely Negroes manage these matters among themselves." Her thin lips seemed even thinner now as though she were speaking of a cat chewing kitten strings.

Molly explained that every respectable plantation considered an excellent mid-wife of prime importance, and all she wanted to know was the name of the best mid-wife in Rivertown.

"A white mid-wife wouldn't attend Julee."

"Why not?"

"What white woman would have a mid-wife who had attended a black woman?"

"Down home black midwives attend both. I don't see—"

"Things are different up here," Hester said briefly. "You should have thought of this when you brought Julee and Matt north." Hester paused a moment and then went on accusingly: "And— since you've brought up this subject—there's something I've been wanting to ask you for some time, why aren't you in the same condition yourself? Is there anything wrong between you and Levi?"

Molly didn't think this was any concern of Hester's, but her own fears made her say, "No, there's nothing wrong." And in her heart she knew there was nothing wrong with her bedtimes, even if she hadn't been "cotched," but in their up-times a great deal was wrong.

Back home later that day she told Julee not to worry. When her time came Molly promised to see that she was properly attended.

"I not worryin' Miss Molly. Matt he say he want me to keep see-rene. No'm I ain't worryin' none—not even one teeny bit 'cos I know you get a good granny-knot tied in my baby's little black belly."

Rivertown was a strange place, Molly thought to herself. It rejected slavery on principle, but when it was to their advantage the local people condoned the practice. On Sunday they listened to Reverend Staap preach on the subject, "We are verily guilty concerning our brother," and on Monday they would deny "their sister" Julee a white mid-wife. The whole thing was deceptive, like seeing a stick in the water. Perhaps it was really straight and only appeared to be bent. Yes, it was mighty confusing to live where two whole different schemes of life existed side by side on the forest-clad banks and cliffs of Indiana and Kentucky, divided only by the river.

Molly said, "Perhaps I can find some way to send you across to a plantation granny."

"No-o-o *mam!*" Julee howled. "Not even if you whups me. Us wants dis little nigger born free this side Mr. River. Yas'm! You jest hist you'self on Prince an' ride you'self on board that ole ferry boat an' cross over an' find that granny-woman an' make *a-range*-ment she come here. Yas'm!"

Molly, fearing Levi would object, didn't tell him she intended to seek a black granny for Julee. She waited for a day when he went far interior to arrange with some farmers about shipping south their on-coming spring produce. Soon after he left the house she directed Matt to hail Seth Douglas' ramshackle ferry. It was a clumsy scow, propelled by two blind horses, one to each side wheel.

Seth Douglas was seedy—an old bushnipple, who took a lively interest in everything about him. His tiny eyes never missed a trick and sparked like jet buttons with what he saw. He wore a broad-brimmed hat, aslant with the weather, and a buckskin vest with the hair still on it, letting it hang loose and open so the air might circulate freely around his old red flannel shirt beneath.

In answer to Molly's question about where they might find a slave-owning plantation, Seth said, "Yes, Ma'am, there's farmers acrost ownin' slaves—man up Rabbit Hash Trace by name of Mason's got the most, so come aboard if you're a mind to." Seth

138

ran a quick eye over Matt, "I can't rightly say if he's in the market for any." Then he cranked up the landing apron, set the gears, released the brakes, and started his two horse-powered engine to cogging the wheels to carry them across the river—divider of slave and free states.

On the other side he lowered the ferry's landing stage to the Kentucky shore. "Jist bear right at the top of the knob and follow the trail to Mason's."

Molly and Matt soon came to a clearing, fields and corn cribs, smoke house, barns and outhouses of all sorts and a two-story house of hewn and squared timbers. But the best sight of all was the slave quarters, a row of one and two-room log cabins chinked tight, with smoke curling from every stone chimney. Molly just knew how they would look inside: floors swept clean and white, the bed in the corner big and tall, stuffed with hay and straw and shucks and a trundle bed pushed under, swing pots filled with bubbling grits over the fire. Oh, one could tell that this was a plantation. It wasn't a big one, but it was respectable looking and surely it was large enough to boast a nice black granny. Feeling encouraged Molly rode Prince, plastered with Kentucky mud, right to the front door of the main house.

Later back home, Matt summed up their visit to the Masons' when he said, "Visitin' us own kind of folks is prime good!"

Oh, it was good—good! Aunt Nicey in fresh apron and tignon sat in her chimney corner and said that in her day she'd fetched as pretty a crop of ninnies as any Young Miss had ever seen, and directed Molly to go home and see to it that Julee "wropped" her belly good and tight in red flannel—red was the strong color —and if Mister George and Mistus Mary was a mind to send her, she'd admire to granny on the other side. If things got bad 'fore she got there to jest put a sharp axe under the bed. It cut birthin' pains right quick.

Mr. and Mrs. Mason both said they wouldn't hear of Aunt Nicey's services being paid for, whatever was Mrs. Blaisdell thinking of, wasn't she one of their own kind needing help? Molly said she'd be pleased to accept the favor in the spirit it was offered, but she couldn't unless they'd accept some favor from her.

And that was how the horse-breeding business came about that so infuriated Levi. He hit the beams when Molly told him

139

she had been over in Kentucky and arranged for Julee. "I don't like to be beholden for that kind of thing," Levi contended.

"We're not beholden to the Masons."

"Molly! I told you I didn't care what arrangements you made as long as it didn't cost anything."

"It isn't costing you a penny," she snapped at him. "I made a deal. I can trade as well as you can, Levi Blaisdell, and you can't stop me from doing what I want to with what is mine."

He cast a suspicious eye at her and said cautiously, "All right, Sorrel Top, don't get touchy. Maybe you'd better tell me what you've done."

So she told him how one thing had led to another. Mr. Mason had admired Prince even if he was covered with mud, said he looked as if he had a strong Morgan strain. Mr. Mason said his own breeding wasn't up to scratch, he'd like to improve it, and the upshot was that she bartered Prince to serve Mr. Mason's mares in exchange for Aunt Nicey's services with Julee.

"Molly! You talked horse breeding?"

"Oh for heaven's sake, Levi! I know more about horses than you know about boats."

"Who's going to see to the servicing?"

"Why, Matt."

"That's not sound trading, Molly. You came out the little end of the horn. It appears to me Mason got the best of you."

She let a smug little smile play around her lips and said carelessly, "Oh, I don't know, every third colt that stands is mine."

"Eh? Honey, you sure do take the rag off the bush. Horse-trading!"

"What's wrong with horse-trading?"

"Well, Sorrel Top, reckon there's nothing wrong with horse-trading, except ladies don't do it, that's all."

"Maybe I don't want to be a lady."

"Maybe you don't, but I reckon you'd make things a sight easier for yourself if you did. And you're my wife, understand, and I don't want you riding 'round talking breeding and trading with men."

Now wasn't it silly for Levi to make such a rumpus when she had done so well. Molly was very proud that she had arranged matters so satisfactorily and eased her mind about Julee's time. True, she had learned of a new difficulty to puzzle her.

140

Mr. Mason had said, "We heard there was a bride up from the South with a couple of servants. We wondered how you were making out owning slaves in a free state."

"I haven't had any trouble. No one seems to care much one way or the other."

"Probably nothing to it, but I heard matters were getting stirred up over there—mostly by the women. Wondered if it had caused you any trouble."

To this she gave a little laugh and said so far her only trouble had been the question of the midwife for Julee.

Mr. Mason said: "There's more runaway slaves sneaking across. They think if they can get through to Canada, they've reached the last gate to heaven. But there's no way to make a living up there; they only starve to death in the cold. I haven't lost any myself, but my neighbor up-river has, and of course he didn't dare do anything about it. As soon as we get that Fugitive Slave Law fixed up things will be different. Then a man can go after his property. I don't know, sometimes I think I made a mistake to settle in the border country."

Molly remembered then Sam Higbet saying that if they ever tried to enforce that old Fugitive Slave Law, they'd put the whole country in an unhandsome fix, upturn the whole business and spill blood.

It was disturbing to add what she heard on one side of the river to what she heard on the other. Certainly the law must be right. Stealing a man's slave was *stealing*, after all. There *should* be a law that a man could come across the river and get what belonged to him. And anyone who helped a slave escape *should* be punished for it was no better than horse thieving—to help a slave to escape.

CHAPTER XV

Late in february of '39, matt went for mason's black Aunt Nicey to granny knot Julee's ninny—a fine boy, whom they named Quercus. Julee said, "I got there fustest, but never you mind Miss Molly, you get cotched sooner or later."

Early that summer, Seth Douglas ran his ferry up to the Blaisdell landing with a message from "acrost." He said, "Well, when you're ready to fetch that colt of yourn from t'other side, give me a hail. Mr. Mason tole' me there warn't no hurry but the mare had dried up."

That evening, when Levi came in to supper, Molly boasted that Prince was sire to a colt which by the agreement with Mr. Mason belonged to her. "I'll take Matt and go get him."

"I need Matt. You can't seem to get it through your pretty little red head that river business is seasonal. When we hit a season, everything else must go by the board. I need every man Jack I can find. I could plain kill Gaithe. He either sits 'round like a squash or goes roaming like he wasn't even acquainted with himself. He's staying a young-un too long; he ought to be done worrying himself about having feelings he isn't used to. I tried to talk to him about how it wasn't wicked and sinful and how it was high time he had a girl, but I warned him to stay away from the shanties in the lower end of town."

"How did he take that?" Levi didn't seem to understand that an experience in a Rivertown fancy house would throw a sensitive lad like Gaithe into hell fires of guilt and damnation.

"Didn't seem to like it, pulled some poetic nonsense on me. But I told him he was a damn fool mooning around and that he'd get out of his doldrums mighty quick if he'd just get himself a woman. And if it was Salena he wanted, why didn't he go after her and marry her—she's old enough—sixteen—and holy cow!"

"What happened?"

"Damned if the young-un didn't pitch into me. Caught me unawares and landed me one on my jaw. 'Course when I saw he was really spoiling for a fight, I let him have it." Levi grinned. "Too bad you and Salena weren't there to see it. A good fight. Hell, that kid was slipperier than an eel, each time I thought I had him down he'd snap up like an India rubber man. 'Course, when we got to butting with our heads, I had the advantage and soon had Gaithe's ears pinned back. Reckon you never knew that down-river they used to call me 'Butter Blaisdell?' Yep, I've got a thick skull for a rough and tumble."

Really! How *could* Levi! Brothers fighting, and Levi of the thick skull refusing to admit the reason why Gaithe locked staghorns with him.

Molly came back to the problem of getting the colt. "Alright, I'll go by myself if you need Matt."

"No you don't, Molly. You can't ride off into the country without a man. I'll send Gaithe."

"I don't want Gaithe."

"Oh, Gaithe's big enough to protect you. I'll send him word he's to take you across."

Molly shrugged her shoulders at her chuckle-headed husband, but when Gaithe cupped his hands to his mouth and made a hail "O-o-ver" to Seth Douglas, she found that Levi had suggested Salena Cranch might like to go with them.

Salena! She was no longer the gangly, flat-chested girl, who had frolicked at Molly's in-fare, been goggle-eyed at the bride's gimcracks, and eager to help settle her and to show her the secret of catching "emptins" to make yeast-bitten cold bread. She had grown taller, was slender instead of slattish, had filled out in the right places. Now Gaithe couldn't taunt her with being a green-apple nubbin, not woman enough to go west.

But Gaithe hadn't noticed the changes in Salena: her skin, olive, overlaid with pink from the summer sun, her hair, brushed to a soft dark sheen. Salena had sobered and grown quiet. Folks said it was on account of her pa, Asa Cranch, who as everyone knew only half stayed in his rightful mind. The other half was everlastingly occupied with trying to catch sight of religion. This must be more than a little hard on Salena now that she was grown up.

But Molly knew that Salena wasn't really bothered by her father for, as she put it, "When you come right down to it, most folks look pretty foolish with their carryings on. Can't figger Pa's any worse than the next one when you look at it all around."

So the three of them, Molly, Salena and Gaithe, were waiting on the shore when the ferry pulled in and with much to-do Seth Douglas lowered the ferry landing stage for them to ride their horses aboard.

As they got under way Seth settled himself on his steering oar and winked at Gaithe, "Reckon you're up to handlin' two young ladies on a fine day like this?" Poor Gaithe! Beet root red, he looked off to the Kentucky hills, not daring to turn his gaze closer to hand.

"You goin' show 'em the big tree?" asked Seth.

"Mebbe," Gaithe said.

"What big tree?" Molly asked.

"Just a ways off the main-leadin' wagon road. Ain't you ever seen it?"

Molly shook her head.

"It's a sight to see."

Molly, anxious to get to Mason's and see Prince's colt, said, "We'll stop on our way back."

"See that you're down here betimes. I don't aim to be circumnavigatin' this river arter dark."

It would have been a lovely summer outing for the three of them if it hadn't been for Gaithe's mood. He rode up beside Molly and pressed his horse in close beside Prince. "Why did you have to bring Salena?"

"That's a foolish question. You be nice to her." She gave Prince a smart touch with her heel and quickened her hands on his reins and soon left Gaithe and Salena trailing behind on their heavy old work horses.

She arrived at the Mason plantation far ahead of the others. By the time they trailed in, (Salena quiet and calm, Gaithe fit

144

to be tied) Mr. Mason was already showing her the colt he had had brought from the paddock to the house yard. The colt was a beauty, a bonny son of Prince, the same bay, the same black mane and tail, the same strength already showing in his shoulders. "He's a darling," Molly called to Gaithe and Salena.

Gaithe hardly bothered to say, "Howdy," as he came over to where she stood letting the colt nuzzle her hand. Across the colt he accused her, "You ran away from me."

"Isn't he a beauty, Gaithe?"

"No! His legs are too short. Why did you run away, Molly?"

"Salena dear," Molly let her voice trill, "what shall we name him?"

"Call him Levi," muttered Gaithe, twisting his hands in the colt's mane. "He's all you think about."

Mr. Mason said cordially, "You young folks will take dinner with us, of course."

"Thank you, Mr. Mason, it'll be a pleasure indeed to sit at a plantation table again. I carried along a few things I thought Mrs. Mason might enjoy. Captain Cleve of *The Rising Sun* brought me hampers of fresh things from New Orleans. There're oranges, bananas, and coconuts and my kin at Quercus Grove sent me a whole hamper of fresh asparagus. I'd consider it a compliment if Mrs. Mason would accept some. Gaithe, please undo our saddle bags."

If she talked long enough, fast and hard enough, maybe Gaithe could collect himself. She wished to heaven Levi hadn't insisted that he bring her.

"And Julee and Quercus sent Aunt Nicey a tignon in gratitude that they're both doing so well. Thank you, Gaithe." She gave him a look which told him to behave himself while she had a good southern visit with the Masons.

It was late when Molly finally tore herself away from Mr. and Mrs. Mason's hospitality.

"Why couldn't you leave?" grumbled Gaithe.

"I had to be polite," said Molly.

"We won't have time to go to the big tree. Seth Douglas won't run his ferry after dark."

"There's time, Gaithe," said Salena. "No telling when you might be over to Kentucky with Molly again. You ought to show her the big tree while you've got her here."

Darn Salena! Molly couldn't for the life of her tell if Salena were being sarcastic or not. There were times when she'd like to take Salena and shake her till her teeth rattled. She had no business being so calm; she ought to be raring up on her hind legs and pawing the air with vexation that Gaithe paid no attention to her. But perhaps Salena thought that someday Gaithe would realize that Molly was not for him and would eventually come and claim *her*—his pearl. Darn the girl! She might exert herself a little bit—get up a little spring sap and try to sweeten Gaithe for herself.

It was the biggest tree in the world! A tree which had tossed its branches in the sunlight, had watched the stars come out, and meteors fall for a thousand years. A tree which had withstood the destructive eddies and whirls of tornado winds. A tree ninety feet in circumference. A tree so big that it would never be felled by mere men swinging their puny axes.

"Ride in, Molly," said Gaithe, for the tree had a great natural opening through which a horse could enter. But Prince refused the entrance.

"I'll hold the horses," said Salena. "Take Molly inside the tree, Gaithe."

There was an insistence and sternness to Salena's voice that Molly had never heard before. It was as though her voice said, keep going, keep going.

Gaithe helped Molly dismount and led the way inside the tree. At first it was dim, but gradually from the streak of light which came through the opening its immensity could be seen like the lofty groined vault of the banquet hall of some mighty king. And it was thrilling to stand within the great heart of this living tree and to know that far above, as it had done for centuries, its wide-spreading branches were sheltering a new generation of birds and small animals.

She forgot her vexation in the wonder of it, "Oh, Gaithe. It's a gorgeous tree!"

Then like a labber-sided pup he lunged at her. Awkward! Clumsy! Inept! In the half light in the hollow heart of the tree he caught her, knocking her riding hat askew. But there was a fierceness and determination about him which was frightening. Hasty hands in the grip of passion sought, midst the frills of her jabot, her rounded breasts firm in the tight basque.

146

"I love you, I love you. Oh God! How beautiful you are! Levi can't have you. I need you! I need you! He doesn't need you. He needs nobody but himself." Gaithe cried to her for help. "Molly! Molly! For God's sake don't run away from me," his tone became more demanding, "I must have you, Molly! Molly!"

She had started to struggle, but realized at once that this only aroused Gaithe to a greater gust of passion. She had thought no one but Levi could be so strong. She braced herself and stayed quiet in spite of the blood drumming in her ears, while she tried to figure out how to cool this outburst of Gaithe's, these passionate words, this hot animal breath, these clutching hands, these pressing lips.

A sound was heard from outside the tree, the horses were pawing the ground, impatient at the delay. It was Prince who trumpeted his stallion authority, announcing that it was time to have done with such foolishness, to cut the play-party and head for the ferry.

Prince's warning gave Gaithe pause, and in that moment Molly raised her hand and struck his face. A stroke of lightning could not have been more unexpected. The electric shock of it snapped Gaithe to his senses, and he let go of her. Like a blind man he put out his hands and groped for the opening in the tree.

The world outside was awash with blood-red light, for the sun had slipped past its last quarter in the western sky.

They had to ride hard to make the ferry. Silent—all three.

"See the big tree?" asked Seth Douglas.

Molly nodded.

"Enjoy it?"

In a flat dry voice, Salena said, "A sycamore is a right strong tree. Any river body knows you tie up to one in time of trouble."

Now what did Salena mean by that?

Molly was heartsick. Everything *was* in a mess now. And who was at fault?

Back on Indiana soil Molly, Gaithe and Salena said only the simplest words of parting, each absorbed with what had happened on the other side. Without a question Salena must have guessed what had gone on inside the big tree.

A few days later Molly heaved a sigh of relief when Levi came storming in to say that fool Gaithe had up and let himself out as a hired hand to Farmer Campbell back in the interior.

"He could have had a better job with me. Someday I might even let him be a partner. Blaisdell Brothers! Sounds pretty good, eh, Punkin?"

"Yes, fine."

"Oh well, perhaps it's just as well. He's still got some growing up to do—and you don't help matters any."

Molly didn't answer. Maybe Levi *did* know that his brother was in love with his wife. But he didn't seem very worried. Anyway thank goodness, Gaithe had taken his wretched self out of town.

CHAPTER XVI

THE SUMMER WORE ON, AND WITH GAITHE SAFELY OUT OF TOWN
and Levi at home, Molly was happier than she had ever been in
Rivertown. She felt secure and beloved, the countryside was
beautiful, and she and Levi worked together to make their
yard and garden the prettiest on Front Street.

There had been but one fly in the ointment. Molly had heard
that Gaithe, on one of his infrequent visits to town, had fought
openly over her. It had been down at Berman's where the liquor
talked louder than usual, and Gaithe had heard Gus Davis mention Molly's name in the saloon.

Gus insisted afterwards that he had only said that Molly was
"as bright as a button" and not that she was "a bright button to
take to bed."

But to Gaithe her good name had been sullied and, being
drunk, he had locked with Gus and knocked the daylights out of
him.

When Molly heard about this from old Miz Davidson, who
worked her old gums on every morsel of gossip to get its full
flavor, she was terrified that folks would suspect what ailed
Gaithe and that Levi would hear of it and think he had to do
something about the matter. But nothing happened. Only Hester
seemed even colder than ever to Molly and renewed her efforts to
focus Gaithe's attention upon Salena whenever he came in to
town for Sunday dinner.

It was on such a Sunday toward the end of summer that Molly
was forced to realize that Gaithe's passion for her, instead of

simmering low to a final quietness, was just under the boiling point and needed but a spark to bring it to a full rolling boil.

The night before, satisfied in Levi's arms, she had heard the first big fat raindrops hit the roof and had gone to sleep to the music of a steady downpour. Morning came with the sky washed blue, and the sun sent down great shafts of light to golden the river.

It was one of those mornings when she wanted to do everything and nothing. She bustled happily through the daily chores in order to get out of doors.

As she was standing on tiptoe to replace a trumpet vine which had broken loose from its piazza mooring in last night's rain storm, her arms were pinned above her head by someone very strong who covered her eyes with his hand. She thought it was her husband, of course, and fought like a wild kitten. But the tall, lean body pressed close upon her. She squirmed and waved her hands until they found hair and sunk her fingers in it and gave a yank. She fought just hard enough and let him force her fingers from his hair, and pin her arms to her sides. When he turned her, she closed her eyes for his kiss. Her mouth was crushed by his. Too late she realized it wasn't Levi.

It was Gaithe.

"You fool!"

"I'm not a fool, Molly. You are. You kissed back."

"I thought you were Levi."

"You don't love *him*. You know you don't. I love you. We love each other. Come away with me. We'll go west."

"If you think. . . ."

"I do Molly. I'm sure . . ."

"Don't! Don't! Gaithe, don't, you're going to ruin us all."

"No I'm not, Molly. I've done a lot of thinking out at Ephraim Campbell's. We can go west, where nobody will know us . . ."

"Go away, Gaithe. Go away—go west yourself. Only *go*, Gaithe, and leave me *alone*."

"I won't go, Molly—without you."

Molly ran into the house, where she stayed until it was time to go to church and afterwards, as usual, to Hester's Sunday dinner.

Sunday dinners at Hester's were not fun and frolic. The stiff white tablecloth and napkins must be treated with respect, for they had to last many Sundays. And in addition to the white tablecloth and napkins, Sunday dinner also meant the best pressed-glass goblets, the coin-silver teaspoons, and "chicken fixin's." For today, Hester had killed a couple of hens, "not laying good," and stewed them in a black-iron, three-legged pot hung over her cherished fire. The chicken done, she had dropped in great spoonfuls of dough which came out pallid, heavy, soggy balls which she called "dumplings."

Hester claimed the plainer the food the better it was for the body, and warned Molly to leave off feeding Levi those southern hot breads and New Orleans Frenchifried vittles or he would get stomach trouble.

Levi had recently said, "Something's come over Ma's cooking. It's not as good as it used to be."

Sunday dinner at Hester's was something to endure, but to-day's was especially difficult for Gaithe was there and Salena Cranch and her father.

The meal was eaten in silence broken only now and they by requests for, and offers of, food—"pass the jell," "have a dumpling," "don't mind if I do"—and a one-sided conversation Asa Cranch carried on with himself about his search for a glimpse of religion.

Seated there, trying to choke down the tasteless food, Molly watched Gaithe fearfully. His eyes were kindled to an irrational brilliance, his cheeks flushed to a feverish red. If only there were some way she could conjure him off. He looked as though he were about to explode, like a firecracker, right on his Mother's white tablecloth and upset all Hester's ceremonial Sunday table fixin's.

If only the boy would go far away! There were tricks, for those who believed, to make a man run away—his tracks could be thrown into running water, a lock of his hair could be put into the gill of a fish and the fish returned to the river. Best of all would be if Salena would win Gaithe to her by secretly laying hands on the back of his neck.

But Salena did nothing. She was a mighty still person who listened and observed, but, so far as anyone could tell, paid no attention to what she heard and saw. Sometimes that kind, when

151

they did break loose, were worse than the trigger ones. Salena was certainly not stupid. If she really wanted Gaithe, she'd figure out a way. Maybe she was just biding her time.

Molly looked at Salena's father, Asa. Each time she saw him she was surprised anew to realize that this pleasant-looking, mild-mannered little man was as crazy as a hoot owl. He was so unassuming, so clean and neat, so industrious, never causing any trouble or kicking up any rows—his only eccentricities being a tendency to talk quietly to himself and to allow his hair to grow long and fall into soft curls on either side of his narrow sensitive face.

Mr. Cranch said, "Been lookin' for my luck to change." His eyes grew wary when Molly asked why, but he said that he'd been given a sign to expect something. "So it's no surprise to me that there's a religious camp meetin' got under way out to Symmes Woods. This one's been goin' since Thursday, ought to be a ding-buster by now and no mistake. We haven't had a big old-fashioned camp meetin' for many a day in these parts, so long ago I've lost remembrance of how one stinks, but I aim to get out there even if I have to walk."

Ira said, "I'll hitch up a wagon and we'll all go."

Hester said, "The way religion is carried on at a camp meeting is a disgrace to the Lord. If you're all a-mind to go I don't reckon I can stop you. The best I can do is stay home and pray that none of you come to any harm." She gave Gaithe the longest gaze and looked at Molly with the greatest sternness.

Asa Cranch said: "A camp meeting is like standing at the gate of heaven whilst at the same time a body is at the gates of hell. It's a twixt and 'tween place. That little feller Religion might've got himself caught in a snare, can't work himself loose. Keep a sharp lookout, and if you see anything let me know."

Long before they got to Symmes Wood the spring sun had set and evening came quickly on the road beneath the great forest trees. Molly was kept busy evading the hands and lips of Gaithe, who had arranged the seating so that he shared the back bench with her, while Levi drove.

Pretty soon the road became crowded with men, women and children—some laughing and talking as if they were headed for a picnic, others solemn in their preparation for the religious experience, still others shouted "Glory! Glory! Glory!" Some

152

rode in wagons sitting on their bedding, holding their cooking utensils; others rode horseback, sometimes two to a horse— known as "riding twice."

Asa Cranch was delighted and said it sure looked to be a meeting of the biggest size and he'd heard they'd rounded up some crack preachers, all in love with sin and as good at this business of wrastling with Satan as Lorenzo Dow had been in his day.

Yes, siree, these folks looked like they'd give the preachers a mighty harvest of glory. With right good will they'd join right in to do battle with the devil and his legions. These folks would lambast that Ole Feller Sin again and again, they'd let it out with a shout, they'd exercise it with the jerks. In fact Asa was so carried away that he clapped his hands as in a square dance and cried, "Swing your partners, Satan!"

Salena said, "Hush, Pa."

In Symmes Woods a great company of sinners had come together to be forgiven that they might once again rejoice with singing in Thanksgiving. Their songs of praise in simple child-like tunes could be heard long before Ira's wagon reached the clearing.

> *Ye stand upon a dreadful steep,*
> *And all beneath is hell.*
> *Your weighty guilt will sink you deep*
> *Where the old serpent fell.*

Molly's sharp eyes took in everything about the camp meeting at once. Twenty acres of superb forest trees had been cleared to form a great square, where a few of the biggest trees with dense foliage had been left to provide protection from the elements. Around the edge of this forest enclosure were the tents of the sinners. As in the feast of the tabernacles, boothlike tents were erected of uprights and cross pieces and enclosed with thick, fresh-green branches, old coverlets and quilts.

The vast open space enclosed by the wagons and booths was given over to the serious business of saving souls and regaining the back-sliders. At each corner of the square, logs had been raised as for the beginning of a small cabin outhouse and filled with earth and sod, on which at night burned bright fires of crackling pine wood. Near each was an altar or pulpit or stand

153

for preaching, a large platform erected between two maple trees whose trunks were the columns of the temple, their branches the vaulted roof, their leaves a fresco painting. The platforms were railed to provide safety for the preachers, who jumped, jerked and swooned. Below each platform was the pen, a rail-fence enclosure where the stray-sinner sheep were herded into the fold of salvation. Here several saplings cut breast high had been left for sinners to cling to while exercising the jerks.

Asa Cranch peeked into one tent and beckoned Molly to look at the young folks who had been preliminarying all day a-wrastling at last with that Ole Feller Satan. Before a mound of straw a young man had his arm around the neck of a girl. Her hair was an untidy muss over her shoulders, her head was thrown back, her face worked as if she were having a fit, her mouth was wet with slaver. Unpretty! The young man moaned, "Sister, dear Sister!" and pushed her bodice low and placed a kiss in a pale hollow. Asa Cranch's long thin nose twitched while he narrowed judicial eyes upon the close-pressed bodies of the boy and girl. "Toad stools!" He pronounced, "Nary a smell here but toad stools! Come on, we got to get nearer the altar."

Molly, too shocked to move, did not follow the rest of her group. Gaithe lingered beside her. He tugged at her arm, "Come Molly, come. Come away with me now! I'll find us an empty tent."

She pulled away, only to have his arm enclose her waist in a tight grasp. "You're afraid of me, Molly. Don't be afraid. I swear to God I won't do anything, I swear—only come." His hands trembled, his whole body tightened under higher and higher tension. He gazed at her greedily, full of craving, his face burning. He looked as though he might seize her in front of the whole camp meeting. "Only this once, come with me."

"Gaithe!" she said sharply. "You're a crazy simpleton. It's high time you got ahold of yourself. I'm your brother's wife. What you want is a sin—a grievous sin." Any slight interest Molly had ever had in Gaithe was gone completely. "Come along now and learn from the preachers the enormity of your sin."

Like a man in a daze, he stumbled after her down the saw-dust trail toward one of the pulpits.

Asa Cranch had found seats for the party after stepping over and around the sinners prostrate upon the ground who had

154

been knocked over by preacher shouts, "And o-ho, sinner, git knocked down yourself before you die and go to judgment. The devil don't fight fair so gouge him, gouge him. Put your thumb right in his eye-socket—that old scally-wag—and fall down, fall down, sinners, all of you. On your knees . . . !"

Asa said he was never so disappointed in his whole born days; he wished he hadn't come. 'T warn't no use thinkin' he'd catch sight of the little feller at this camp meetin'—it was enough to make him straight shirt-tail it out of there.

Molly forgot all else, so appalled was she by what was going on before her. Her attention was caught by a girl quite near her who rose from her seat and was so pale she looked as though whitewash could be scraped from her face. She clasped and unclasped her hands and sat down again only to get up, sit down, get up yct again. A trembling seized her, she let out a sob, and tottered to the anxious bench where she burst into hysterics at the shouts which went up for her and the tumbling words, "Sister! dear Sister!" The girl's sobs grew to groans, and finally to low animal moaning, followed by violent jerks of her arms and legs, her eyes wide open but vacant.

A preacher ran practiced eyes over her body given up to passion and declared with authority for all to hear, "Jesus is with her!" Shouts went up, "Glory!" "Oh Lord Jesus!" "Amen, Amen!"

The preacher, now drunk with his success, went to frantic excesses and dealt with drinking, fighting, gambling, stealing, killing, and fornicating. His fancy carried him to have an argument with Satan himself as to which was the greatest sin to be committed in fornication—a man to go unto his wife and hate her, or a man found with a married woman, or a man who lays hold on a virgin and forces her. He took all sides of the debate and funned and frolicked with fornication arguments. Oh! He was a powerful big preacher who could stir up folks mighty quick and keep them a-going until he had them all at the very gates of perdition bound with their own sense of guilt.

Asa Cranch said, "Guilt! If 'twarn't for guilt these preachers'd have no cash crop."

Asa's words broke Molly's absorption in the scene before her. Once again she was conscious of Levi, Ira, Salena, Asa and Gaithe.

Gaithe!

Gaithe rose to his feet, he sat down, got up again, sat down. Like a person hypnotized he was doing what the girl had done. He clasped and unclasped his hands, his eyes were open but their vision was turned inward upon his own sin.

Asa Cranch cried, "He's tuk! By gum, he's tuk!"

CHAPTER XVII

Levi stepped out of his Sunday pants and flung them carelessly over a chair. He was still wrought up about Gaithe being "tuk." "Animal, pure animal! Those folks out at the camp meeting have fornication mixed up with religion. The preachers scare some people to death with their sheet-lightning peeks into the dark ugly places of folks' dirty little minds. They ought to be run up Salt River. I'm half inclined to do it myself."

"Don't you dare!" Molly was badly frightened by the turn of events and wanted no more stir about it.

"But, Molly! Look what they might have done to Gaithe. That young-un is just prime for going off half-cocked. He still hasn't come to terms with himself. Those preacher fellers can't do harm to some folks, but you saw for yourself, Molly, how a person like Gaithe can be hypnotized. If Pa and I hadn't stopped him, he'd have hit down that trail same as a dog that's sniffed a whiff of a rabbit."

Molly wondered if they had made a mistake not to let Gaithe be "saved." He had great need, as she well knew, of having his animal spirits drained off. But together Pa and Levi had broken Gaithe's spell. They had closed in upon him and protected him and got him safely away from the camp meeting. Yet now Molly was disturbed because the boy was still so keyed up. Such an abundance of immoderate feelings was bound to come uncapped and find release somewhere.

Gaithe had taken Salena home alone. Levi had whispered insistently to let him. Salena was a steady girl who would know how to handle Gaithe. Perhaps, Molly had thought, this is the chance Salena needs to lay her hands on the back of his head—then everything would be solved in the best possible of ways.

But a short time later Molly was awakened out of a sound sleep by someone crying, "Levi! Levi!"

It was Salena on the porch outside the bedroom window.

"Levi! Levi! Get up, Levi! Go get Gaithe before he does something to himself."

"Where is he?" Levi already was out of bed, fumbling for his pants in the dark.

"Down to my house. We . . ." Salena's voice broke. "He's making wild talk, he don't half know what he's saying. I don't want Pa should find him. Pa might . . ." she hesitated and added lamely, "if he found out, he might make . . ."

Molly felt a shiver pass through her, a fear that real harm had been done. Oh, not that it would be so terrible if Gaithe and Salena . . . but what if he had *forced* her. There was a quality to Salena's voice that made her afraid for them all.

Levi fell over the rocker of a chair in the dark and cursed. "For God's sake, Molly, get up and make a light. Take care of Salena. Find out what happened. I'll soon get Gaithe in hand. I've been wanting to trounce him for quite a spell."

To Salena he said, as he ran past her out onto the porch, "Go in to Molly. Don't worry. I'll bring him in, don't you worry, Salena."

Panic filled Molly. Her hand lighting the candle in the common room shook. To try to still it she rattled down the ashes in the Buck's Patent Stove and added a fresh stick of wood to the fire. She filled the tea kettle with water from the pail on the bench and set it on the stove. At last she had herself sufficiently under control to ask the question, "What's happened?"

Salena had grown quiet and sat unmoving on the stiff old settle. Her stillness put Molly into as much of a quivering fuss as her former excitement had done. "Tell me what's happened between you and Gaithe, Salena." Molly's voice was firmer than she felt.

"I'll tell you all right," said Salena in a hard dull voice. "I've been pining to tell you for quite a spell, Molly. It's all your fault that Gaithe's in the fix he's in. You play-partied him, Molly, without it meaning a thing to you. You egged him on because it pleasured you. You never bothered to study out how it might fetch up in an unhandsome fix.

"Then you got scared, when Gaithe's feeling for you growed up into more'n you could handle. You should have seen your face that day we went across to Kentucky when you came out of the big sycamore tree. And I was satisfied it had happened because I thought it'd show you you were goin' too far with Gaithe. But I reckon I was a fool to think it would fetch Gaithe up to look where he was headin'. I wouldn't care so much if you really loved him, it would be more honest if you did, and I'd feel better about it. But you don't love any other body than your own self, Molly . . ."

"Salena—!"

"You'll hear me out. You want to know what happened tonight between Gaithe and me? I'll tell you, Molly, because you were—there."

"Salena!" Why the girl was beginning to talk pure nonsense; she must be crazy.

"There's no argument, Molly. You egged Gaithe on, he fell in love with you and he can't fall out. He came into the house with me tonight and I let him because I knew he was still het up by the camp meeting. And pretty soon he began doing love things to me, the kind I'd fancied him doing time and time over, and mebbe I was kinda stirred up, too, by the meeting and all and the first thing I knew Gaithe was a-rarin' for me—and I guess mebbe I let him—. I've loved him so long and always before he treated me like I was no more than a green-apple nubbin. I was so happy to have Gaithe know I was a woman—too. I even made a little prayer of thanksgiving that at last everything would be all right for the two of us."

"It is, Salena!"

"No, it isn't."

"Why ever not? It is no great sin if you and Gaithe—Levi says so."

"But it is, Molly."

"Oh Salena!" Her voice was impatient.

"You don't need to get mad at me, Molly. You see Gaithe wasn't making love to me, Molly. It was *you!*"

Molly gasped.

Salena went on in the same dry, flat voice: "When Gaithe

159

began it was beautiful, just the way I'd always imagined, those poetry things like you and him read together. Then he got strange and left off saying the pretty things about how all he wanted was to sit against my feet and kiss my hair, and swore it was a lover's lie, he wanted a lover's all. And I guess I kinda liked the things he did even when he got to rarin'—."

Salena sat quieter than death. Her open eyes stared at what had taken place between her and Gaithe. Molly was afraid to break in upon what Salena was seeing, something awful must have happened. When Salena had finished looking inward she roused herself and turned unseeing eyes upon Molly. She spoke as from a long sick bed of pain, worn to a lassitude by fever and hurt, near the zero of illness. "It was when he said your name— Molly—that everything went kim-kam and I knew that to Gaithe I wasn't me—I was you."

Molly was shocked as her mind took in the meaning of Salena's words. The impact of how it must have been for Salena left her speechless, at a loss to know what to say. Salena had no right to blame her because Gaithe had fallen in love with her. She wasn't to blame. It wasn't fair of Salena to blame her, if she had to blame anyone she should blame Hester. Hester, who tried to bind all others to her ways. If only Hester had been a little kind to me, Molly thought, given me the mother's love I longed for; if only Levi had some understanding how difficult it was to adjust to a new kind of life. If only—if only—In a way it was Salena's own fault, too, because she hadn't done a single solitary thing to try to win Gaithe. But Molly's self-justifying thoughts were broken in upon by Salena's bitter voice.

"You want your own way just to pleasure yourself. You want to live your whole life like a play-party. And when you can't, just as easy as shelling peas, you put the blame on somebody else and won't play. You run away. It's you, Molly. It's your own self is to blame for this fix Gaithe, you and me are in. Everybody, Levi too, would be better off if you'd never come to River-town."

Salena's accusations were like slivers run under a finger nail. Why, Molly thought, I'm not to blame for anything. Nobody ever blamed me for anything except Hester—and Levi, himself, said not to bother about Ma, just to step around her. Salena had

160

no right to lash out at her this way. True she had taken pleasure play-partying Gaithe, but she had meant no harm.

Only now she wished she hadn't. If only—Molly went on and on in her own mind, but finally each time came back to Salena's words, "You egged Gaithe on because it pleasured you, without studying where it might fetch up."

She was surprised that it mattered to her what Salena thought of her. She remembered the awkward gangling girl, dressed in Hester's brown cast-off, so, so lively, so eager to see all the bride's gim-cracks and so in awe of the silver coffee pot and the fragile Sèvres cups. A warmth of affection for Salena, her first friend in Rivertown, spread through Molly to be followed by a new feeling, a kind of bearing down through and through her, settling into a definite gnawing pain. Into her mind there crept the thought that this pain had a name—remorse.

Deep sorrow that she could have been so self-centered, so thoughtless as to cause so much unhappiness bit deep into her. She wished there were some way she could go back and begin again, do differently. Salena had held a mirror for her to have a look at herself, and she did not like what she saw. What could she say to show Salena she was sorry? But being sorry could not put things straight. Regret didn't change anything. She would have to *do* something. Yet the knowledge that she didn't know what to do crushed her. It was terrible to want so badly to make everything come right and not to have the slightest idea of how to go about it. This was a new kind of aloneness. It made her feel old.

The sticks in the fire having burned through, fell apart; the candle on the table guttered low. She and Salena had been sitting for a long time without looking at each other or saying anything. It was with relief that they heard Levi's step on the porch. Levi's step—and another's.

It gave Molly something of a shock to see Levi and Gaithe looking so normal. There clothes were rumpled no more than usual, their hair only naturally mussed. She had half expected that they would come in with their heads broken, their clothing in shreds, their bodies bleeding, ready for bandaging.

Levi, with a kinder hand than usual, pushed Gaithe forward into the room and said, "Gaithe wants to see Salena alone."

Levi's attitude said, there's nothing to worry about, I've got everything ship-shape. I've talked sense into this nincompoop, he's going to do the right thing by Salena.

Molly got up to go, but was stopped by Salena, "You and Levi don't need to go, Molly," she said. "I know Levi's told Gaithe what he has to say. Well, he doesn't need to say it for I won't do it."

Gaithe left for the West within the week. If he hurried he might get to St. Louis in time for a meeting, announced in the *Messenger*, to make preliminary arrangements for an expedition to Oregon.

Levi said it was the goldarndest thing that nobody could budge Salena Cranch and make her go along with Gaithe. Christ-a-mighty, Gaithe had asked her again and again. Pa had offered to outfit them with a wagon, Ma had offered to supply it—and still Salena wouldn't go.

"What ails the girl, anyway? Talk to her again, Molly."

It was useless. Salena said, "It's not good enough, Molly, unless Gaithe feels the way I do. He's got to love me right here in Rivertown and not out on the prairie like he *says* he will. I want him to love me here and not out in a sod house where he's got no choice."

Salena, half orphan, with a doodledy father, brought up mostly by herself, had her own set of standards and values. Molly had to admire her for holding out and wondered how she had come by such strength. The first time Molly had seen Salena she had asked her if she liked Gaithe. Salena's reply then had been simple; she had said, "Do I like maple molasses?" She still loved Gaithe with her whole heart, but just as simply, she expected the same from him. If he couldn't return the quality of her love, she didn't want to marry him.

Molly asked, "What if you—Salena, what if you have a baby?"

"I'd make out. Don't reckon I will. But if I did, I'd make out."

"What if you never see Gaithe again? He might not come back. Not many return from the West."

"He will if he wants to. He will if it's right he should."

Nothing budged Salena, not even when she saw Matt readying Tuck, the horse Ira had bought for Gaithe's journey west.

Matt fussed and fumed while he put Tuck in prime condition,

and was full of advice on how Mr. Gaithe was to care for the horse. Tuck was fitted with saddlebags, blankets, a sack of his own feed, cooking utensils—oh, so many things that were necessary to a long journey across the country.

When ready for the trek west nothing could be seen of the horse but his head fore and his tail aft and his sturdy Morgan legs beneath the load. On the hinder part of the pack was a pair of hobbles hastily forged by Ira in his shop. Levi brought a collar and bell for Tuck's neck. " 'Tween hobbles and bell you ought find him quick enough of mornings."

Hester, white and tight-lipped and grim saw to her son's woolens. Salena brought fragrant loaves of bread fresh from her oven, while Molly fitted in boiled ham and cheese.

The bell on Tuck's neck tinkled.

And Molly listened to it long after Tuck and Gaithe had disappeared from her sight. She turned back to the log-cabin, dogtrot house where Levi expected her to stay and be a boatman's wife. Resentment welled within her and her determination to find some way to make Levi go west too, hardened and took on an added strength.

CHAPTER XVIII

Money was tight the winter of '39–'40. There had been a crop failure and there was nothing to ship south. There was no corn to fatten the pigs, so the farmers turned them loose "to root, hog, or die." Stock without pasture or feed were killed for their hides. The warehouses stood empty, the distilleries were closed down, the spindles in the factories twisted no cotton. The trees of the forest were the only cash crop.

Toward the end of November, Levi made one trip south with lumber and found New Orleans was giving good prices for everything *but* lumber. He returned by steamboat, working his way by wooding for the boat, calling for the "ole white pitcher" with the other common men. He warned Molly not to ask for credit down on Main Cross. He would dip into his strong box for the essentials, but she'd have to wait for a fancy chamber set, Queen's ware, handsome with gold, to go with her tin bath tub. And he raised a merry rumpus one day when he found out she'd been down on Main Cross and bought perfume.

"But Levi, my favorite frangipane gave out."

"Not essential. If you won't take it back, I will." And he did.

Molly's house held the essential bed, table, and chairs, her larder the essential food, no better than cabin rations. Sugar went to twenty cents a pound, butter to fifty, and coffee—it went up and up and up, so that instead of being black and bitter strong, the brew she drank looked like mud-riled branch water. She would be ashamed to offer it to a guest.

But there was no entertaining in Rivertown that winter. Minnie

164

said folks wouldn't admit it, but there wasn't a home in the whole town where things weren't at a pinch. Nobody was reckless enough to say "Come at candle-light next week Thursday and set up with us for a bite."

Even the rich ones, like Judge Haines on High Street, were having a hard winter. There just wasn't enough in anyone's cellar to throw it around. And as for Molly decking herself out in her fancy clothes, Minnie doubted if folks would take kindly to the notion, even if they knew her belly was no fuller of dull dry rations than their own.

Not only was money tight, so were the living quarters. Molly had complained that she couldn't possibly cook, eat, and sit in one common room.

Levi said, "You will when ole Ma Nature tells you to. The caterpillars were dark from stem to stern, and that means a dark cold winter, and the hornets are building high so they won't get buried in the drifts of snow."

The first damp chill set Molly's teeth to chattering, but stubbornly she remained out of the common room. Only when the frost blocked the windows and the air deepened to blue cold, was she willing to button up in the kitchen. She brightened the room as well as she could against the dull-gray skies with some of her knick-knacks and curtains made with much finger pricking. Her residence in Rivertown had been too taken up with bare essentials to allow for much interior decoration.

Julee said; "They cozify, Miss Molly. You mighty handy to figger them out, but what Mammy Fay say when she know you cut up you' summer-morning calicoes to prettify you' cabin?"

Levi occupied his evenings sketching on innumerable sheets of paper—sketching and discarding. With all the other household duties going on in the same room, the mess and confusion finally got too much for Molly. One evening she snapped at him, "Get your papers off the table so Julee can set it." Then remembering her empty frangipane bottle, she added, "Buying and wasting paper! You throw away what you draw. What do you think you're trying to do?"

Levi tipped back his chair, took a deep breath of satisfaction and said, "Steamboat! Working out how I want her built."

So all her arguments had been in vain!

There had been a time when she had thought it might not be

so bad to be a captain's la-de-da lady and travel up and down the rivers. But then she had found out that the wives were expected to stay up the hill and watch over the house and the young-ones. Anyway it was ridiculous of Levi to think he could ever own his own steamboat! How could he ever get thirty thousand dollars together when she couldn't buy even an ounce of perfume? And here he was setting coffee cups on chairs, cluttering the already overcrowded place with drawings for something he couldn't possibly afford. It made her explode like an overloaded boiler.

"What would you have done with a steamboat this summer? Hung it up on a sand bar to dry and split its seams!" She'd seen sorry sights of steamboats come to grief, gray forgotten hulks. Oh, a steamboat was a fine thing when someone else took the risk.

"Takes time to design a boat," Levi drawled. "Maybe this is an off year, but even if I had the money to build, I wouldn't know how to go about it. This is a good time to figure out just what I want."

Molly thought that as long as the steamboat remained a figment in Levi's mind and no more than a few drawings, she would still have time to make him give up the river and go west to live as a husband should. But the night he burst into the kitchen with an armful of lumber and made a great to-do, pulling off his wide-brimmed hat filled with snow, and creating a miniature snow storm by sailing it across the room, she was set back hard on her heels.

With one sweep, he cleared the old trestle table. "Get some of this clutter out of here. I've got to have elbow room." He dumped the lumber down on the table.

"Levi Blaisdell, if you start some new kind of whittling in this room . . . !"

"This old table will be just the thing. She'll be five feet long."

"Levi! What are you going to do?"

"Why, build a model of my steamboat to scale. What d'you reckon I've been making all those drawings for?"

Levi now claimed the common room for his own. She and Julee had to manage their housework and cooking with the least disturbance to the boatmaker and his friends, who came with free advice regarding the steamboat, while they added their boatpin shaving litter to the mess Levi had already made on the clean polished floor.

"What you fussing about? Take up the scatter rugs. Then all you got to do is sweep the shavings into the fireplace."

She carried the fragile black and gold japanned tables and delicate china back to the safety of the cold, unused best room. Once she insisted upon having a fire built in there and put on her lavender brocade, which bulged almost to bursting over the necessary layers of flannels.

The snow came down thick and fast, and no visiting ladies teetered along the rough puncheons laid end to end, which was the sidewalk to the Levi Blaisdell house. The first snow had been a beautiful sight. But not any more, when it held her a prisoner within her house, her windows barred with icicles. At night water froze even in the kitchen pails, and by morning their clothes were ice-stiffened. Once up she had no desire to venture outside beneath the clouds which hung heavy and dark above a river grown black. She was shocked when she saw huge cakes of ice on the river and realized that ice could hold her a prisoner as effectually as sand.

Oh! This river Levi was tied to was a hateful thing—worse than another woman trying to take him away from her. She had known it would be like this—even though she wouldn't admit it—since that first evening when she had humbled herself to ask him about the shear on a boat. And now she was going to have a chance to find out, because she was sure Levi's model would have the shearest shear between New Orleans and the Queen City.

So she shivered and returned to the common warmth of the kitchen room where Julee giggled, "You' nose, it look like a lit candle."

Gradually she thawed out in the heat generated by the fireplace, Buck's Patent Stove, and overheated bodies done up in red flannel. Here the close air was filled with talk of proper diameter for cylinders, how many buckets to a wheel, how many staterooms for "live lumber," how much room for freight? At times the arguments grew heated, but on one thing these rivermen all seemed to agree, the real money was in freight and Levi was smart to model his boat to carry the maximum.

Sam Higbet said it was getting so everything from a pitch

fork to a sawmill was shipped south. And Cal Preble agreed it was pure fact that the South depended upon the North, which gave them a right handy market.

"Properly speaking," Sam said, "trade faces South. 'Bout all a southerner does for himself is to get born and die—the northerners do all the in-between for 'em."

Encouraged by the laugh this brought, Sam went on, "Sure, when they get born, what they got to cover 'em? Northern muslin. Where do they get their Bibles, brooms, buckets, shoes, hats, an' knives?" Sam snapped his knife shut, "Furniture, crockery, all kinds of machinery, wagon wheels? By Jumpin' Jeems, they even ride to their very graves on northern wheels and they're laid out in northern clothes. How you reckon they'd dig their bury holes 'thout northern spades? Even their tombstones are northern slabs."

"What's ailing' you, Sam, it's not like you to get up a big head of steam. What's put the fat to your fire?" Cal asked.

Sam hitched his chair, snapped the blade of his knife open, ready for attack. "Been readin' the Cincinnati paper, which is kinda riled up by talk of enforcing that old federal fugitive slave law. A law to give a Kaintuck slave owner the right to cross that river out there," knife pointing, "and come right into this house if he's a mind to, search out his runaway slave and take him back across to Kaintuck—*by force!* And by Jumpin' Jeems, I for one don't like it. Bound to make trouble."

"It'd be his property," Molly put in.

They all looked startled, they must have forgotten Miss South was there.

"Property maybe, but a human bein'!" Cal Preble said indignantly.

Sam said, "I don't argue the right and wrong of owning 'em. I only say we're headin' for trouble if they pass a fugitive slave law. It'll stir things up to a fine how-de-do."

"But no one likes to lose valuable property," Molly said. "And Sam Higbet, I want to know where would the cotton mill down on Front Street get anything for its spindles if it weren't for the South?"

Levi slipped a piece of wood neatly into place on the hull of the boat model and said, "Yup, all that makes for good trading. Don't want anything to come between the North and

168

the South." Naturally, Levi visualized his chimerical steamboat plying in trade on two thousand miles of celestial water—one end of which was dried up for six months and frozen for the other six months of the year, while at the other end floods and fevers flourished!

Wintering Levi was no better than summering him. Even when he was up the hill he carried the river with him. But Molly was still determined to make him go west.

By Spring, she was in what Rivertown ladies called "an interesting condition." However until she was certain, she didn't say anything to Levi.

Actually she had no idea how Levi would feel about a baby. Somehow she hadn't been able to visualize him as a papa, but she could clearly see herself hanging over a cradle. She hugged her hopes close to her breast waiting for further signs of surety but planning a rosy future of happiness. Upon her own child she would pour all the mother love she herself had been denied. Each day she would carry the new weight with delight until at last its little hand lay upon her breast. Oh! Never would a child have such love bestowed upon it! She would see to it that nothing was lacking. And as soon as she was certain she would tell Levi—maybe before he went South.

But Levi was grumpy these days because spring business was poor. Again everyone had timbered for a cash crop. Thousands of immense trees had been felled in the primeval forests along the Ohio and its tributaries, and the huge trunks lashed into great rafts strained at their chains.

From her doorway Molly watched the unwieldly acres of logs float past, a menace to all other navigation. The river seemed one huge floating raft. The market would be glutted again; there couldn't be buyers for so much timber. And once New Orleans was reached, they'd have to break up the rafts and let the mighty timbers find their own way into the gulf. But Levi was going out with dressed lumber, which might give him an advantage and maybe he would bring home some cash.

Then she would tell him her happy news, whereupon he would cherish and worship her anew. He would give her a great deal of money and tell her to go to the Queen City, and buy everything she wanted for the baby. And while she was about it, why not get an armoire like the one at Rutland Hall and what about a pair of love seats for the best room now that they were to be Levi Blaisdell, wife and child?

However one evening before he left, Levi swaggered in, once again as cocksure of himself as though he were the great-grandson of God. He took his red and black log book from the chimney cupboard and brought it to the table.

"Watch me, Molly," he said. He wrote painstakingly until at the end he made a large mark with a great flourish. Oh! By now she had been wife to Levi long enough to recognize his leaping-trout-of-the-waters symptoms, and to be a bit wary of his exuberance until she caught the clear meaning of it.

He patted the page of his log book. "It's a great day, Molly." He expanded his chest like a man of great abilities who could do anything in the world single-handed. "Yep, I've dreamed of this day since I was no bigger than a minny-fish. It's been a long time a-growing and I reckon nothing's going to stop me now. I'm right out there now—on my way!"

"Levi! What have you done?"

"Done? I've bought my steamboat—at least the lumber for it."

A mighty thump struck her heart, sending the blood pounding through and through her, gorging the tiniest farthest blood vessels, pressing on all the little nerves, making each and every one cry out, no, no. She thought of the pinched and tight winter, "Can't you get along, Molly? Don't want to dip into my savings." Oh, she hadn't been actually hungry, but she had grown infernally tired of scrimping while all the time Levi had money enough to buy lumber for a steamboat!

"Dressed lumber will never be so cheap again; prices will go up. I figure it won't be eating anything while it seasons till I can get around to building."

Stacks and stacks of lumber—waiting—waiting to become the gleaming white steamboat conceived in Levi's mind and quickened into a miniature life by the model occupying too much of her kitchen.

Levi said, "You'll have to make out, Molly, same as you've been doing for a mite longer."

That did it! "You mean I can concoct a river water sauce to pour over your whittlings?"

She hadn't gotten over her pique when Levi floated south with his load of dressed lumber. Neither had she told him she was with child.

Oh my no! The tables had been reversed, the big happy news was Levi's precious steamboat.

Perversely she wouldn't confide in him, before he left, although she was pretty certain of her condition. She was also almost afraid that Levi might just say, "A baby, huh?" when she wanted to throw herself into his arms and cry in joy, "*Our* child, Levi, *our* child!"

After he left she took to studying her body and examining her face in the mirror to see how much of her delicate girlhood had slipped away. She had heard that a certain expression came to a woman's face which always revealed the inner secrets of her body. Surely this growing maturity she felt would show; this firmness and strength born of a new purpose in life. But once it flashed across her mind that it was not right for her to exclude Levi from sharing this great tenderness she felt while waiting for the quickening of life. Still she welcomed each little sign, even if it brought discomfort; the morning nausea, the blue shadowed eyes, the brown pigmentation of her firming breasts. But the morning she couldn't fasten the band on a petticoat she told herself it was high time she quit her daydreaming and decided what she was going to do.

Naturally, she couldn't go on living this way now that she was going to have a baby. But since the lumber for the steamboat had been bought, she knew it was no time to argue with Levi about going west. Perhaps it would be better to stay in Rivertown until the baby came. In the meantime she had to change her way of living. She doubted if Levi would do very well with his load of dressed lumber in a glutted New Orleans market. And although she had never thought much about money, she realized now that Papa must be very wealthy to have been able to provide so amply all those things which she had taken for granted: spices, wine, coffee, sugar and confections, damask-covered walls between gilded dado and cornice, tall case clocks, jades on a mantel shelf, a Chinese fret in a brass fireplace fitting, and mirrored girandoles reflecting Papa's fancy that he was a landed English gentleman residing only temporarily in America.

How had he made his money? Molly wished she had listened

171

to business conversations carried on at table. All she could remember was that you sold something for more than it cost, or you traded something you could no longer use for something you could. This sounded simple enough, but there must be more to it than that.

Then she remembered that after the past year's crop failure, Levi had said that competition would be keen and there was apt to be fancy throat-cutting. The chap who would be sitting on Easy Street would be the one who had bound the farmers ahead of time in some kind of deal which gave them a little extra slice of something they wanted over and above current prices. Levi had already been out in the country trying to contract with them for next autumn's business at quoted Cincinnati prices. But he hadn't gotten anywhere because he hadn't been able to clinch his deals by offering that little extra profit which was money or which could be turned into money.

If only she could think of something. If she could clinch the fall business for Levi she could then insist that she must have her fair share to do with as she pleased—yes, even buy frangipane, if frangipane was what she wanted. At the moment what she wanted most was yards of the finest lace whipped into the finest linen to make long clothes for the baby.

Perhaps she could dicker with the farmer's wives for her fine trousseau. But who in the hills would have need of a white cashmere cloak trimmed with red ermine? She could hire out Matt, no doubt, but a Rutland did not hire out her slaves, and in any case one slave could not provide the wherewithal for the many deals she contemplated. Her arguments brought her around to Prince, which is where she had expected to arrive all the time.

It was obvious now. There was nothing else for her to do but offer the farmers Prince's splendid strong strain of Morgan blood. He'd service their mares and instead of stud fees she'd contract for the crops at Cincinnati-quoted prices.

But that didn't give her that little extra something. She'd be Papa's shrewd daughter and, where she could, she'd get every third colt for her own and presently she would have horses to ship to the southern horse market. This, she knew, was profitable, because both Papa and Uncle Philip bred Morgans for the trade.

But when Julee heard she was to be left alone daily with Quercus while her mistress and Matt rode off to get lost in the hills and maybe never come back, she set up a howl that could be heard clear across to Kentucky. Finally Molly had to say, "Come along, but you'll have to ride one of the work horses."

They rode out every dawn and rode in at twilight; Matt on Woodpecker carrying Quercus, Julee on Bess, Molly on Prince. Saddle bags were stuffed with food, bottles of wine, and a measure of oats for each horse.

Molly knew nothing could be kept secret in Rivertown, so she wasn't surprised to find Hester waiting for her one evening.

Her mother-in-law lost no time in coming to the point, "You can't ride a stallion around the country and barter his services."

"But I am." Molly drew off her gloves, her riding hat, and laid them on the table in the wide hall. Then she loosened her jacket so that Hester might not notice how tightly it fit.

"You never asked me if it was proper and suitable for you to do this."

And for a very good reason, Molly thought. You would have forbidden it.

Hester went on, "It has taken every ounce of my patience to put up with what I thought were the mistakes of your youth, but now you are becoming so brazen that it is my duty, with Levi away, to forbid you to continue this disgraceful performance."

Instinctively Molly struck back with, "By what right can you forbid me?"

She was tired from a hard day and would have loved to lean her aching head upon a mother's breast, feel comforting arms about her and murmurs of, "There, there, we'll have you in bed in a jiffy."

But Hester was distraught and ruffled. She tapped her foot as an angry turkey drums his wings, while her face turned as red as a turkey's wattles. "Have you no respect for your husband's mother?"

Molly wanted to tell Hester that she had. After all, wasn't she herself going to be a mother? She would have liked to have said that she was sorry she had walked down the church aisle in improper dress, singing improperly, that first Sunday. It was the only thing she had done deliberately to offend. In everything else she had acted innocently. She could even show the urgency of what she was now doing. She really wanted to try and make Hester understand.

But the older woman's voice rose louder in the big hall now growing dim, "I'll not stand by and see you besmirch our good name. I forbid you to disgrace us."

For a moment the old childish doubt of her identity swept over Molly. Papa called her Mary, Mammy Fay called her Marie, while Levi had proclaimed her a new person with a new name, Molly Blaisdell, which Hester now insisted belonged to the clan.

She stiffened against her Puritan mother-in-law and said, "I must be my own judge of what I do and believe me I am doing nothing wrong; I am doing something I *must* do."

Then instead of trying to break the barrier between Hester and herself, she picked up her hat and gloves and held them in such a way as to shield her body from too close scrutiny by her mother-in-law's censuring eye.

CHAPTER XIX

THE DAY MOLLY FOUND MRS. WORKUM BROUGHT HER JOY AND relief.

She had enjoyed riding Prince in the open country, feeling free of the town which hampered her. On these trips into the interior, once they had climbed up over the second rise back of town, they were in fine rolling country, good farming land.

She had expected to find only the most primitive pioneer cabins crudely furnished with hungry children benched at a puncheon table or sleeping on beds of leaves swept into a corner. Instead she found Mr. Ephraim Campbell's new brick house almost finished. The bricks had been burned right on the place, were rough, of different-size and shapes, streaked and freckled in the drying. Mr. Campbell had got ahead and obviously was a leading farmer in these parts.

He told Molly that she'd got on to a prime idea and he didn't see why folks wouldn't cotton right to it. What's more, he not only promised to go along with her but said he'd be seeing folks and would help spread the word that Levi Blaisdell, through his Missus, was offering a right good deal. For a start he told her she could do no better than to tackle Homer Workum up the road on the next quarter section.

Molly, with her entourage, consisting of Matt, Julee, and Quercus, rode between the forest lanes of hickory, black walnut, beech, oak, and buckeye until she came to a fence, part stone, part split rails zigzagged like feather-stitching, enclosing freshly turned and seeded fields, guarded by scare-crows clothed in tattered, raggedy homespun.

175

In the midst of the cleared land was Homer Workum's two-storied log home and snuggled up to it were the small tight barns and out-buildings of a farm family who had fought their way through the wilderness, won their struggle of felling the forest, stood up to the big butts until they too had vanished.

There was nothing tangibly unusual about Homer and Sarah Workum's place, either without of within, but, when Molly rode away after her visit, there was a new lift to her chin. There was nothing new in seeing spotted cows, their white bellies so full uddered that their teats stuck out every which way, or in seeing pails scrubbed white. Or for that matter in the long tresses and skeins of yarn hung on the kitchen walls, the spinning wheels and looms, the long rolls of linen pegged at the corners bleaching on the new green grass and dampened with water hour after hour.

Perhaps the key to the difference between the Workums and other folks lay in their attitude about what they were doing. Everything they did was done with spirit, courage and laughter. Like the side door which didn't yet have a stone step.

"Probably never will have," admitted Sarah. "The young ones are mighty spry and learn fast enough to roll over the threshold and us grown ones learned to stretch 'til now we're used to it."

Sarah Workum did endless hard work and except in sleep her hands were never quiet. In the evening her needles clicked, or her wheel spun, while she watched over the fireside studies of her children.

Without her there would have been no home, only drabness, fear, and loneliness for it was on Mrs. Workum that her man and the children depended, not only for the finished products of the field, but for companionship, and teaching. Sarah Workum was the highest of her kind—a woman who when she lay down weary at night had the satisfaction of knowing that she had done as well as she could whether it had been a day of sunshine or shadow, a day of joy which no one could take from her, or a day of sorrow which would pass.

Molly couldn't define the out-going warmth of Sarah Workum, but perhaps that was why she had found it so easy to tell her, a complete stranger, that she was going to have a baby when she hadn't even told her own husband, Levi. Sarah Workum was the kind of person who could feel and understand how much she wanted a baby though she didn't tell her she wanted it mostly to fill that horrid place inside her which was fear, nor that she was glad to give Hester such concrete evidence that she and Levi were not strangers.

No, it was just joy to talk of the baby and what preparations she must make for its arrival. The air was filled with chatter of how many flannel didies to hem, how long the dresses should be, how to make the lying-in quilt. And according to Sarah Workum Gramma Pilcher was a good granny even if she was white and folks would like it better if the colored one from across the river wasn't sent for.

"But my gracious, what am I thinking of—here is Homer in for his noonin'. While I stir up a smart fire and make fixin's you two can talk business. Homer, this is Miz Molly Blaisdell come to fix up a deal for Levi who's down New Orlean's way with a spring load."

Each day became harder for Molly. She rode farther and farther for she was meeting with such tremendous success that she couldn't think of stopping. At this rate she'd have the whole country's produce sewed up in contracts for Levi.

One day Julee complained that her rump was so worn out she couldn't sit Bess's old broad back again and she'd rather stay home alone with Quercus no matter who might come and carry them off, but maybe Miss Mary Marie better give her a pass.

"But Julee you'll be at home."

Julee said, "Yes, Lordy Jesus, us not goin' anywheres but you make us a stay-at-home pass sayin' us belongs to you, if any 'paterollers' come."

So! By some mysterious grapevine Matt and Julee had learned about fugitive slaves but to pacify Julee she gave her a "stay-at-home" pass and was glad not to have Julee and Quercus with her for she and Matt could make better time alone.

That evening when the two returned home, Molly got out of the saddle so tired that her whole body was a-quiver.

Julee said, "Oh! Oh! You look like you take as big a lickin' a gal ever toted."

Molly had reached the very limits of endurance. She was tired all over, and was no more than a wooden-jointed doll as Julee removed her soiled riding habit and clothing. She dropped across her bed and was too tired and sleepy even to finish a cup of soup.

"I'm all right, Julee, you may go. There's nothing wrong with me a night's sleep won't mend."

Even before she was entirely awake she was conscious that someone very close to her was breathing heavily. Then she realized with surprise that it was herself and she felt a general unease in her body. It might be the smoked hams of squirrels she had eaten at the "noonin'" at the Hazlip farm. She hadn't wanted to eat them but she couldn't offend Mrs. Hazlip who had so little to offer after a lean winter and who was proud of her resourcefulness in "parsarvin' the best of the critters by saltin' and hangin' in the chimney to smoke."

Now Molly regretted saving Mrs. Hazlip's feelings and leaned over and gave "the critter" to the night bucket and felt a little better for a time. But her pains persisted in waves, a cramp, followed by an ebb. One cramp came mightier than the rest and shook her whole being.

This then must be the quickening Mrs. Workum had told her to expect. That cherished moment when she would feel the first movement of her child, to know that it lived. And surely a child who gave his mother such pain at the moment he quickened must be an exceptionally strong child who would be fearless like his father, and for every pain he gave her she would love him all the more.

It must be close to dawn, almost time to get up. Julee would be in soon to prepare her for another day in the saddle, but now she would tell Julee that the trips into the country had to be over because of the child.

Oh! wouldn't Levi be surprised when he came home. "Are you sure?" he would ask. And for answer she would take his hand and guide it to her swollen body and let him feel the kicks of their child who surely would be born with spurs so sharply was he jabbing her.

Mrs. Workum hadn't told her that quickening hurt, nor had Julee ever complained; certainly this should not be cutting her in two. That cutting pain must happen only the once, there wouldn't be another one.

There was!

She was so shocked by the cramping pain that her breath stopped. When her breath came again a big thistle of doubt jabbed her.

She screamed, "Julee!"

The following October Molly stood in her back doorway and looked at the long line of wagons waiting their turn to go down the gully road to fill Levi's flatboats. Levi was proud of his boats this fall. It had taken a four-ox team to bring in the ninety-foot poplar tree trunks cut in the spring before the sap rose and left to season until needed for the gunnels of these ten big boats. Each of them was held together by two thousand, white-oak boatpins, every one of which Molly was certain had been whittled in her very own kitchen—twenty thousand boatpins. Yes, Levi would come home from this trip with bags of gold, for each load might bring five thousand dollars in New Orleans, giving him a good commission.

The long line of wagons held tons of various kinds of produce which assured Levi of "straight" loads, the kind he liked. Levi was not one to mix potatoes, apples, flour, beans, brooms, and buckets together on one boat. "Piddlin'." No sir-ee if Levi were going to carry potatoes he wanted a full straight load of potatoes in a flatboat.

"Gosh-a-mighty," he said, "you reckon I want to go 'round a New Orleans wharf begging this one and that one to take a mite of this, a mite of that off my hands?" Yes, Levi was jubilant at the long line of wagons. He flew around as if he had hot grease in his pants trying to boss everyone at once. He'd hardly take time to eat so she had to tell Julee to fix cabin rations of corn bread and bacon only for Mr. Levi's breakfast to be stuffed into his pockets and munched when he happened to remember he was hungry.

The excitement of such a sizable business sustained him. Levi allowed he knew more ways to transact business than a country man did to whip a mule, but dod-derned if Molly hadn't turned a smart trick standing Prince at stud.

"You did it Half-Pint, I love you. If I was starving and had only one hoe cake I would give you half—the biggest half. With this load I can lay a cradle for my steamboat."

So a cradle for a steamboat was to be her gain for those long hard days in the saddle last spring instead of a cradle she could rock with her toe.

If Julee hadn't lost her head that night and sent Matt for Hester no one would have known she had lost her baby. It was dreadful to have Hester accuse her of deliberately bringing on the miscarriage by riding horseback. And when Hester had done with her she was left to brood alone. She was not to have a different and better time after all; she was lashed and flung back to her old feeling of being bound and lost in the world, not knowing who she was, and nobody caring.

And, of course, there had been nothing to tell Levi when he returned except that she had made a bargain with the farmers for their autumn business. She wouldn't have ever told him about the miscarriage, but Hester was not one to miss such an opportunity to be righteous.

She was relieved that Levi did not blame her, but she did expect him to soothe and reassure her, to give her consolation, to bind all the bruises and contusions of her shattered life. She was not prepared for his light dismissal of the whole business even though he was sorry she'd had the pain and the trouble. "Still there's nothing to cry about," he'd said, "there'll be plenty of babies."

Oh, Levi hadn't come right out and said that her business deals were more important to him than losing their first child, but he had certainly acted that way.

And now each flatboat had to be loaded evenly, each corner must draw the same amount of water so that the entire boat was safe from snags, sawyers, sandbars, rocks, and a thousand other hazards of floating a valuable cargo all the way to New Orleans. Levi was hustling to get everything checked before taking off.

"Goodbye, Molly."

Everyone agreed it was quite a sight to see Levi Blaisdell's ten big flatboats go out, the broadhorns slashing the water, while the boatmen sang, *Hi-o, away we go, floating down the river on the O-hi-o.*

Then Molly was alone again in the lonesome house wrapped in a cold fog that sent mildew into her bones.

CHAPTER XX

MOLLY HAD HAD A COUPLE MORE "MISHAPS" AND THOUGHT perhaps that was why she was ready to fly the cat hole. There must be something wrong with her; it wasn't credible that a new life conceived in the passion she shared with Levi shouldn't be strong and grow to fruition.

With some diffidence she broached the subject to Minnie Preble. Minnie said she'd had the same trouble in the beginning. Land of Goshen, all Cal had to do was wink at a bedpost and she got caught but couldn't carry. But now! Just look at the young-uns down to Preble's, you couldn't put your foot down without stepping on one. Molly didn't know when she was well off in Minnie's opinion.

These days Molly took over most of the care of Julee's ninny, Quercus, who proved to be an excellent companion. She could speak freely to him, he never misunderstood her, nor rebuked her for unseemly conduct, nor repeated anything she told him in confidance. When she shed bitter tears he had a way of pulling her red hair with his tiny black fists to tell her he'd give her something worth crying about. And he'd squeal his delight when she said, "You're a bad, bad boy." If she fed him he'd blow the gravy-soaked bread to show her what a clever comedian he was and if his performance didn't meet with her applause he applauded himself.

Yet Molly was dissatisfied and disappointed with her life in the town, the way she had to live. And yes, with much of her life with Levi. If ever the time came that he did not, at night, wipe clean her slate of frustrations and vexations! She was building up and building up—and had been for quite a while—one devil of a row with Levi. It had to do with a great many little daily things, not one of which, if taken singly, was so terribly important but if she put them all together and stirred them in one pot they became a witch's brew that made her want to whirl and scream.

Levi himself was depressed when he returned from one of his trips south. "I did some checking. 'Pears steamboats might be a mite overbuilt. Many a boat's tied up or just making out moseying along the willows. A fellow could pick up an old tub right cheap if he had the money. Wouldn't be the same as building your own though. And I've got ideas. So, reckon I'll flatboat a spell longer."

He wrote in his journal. "Steamboats overbuilt, won't lay my keel for a spell." He lacked his usual flourish when he returned his journal to the chimney cupboard. His normal exuberance was drained out of him like liquid from a bottle.

He turned sadly. "For a fellow like me it looks as if catching a steamboat is harder than climbing a sapling heels up."

Molly struck swiftly with belittling, pride-hurting words—fighting words. "You're a goose to think you can ever build a steamboat. You think you're a ring-tail roarer who can lick this river. But you're as dumb as a dead nigger in a mud hole not to recognize you can't."

Levi's face grew set and hard.

It was a dangerous time. The air between them was unfriendly. Always before Levi had been amused at her spit-fire ways but this time she had caught him at a moment when his own sap was too far down. His expression held no amused tenderness for her now. He didn't, as was usual with him, try to make things easier for her when she was so unsure of herself—had learned so little about herself. Molly didn't know this Levi and it frightened her.

He shouted, "Wish you had run back to your dumb niggers and your Louisiana mud hole."

"Don't shout so," she screamed.

"Don't you shout at me."

"I'm not shouting! I'm only *telling* you."

Levi won the battle when he yelled at her. "You're a baby—wearin' three-cornered pants. You're not fit to be a boatman's wife." And he flung himself out of the room.

When she had done crying she set up her row of excuses, like bushes to hide behind. She was so terribly frightened of herself and those undefined thoughts that hid in the dark, beneath the bone, deep in her brain. She was so frightened of this unknown part of herself which in some way bound her a slave to her unhappy self. If only she could free herself . . . And she began all over again with the excuses. If only she could get Levi away from the river.

But Levi was so much stronger than she. His dejection about the steamboat had been brief. Soon again he was a rip-staver riverman who bragged that when still in his cradle he had sucked on a tit-rag soaked in river water and whiskey. He was whole again in self-confidence, while she remained chopped up in little pieces. She hated him for his one-ness.

She especially hated his fiddling with the model of his steamboat. It didn't make sense the way he kept shifting things around in the hold and lower decks. He was as finicky and as notionable as a woman trying to figure out where a new piece of furniture would look best. One day he had his miniature wooden boilers in the hold, the next they were up on deck forward, then aft. He was everlastingly trying to figure out how to get the most speed and the most cargo space for his boat. In anger she had Matt move the model to the wide dog-trot hall. To Levi she said, "During warm weather you can work on it out there."

Levi replied, "This is goin' to be a bumper-crop year; a few more of these and I'll be in the money."

That autumn she saw what the boatmen meant when they spoke of Fall Business. Everything was in demand, beeswax for candles to be sent to far-off Catholic France, ginseng to fill the orders from far, far eastern Canton, tobacco for England, flaxseed was in good demand, and hay and more hay, tons and tons of it, bushels and bushels of wheat, everyone said the best in years, its berry large, plump, smooth, and well filled. There were barrels and barrels of potatoes, sack upon sack of barley and oats, bags of onions, corn and more corn. Oh! After the lean times it was wonderful to see the bumper fall business.

Competition was keen to get to New Orleans before the great glut of plenty tumbled the market. The farmers couldn't get the stuff to the landings fast enough. Some shippers pushed off with their flatboats half loaded, expecting to pick up the balance at way-points. Others rushed into the country and advanced their prices to the farmers to get delivery of the produce. Experienced boatmen were scarce. Levi said he not only needed every Jack man but by Jeems he could even use a Jenny.

"How about it, Molly? You're always bragging about how you checked plantation stores and handed out rations at Quercus. There's not a mite of difference to doing it in barrels, hogsheads, and tons, instead of pints, quarts, and pounds. We could move the wagons a sight faster if you'd help. With your quick neat hand on the figures releasing me, I'll lay money on a barrel head I'll get to New Orleans as soon as anyone and *then* watch the profits I'll bring back. Come on, Half-Pint, I need a clerk to do the manifests."

So there Molly perched, "from kain to kain't" on a very high stool before a crude desk with a sloping top placed in a wooden shed, bent over the manifests she signed, *M. Blaisdell, Clerk.* She wouldn't admit it but presently she grew excited and thrilled to see the long line of wagons waiting to come down the gully road. She got used to the drivers of those wagons in their calf-spotted coats, high boots (some with red-leather tops carefully displayed), red comforters around uncollared necks or dragging from coat pockets, puffing away on long nines between their teeth.

She got so she could look upon them with a stern eye and say, "This completes the one hundred barrels we contracted for."

She might have been Mammy Fay saying, "You've had your hundred pints of flour, Orris. Tell your wife to be more careful next time."

The men shuffled their feet a bit and said, "Yes, Ma'am. Heer'd you wuz strict and knowed if one potato wuz missin'. Heer'd nobuddy could put anything over on you. Allus knowed I couldn't fool Levi. Right proud to do business with his Missus. How about these few coops of chickens?"

But Molly was firm, "No chickens." Levi wouldn't piffle with a few of this and that. Levi dealt only in hundreds and thousands.

"I'll take three dozen chickens for myself but I'll only give seventy-five cents a dozen. That's the quoted Cincinnati price."

The farmer grumbled but let her have them. She'd tell Julee to roast the lot of them and send Levi off with a good ration of fresh meat. She'd show Hester she knew how to ration a flat-boatman.

One day her hill friend, Mr. Workum, came with his loads of produce.

After Molly had asked about his family and checked his contracts he hemmed and hawed, but finally said, "Mrs. Workum sent along a couple of barrels of soap and wondered could you take them off her hands and oblige her, Ma'am?"

Molly remembered the happy day she had spent with Mrs. Workum making "woman talk" and the unhappy time which followed when she had her first "mishap." Remembrance of Mrs. Workum's partnership with her husband gave Molly an understanding of why helping Levi with his shipping gave her a feeling of security she hadn't had before.

In her mind's eye she saw how Mrs. Workum had labored to produce the two barrels of soap; the carefully hoarded fat, the rye straw in a barrel with the sawtooth bottom through which the wood ashes drained down onto the leachstone and the necessary lye dripped into the pail. Probably Mrs. Workum had labored with extra care over this soap which she hoped to sell in order that she might have money to buy some longed-for cherished bit of luxury.

So Molly said with authority, "Why certainly, Mr. Workum, set the soap off the wagon."

When Levi saw the two barrels of soap he said, "Gosh all fish hooks, Molly, two barrels of soap! Piddling! I thought I told you always to take a hundred of anything or none."

"I'll wool-lightning out of you if you don't take those two barrels."

Levi laughed, "Whoopity! That's my Mississippi snapping turtle. Thought I'd lost *you* up Salt Creek."

She nudged him happily with her elbow and said, "Go 'long with you."

Levi pushed off on his first trip with eleven broadhorns, every-one of them loaded, and worth fifteen hundred dollars. There was plenty of money tied up in those cargoes for Levi had advanced heavily to the farmers out of his precious steamboat savings.

"But in return for the advance, Punkin, I'm gettin' an extra five-percent commission." Levi said the farmers liked a shrewd deal from him because then they knew he dealt the same way with the fancy-vest boys in New Orleans. In the end everybody was ahead.

"And you wait, Punkin, 'til you see the pork this year. Yes, siree, this is a year for hog."

Levi made twenty-five hundred dollars on his first fall trip.

With this money he contracted to have a pork house hastily put up on the back of their property. He rode far into the country to contract for hogs.

"There's more money in dressed pork, Punkin. Why should I pay a middleman's profit?"

Molly had hardly seen him before Levi was off with another fleet of flatboats. He still carried hay, wheat and corn but he added many head of horses and mules. "That's what decides how wide to build a flatboat, Punkin. A row of horses down each side, just room enough to feed them and shovel out. Takes eighteen to nineteen feet."

Levi made one more trip before the pork business started.

When it began Molly said only every fifth hog she met was a man. Levi said, "When they really get coming you can't go out in the streets."

It was true. Molly got caught downtown one day at Main Cross and High and had to run up the nearest steps to escape from the mass of hogs filling the street. The experience was frightening.

First had come a man riding horseback who yelled, "Hawgs!" From a bag laid across the horse's withers he drew handfuls of corn which he scattered in the street. His voice was hoarse from crying, "Pig—oo—ee! Pig—oo—ee." Men with long sticks were stationed at alleys and cross streets to help the drovers keep the hogs trotting. At the rear came the fattest porkers with special drovers to prod them on their way. They were tired from carrying so much fat.

Levi said there had been a time when the pork business hadn't amounted to anything because the hogs' legs used to be too spindly to carry any weight. Then somebody with brains bred the White China pig to a Poland hog . . . "and you'll see, Punkin, we've got pork business."

She understood what Levi meant when she came upon the

186

hogs that had "guv out" and were riding their last miles in wag-ons. Cal Preble called to her from one of them, "How you like your hawgs, Molly?" They were Blaisdell hogs being driven to the new Blaisdell Pork House which was a slaughter house in her own backyard.

Back home Molly kept close within doors. She had seen all Levi's neat arrangements for slaughtering.

"A man drives the hog in this little pen, Punkin. Another stands up here and knocks him on the head, the man alongside reaches over and sticks him in the throat—."

"Levi, please!"

"Honey, those hogs are our steamboat. Don't you *want* to know? There's something wrong with you if you don't have any curiosity about making pork."

"All right. The hog is killed. I don't mind once he's dead. What happens to him next?"

"Then two men haul him to this vat where two more scald him and another rakes off his bristles. Does it in one and a half minutes. Then he's hung on these hooks with stretchers between his legs. Two men split, gut him, halve him, throw him down, off with his head. Guess how long since he was a live hog?"

Molly shook her head.

"Three and a half minutes. Hope my boys can cut it to three."

"All right. It takes three minutes to turn a hog into pork." She wished Levi would have done with this business.

"Then they're cooled and packed in brine. A great business—pork business, but I haven't the feeling for hogs I've got for the river—and a man's got to do what he feels for."

"What about a woman?"

"Oh, she'll go along with her man."

She thought of the thousands and thousand of boatpins whit-tled to hold together the huge flatboats needed to carry the loads of produce necessary to build Levi's steamboat, the brown flitches of smoked bacon and enormous hams, the barrels of salt pork, the tons of hay, hundreds of bushels of corn, wheat, and oats. It seemed to her that all the corners of her life were filled by these things. The corners might grow and multiply but they would still be held to the focal point, Levi's dream of building a steamboat, which to him was a way of life.

Another gray day of loading flatboats begun in a drizzling rain

187

ended in a snow flurry. Tired, dirty, wet, and cold she closed her book of manifests, uncurled her toes from the rung of her high stool, and wearily uncramped herself, clutched her long, bedraggled skirts and climbed the muddy wagon-rutted gully road to the old dog-trot house.

That evening Levi said, "Reckon I'll have to move my boat model back in the kitchen. Time to button up again for another winter." He fiddled with his boat model which seemed to rest him while she thought of the Workums and her new-found partnership with Levi. If she followed his notions willingly and helpfully, would she gain the security and inner peace of Mrs. Workum?

Levi came in from the dog-trot hall and said, "You know, Punkin, I think I've hit on it at last. I've got a notion that if I put the wheels further aft I can get more speed. Stands to reason she'd help herself more."

Molly closed her eyes for a second. Here was another one of those moments of her life when she stood clear and free in the present, a moment of reality with a decision to make. She steadied her voice to say, "Stands to reason."

Levi came over to the table and showed her a piece of wood. "Finest walnut I could buy."

"It's lovely wood, Levi." She sighed very slightly.

Levi put his arms around her, hugged her close, and dropped a kiss on top of her head. "Honey, it's just the way I imagined it would be."

"How, Levi?"

"Oh, you and me. You doing whatever it is women do, me making my boat, both of us dreaming together how it's going to be."

Levi made his last trip of 1843 south with a great load of porkers. That year Levi Blaisdell was King Pork of Rivertown.

While he was gone Molly had Matt move the steamboat model back into the common room of winter—the kitchen. For the first time she really studied Levi's model and quickened at the thought of how she would look rounding to for a landing. Her lines were graceful, slender, and long. Her tall smokestacks would have the very best filigree work touched up with plenty of gold pluming their tops. On her paddle-wheel boxes bright pictures would be daubed. But to Molly's eye the guard rails looked too plain. If a boat was feminine "she" should look dressy, as if she were going to a party flounced in laces.

Molly rummaged in a trousseau trunk for lace which she starched to board stiffness and fastened it to Levi's plain guard rails and admired the result.

She studied the inside of the boat, the ladies' cabin. In a flight of fancy she carpeted it with pink and white flowers; to each stateroom door she put a porcelain knob; she hung great chandeliers of glittering glass drops to reflect the light of hundreds of candles. She let her eye wander forward. Here would be the dining appointments with the finest napery, the best china (no little heavy bird-bath crockery on the Blaisdell boat), the heaviest silver, the finest cuisine, served in the best manner. After the tables were cleared and pushed back the orchestra would play for dancing—the minuet, a cotillion led by the captain's wife.

Everyone would say, "The Blaisdell boat? She's not one of the biggest but, upon my word, she's the latest and is so refined in her appointments."

When Levi saw the starched lace on the guard rails of his model, he said, "Good God, Molly, lace from your petticoats—on a steamboat!"

"Sets her off doesn't it?"

Levi studied on it, Hoosier fashion, a right smart spell before committing himself. "Gol-derned if it don't. We'll deck her out."

With the profits from the pork business Levi's glorious moment came. He wrote in his log book, "Started laying the keel."

The following spring, in spite of a speedy close to spring trade in the south, the flatboatmen were still away on the first day of May and so missed the annual celebration in Symmes Woods. Everyone said it flatted out without the boatmen to put some get-up and go to the affair.

When the boatmen got home they were feeling rambunctious because business was steady at last. There wasn't a one who wasn't Mr. Bang-All. They claimed to have been swindled by folks not waiting for them to have the May Day party and dod-blast it if they just wouldn't have one of their own just to show folks they shouldn't over-reach themselves when dealing with boatmen.

They didn't fool anyone, everyone knew they were just spoiling for a frolic. There was no holding them.

At the head of the Blaisdell gully they sawed and hammered away. They drove boatpins to make a float like a flatboat, complete with a steering sweep behind, a gouger in front, and token broadhorns on either side—they couldn't have got the float through the streets with real ones. When the float was finished, they hitched a six-horse team to draw it with Cal Preble riding the wheel horse. On its hatch was Fiddler Jim to furnish a tune. Beside him was Levi blowing his boatman's horn.

Ahead of the float went the boatmen with a great thick rope which reached from gutter to gutter. With it they swept the streets clear, tripping anything in their path. Citizens, hogs, dogs and cows skipped out of the way of the boatmen headed for their frolic.

They went up and down the streets stopping at the houses where the women, including Molly, had hung white napkins at their doors to show that the boatmen could expect a donation of viands. With whoops and hollers for each woman the boatmen piled their cargo on the float. At Berman's a mighty shout went up at the sight of him waving his white apron. Eager muscles heaved his barrels of "red-head" aboard. With a roar a half dozen boatmen swarmed upon Berman himself and hoisted him up alongside his barrels. It was useless to struggle against the boatmen bent on an outing.

Their cargo collected they formed a parade and it was no funeral-like procession that headed up Main Cross.

The Rivertown Roarers, dressed to the nines in brand-new blue uniforms appropriately bullioned and pomponned, rode in their elegant new bandwagon—a huge twelve-seater carry-all. The end seats, front and rear, were higher than the four middle ones. All exposed woodwork was brilliantly painted, the under body blue and the upper parts flame red. It was overlaid with gold scrolls and blue, green, red and yellow curlicues. The driver's box on either side was decorated with portraits of what was no doubt the goddess of music. Four plumed horses pranced to the oompah of the silver cornets of the Rivertown Roarers. If a player bogged down in a piece beyond his skill, he clowned his way out of his difficulty.

Wagons, short-tailed drays, high-wheeled carts, loaded with

the fun lovers of Rivertown both male and female, happily followed the pride of the town, their own Rivertown Roarers.

"It's different when the boatmen are here."

Molly realized with a rush how used she had grown to these tall, broad-shouldered, deep-chested men. Papa had named them buccaneers, bandits and bullies. But she was growing really fond of them.

These rivermen were a lusty lot. Beside them, other men seemed colorless and pale—wishy-washy. Levi, with this love of the river coursing through his blood, was one of them.

Now she was able to laugh when Levi picked her up and set her on the float on top of a barrel of "red-head." She remembered her jolly wedding procession, the kin escorting her with her bridegroom to the steamboat. What would they think if they saw her now? And Mammy Fay, what would she have to say to her Young Miss who wore a sunbonnet and sat on a barrel of whiskey and rode to a boatmen's picnic?

When they got to Symmes Woods nobody bothered to look for late May flowers. Berman lost no time in opening the bar on the flatboat float to hush the rivermen who milled around like sheep.

They bleated they had an unusual thirst straight from Salt River. Ba-a-a. One after another took to ba-a-a-ing at Berman or butting each other with their heads. The opening of the bar was saluted by a crack from the little cannon set up on the float. The Rivertown Roarers oompahed the flatboatmen's song, *Hi-o, away we go, floating down the river, on the O-hi-o.* Everyone lifted his cup in salute to La Belle Rivière. Old Fiddler Jim struck up the other favorite, *Dance, boatman Dance, dance away; Dance all night till broad daylight. And go home with the gals in the morning.*

They danced on a platform, several cotillions at once. They broke into the rougher and livelier country dances of an earlier pioneer time. These tall men could swing any girl right off her feet.

And when the women were not dancing they spread snowy cloths on long puncheon tables in a great low shed open on all sides. They used sharp elbows when a man hindered their work by throwing an arm carelessly about a tightly laced waist. If he discovered the waist belonged to his wife, or even if it didn't, he bent and gave her a smacker. A woman was helpless with a giant riverman newly returned home. If he tilted your head back for a kiss it was better not to rouse him further with too hard a poke in his ribs. You'd better let him have a little favor and then say good naturedly, "Go along with you now, make yourself useful, bring the baskets."

The women served a bountiful repast to these men who had cooked their own "grunts and grits," as they called smoked hog and hominy, over a crude fire on their flatboats while they floated south. "Gosh all hemlock!" the rivermen roared. "Tastes good!"

There was no end to the food on the plates and no bottom to the cups. Now and then someone rose to propose a new toast. Nobody listened but everybody cheered and drank to the toast with right good will. The men belched, picked their teeth, and leaned their elbows on the table. Fiddler Jim was begged to rest, nobody could possibly dance when so glutted with food and drink.

The crowd broke up and wandered off in small groups to wait for recovery. Knives came from pockets for boatpin whittling, others brought forth dirty decks of cards and played Picayune Poker. The women engaged in what Levi termed, "jaybird-jabber."

Levi, Cal Preble, Sam Higbet, and others who liked to work their gums engaged in Hoosier tall talk.

"Yep, it won't be long now," Levi said. "I'll have me a steamboat."

"It's a great age we live in."

"Must have been a sight when the country first began to fill up. Reckon we dreened off the best blood of the East."

"Smartest thing was when we bought Louisiana Territory."

"Sure, sure. You'd think any fool would have seen nature meant us to have the whole of the Mississippi."

"Should have bought Texas, too."

"Yep, ought to go all the way from Atlantic to Pacific."

"We're already a great inland empire."

"The flatboatmen did it."

"Reckon we're about the last of the flatboatmen. The steamboats are runnin' us off the water with their fast time."

Sam Higbet, ever a gloomy gus, said, "Looks to me like we're maybe headin' for trouble."

"How, Sam?" asked Cal.

192

"There's too much talk of a Liberty Party."

"We got it already right here," Cal said. "Heard the planters are gettin' so they're 'fraid to bring their servants to Cin., 'fraid they'll get notions and slip off."

"Heard up to Bluffton, folks were having horses taken, they find them turned loose eight or ten miles from home."

"Yeah, things are gettin' bitter."

"Makes folks push west."

"Country'd be too full if some didn't move on."

"Pacific Ocean will fetch 'em up by and by."

"Yeah!" said Cal. "The Pacific Ocean! Reckon we'll live to see the National Road go clear across?"

"Maybe a railroad," said Sam.

Both Levi and Cal shook their heads. Such a thing could never happen.

Levi said, "There's only one thing a railroad might be good for. To bring produce and passengers to the steamboats."

"Yep," said Cal. "Railroads can't jump across rivers."

"You boys better get on the steamboat bandwagon," Levi advised them.

But Sam and Cal said that business was too chancy for them. Too many accidents. An ordinary packet cost maybe thirty thousand dollars and only God knew if she'd blow up her first trip out, run on a sawyer, catch fire or come to an end by any one of the thousand things that plagued rivermen. A lost flatboat was bad enough—but a steamboat!

At the boatmen's picnic Molly accumulated more than a sunburn and chigger bites. Little thorns of doubt and discouragement pricked her new-found security in going along with Levi's notion of a steamboat.

CHAPTER XXI

QUERCUS, JULEE'S NINNY WAS FOUR YEARS OLD. HE WAS A SWEET baby, fat and slick as could be. Julee said, "He the jigginest little bugger ever was, he dance and sing the mostest—a juba ninny."

Molly watched Quercus out in the back yard doing a "Juba" taught him by Julee. The little monkey put plenty of meaning into his silly song, *Juba, Juba, Juba up 'n Juba down, Juba all aroun' the town.* Quercus stamped his right foot on the strong accent and clapped his hands on the weak just as well as any plantation negro cutting loose on Saturday night.

Molly rewarded his dance with a biscuit and said, "Quercus, how'd you like to be a fly-sweeper?"

"What am dat, Mistus Molly?"

A lump came in her throat at the memory of little Ambus in the fly-swing over the long mahogany table at Rutland Hall, Little Ambus catching biscuits and shining his black face with the fat of bacon and ham.

She had not been back to Rutland Hall nor seen any of her relatives since she had come to Rivertown. Oh she could have gone, but she was held back by her pride. In all these years there had never been a time that had been right for her to go south for a visit, and certainly she had not wanted—or invited—any kin to come to see her in what Julee called "that old rottendy dog-trot house."

"Mistus Molly!" whispered Quercus, "Us wants another biscuit." She filled his hands with biscuits because she was sorry he wasn't on a plantation where he'd have lots of other ninnies to play with. And later on she made him a pair of white pants, a shirt, and red calico slippers to cover his black feet. When Quercus got them on, he couldn't stand still, but had to juba, juba up and down.

Then she got Ira to make a swing to hang from the ceiling beams over the table. But alas, there were no peacocks in River-town to furnish tail feathers for a colorful graceful fan so that Quercus, sitting in the swing over the table, could sweep away the flies. And wild turkey wings proved to be too short. Quercus couldn't quite breeze the flies with them. But when his swing perch was lowered Quercus's little red calico shoes swung too close to the platters.

Julee said, "Lawsy me, what you try to do? The Lord God his-self couldn't make no fly-sweeper out o' Quercus, he too hoppity."

"Us too hoppity, Mistus Molly," echoed Quercus.

"No, Quercus! You swing too hard. Easy! Careful! *Don't* stick the feathers into the gravy. No, Quercus! No!"

"Us wants down, us not like." Quercus's black face crumpled. "Quercus!"

He dropped the turkey-wing fan, opened his mouth, which was as red inside as a ripe watermelon, and howled.

Julee said: "Ole rottendy place! Us got no biggedy folks food to breeze the flies off of. The Lord God hisself couldn't turn this ole rottendy cabin into a biggedy place. You plumb foolish you try." She rolled savage eyes from her mistress to her son. "Hush you mouth, you Quercus, us takes you down, you don't have to brush flies from cabin-ration vittles." She lifted Quercus from the swing and held him close. She scolded Molly, "Us keeps tellin' you it's not the same."

Yes, Molly knew these years in the North must have been dreadfully lonesome for Matt and Julee without the fun and frolic of their own; the barbecues of roast pig celebrating the completion of some big seasonal job; the Sunday visiting; the music strummed on gourd fiddles, timed by the click of the clap-ping bones made from the ribs of beef. At these good times Matt could out-dance any one else. His feet trip-hammered a rhythm better than the drum beat. All the movements of his dance were made from the hips down. He kept his body so steady that he could balance a glass of water on top of his head, while his feet jigged right and left, and never spill a drop. For an extra show-off he'd finish up with a whirl 'round while everyone held his breath to see if he'd make it this time and they could yell, "whoopity!" Yes those had been happy times at Quercus Grove, Molly thought.

Julee's voice cut in, "Matt and me, us scared. Us knows River-towner folks hubbub 'cause 'o Matt an' me—us black. I wants to go home 'fore Matt he gits into trouble. Matt, like always, need steadyin', he gits too big for his britches, he strut all 'roun' town. I tells him he want watch out, some night he git a hand laid acrost his big mouth an' he git took acrost the river to sure misery. You oughts to do something, Miss Molly."

For some time now there had been matters afoot which disquieted her. They hadn't all happened at once nor had they at first seemed to have any connection with one another, but gradually a pattern could be discerned. Like a picture puzzle each piece began to fit into another and gave meaning—even faraway happenings.

Like the Liberty Convention which had been held in Buffalo. The *Messenger* wrote a hot-headed piece lambasting the meeting. Editor Folsom claimed nobody had any right to take away private property and slaves were property. Such talk should be put down; it caused bitterness and made enemies, divided folks, brothers even. And if it went on it could raise up that old trouble about Union again.

When Molly asked Levi his opinion about all this, he just said that it was bad for business to stir up the South against the North.

Another time she turned to Captain Cleve in his "settin'" room on board *The Rising Sun*. Lately she had been making more frequent visits to see him. She was growing more and more disgusted these days, but after she had sat with Captain Cleve she always felt more of a person. He satisfied in her a half-felt need to reach out for something a little bigger than herself.

The captain settled himself and rocked comfortably, while he considered her question. She had asked, "Have you heard anything about trouble between the North and the South, because of slavery?"

He said, "Yes, a body hears plenty of argufying on the subject and there's a fallin' off of Southerners journeyin' north except strictly for business. Planters aren't bringing their families

196

to sojourn in the Queen City and at the resort places like they used to. Reckon they want to show the North. Also they're afraid to bring their servants 'cause they're scared they'll get notions and be enticed away. There's a lot more running away than there used to be. They're getting help these days; there's some kind of a system a-operatin' to carry escaped slaves to freedom. Any hurricane about it in Rivertown?"

"They got up a terrific blow about it at the Lyceum one evening when they tried to debate, *Ought Slavery to Be Abolished?* Levi had to hold me down to keep me from spouting and I would have the next time only there wasn't any next time." Molly laughed. "The committee got scared and substituted nice safe debates like *Did the Allied Powers of Europe do right when they banished Napoleon Buonaparte to the Island of St. Helena.*"

Captain Cleve shook his head. "There's so much agitatin' again over this pesky question of slavery that I'm afraid for this country. It would take me from here to New Orleans to lay out the different angles but right now the hot potato is Texas. And it's not only Texas but all the new territories opening up by folks pushing west. And incidentally the South's not very smart to slap on these new wharfage taxes when the West is already pullin' folks and we're already paying through the nose with ad valorem taxes."

"Can't something be done?"

"Only if folks are willin' to study on the problem 'stead of just gettin' up a head of steam over it. Once they get it to the moral stage, the right and wrong stage, neither side listens to the other, they've already lined up. Take you for instance, reckon you ain't never questioned your right to own Matt and Julee in Rivertown but you're breaking the law when you do."

"I am?"

"Sure. Nobody has bothered you because most river county folks have always been sore about the old state ordinance against slavery."

"Captain Cleve, do you think I could have trouble over Matt and Julee?"

"It all depends on how stirred up folks get. There's some who think that this here secret system I spoke about a while back is a-operatin' through Rivertown. That could rile folks up, but there's a strong feelin' for the South here because of trade, so you probably won't have any trouble. Howsoever you better keep your ear close to the ground."

For some time Molly had been puzzled by the mysterious carryings on at Hester's. One evening toward candlelight she had dropped by her mother-in-law's to return a bowl. At the gate she met Mrs. Hopple, Mrs. Butterfield, and Old Miz Parsons, the wizard cutter of Rivertown's sewing circles. Molly spoke pleasantly to the women each of whom clutched a large bundle to her bosom. They acted huffy toward her, but she wouldn't have thought much about that. However when she went in the side door of Hester's house, following Rivertown's custom of entering unannounced, the indominable Hester seemed routed in confusion.

The room which was always so neat and tidy was in disorder: chairs were every which way, the table and floor a clutter of scraps as though cutting had been done hurriedly with no time for cheese-paring neatness. And Hester herself was trying to stuff large piles of cloth into a cupboard before Molly could see them.

The cloth, Molly noticed, looked like homespun. Ladies at a sewing circle never sewed on homespun. Homespun, used only for the roughest work clothes, did not lend itself to articles for a church fair, nor was it brought out to display before the public eye of a social sewing bee. And why on earth, Molly wondered, should Hester have so much homespun anyway, heaps and piles of it, with only Ira to provide for?

Somehow or other Hester had crowded the last of the coarse cloth into the cupboard and finally got the doors shut and shielded them with her ramrod back. It was odd to see her in so much confusion. Her hands clutched and unclutched the folds of her bodice as though trying to discover if she had lost something she had hidden in her flat bosom.

Molly, who had always been afraid of Hester, was astonished by her mother-in-law's obvious panic and a little sorry for her too. After this, she was certain, she could never hate Hester so whole-heartedly because after all Hester was human too, and run through with fear like anyone else.

"I brought back your bowl," Molly said politely. "Levi sent his thanks for the blanc-mange."

For answer Hester clutched again at the folds of her dress.

Molly tried again, "It is getting on to candlelight, I must hurry back to see to our supper."

And Hester let her go without having spoken a word.

All the way home and for some time after that Molly puzzled the question, "What is Hester up to?"

Then one day Asa Cranch, without knowing it, added another piece to the puzzle.

Molly had grown used to Mr. Cranch, even liked and enjoyed him, which was probably why he didn't mind telling her some of his queer ideas. Most Rivertowners, he said, treated him as if he was crazy, when he warn't at all.

Folks had begun to say that Asa Cranch was so mixed up you couldn't believe a word he said. He'd told so many tall tales about all kinds of imaginary cubby-holes he'd discovered in his search for religion that nobody would listen to him anymore.

Molly had got used to having him drift in and out of her yard, the out-buildings, at times even the house itself; she knew he was harmless. So one evening when she was airing herself on her front piazza, he eased himself down onto the top step, saying, "Clean tuckered out, I am."

"Have you been on a hard job, Mr. Cranch?"

"Yep. Miz Blaisdell said she had a mite of work she wanted done. But law's sake, it warn't no piddlin' job. I enjoyed it right smart though, what with one way and t'other. Thought I might be goin' to have to move on to greener pastures as you might say. Thought I'd turned up every likely place in Rivertown. Then by cracky if up don't jump a hull place I never even dreamed of. I never knowed Miz Blaisdell had that there big cellar to her house. She says when she first come here she used to be a-feared of buccaneers and bandits—even Indians mebbe. She said in those days folks allus had a way to get out if they got hedged up. You never seen that old cellar of her'n I reckon?"

Molly shook her head.

"'Course not," Asa said. "And don't reckon you'd find it now if you didn't know where to look in the woodshed. She said she had Gaithe dig a way 'tween the ole cabin cellar and the one under the house. But Gaithe left a-fore he got quite finished. I finished it now; that's why I'm so tuckered out. Guess Gaithe got kinda busy what with one thing and another a-fore he lit out for the West.

"Acted like he'd had a good stiff smell of brimstone, an' his ma a-drivin' him to do somethin' he didn't want to do."

Molly said quietly almost to herself, "Why would she want more cellar room?"

Asa overheard her and answered: "She said she needed more room, but shucks, now she's only got her and Blaisdell. 'Tween you and me and the gatepost I got a notion Miz Blaisdell's a mite teched . . . Well, reckon I gotta push off for home and supper."

Molly was left holding this large key piece of her puzzle. She was afraid to lay it down and fit it into the other pieces. She didn't really dare to look at the whole picture.

CHAPTER XXII

MOLLY HAD NOT SLEPT THE ENTIRE NIGHT. SHE HAD GONE OVER and over in her mind the problem of what to do about Julee, Matt, and little Quercus and was no nearer a solution than she had been before going to bed. She both welcomed and dreaded the break of this day.

Matt was in jail. Rivertown was in an uproar. And Levi, who would know what ought to be done, was down river with his '44 May butter.

In the pre-dawn darkness Julee's regular breathing showed that she and little Quercus were sound asleep on the husk mattress dragged in from the cabin and placed on the floor by Molly's bed. Julee had been afraid to sleep in the cabin now that Matt was gone. And with Quercus held tightly in her arms, she had said, "You gots to make this come right, Miss Molly." Then she had gone to sleep, leaving her mistress to struggle with the problem of owning black servants in Rivertown.

Not only did Julee look to Molly "to fix things right," but every Rivertowner expected her to resolve her dilemma to his own personal satisfaction. Her own wishes in the matter, if any, were not to be considered.

Some people said that Molly wouldn't be in this pickle if Seth Douglas hadn't ferried the stranger over from Kentucky in the first place. Some claimed Seth should have recognized a nigger stealer. Others said anybody could've told he was an agitator coming to Rivertown to stir up trouble over slavery.

If only Levi were home to tell her what to do, but he was

hundreds of miles down river where owning slaves did not present the problem it did in Rivertown. Oh! there were plenty to tell her what to do, every Rivertowner stood ready to give his downright opinion, oh! every soul knew exactly what should be done about Matt, Julee, and Quercus—that is everyone but their owner. And she was the one who had to decide and decide quickly. She couldn't wait for Levi's return.

Sam Higbet had summed it up when he said, "No blood's been spilt yet, Molly, but there's a parcel of puling, fanatical moralists in this town who favor themselves as chosen by the Almighty to invoke His Higher Law. They hanker for an excuse to arm themselves and rabble rouse against the South Side Viewers who they've decided carry two-pronged forks. There's a snag of trouble, Molly, and if you don't look out there'll be broken heads—worse if you don't get your man out of jail. Been readin' about some places havin' regular riots over slaves."

"But Sam, Matt hasn't run away."

"Sure everybody *knows* that, but folks let go their reason when they get stirred up. No, Molly, you got to get Matt out of jail. If you don't, in two shakes of a lamb's tail, folks will start knockin' the place to pieces, some tryin' to take him out of jail, others tryin' to keep him in."

"But Sam—."

"Yeah, I know, Molly, same as you do why Berman slapped your man behind the bars, but you better take him out of there before folks' passions stir up a fracas to set the Ohio River afire. We don't want trouble in Rivertown over your blacks."

Molly didn't want to leave Matt in jail but she didn't know what would happen if she took him out. He might run away; he might take Julee and Quercus with him.

It was pathetic to see Julee's terror. Julee was no help in her own trouble, she could only huddle in a dark corner with Quercus and tremble, too scared to peep out a window.

"Julee! Come, come, fix us a bite of supper," Molly encouraged her.

But Julee only cringed and said, "For Gawd, Miss Molly, don' make a light." So Molly brought cold corn bread and buttermilk, but only Quercus ate—Julee had "no feel for vittles."

Later when Molly went to see Matt, safe in jail, he was a

contrast to Julee. Matt was mighty proud that Rivertowners were argufying over him.

The townspeople had come out in the open and shown which side they were on. Oh! The South Siders hadn't pulled butternuts from their pockets the way they did in some places, but they'd let their side be known all right. And the black abolitionists weren't backward in shouting bitter words either.

Matt said, "Us heer'd Ole Mistus Hester come to us fight. Ole Miss she flutter, honk, and hiss like ole goose when her stole nest is found. Us like to bust laughin' every time us think of it. Ole Miss won't give us no hot bread, no bed, but her stick up for us black folks."

"Matt!" Molly spoke sternly.

"Yes'm."

"Matt, I want you to tell me exactly what happened."

"Yas'm, Miss Molly." Then Matt explained how he and Julee had gone after work for an evening walk in the town, leaving Quercus with their mistress to keep her company. Matt said that they both had enjoyed themselves a great deal strutting up and down on the streets with the white folks and looking in the windows of the shops. They covered the whole business district and window shopped in every store in town but, Matt stressed, neither he nor Julee had acted biggedy.

"Yes, Matt, I believe you," Molly said. "Tell me the rest exactly as it happened."

So then Matt explained that he and Julee were still walking up and down like before when they came to the alley between Walnut and Poplar Streets and then a strange white man suddenly stepped out of the alley. Matt and Julee would have brushed against him if they hadn't leapt back quickly. As it was, they never touched him, but the man was hopping mad. He swore at them and demanded a match.

At this point of Matt's story it flashed across Molly's mind that the man had wanted the Negro to give him a brush as an excuse for an altercation, and failing that had asked for a match. Anyone would know that a darkey wouldn't have one of those new friction matches. A block of locofocos was so rare that it was treated with great respect and guarded in a tin box; no colored man would have one on his person. "What did you say, Matt?" she asked.

Matt had explained he didn't have a match, but now the stranger said, "Then I'll give you one straight from hell! I'll learn you to make braggy answers." And right away he upped and struck Matt right across the face. Matt was scared and sure this must be a patroller after escaped slaves. In fact, he was so scared that he could not remember exactly what happened after that. Folks came flocking out of the stores and Matt told Julee to run. People got excited and yelled fighting words to one another. Some of them lined up with the stranger and said they were going to learn Matt his place. Others called, "Slavers! Slavers! Black bloody slavers!"

"Yas'm," finished Matt, "this am been a day! White folks fightin' over this nigger."

"Never mind, Matt," Molly interrupted. "You stick to telling your story of what happened."

"Yas'm. Mr. Boss Berman gits a-holt o'us an' says, 'Boy, looks like you got us a sure nuff fight. Git you outten here 'fore you lose you' black skin! Us know us kin trus' Mr. Boss Berman so us stick close to him. He make big talk both sides but all the while he jostlin' us outten the crowd an' bring us here to jail an' say, 'Mister Jailer Tuttle, you locks this man up to par-sarve him 'cause he might git hurt an' put folks in more of a pickle-muss than they's in.' An' Mister Jailer Tuttle say, 'Come along Boy.' Us some scared 'til us sees you an' know Julee Girl make it home. Us know you fix things right."

No doubt, Molly thought, Berman had acted wisely to whisk Matt into the safety of the jail, perhaps his black presence would have excited the crowd to violence and perhaps she would not have been able to break up the fight.

Actually she and Quercus had been sitting on the cooling board out on the river bank singing juba songs, when Julee came on a dead run. Julee ran so fast that her skirt tail stood straight out in back.

It was a garbled, exaggerated story Julee had told of the whole place strewn with mutilation. "They's fightin' in front, in behin', an' both sides, an' Matt he yell for me to run an' I ducks through an' makes the hot footses. Oh Miss! Tracks you self down there 'fore they takes Matt. He got no pass. That pateroller steal Matt—Oh! Oh! Us never see Matt again."

"Hide, Julee! Take Quercus and hide!" Molly shouted and ran

as fast as she could down to Main Cross. She guessed she'd have something to say if anybody stole her property.

She arrived breathless with haste.

Quite a large excited crowd was gathered in front of Johnny Briggs' store.

"Where's Matt? Where's my servant Matt?"

"Sh! Molly," said Gus Berman. "Matt's safe, I took him to jail. That cuss-holler stranger is the trouble, not your boy Matt."

The crowd fell back as someone shouted, "Here's Molly."

She stepped into the center of the ring formed by the River-towners and faced the stranger. She tightened her right fist and wished it held her riding crop. She'd love to lay it across his pasty-pudding face for having molested her servant Matt. This was only a dog of a man to be sent running on all fours with his tail between his legs. She addressed him furiously:

"You! You low-down southern white man. You aren't looking for your property, your kind never owned a Negro. You can't molest my servants."

The man shuffled his feet and looked to his Rivertown sympathizers for help, but got none now that Miss South was there. Under her tongue lash and haughty demeanor the stranger shifted his bellicose manner to one of greasy placation. He shamefacedly pulled off his hat and said, "Escuse me, ma'am, I didn't know there was any quality here-a-bouts—."

Molly snapped him up without letting him finish, "or you wouldn't have come to Rivertown. There's plenty of quality in this town and we don't want people like you coming in here making trouble."

She heard a murmur of approval run through the crowd so she hurriedly followed up her advantage. "If you're a patroller looking for someone else's property you have no right to cross the river, to set foot in this town, this is a free state."

There was a surprised buzz of approval followed by a shout from Rev. Staap, "It's free, we aim to keep it that way."

"I'm not a patroller, ma'am."

"Then what are you up to? You're a white rat of a man to come among decent folks stirring up trouble. You should have been hung when a potato vine could have done it."

"Go to it, Molly. Pour him back into his jug," shouted Johnny Briggs.

"Anyone can tell by just looking at you that you're as crooked as a ram's horn. There's no room for you in Rivertown. I'm telling you to go back where you came from and tell the people who sent you to keep you away from here. We don't want your kind around here. Get out and stay out."

"Yeah!"

The crowd took over.

"Yeah! He's a crook. Six jumps ahead of the sheriff."

"Light out for Texas, stranger."

"Yeah! Reckon we might tie you on the back of a mule."

"Riverin' him'd do better."

"Yeah!"

The stranger fell back a step or two and a dozen or so men led by Johnny Briggs moved slowly forward.

Johnny said, "You better git goin', stranger."

They headed him down Main Cross toward the river and the ferry. Like a suck-egg hound the stranger slunk out of sight.

And the crowd dropped off into groups to argue the case of the stranger Seth Douglas had ferried into their midst.

Everyone expressed his opinion freely to Molly. They said it in different ways many times over.

That evening Reverend Staap and a committee of ladies, Sister Parsons, Sister Hopple and Sister Butterfield, representing the abolitionists of Rivertown had lanterned their way along the Blaisdell puncheon walk to wait upon Molly. They sat on the edge of their chairs their backs stiff with the purpose of their mission. The women pulled their black shawls tightly across their breasts, folded their black mitted hands on their black reticules and turned their eyes upon their leader and spokesman, Reverend Staap.

In a pulpit voice he asked, "What are you going to do about your slaves?"

All four pairs of passionate eyes asked the question.

Molly asked, "How do you mean?"

Reverend Staap was a humble-looking minister, rather seedy in his black-turned-green clothes, but when he spoke of the moral wrong of slavery he was Nehemiah confessing the national sin and appointed by God to rebuild the country. He was sincere in his passion that slavery was a crime, a dark stain upon the fabric of the country.

Molly listened to his awkward homely comparisons of how the cleansing of it was to take place, as the rotten stone rubs the brass, as alum purifies the water, as the white-hot iron cauterizes the wound, so would the abolitionist rid the country of its abomination, and there was no better place to begin than right here at home.

It was soon apparent that the committee expected Molly to free her slaves. The minister voiced this general sentiment when he said, "Today you yourself declared publicly that this is a free state and yet you hold slaves."

"To all intents and purposes they are free. I would never put them upon the block."

"But do they have their papers of manumission?" asked Sister Parsons.

"Well, no, they don't."

"Then they're not free," snapped Sister Parsons.

"They wouldn't know how to take care of themselves if they were free. They need my protection. You saw today for your-selves that they aren't safe. They are in danger of being stolen and sent to the block."

"Not if they have papers."

"Papers can be taken from the helpless and destroyed."

"We'll see that they are protected, if you'll free them."

"Very well, suppose you can, how will they live? Will you, Reverend Staap, give them work, pay them wages so that they can take care of themselves, buy land, build a cabin, buy food and clothes?"

Reverend Staap hemmed, hawed, hitched about and said, "Times aren't too good. I have my own family to look out for."

Molly questioned each of the ladies with her eyes.

Sister Parsons said, "We talked it over, Molly, and nothing would have to be different. We're only asking you to manumit your slaves. We thought we'd let you keep on much as you are, let them live with you same as they do only they wouldn't have to work for you unless they wanted to, and if they did you'd have to pay them. They could work for other folks too. If we had them do anything for us we'd give them a little something, maybe some vittles or clothes."

207

A little something! So-o-o-o! She was to manumit Julee, Matt, and Quercus to become the slaves of the abolitionists of Rivertown. A fine how-do-you-do! She'd not free them to be at the beck and call of Sisters Parsons, Hopple and Butterfield. People like the Reverend and the Sisters loved the blacks only in the abstract. Like Hester who, when they were on her very own doorstep, would not admit them to her house but fed them outside.

Molly hung onto her temper; she knew she must not tell the abolitionist committee what she thought of their proposal. So she bowed them out with a promise that she'd think over what they had said.

It puzzled Molly that Hester had not come, well, maybe not with the committee, but at least called on her privately to issue an edict regarding Julee, Matt and little Quercus. Hester with her righteous air of condemnation had never hesitated to speak out on all other matters to her daughter-in-law. Why did Hester withhold herself now in a matter of such importance?

Then at last Molly was obliged to slip into its place the final piece of the picture puzzle. She could no longer ignore Asa Cranch's tale of digging the passageway into Hester's secret cellar.

Hester's house was certainly a part of that secret system operating to help runaway slaves. In Hester's house they were hidden. In Hester's house a secret sewing circle met to make clothes of homespun for the hidden slaves.

Questions, dark, ugly, terrifying questions popped and crackled through Molly's mind. Her husband's own mother! What about Ira? Did he know? Was he a part of this? Of a certainty she knew Levi was not. But who? Who? Who would help Matt to run away?

The true core of the matter was that she did not care to lose her servants by any method, she didn't want them stolen by some southerner nor made fugitive by a northerner. And she really believed that they wouldn't be as well off freed as they were with her.

On this last point Minnie Preble violently disagreed saying: "I'm not given to rabid action like some women in Rivertown, I won't lift a finger to help a slave escape but you got no right, Molly, to hold slaves. I don't see how you can own a human being. I just don't see how you can do it. I like you, Molly, and I've been your friend ever since you came to Rivertown but I don't know—if you won't free your slaves—I doubt if you can count on me any more." Minnie's eyes pleaded with Molly not to force her to such action.

The following day the bells of *The Rising Sun,* rung with authority by her pilot, Scoot, were a welcome sound.

Captain Cleve at ease in his rocking chair listened to Molly's story. "You're plunged square into this plug-muss, my dear girl. What do any of these folks, north or south know about slavery? The northerners read about it clear back to ancient times and marshal their facts according. But how many of 'em have lived below the Mason and Dixon line? Slavery isn't the simple thing some folks think. It's more than a question of right and wrong, profit and loss. Reckon a body would have to live in the South to know that it's not something that can be taken off or put on like a coat." And Captain Cleve enlarged upon the respective viewpoints of the North and the South.

To these abstractions Molly wailed, over and over, "But what am I to do about Julee, Matt, and Quercus in Rivertown?"

Captain Cleve narrowed his eyes and squinted at the river. Finally he said, "This rumpus will quiet down soon as they get Texas settled. Why don't you let me take 'em back to Quercus Grove 'til it blows over?"

Molly wakened in broad daylight to unusual stillness. She listened. She sharpened her ears and strained to take in the meaning of this new quietness. It was the absence of little familiar sounds. Lacking was the commotion and stir of a household breaking out a new day, the creak of the chain drawing fresh water from the pump, the tread of feet heavied with morning tasks, the fall of the axe, the splintering of kindling wood, the slam of a door, the rattle of the ash shaker in the Buck's Patent Stove, the clatter of the iron tea kettle set over the open stove hole, the crunch of the coffee grinder.

That Julee! Late again with the morning coffee! Julee was getting careless, taking on more of Matt's slack ways, she's have to take hold of Matt and Julee with a tighter rein. It would be her fault if they became of no account.

The silence was broken by a full, horse-size, long-drawn-out commanding neigh from Prince in his stable across the back yard. He was not giving a welcoming whinny; he was angry, letting loose his stallion trumpet, kicking, and stomping the heavy timbers of his stall. Prince didn't like neglect any better than she did. Matt had better get out to Prince before the stallion hurt himself.

Matt! Julee! Little Quercus!

Then she remembered. They were not oversleeping themselves out in their cabin. The cabin was empty. They were gone. Yesterday she herself had put them in Captain Cleve's care together with a letter to Uncle Philip asking him to take them until the ruckus in Rivertown quieted down. By now her servants were far down the Ohio River being carried back to the broad Mississippi. There was no Julee to bring to her bedside the round silver tray with its shining pot holding hot strong bitter-black coffee to be poured into the thin Sèvres cup.

Then Prince's repeated high trumpet call and renewed stomping brought her off her bed, into her clothes, and out to the stable to quiet him. She led him to the drinking trough where he pushed the stale water about with his nose and turned a resentful eye upon her and refused to drink until she had pumped fresh water into the trough.

On the way back to the house after she had given Prince more than an ample amount of oats and hay she saw Julee's cabin door standing open. If she didn't close it wild animals would get in, foul it, destroy it. The cabin was forlorn with the emptiness of hasty departure, bed tumbled, furniture out of place, rag rugs and shuck door mat askew. The fireplace where Matt usually kept a roaring fire was a wide black hole, the pot hooks above the gray ashes were empty, and black iron kettles littered the cold stone hearth. Molly hastily closed the door of the cabin and ran to her own kitchen.

From its accustomed place in the cupboard she took the gleaming silver tray with the coffee pot and dainty china cup and brought them to the kitchen table. She turned to the stove, cold and black. Behind it the wood box stood empty. She went to the woodpile for firewood of which there was an ample supply on hand but no kindling. Chips which she gathered into her skirt would have to do. She rattled down the ashes in the stove with angry thoughts for the smug Rivertown women who were probably saying, "How you reckon Molly Blaisdell's makin' out this mornin' workin' her own ash hopper?"

Well she'd show 'em! But the chips burned out before the heavier wood caught fire. So she gritted her teeth and stood up to the wood-chopping block as she'd seen other women do. She anchored a likely piece of wood against the block with the sole of her shoe, her heel firm upon the ground and came down with a blow from the hatchet, hoping she wouldn't split her foot in two instead of the wood.

The fire took hold with fresh chips and kindling wood. At the cistern she filled the great wooden water pail and found that she couldn't carry it into the house. She had to reduce it to her "Half-Pint" size.

How would she ever be able to do the housework with no Matt, no Julee?

At last in triumph she had made and brought to the kitchen table a pot of coffee to go with some leftover cold biscuits rummaged from a stone jar. Tears stung the back of her eyes but she would not let them flow. She gave a wry smile at the unused silver coffee pot. She laughed a little in remembrance of how she, Matt, and Julee had first set up housekeeping in this kitchen and how Julee wondering if they were missed at home had foolishly followed Matt's advice to stick her finger into her dish water, take it out and see what kind of a hole it left.

Swiftly Molly seized the silver coffee pot, stood on a chair and pushed it far back on a high cupboard shelf. She said aloud. "Us our own Julee now," and set to work to put her house in order.

That night she tumbled into bed a scarred woman from her battle with work. She had shovelled out Prince's stall, filled it with fresh straw, she had righted Julee's cabin, scrubbed, and scoured her own house, dusted everything including the exquisite figures on the pip-squeak music box. It was with considerable satisfaction that she said, "This *am* been a day."

CHAPTER XXIII

WHEN MOLLY TOLD LEVI THE STORY OF WHAT HAD HAPPENED to Matt, Julee, and Quercus she did not mention her own conviction that his mother was an active abolitionist in the secret system to help runaway slaves.

Molly lacked proof of Hester's fanatical enterprise; she only had her suspicions. If she conveyed them to Levi she'd probably stir up a heap of trouble for this would be one time when he would not "step around" his mother. Better to let a few slaves escape than to bring on a fight between Levi and Hester. Beneath her mother-in-law's prim severity was flaming passion, which if once fully aroused, could bring on disaster. If Hester's kind buckled on the armor of the Lord they did not hesitate to do violence, break everything to pieces when necessary. No, it would be better not to tell headstrong Levi what iron-willed Hester was doing.

Neither, Molly decided, would she try to find out if Ira was party to the runaway slaves. The less she knew about such things the better off they'd all be.

Levi, knowing nothing of all this, simply said, "Wish you hadn't sent off the blacks, Half-Pint. How're you going to make out without 'em?"

"Oh, I'll manage," she assured him.

"Reckon you can? Other women do—but—," he let his voice trail off. Plainly he wasn't convinced that she could work her own ashhopper as well as Minnie Preble or any other woman in Rivertown.

She restrained her impulse to tell him of her aching back, her arms pulled from their sockets, her cramped knees, her roughened hands. She found herself wanting Levi to believe that what other women could do she could do as well. So she said lightly, "Oh pooh!"

Levi rewarded her with a grin of approval and said, "Good for you, Molly. I always knew you had it in you. Ever since I first saw you with that cute little umbrella, I knew you had the makings of a true boatman's wife. Hurrah for our side! But look here, Punkin, if you aren't going to have Matt and Julee, why don't you sell them? They'd bring two—three thousand dollars, even Quercus might bring a couple of hundred."

Sell them! Sell Matt! Sell little Quercus! Even sell Julee! Levi had been in the South time and time again but he had no understanding of the gradations in slave owning. It was useless to try to tell him how she was tied to Julee by a thousand nerves, which were manipulated like puppet strings by Mammy Fay. Sell Julee! Even to think of such a thing was outrageous, but she couldn't explain it. . . . She said, "A Rutland doesn't sell slaves. A Rutland—."

"All right! All right! Forget it! Don't get to raring like a Rutland horse. I only thought—."

"Well you got another think a-coming."

Molly was surprised at how quickly the turmoil in Rivertown over her slaves subsided, neither side being particularly concerned about how she was managing without them except perhaps the jealous ones, who hoped that she was having a miserable time.

The abolitionists had grown exceedingly cautious. Reverend Staap ceased preaching on the subject. No one came to see Molly to admonish her for returning her servants to Mississippi, a slave state.

Only Minnie Preble, as gentle and soft as her gray Delaine dress, continued to plead with her about sending Julee, Matt, and Quercus south to Uncle Philip. One day to Molly's horror their differences of opinion grew to the shouting stage and both of them hurled words at each other without listening to what the other said. Minnie's usually composed face grew red; the cords and veins of her neck above the gray fold of her collar stood out angrily. Molly was shocked to see the transformation in her friend.

She cried, "Oh Minnie! Let's not you and me fight over this wretched business."

Minnie subsided but she was awkward and strained on leaving Molly's house. And after that when Molly went past the Prebles' Minnie didn't stick her head out her door to bid Molly to come in and "set up, take a chair." Nor did Minnie now run along the puncheon walk to Molly's when she, "had a minute to pass the time of day."

Molly saddened at Minnie's distant politeness. She missed her quick little glances of affection, her drolleries, her good will, and kindliness. There wasn't another person in Rivertown who could have hurt her as Minnie Preble had done by withdrawing her friendship, not even Salena Cranch.

As time went on Molly grew low-spirited and her early rising, without the help of the little pot of strong black coffee, grew more difficult. And presently, after a quick look at Levi's almanac calendar, she knew the cause of her wretchedness. But she supposed this would end like all her other pregnancies in a miscarriage. She had lost count of her disappointments, had grown weary of paying the price of the first miserable weeks only to have no reward for them. She dragged through the days and dreaded going through yet another mishap.

Then one morning she wakened bursting with a feeling of good health and well being; she felt glorious. She bounced out of bed and gave the old Buck's Patent Stove the kind of a shaking it hadn't had for many a day. No longer did the sight of white hog fat in the frying pan turn her stomach wrong-side out.

At the table she said to Levi, "My, but I'm hungry!" and ate a prodigious amount of bacon, fried eggs, grits, and biscuits.

Levi looked first at her empty plate, then at the last fried egg upon his own and said with a wide grin, "Here Miz Blaisdell, have another egg," as he slipped it onto hers. "You better get back your strength. It appears to me you might be eating for two. Reckon this one's going to stick."

The first time she felt the baby move within her body she laughed right out loud, patted her belly and cried, "Juba! Juba!" She wanted to run down Front Street, all the way up Main Cross to High shouting, "Juba, Juba, I'se cotched." She wanted everyone to know the miracle of the new life she felt within her and she longed to share with others her feeling of utter bliss.

One evening a few days after this Levi said, "The Prebles' have got a mighty sick young-un tonight."

"Which one?" Molly asked.

"Dan'l."

"What's the matter with him?"

"Ole Doc Everett can't make up his mind whether it's congestive fever or the quinsy croup, Cal says."

"What's he doing for little Daniel while he's 'figgerin' on it?" Molly knew that little Daniel Preble could easily die while ole Doc Everett maybe-yes-ed, maybe-no-ed. And while Minnie and Cal had more young-uns than they needed they couldn't spare any of them, least of all Daniel, the favorite.

But Levi was still talking: "Cal said Dan'l puked the calomel fast as they held his nose to make him swallow it. Doc Everett's bled him a couple of times, figures he'll do it again tomorrow if—."

"If Daniel is still alive!" Molly felt her own child move within her and her whole being cried out as she grasped the meaning of how poor Minnie must feel.

"Reckon that's about the size of it. Don't know how they'll get through the night; Minnie's right tuckered out. I told her I'd go get Ma right after supper to come set up with the boy."

"Why *Ma?*"

"Ma's handy in a sick room."

"So am I," Molly said, remembering the sick house at Rutland Hall and how she had helped Mammy Fay tend bowel complaint, the shakes, breaking-out, lung fevers, oh, all sorts of diseases.

"But you and Minnie aren't speaking, are you?"

"Levi Blaisdell, I'm ashamed of you, as if I wouldn't go to Minnie when she needs me." And with that Molly turned her back on her husband and went to look in her trunks for the mysterious herbs Mammy Fay had packed " 'gainst the sickness." Of course she herself had no idea what the herbs were, but they were labeled for the disease to be treated. Mammy Fay had made them into neat packages and had told her Young Miss to write plainly what symptoms each herb was to be used for and how to brew and dose them.

215

Levi said quietly, "I knew you'd never let a quarrel keep you away from Minnie when she needed you, Molly, and I'm downright proud of you, but maybe you ought not to go. Dan'l might have something catching. I don't want anything happening to you or our own young-un."

"Oh! I won't catch anything." But it was mighty nice nevertheless to know how Levi felt about her and their child she carried.

In a few moments Molly had covered the short distance to the Prebles. She went quietly into the sick room and put her arm around Minnie, who sat beside "Poor little Dan'l." He looked about done for.

Minnie let her body sag and rested her head against Molly's filled-out body. "Molly! You came!"

Molly patted her friend's shoulder and said, "There! There! We'll soon have Daniel out of this."

"Dr. Everett said there was nothing more to do. Not to call him tonight. He'll bleed him again tomorrow."

In a teapot Molly brewed Mammy Fay's herb labeled "Lung Fever." When she began to dribble it from a spoon between little Daniel's parched cracked lips Minnie let out a cry of protest, "Dr. Everett said not to give him even a drop of water, unless I wanted to kill him."

Molly paid no heed to this warning. Instead she gently pushed down on Daniel's chin and with great difficulty managed to get him to swallow the tea. Soon he was able to take a spoonful at a time, and presently Molly held his head up and put the spout of the teapot into his mouth and let him drink freely.

Minnie said, "My gracious, but he's thirsty."

After that Molly brought a tea kettle filled with sweet herb-smelling steam and rigged a blanket tent around little Daniel's head. Minnie didn't protest when Molly brought a basin of water and cleaned Daniel and his fouled bed. All she said was, "I wanted to do that but Dr. Everett said not to move him, he was too weak. Dr. Everett says there's nothing to do but bleed him and give him calomel. But if Dan'l's going anyway somehow I'd rather let him go as easy as I can. It don't seem right not to let him drink if he's that thirsty."

Dan'l's poor little body seemed to be on fire so Molly covered him lightly with a soft quilt instead of the hot feather-stuffed puff. All night every half hour she brewed fresh tea and let Daniel have all he wanted. She persuaded Minnie to lie down while she watched with a lone candle.

Toward morning she had a bad time when she sat alone with death. Little Dan'l went into a sinking spell, the high color of fever drained from his face, his breathing stopped, started, became rapid, stopped again. It was touch and go for the child. Molly wished she knew something more to do but she didn't; she could only hold her breath when Dan'l held his, and breathe when he breathed. Suddenly her own baby moved. Oh God! Save Dan'l! she prayed. She searched her mind desperately for any cure of Mammy Fay's she might have forgotten.

Perhaps she ought to call Minnie and Cal? No, she decided to wait a bit longer because it seemed to her that the child's breathing was a little more regular. She held the candle closer within the steam tent and thought Dan'l's color was less like marble. Slipping her hand beneath the quilt she found that his body instead of being dry and burning was moist and cool now. She pulled another quilt over him and tucked it in close about his little shoulders.

Then she watched until Daniel's breathing became regular and she knew at last that he was out of danger. Instead of the final waxen sleep he had fallen into a baby's delicious flushed nap. Molly uncramped her stiff body as the first streak of light broke through the window and she blew out the candle. If ever she had to sit through such a night with her own baby! Oh God! What women endured!

Later that morning Minnie declared gratefully that if anybody in Rivertown had anything ornery to say about Molly Blaisdell they'd have to reckon with her and Cal after what she'd done for their little Dan'l. "As for your owning slaves Molly, I won't let it stand between us because someday, I'm sure, you'll free 'em."

And after that horrible night Levi said proudly, "Honey, I knew you had a woman's hands." He had taken them and turned them over and looked at them, rather short fingered, somewhat square, calloused, bruised, and grimed by housework. Molly looked at them too, in some wonder that her hands, which soon would gently hold her baby, had learned so much about the art of being a woman. She was fulfilling herself at last and she thought she was rid at last of her old childish burden of fear. She was very happy.

There were endless pleasant talks with Minnie Preble about the virtues of tiny shirts and bands. And now Molly was grateful for the long meaningless hours spent at Rutland Hall with embroidery hoop and frame. Tiny stitches were full of meaning as they formed yard-long skirts of the finest cotton. Yards and yards of handmade lace like cobwebs were whipped onto the sheerest linen. Small pillows and little quilted coverlets were stuffed with the softest down.

Levi said, "You better have Dr. Everett."

"I don't want a doctor."

"Well, then, Honey, maybe you'd like me to send for Mammy Fay?"

Now, that's pure generous of Levi, Molly thought.

But when she recalled Mammy Fay's dolorous tirade about how dear little Mama died because of Papa's getting the doctor man Molly decided that she couldn't bear to listen again to that unhappy time of her own birth.

Neither did she want to be reminded through Mammy Fay of Papa's captious disposition, with his picayune objections to everything that she did, his carping spirit which never failed to warp her. No, she didn't want to give birth to her child in such an atmosphere. She wanted it to be born in an air of happiness. It was dear Uncle Philip who had claimed that happiness was to be found in the daily air we breathe. So she said, "That's mighty generous of you, Levi, but I'll make arrangements with Gramma Pilcher. Everyone claims she's the best white granny woman in six river counties."

"You do what you think best, Honey. I want my best girl to have everything. We mustn't have any mishaps, now that we've got this far."

She gloried in her first pains. Pain was a small price to pay for so precious a thing even when it grew to thumb-biting proportions. All but fainting she walked the floor at the direction of Gramma Pilcher. Finally, she had been bearing down for hours with the aid of a sheet fastened to the bedpost, Gramma Pilcher said, "Reckon we got to coax the wee feller a mite. Reckon he's skeered to come out on his own in this world of travail." Then she helped Molly, who was worn out and exhausted, onto the bed. "Hold real still, Honey."

Putting a goose quill up Molly's nose she blew a pinch of dried snuff up it. At once Molly started to sneeze prodigiously. She gripped her belly, where her skin was taut as a drumhead. Violent spasms seized her. She clutched her burden to hold it within her but it slipped from beneath her hands. In a moment she held only her own shrunken, loose-skinned, flaccid belly. She lay still now, a woman depleted, her strength sapped by the fierce struggle of giving birth to her child.

"That fotched him," said Gramma Pilcher. "Nothin' like a pinch of snuff to oust 'em of a warm nest."

Molly opened her tired eyes when she heard Gramma Pilcher say, "So you don't want to tell your little mama you're here?"

Oh my God! Had she gone through all this to bring forth a dead baby? She turned her weary eyes to Gramma Pilcher who held a red mite upside down by his heels in one strong bony hand, while with the other she clapped a smart whack on his little red behind. The thin baby wail was a mighty welcome sound.

Gramma Pilcher said, "That larned him he's got to do his own breathin'. He can't stop now 'til God stops him."

This was Molly's first look at her son. At the moment his appearance didn't tend to invite favor but he was flesh of her flesh, and bone of her bone. She closed her eyes well satisfied.

When Gramma Pilcher was ready to leave she told Molly babies warn't as much of a rarity in these parts as she might think. Hoosier babies had a way of growin' up 'tween the corn rows, so she shouldn't worry none. Granny further advised her to be careful a cat didn't come 'round to steal his breath away. She should give him suck whenever he hollered and in between let him worry on a bacon rind. Only Granny said, be sure and tie a string to it so's to get it back in case he swallered it. And finally she urged the young mother to start pot likker right soon so he'd likely survive. An' if he didn't it'd be 'cos the Lord seen fit to take him away. "What you name him, Honey?," she finally asked.

"Philip," Molly said.

Little Philip breathed happy air.

He was as beautiful as sunlight, as pleasant as flowers, exquisitely formed. "Look, Levi, would you believe it? He has exactly ten fingers and ten toes. Each has its own perfect tiny nail."

For the first nine weeks of his life Molly bit his nails instead of trimming them so that he would not live the life of a thief nor have to scratch for a living. Philip's blond hair grew long and silky but she would not cut it until he was a year old in order that his life not be cut short. She taught him to juba his hands right and left, up and down, before he could talk. Juba, juba were the first words he spoke. As soon as he could toddle he learned to dance to his juba. Truly Philip was a jubilee child.

By the time he was three you could see both his mother and his father in him. He had Levi's long fair body full of romp and gaiety; he thought life was made to his order and just for him. He had Molly's light impetuous movements.

Molly had him for just three years.

Then the women came, brimful of platitudes. Unwanted, unbidden by Molly, they nevertheless followed the custom of coming to sit in the house of the bereaved. They told her that her darling had never been hers. God had loaned him, only, and now He had taken him back.

CHAPTER XXIV

It was a bitter thing to be a woman.

She heard the whispers of the women who sat in her parlor, "She ought to give in . . . it's bad not to cry . . . what's gone is gone."

Molly, sat on a stiff straight chair in the bedroom, staring at the same spot on the wall, unable to rouse herself sufficiently to tell the women to leave. She wanted to be alone.

"Drowning doesn't hurt, Molly," everyone said.

How did they *know?* They had never drowned. Philip had reached out his arms to his mother to save him and she hadn't been there. Waves of despair washed over her now and pulled her down into a deep current of grief.

"God punishes idolatry," Miz Butterfield and Miz Hopple told her piously. They said Molly had overloved Philip, so God had taken him from her.

Nevertheless like every other Christian Rivertown woman these ladies did their duty and brought baskets of vittles to the grief-stricken house. They remained to visit in the parlor, the hall, and the kitchen, where Hester had taken over for her daughter-in-law.

Hester was ashamed that Molly didn't thank these people herself for the covered dishes, the cold bread, the pies, cakes, and cookies which they had brought to tide the Blaisdells over little Philip's funeral.

"She won't eat a thing, and there's more than enough, so you might as well set up and have a bite with the rest of us," Hester told the visitors at last.

It sounded like a sociable. In Rivertown even grief wasn't your own business, Molly thought, bitterly, as she listened to the rattle of dishes, the murmur of voices of folks at the festal board. "Pass the jell . . . Have some more chicken and dumplings . . . Her cake's a mite heavy . . . Too much saleratus if you ask me . . . Never cared for clove cake myself."

How could they! How could they! When her darling lay in his little white coffin out in the dog-trot hall. How could they! It was their fault that Philip had drowned. In her anguish she struck out at anything she could possibly blame. *Anything* but herself.

She should have been able to send him to Hester, his grandmother, while she struggled with her canning so necessary to the Blaisdell's welfare in the coming winter. But now-a-days Hester never urged Molly to come to her house. In a thousand little ways she let her know that she wasn't welcome. His very own grandmother had no time to care for adorable little Philip. So now Molly blamed Hester for Philip's death. Then too, Rivertown's new grappling hooks hadn't been very effective in locating the little body where it had lodged up against a sawyer in the river. So not only Hester, but the whole of Rivertown was a part of this crime. Her neighbors had pushed her into the position where she had been forced to send her slaves south. It was their fault that she had to do her own canning with Philip underfoot; it was the fault of those women who were passing so freely through her house, and those men who were standing about so awkwardly out on the piazza with Levi.

Oh! She could hear them, they even talked river and whittled boatpins while her darling . . . ! Molly's nostrils twitched when the women burned coffee in saucers and ran around with burning string in an effort to neutralize the stench of death.

Without rapping, someone opened the door of the bedroom and quietly came to where she sat staring at a spot on the wall. Minnie Preble's voice said, "I brought you a cup of coffee, Molly. You ought to eat something, keep up your strength—for the funeral."

"I don't want any." Why should she keep up her strength? For what?

"Molly, Levi needs you—you got to think of him as well as yourself. Cal just found him down in the shed mourning over those boots he had made for Philip. He told Cal 'He never grew big enough to fit them.' Cal said it like to tore him to pieces to see Levi cry and not to be able to help. It's a fearsome thing to be snared in a hole of self-blame. You ought to help Levi, Molly. It'd help you, too, to help him. Go take his hand . . .'"

Molly sat silent.

Minnie sighed, "Levi took a sight of pleasure in having a son to be a riverman."

There had been many a family hassle over this point. Molly always began, "No son of mine . . ." And Levi always came back with, "Don't mollycoddle the young-un," and he'd say to Philip, "Who are you?" Philip would answer, "Butter Blaisdell," and bend over, double his fists, and ram his head straight at Levi who, to the child's ecstasy, would pick him up by his middle and swing him end over end to perch on his shoulder and carry him off down the gully to the river workshed.

Molly, in agony for her son's safety, would beg, "Oh Levi, don't, please don't." But Levi said, "Gosh all fish hooks, Molly, he's a regular ripstaver."

Philip would turn round baby eyes at her and solemnly repeat, "I, a ripstaver, Molly, I, a riverman, a ripstaver riverman."

Molly would grab him, hug him, smother him with kisses and demand, "Who do you love?" Philip would shout, "You!" but he would pull away from her and run off.

Philip was a lively child. And as long as she could hear him juba right and left she had no great cause for worry about him. It was always his silences that sent her looking for him. In the beginning it was the impenetrable forest across the gully she feared. She had heard of children wandering off into that endless, overgrown tangle among the big trees. One child had been found way up towards Bluffton, his little dress in tatters, his little body scratched and bruised. But gradually Molly forgot the forest because time after time she had to go down the gully path to find her riverman baby.

With Philip underfoot trying to can the fruit sauces to perk up the winter's starchy fare was a hair-raising experience. He was into everything trying to help. Molly was terrified that the moment she wasn't looking he'd pull a scalding kettle over himself or that his little dress would catch fire, and then he'd be burned to death or scarred for life. That very thing had happened to the Carter baby. "No Philip—no! Don't Baby—don't!" Philip said,

"Levi lets me help." "Don't Philip, don't touch the pan of syrup—don't, Baby, don't!"

At noon Molly said, "Levi, I can't make any headway with Philip underfoot. Will you take him so I can get through?"

"Philip help Levi," her baby shouted, happy to escape her restrictions.

Philip had busied himself happily near the shed while Levi worked. Suddenly the father was conscious of a prolonged silence and went searching for the boy. Calling Philip's name, Levi covered the river bank, then headed for the house. . . .

It was five long nights and four long days before the searching parties found him. And then everyone said, "It's lucky the body fetched up on that sawyer or reckon it'd been carried all the way down-river, might *never* have been found a'tall." Never to have known what happened to Philip, never have had his body in the little white coffin to carry out to Cedar Hedge, never have his little grave to keep tended, never have a place where she could lie dead with her baby later on. For not all of her died then. Only a part of her died with Philip.

What remained lived on in a cold soup of solitude.

She tried not to blame Levi, for he grieved too, but one day she heard him whistling at his work down in the gully. She closed the doors and windows that she might not hear him. Perhaps it was true that men recovered from grief more quickly than women.

But Molly grew techy and wore her feelings on her sleeve; whenever Levi happened to brush her she would burst out into a storm of tears to be followed by days of huffiness. Days of soreness within herself made her jittery and crabbed.

Over the years their physical union had reached that perfection of husband and wife who have lain together often. Each knew what the other needed and expected in order to have satisfaction, and through their giving each lost self and became one with the other.

But now Molly was unable to do her part. At first she couldn't let herself go because thoughts of Philip dragged her to her own death wish—at a time when Levi wanted life and creation. Then the fear came upon her that she might conceive again; she vowed she wouldn't go through that all once more. She took preventative measures. She rummaged in Mammy Fay's store of supplies sent north with the bride, young Miss Mary Marie. Mammy Fay had said, "You have your babies when you want them." Molly found Madam Restell's Powders and studied a volume Aunt Lucinda had given her called, *Married Woman's Private Companion.*

Levi grew testy and said, "I don't know what's come over you, Molly."

Molly turned her back on the river as much as she could, but there was no way to avoid it, it was always there, a constant reminder of her own particular hell. After Philip's death, when she had first been able to lift her heavy eyelids and had seen the river, she had cried, "Levi, take me away."

"I can't Molly—the boat . . ." So he cared more about his chimerical steamboat than he did about the death of his son—about her.

She begged him to give up the idea of the boat, to sell out, to clear out, leave Rivertown. "I hate it here."

"I'm sorry, Molly. I know it's hard on you just now, but it'll grow easier. I can't leave now—this is where my chance is."

Levi had stopped off at a convention in Memphis and was all steamed up over a speech he had heard by John C. Calhoun. "He said if the present rate keeps up, by '86 we'll 'need forty-four thousand steamboats and flatboats to carry our produce and passengers south, and New Orleans will have sixteen thousand sea-going vessels docking there to carry the loads to foreign parts.' There's no better place in the whole United States than right here; I'm getting into steamboating at just the right time. You can't expect me to throw away the chance of my life."

She couldn't forgive Levi for being able to go on so easily after little Philip's death nor for his lack of sympathy and understanding of how she felt. She followed a dull round of household chores, done sloppily, with no spring in her step, no quick movements of her hands. All of her was tired.

Levi said, "You used to have a master hand for smarting up—yourself, the house, and the vittles, what's come over you?"

And when he ran into a bad piece of luck on a wheat deal she didn't care and had no sympathy to offer him in his clutter of trouble. She was too wrapped up in her own.

Because of rumors of privateers on the ocean, insurance rates had gone so high that nobody dared to ship the wheat Levi had contracted for in Cincinnati. Prices tumbled. He got forty cents a bushel for the wheat he had paid sixty for.

Molly didn't give a hang about the whole business and she only half listened to his fighting words against the whole country. "Warmongers!" shouted Levi. "I hope they fall in Satan's frying pan and their souls burn in hell."

He glared at her so fiercely that she roused herself to say, "Who?"

"Sweet Jesus! Don't you even look at the *Messenger* anymore?"

"I read more than you do. Who is it you want to go split brimstone matches with the devil?"

"The warmongers in Washington."

"Oh! That!"

"That! Do you call it 'that' when the whole country's being thrown into a war with Mexico. No good's going to come from it. Who wants a country nobody can use? Who wants to go fight Indians? Who wants to go bleach his bones in Mexico!"

But Molly didn't care where anyone's bones bleached, her own included.

Levi raged on against the president of the United States declaring, "We're Polked! We're getting thrown into a war with Mexico which will sicken us like so much poison and cost us fifty million dollars for the privilege. Damn fools!"

Then the real reason for his ranting was made clear. "By the time I get the money for her upper structures" (*her* being the steamboat) "her hull will have dry rot, won't be fit to launch."

Molly was too beaten really to take advantage of this wide barn door Levi opened to her; only from habit she said, "Leave the river, Levi."

But Levi was stubborn and having aired his shirt said, "Oh! They'll finish this war business quick enough I reckon; they'll go down there, splurge around for awhile in their fancy braid and buttons, kill a Mex or so, swap a horse now and then, and think they're old 'Rough and Ready.' This is nothing more than a setback." And once again he was raring to go with his sap coursing through his long powerful frame.

That evening he found her in the gloom, stiff and straight in her chair, the only sound the tick of the clock. He came and knelt beside her, tried to take her into his arms. She pushed him away, got to her feet and said fretfully, "Your supper, I must see to your supper."

Supper was a sorry affair, eaten in silence, the cleaning up afterwards negligently done. Then, automatically, because it was the next thing to do, she removed her clothing and went to bed where she clung in misery to the side rail.

When Levi came to bed, he moved closer to her than he had done in some time. He said, "Molly! Molly, darling." Thank God he didn't try to touch her. "Life has to go on, Molly. Believe me, I've done a lot of thinking. There are some things we can't understand, but one thing I am sure of: Grief shouldn't turn us away from life. You have to learn to roll with life. But you are turning away, Molly. You're in a kind of living death. Oh! My dear, my own one, try, won't you *try* to climb out of it? Come on, Molly, climb up, come with me. It's almighty lonesome without you. Molly! I need you!"

He laid his hand upon her hip and turned her toward him.

"No!" she moaned.

Then she lay passive as he gently had his way. She hated him for taking her like that. And she hated herself for her withdrawal when he was so good, so *right,* so tender.

Molly always thought that the new life she now carried had been conceived on that wretched night.

For the first time she hoped for a mishap. She even tried to bring one on by saddling Prince time and time again and riding him like a demented woman. She would come in and topple from his back in a sickening faint.

Nothing happened, nothing was shaken loose, no pain came to jack-knife her double. The pregnancy was repugnant to her and she blamed Levi because he had put her in such a fix.

She loathed herself for loathing Levi. So she picked fights with him, but could have wept for him when he wrote in his log book, "Can't launch my hull. No money for superstructure."

This time Levi literally had hit a snag. He had lost a valuable cargo near Goose Island when the bottoms of two of his flatboats were ripped out. He wanted to travel straight down to Washington and tell those fools what he thought of them for stopping the service which kept the river clear of snags and sawyers . . .

But Levi never saw her tears of sympathy for him. All he saw or heard were self-pity and fighting words. "You're a fool to stick with the river." She shouted at him, "If there's any animal that's harder to live with than you it must be a mule."

"What a way to talk! Thought you had a high opinion of yourself as a lady."

"You've dragged me down to your level with your coarse tongue!"

They tried to outdo each other with reasons why each should not have married the other—pure fighting words.

Her child quickened within her and her burden heavied as the weeks became months and one night Gramma Pilcher was sent for. Molly had come to her time.

"What you figger on calling this latest found?" asked Gramma Pilcher.

"I don't know," said Molly, frayed, at loose ends, all pertness gone from her.

"Seein' she's a girl why don't you call her after yourself?"

"No," was all Molly said. She had no wish to extend herself with any of her mixed-up names.

Gramma Pilcher cocked her head on one side, and looked at the scrap which lay across her knees and announced, "She favors Cory."

"Who?"

"Cory, Cory Blaisdell, the girl Miz Blaisdell lost when the cholera plague went through here. Reckon you never saw her; she was before your time. And when Miz Blaisdell saw this one a few minutes ago I could tell she was took with the same notion."

Molly didn't care if Hester named her Cory. To Molly she was an unpleasant baby through and through. Right from her conception not one moment of pleasure did she give. She was a puling, puking infant, and as Levi said, "Open at both ends."

Hester said, "It's your breast milk that ails her. It's like poison to her. Poor Cory Baby. You better wean her. Let me take her home and put her to rights."

Molly didn't protest; she let Hester claim Cory.

Matters between Molly and Levi were no longer strained to the cat and dog order but the physical bond with which Levi had held her from the beginning had slipped too many notches to hold her in security now. Once again she was plagued by restlessness and the childish need for escape—to run away. Without any regard for what Rivertowners might say she saddled Prince and rode alone far along the new roads that were opening up in the interior.

Now a fairly good road went all the way up-river to Bluffton. There was talk that it would soon be built into a regular turnpike, maybe eventually connect with the national road which presently would reach across country as far as St. Louis. They might even extend a branch of the Blufftown road right into Cincinnati to connect with the Little Miami railroad which ran north all the way to Lake Erie.

Levi had been right upset when he heard that some mail from the west had come overland by way of Chicago instead of going around by the waters of the Missouri, the Mississippi, and up the Ohio. Levi said some fool had made a mistake not to send it by the mail boats. He got real mad when Molly questioned him on how long it took the boats to make the trip and then pointed out to him that the overland route was three days shorter. "Bet they start carrying all the mail overland," she said nastily.

Levi replied, "Only a she-monster would think of such a crazy idea." He added with scorn. "And what would you have a railroad do when it comes to a deep gorge."

"Oh, cut off the trees level, and lay the tracks from stump to stump."

Levi looked his disgust. "And what would you do, Mrs. Railroad, when you came to a fine big river?"

"Build a bridge."

"Ha!" said Levi and slammed the door behind him.

Nevertheless business was on the up-swing. Unsettled international conditions due to the Mexican War had kept prices down. The Cincinnati commission firm again asked Levi to buy wheat. He said he would if they'd double his commission so he could recover his previous loss with them. They agreed.

So now he bought heavily at very low prices and held the wheat until the following spring when prices went shooting up like skyrockets. He got his double commission, and he was as happy with his success as a ninny with a little molasses. He claimed now to be, "no piddling man, I've done right good."

And on the day when Levi heard his first steamboat whistle he behaved as though he had a skinfull of liquor. Some folks said the whistle rattled the dishes in their cupboards; others, it was heard, went down on their knees thinking it was Gabriel announcing the end of the world. There were death-bed conversions at the sound of the blast but most folks ran to the river bank.

Levi cavorted up and down like a colt in high oats. He allowed he was going to show 'em what was what. "Just wait 'til they hear the whistle I'm going to put on *my* boat. By gum they'll know when I'm coming 'round the bend, I'm going to have me a blast that'll blow folks right up off their chairs and set them right down on the public landing to watch me round to."

"You better watch out, Mr. Smarty, or you'll use up all your steam blowing your whistle and you won't have any left over to run your imaginary little boat," said Molly acidly.

"You sure know how to squeeze the juice right out of a feller, don't you, Molly? Just because you've squeezed yourself dry, set around in your shimmy tail, you try to make me do the same thing. You don't want me to believe in myself; you don't want me to think I can build a steamboat. You want me to fail and then set down, a twin squash to you. Well, I'll thunder and scissor my way to hell and back before I'll let you do that to me.

"For God's sake Molly, stir your stumps and you'll feel better. Go on down to Main Cross and get yourself some new skirticoats. You used to trick yourself out real cute—but here lately—I don't know—. Get yourself a bottle of that fandangled perfume you used to use. I've got the money."

She just glared at him.

He shrugged his shoulders and said, "Well, suit yourself. Reckon it's your own business if you want to mope. But I'm not going to mope with you. I'm going to lay a new keel for my boat. Wouldn't feel right putting her fine new superstructure on those old timbers. Reckon they've got dry rot by now. Yes siree, I'm going to start all over again, right from the bottom."

She thought with bitterness of the ten long years of struggle for the boat, her lonely times as a boatman's wife with Levi far away, her delight when he returned, followed by her distaste for the routine life, the ceaseless whittling and the boatmen's talk.

If only Philip had lived! Philip would have freed her from her bondage of frustrations and fears.

She snapped at Levi, "What makes you think you'll make it this time? Another keel will dry rot like the first one; you'll knock that one down and another will rot-rot-rot."

"Don't you want me to succeed, Molly?"

"No!" she screamed.

230

He looked at her slowly, giving her a thorough going over. "You think I can't build me a steamboat?"

"Of course you can't." Her voice had the bite of well-aged vinegar.

Levi started to say something but didn't.

She thought she would drown in the silence. Then finally unable to endure either the silence or Levi's cold calm scrutiny, she shouted, "Quit staring at me! You're a sap not to know you're a flatted-out failure; you'll never have a steamboat. You're just a piddlin' man; you can't even get out of a log-cabin dog-trot house." Letting loose her storm of abuse was like getting drunk for some people. Molly paused, took a long breath, and then let go again. Her voice ripped, "You mud cat! You westerner! You river rat! You think you're going to wear the broadcloth, the gold braid, the buttons, and stand on top deck with a silver speaking-trumpet and call out the orders. I tell you you're never goin' to make it. You're just full of yourself and hot air. It takes steam, S T E A M, to blow a whistle on a steamboat and you will never set a boiler on any deck."

Levi made a lunge toward her and she thought for a minute that he was going to butt her with his head. She wouldn't have cared if he had.

Then he stopped and looked helpless and uncertain but only for a moment. "I've had plenty of set-backs, Molly, but I reckon no more than most folks. Reckon the worse one a body can get is when some one, say like a wife, belittles a feller, tries to take his sap right down, tries to make him not believe in his own self. You can't do it to me, Molly. I won't let you! I'm going to have me the God-damnedest biggest, whistle-est, shearest, engine-est, paddle-est steamboat between here and New Orleans and you can't stop me with your down-in-the-mouth talk.

"I don't like the way you've been carrying on, I just want you to remember that. Reckon I can't stop you from hawg and pantering your ownself but I'll be God-damned if I'm going to let you do it to me. You might as well understand first as last that I'm going to build my steamboat. I'll succeed in spite of you, Molly. It won't pleasure me the same as it would if you stayed on board, but I reckon I can get along without you if you're so set on going a-shore."

Molly listened back through the years. She heard the steward on *The Rising Sun* ringing his brass handbell and singing, "All dat ain't a-goin', please to git a-shore." She didn't answer Levi.

He stared at her a long time.

She answered with a stare of her own which told him plainly enough that she was "goin' to git-a-shore."

He dropped his gaze before she did and turned from her.

Yes, it was a bitter thing to be a woman.

CHAPTER XXV

So the summer of 1848 moved on.

Cal Preble, Sam Higbet, and a dozen stalwart rivermen with whoops and hollers had knocked to pieces Levi's old rotting keel. The oxen, Broad and Buck, snaked the heavy timbers out of the way. A new framework was built to cradle the new keel for Levi's steamboat. Broad and Buck, ponderous and slow, urged on by a gad snaked huge fresh logs into position. Fletch saws ripped through oak, poplar, black locust and Allegheny pine. Stout men bent their backs and waited for Levi's "He!-oh!-heave!" then lifted the heavy timbers into place.

Whoopity Boss Butter Blaisdell was having himself a whale of a good time. There was no holding Levi these days. He said prosperity was here at last.

The Mexican trouble was over. Levi himself had seen Santa Anna's saddle on exhibition in New Orleans. The bridle was silver gilt with massive ornaments attached; the pommel represented the head of an eagle made of solid silver plated with gold, its eyes diamonds, its skirt trappings decked out with all kinds of precious stones. Texas, a part of Mexico, California, Oregon now were all a part of the United States. Folks cavorted on high horses because the United States at last was fulfilling its Manifest Destiny.

Sam Higbet said, "Yeah we won, but like Ralph Waldo Emerson said, 'Every sweet has its sour.'" When asked what he meant Sam replied, "Who's goin' to decide what's to be free and what's to be slave? Suppose the Southerners start to move west who's to say they dassent take their black property with them? And what you

233

reckon's goin' to happen when these folks comin' down the Ohio meet up with them? Can't you kinda figger there's goin' to be a ruckus?"

The whole country seemed to be moving down the Ohio River. Immigrants, no place to sleep, little to eat, jammed the lower decks of the steamboats. They were mostly Irish driven out of Ireland by the potato famine and German revolutionaries fleeing autocracy, folks who came to eat and to be free in this great empire of plenty. They were packed in the boats along with fire brick, plows, wagons, nails, and furniture, with whiskey, tobacco, hides, and feathers, flitches of bacon and ham, butter and cheeses.

They were going to the Mississippi but when they reached the Big Muddy they'd go up-river to St. Louis. There they would make up their minds whether to fan out to the northern valleys of the big river, to go to the big bend of the bucking Missouri, to the foothills of the Rockies, even cross over and go beyond, or strike down the Santa Fe Trail to the great Southwest.

Sam Higbet said: "Yeah, the country's on the move, moving right into trouble. We can't seem to set up any government for the new West. We can't settle the argument of where to draw the line between free and slave. This country ought to go back and get born again, start over. But I reckon it's more of a job than folks are willin' to undertake. Folks are kinda short-sighted."

Molly, half listening to Sam's spouting, caught at his words "to be born again, to start over." Sam was stupid. It couldn't be done, there was no way to go back. A country couldn't do it any more than a human being could.

Yet sometimes as she sat squashlike in her chair, Molly was stirred by the sight of the immigrants on the boats. These folks were starting over again, making new lives in new places. Her mind began following them as Ira's did when he, in imagination, went along with the turns of the wagon wheels he made. In faraway places she saw them felling the trees, building their houses, planting—man and woman together like her friends Mr. and Mrs. Workum. If only she and Levi—! But of course she and Levi couldn't.

Levi was building a keel for a steamboat which he claimed would soon be ready to launch. He had decided to call the boat *Hoosier Girl*. Once he had mentioned calling her the *Molly B.*, but Molly had told him in no uncertain terms he might not use her name.

She had tried to shut her ears to the noise Levi was making with his keel building at the foot of the gully, but the crashing sound hit her body again and again, demanding attention. It wormed its way inside her bruised defeated spirit where it throbbed like an ulcerated tooth. She began to hear a rhythm in the noise. It was like a band playing urging her to march. There was the rat-a-tat-tat of the hammers, the chig-chig of the saws, the chop-chop of the axes, the whir of the bandsaw, the clang-clang of iron on iron. There was a crescendo of the men's voices when they dippered a snootful from the whiskey barrel set out by Levi and a diminuendo at evening when he paid them off the head of the empty barrel.

Each day Molly did less and less as fewer things held her interest. Even her daughter required little of her time, spending as she did most of her days—and even an occasional night—with her grandmother on Poplar Street.

One day Molly was surprised to realize that she had sat out on the cooling bench listening to the music of the men's work on Levi's new keel without even thinking of Baby Philip walking into the hated river. She was shocked to discover that this could be so.

Then came the evening when Levi said, "Think you could stir your stumps to put up Captain Cleve for overnight?"

"Why certainly, you know there isn't anyone like Captain Cleve. But why is he staying?"

"For my launching."

"But only the hull is finished."

"It's only the hull you launch."

"Oh, then it can't amount to much."

"Mebbe you better wait and see. Be glad to have you in on preliminarying the fixings, Molly."

"No thank you," was all she said. Levi could manage his own launching of his *Hoosier Girl*. She'd have nothing to do with it beyond going down to meet *The Rising Sun* and herself invite Captain Cleve to come up the hill to stay with them during whatever foolishness Levi was cooking up.

Captain Cleve said, "Sure thing, proud to. Wouldn't miss bein' on hand for the big day. You are my young folks."

235

She blurted out, "It's not *my* big day."

Captain Cleve's eyes crinkled. He seemed embarrassed because of the bitter words she had spoken. So she added lamely, "Oh! I just meant it was Levi's day."

"It's your day too."

"No it isn't."

"Sure it is, Honey. More so than most women." He leaned closer to her. "I've known you since you were a little tyke comin' on board my very first steamer. Your raisin' was more than a bit peculiar, but I allus figgered if once you got the chance to come to grips with the real facts of life you'd know how to take a-holt. Matters haven't been too easy for you, my girl, and mebbe a few things are still amiss, but you go 'long with Levi. He's real steady, knows how to take set-backs. It's mighty important in marriage that husband and wife are one person in good luck same as in bad."

Molly thought grimly, Yes, in marriage husband and wife are one person and that person is the husband. All a wife is supposed to do is put on her sunbonnet and go along with her man's notion.

Captain Cleve continued gently, "You go 'long on this launchin'." He grinned at her. "How you reckon us men get satisfaction from what we do 'less our women are prideful of us?"

So she was expected to clap her hands and give pleasant recognition to Levi's foolishness! Captain Cleve was a sweet old romantic who through the long years since his wife's death had grown idyllic over marriage. No sir-ee, Molly had no intention of going out on the river bank for Levi's launching; she'd button herself up in the house.

She paid no attention to Levi's preliminary arrangements. Once when Minnie Preble referred to it she told her she didn't know anything about such shenanigans so she was leaving everything to Levi. She told the same thing to Hester and anyone else who asked. As a result she was in no way prepared for what took place.

At first when a few folks drifted out onto the Blaisdell river bank she wasn't surprised; there was little enough in Rivertown to cause excitement.

But after a while Hester arrived and said accusingly: "Whyever aren't you dressed up? Folks are already on their way. Here, Cory, come to Gramma. I brought you your launching dress."

Too late Molly discovered that launching day meant open house at the Blaisdells'. Folks drifted on and off her piazzas, in and out of her house. They swarmed out on the river bank, jostled each other on the gully path, and crowded the river shore, and over-flowed Seth Douglas's ferry boat. Everybody came—the Lyceum-cultured elite, the Bible-thumping brotherhood, the purple-nosed profane, the lazy scoffers, the ever-hopeful whittling rivermen. They all came, the men white collared or red necked, the women laced to primness or wide-open for baby. The town's young fry came to get in everyone's way. Every old houn' dog, every ole hawg, an' every ole cow switchin' her tail.

Everyone felt fine and said, "Tolerable I thank ye, how be you?" "A great day for Rivertown, launching a boat. Reckon in time we might have a regular boat yard." "Yes sir-ee, takes a feller like Levi."

The Rivertown Roarers appeared, resplendent in their bright uniforms on top of their gay bandwagon, busily blaring their brass instruments. Behind them came Berman who without even a by-your-leave took over Molly's front piazza, the front yard, and the river bank. He set up long tables on which he piled free lunch for all. He set out drinks of light wines and small beer for the abstemi-ous and those too stiff to let go with red-eye and whiskey. But the real celebrating refreshment was the big wooden washtubs of eggnog, made, Berman declared to Molly, with the freshest eggs, the thickest cream, the upstandingest liquor, the fleckiest nutmeg. "Levi said I was to spare nothing for his launching."

Berman handed round new tin cups with the rich golden eggnog cascading down their be-dewed silvery sides. He urged the guests, "Step right up, Ladies and Gentlemen. First come, first served. Don't be bashful. Eggnog for all! No bottom to this here vessel." It was a party all right. But not Molly's. Not hers at all.

Nevertheless she found it hard to escape this over-hearty brashly jostling crowd. She couldn't bear to listen to their fine words of praise when she had had no part in this steamboat business. In despair she slipped down the gully road leaving Cory with Hester and retreated into Levi's workshed where over the months he had taken to spending more and more of his time whenever he was at home. At first he had made feeble excuses but presently he hadn't bothered to conceal that he had lost his appetite for her. Now in his workshed she realized how truly far apart they had grown.

If Levi weren't down-river they saw each other at table but they scarcely spoke. After the evening meal he went down the gully path where he tinkered later and later. When he came in she was in bed and if she wasn't asleep she pretended to be. Mornings when she wakened Levi was already up and had the coffee pot on the stove and was off down the gully path to his work and to play with that steamboat model which he was forever changing.

She noticed now that it had a new structure on top of the hurricane deck. She examined it more closely and saw that it was one very large cabin. Every other steamboat had a flat top the entire length of the boat. Levi *had* been clever to figure out a way to use all that waste space. She wondered how he managed to do it. What did he call it? He had more cabins than there were states to name them for. Maybe he'd call this new one Texas. It was big enough.

And maybe this time Levi would get his real steamboat built. If he let her it might be amusing to come on board and play the great lady—the captain's wife. It wouldn't be quite as good as being a Charleston belle-picker but she could blow herself up to be Rivertown's first lady. She'd go aboard Levi's steamboat and outdo the captain himself. She'd be Mammy Fay's kind of a lady. And she decided to start right now by watching this launching; she'd pretend it had been her idea right along.

The hull, side-wise to the river had been built on blocks shored up around the sides with two ways of heavy timber beneath her. Somebody yelled at Levi, who was trying to be every place at once, "Got her greased good?" Levi waved a hand and yelled, "Yeah! Rancid grease of hawg!"

Levi had slicked down his hair. He swaggered a bit while he inspected his hull as though it were an ocean-going vessel. He and Captain Cleve checked the timbers which would slide on the ways to make an easy coast to the river, and the ropes which would hold her until she was ready for the launching.

Importantly Levi ordered Cal Preble, Sam Higbet, and his other river cronies to their stations under the hull. With their mauls they knocked the "shores" out from under. Levi nodded to Captain Cleve with satisfaction when the lashings held the hull steady and Captain Cleve nodded back with a big smile for his fair-haired riverboy Levi. Molly, watching from the shed door, felt a twinge of jealousy. She had a dark ugly thought that somehow it wasn't quite fair for everything to go so right for Levi on his launching day. He and Captain Cleve were climbing the ladder to the deck of the hull for they were to ride her down the ways. And now when she heard the crowd shouting Molly felt like a little girl who had refused to go to the party and then wished with all her heart that she was there.

The crowd grew quiet and expectant until someone cried, "Speech! Speech!" Then everybody cheered and the Rivertown Roarers blasted their brass. Levi waved to the roaring mob, shook hands with himself high over his head and at just the right moment, palmed his hands for silence.

He began, "Fellow Snags, Sawyers, Stumps, and—Other Obstructions—." Molly supposed Levi included her in the last category for certainly she had never helped him except that time when she had acted as his clerk. The crowd loved Levi's spread-eagle speech, there was no holding them, they roared their delight at everything he said. He was their very own Rivertown boy launching his own boat. The Rivertown Roarers let out longer and louder blasts on their cornets.

"Launch! Launch!" Folks stamped their feet and their hands took up the rhythm urging Levi to get on with his fun.

Levi yelled, "Get your cups. Cups for all! Everybody at scratch!"

The crowd milled around to fill their cups for the toast, surged forward, and waited in silence.

In the shadow of Levi's workshed Molly waited too—empty-handed.

The crowd with cups at the ready, quiet and expectant watched Levi closely. A murmur ran around the crowd as it became evident that something was not to his liking. What could be wrong? He spoke to Captain Cleve standing beside him on deck and Captain Cleve nodded his head vigorously. Molly just bet Master Levi had forgotten something important, something which would wreck the whole business—wreck the new hull itself. He looked so strong, so tall, so much himself, and yet no longer the same for this obsession with steamboats had made him harder.

Up to this moment Molly had had nothing but bitterness for this launching. But now all of a sudden she found herself wishing that Levi would not fail in his moment of triumph.

Over the tops of the heads of the crowd she heard his bull-roar, "Where's that girl?"

"Molly! Where's Molly? He wants Molly aboard."

She could not run away. Men ran and caught her. "Here she is!"
"Bring her aboard," shouted Levi.

Willing hands guided her to him where he stood at the head of the ladder, captain of his hull, waiting to haul her on board for the launching. He took her hand and steadied her aboard. He said quietly, "You been running away from me long enough, Molly. I'm goin' to lick hell out of you if you keep it up. I won't have it. You're goin' to ride down these ways with me, Molly, whether you want to or not—I want you and that's reason enough." He held her in his strong left arm. Then he raised his right arm in signal to the men at the ropes below which held the hull of the *Hoosier Girl* draped in launching flags and bunting.

The men lifted new gleaming sharp axe blades. They waited.

Hoosier Girl's moment had come.

Levi shouted, "Cut lashings!"

As one, the axes dropped.

Hoosier Girl was free of the ropes which had held her. For a moment she did not seem to know it, then she gathered herself together. She moved. She stopped. Her flags and bunting hung limp. Molly felt Levi's body grow tense with fear that his *Hoosier Girl* wouldn't take the plunge. But the hull *must* move, Levi's feet pushed on the deck to make her. Molly found her own body tense, her own feet pushing. *Hoosier Girl* had to move—she *had* to.

At last the hull gave a great convulsive shudder. Moved! Poised again. Oh! Would she never gather herself for the plunge! She acted as if she were afraid to make the steep descent into the river. Involuntarily Molly cried, "Move! Don't sit there like a squash. Move!" *Hoosier Girl* moved and gathered momentum. Her flags and bunting lifted in the breeze. The Rivertown Roarers blared a fanfare for her plunge.

Hoosier Girl darted—

Down! down! down!

Levi yelled at the top of his lungs as he rode her down, "Hip, hip, hooray!"

Molly was silent.

Hoosier Girl struck the water with a mighty splash, rolled sickeningly, then steadied herself.

Great cheers went up from those on shore, "'Hooray for *Hoosier Girl!*'" They lifted their cups, "To the *Hoosier Girl!*"

Molly knew that more than a boat hull had been launched. A

new phase of her life was launched as well. This time she was going to be a captain's lady.

The big wave kicked up by the *Hoosier Girl* reached to the Kentucky shore. Hawsers were attached and she was brought back to her Indiana home shore to be finished, her upper works built. Over fresh eggnog the men declared the *Hoosier Girl* had ridden like a queen . . . she had lighted and sat on the water with the grace of a duck . . . she was a daisy . . . looks like she's got speed lurkin' in them timbers . . . Yep . . . how about 'nother . . . don't mind . . . not bad fur eggnog . . . not bad . . . tolerable.

That evening a proud, jubilant Levi wrote in his log, "Launched the *Hoosier Girl.*" He turned to Molly and gathered her close in his arms. He said, "A boatman's wife rides the ways with him. You understand?"

"I didn't suppose you'd want me."

"Punkin!"

That night she let Levi love her with the old vigor and felt vestigial stirrings of her former passion.

Through the days her idea of becoming a steamboat queen strengthened. She would throw herself into this steamboat business and surpass even the captain. If anyone thought she was going to stay up the hill in calico while Levi broadclothed and gold-buttoned himself, he was mistaken.

She had been unsuccessful in the first half of her life, her first cake had been all dough; but now she would build herself a life which would be all sugar and honey with a little molasses too. She'd made a mistake in not being Mammy Fay's kind of a lady from the beginning. Maybe it still wasn't too late if she hurried. Levi would make lots and lots of money with his steamboat; she'd get him to build a fine house. Goodness gracious there were many splendid mansion houses on the Ohio River; there was a handsome Greek Revival down Adams way which had cost forty thousand dollars and would make even Papa's eyes bug out. If Papa had been able to make himself a landed English gentleman in Louisiana, why couldn't she be a great lady in Indiana. She would waste no time.

The next day she looked in her mirror and was horrified at what she saw, an old doll someone had thrown away, instead of a woman who would be just thirty her next birthday. A wisp of a thing, short, thin, slattern in a full dull-brown calico work dress, her skin weatherbeaten brown underlaid with a tinge of yellow.

She took a hand mirror to a window and searched out the traces of crow's feet around her eyes, the wrinkles of a boatman's wife, forever squinting at the river, at the sky. Her hair had grown thinner, bleached, scraggly, without sheen. She put the mirror down and caught her lower lip between her teeth, puckered her forehead and looked at her hands, dirt creased, nails broken. She rubbed the pucker from her forehead; it wouldn't do to get perpendicular lines above her nose. She snatched the mirror which told her they were already there. Oh! Oh! Why had she let herself go so!

She locked all the doors and went to work. She built a big fire to heat gallons and gallons of water.

Hurry! Hurry! There's not much time; you're already an old woman. Unless you hurry, hurry.

She began with her hair. She washed and washed it with egg whites until it squeaked for her to stop. She rinsed it in vinegar and rinsed it again and again. In the last rinse she put some of the pink dye which she hadn't used for years. Just enough to be felt and not seen, the directions said. She estimated the right amount and hoped she'd not come out a fright.

Then she wrapped her head in a towel and ripped off her clothes. She took a hasty look at her sagging breasts, her thin body, and shuddered; she was nothing but an old ribbed cow. Maybe if she stuffed herself with eggs, cream and butter she could get back her figure.

She scolded herself for starting to weep over her broken body; tears left marks on a face. She must learn not to let her feelings show. She must keep bright of eye, make her skin satiny smooth with sweet-smelling salves, brush her hair to a burnish.

Next she put a mixture of white sugar, vinegar, and soda on her face and arms to bleach them. After a suitable interval she removed them and rubbed herself with lanolin paying particular attention to her poor, poor hands with their broken nails. She shook out her hair and brushed it one hundred strokes. She searched out a dressing gown and knew at once that she must go down on Main Cross for a Godey's *Lady's Book*, or better still she'd go to Cin (as everyone now called Cincinnati). A queen didn't buy in Rivertown.

Then dragging a chair to the the cupboard she searched the top shelf for her silver morning coffee set. It was badly tarnished so she cleaned it and then had to do her hands all over again. After that she filled the pot with fresh strong coffee and carried it and a tiny fragile cup with her to bed.

She told herself a woman was foolish to let herself go. When unpleasant things happened all she had to do was to harden herself to meet her own pain and discomfort and as for the troubles of anyone else she wouldn't pay any attention to them.

Molly was dismayed when she discovered that once again she had been "cotched" and was going to carry. But she quickly applied her new wisdom, she would ignore *this* baby as much as she could. Philip had had love, and Cory hate; this baby would have neither; it could look out for itself.

She threw herself into a fever of excitement over Levi's steamboat. It wouldn't be long now, Levi said, before he'd be making good on his promise of their wedding day. He'd ride her up to the front gate of Quercus Grove on his own steamboat.

Levi urged Molly to shopping trips in Cin in search of proper fixin's worthy of the *Hoosier Girl*. "I'll stick to construction, Molly; you go shop round for the gee-gaws."

Her mind was a whirl of pink and white flowered carpet for the bridal chambers, chandeliers of glittering glass drops, porcelain door knobs, walnut and mahogany tables and chairs, china, glass, silver and napery. *Hoosier Girl* was to be furbelowed and feminine in all her appointments. To this end Molly fevered herself to a fast and furious pace.

Levi went out time and time again with his flatboats awash to get the money to pay for those luxuries which Molly in a perverse frenzy bought for Levi's harlot, *Hoosier Girl* saying, "I thought you said you wanted only the best." Levi agreed he did and went down river with another load to get the money to pay for the furfuraw.

While he was gone Molly dressed to the nines and went down the gully path to see that the workmen were on the job in the morning and to pay them off the barrel head in the evening.

She heard a good deal about cut-offs, slides, balances, pistons, and poppets. The words had no meaning to her but she always listened carefully to the men. She put on an act of studying Levi's model and drawings of *Hoosier Girl,* and in the end she commanded them to do exactly what they had told her Levi had said they should do. She was amazed at her own cleverness and was dumbfounded at how easy it was to fool these simple rivermen. They all agreed that it would have been "on-possible" to build the boat without *her* with *him* gone.

So the *Hoosier Girl* became finer than anything on shore. Her guard rails were as lacy as the lace Molly had taken from her petticoat, starched, and hung on the model. Inside, her ceilings were coved, her beams and supports were grooved, filigreed, knobbed, scrolled, shell-worked, and flowered. Gold outlined her maze of broken and irregular curves, gold glinted every turnip knob. She was fabulous.

Editor Folsom almost did *Hoosier Girl* justice when at Molly's dictation, he ran a description of her.

"*Hoosier Girl,*" wrote Editor Folsom, "is a splendid palatial boat soon to enter the Cincinnati–New Orleans trade. Her measurements and equipment are as follows (Levi insisted on these): Length, 182 feet; breadth of beam, 31 feet; water wheels, 28 feet in diameter; length of buckets, 10 feet, 3 inches and 28 inches wide; hold 8 feet; she has four boilers, 30 feet long and 42 inches in diameter, double engines and two 24 inch cylinders with 9-foot stroke; she draws 4 feet light and hardly more than 8 feet with 550 tons of freight, her full capacity."

"Levi," Molly protested, "nobody's interested in those details, let's cut them out."

"Not on your tin bath tub."

"She has forty staterooms affording eighty berths, all apportioned to cabin passengers, the boat officers being provided with quarters in the ample stateroom top deck called Texas. This arrangement affords the officers opportunity of attending to their appropriate duties without the annoyance and interference of others. The staterooms are spacious, capable of being well ventilated. Their appointments in both taste and comfort are flawless, having been selected by the captain's lady.

"The agreements which are provided here can be commanded

244

by but a few in their homes ashore. Exquisite taste has dictated all the details. Everything about *Hoosier Girl* is of the best quality and highest finish; convenience and elegance are everywhere apparent. The floors throughout are carpeted in luxurious taste but none so rapturously as the four bridal cabins. No thought, care, or expense has been spared in the appointments of the cabins hymeneal. But all is in exquisite taste. Even the main folding doors which admit to the ladies' cabin, with their rich panel work, could scarce find a rival in the embodiments of the best architectural and decorative skill of that epitome of taste—old Charleston, South Carolina."

"Why put that Charleston stuff in, Molly? Don't mean anything to folks here-abouts," grumbled Levi.

"Of course it doesn't but it's to stay in."

Levi said, "Cut out the la-de-da stuff, put in the safety part. Folks want to know they're not going to get blowed up, burned, or drowned."

Mr. Folsom looked helplessly from Molly to Levi then decided in favor of Levi, and wrote, "*Hoosier Girl* is supplied with two of Evan's safety guards, one to each outside boiler. Her tiller and bell ropes are all of wire—"

Levi said, "Gosh all hemlock, it must be infernal to have your ropes burn and not be able to signal. Helpless! Put in about that extra hose I've got, a hundred feet to reach any part of the boat. And the life preservers!"

"The seventy-two table chairs have life preservers beneath their seats of such tested buoyancy that they are able to float two persons with ease. All door and windows, nearly five hundred in number, are of lifting hinges and can be detached at a moment's notice as additional safeguards in an emergency.

"Nothing is hazarded in the assertion that there never yet has floated, on the waters of the Ohio or the Mississippi, a boat equal in all respects to the *Hoosier Girl*. If this statement appears extravagant to any man of intelligence let him but visit her at her home berth in Rivertown and ascertain for himself that all the details herein described are correct.

"The discriminating will discern more things of interest than provided by Mr. P. T. Barnum. *Hoosier Girl*, a veritable floating palace, has cost her owner, Levi Blaisdell, Captain, not less than

$33,000.00. As soon as *Hoosier Girl* has completed her trial runs Captain Blaisdell expects to enter her in the Cincinnati–New Orleans service."

"Gosh all hemlock," said Levi when he read all about *Hoosier Girl* in the *Messenger*, "Folsom made a good spout about her."

CHAPTER XXVI

WHEN WORD GOT AROUND THAT A MAN IN CALIFORNIA HAD PICKED up a real gold nugget on the bedrock of a "crick" it was "O.K." (off to Kaliforny), singing a song to the tune of "Oh Susanna." Hardly a boat passed but Molly heard the rallying song of the gold rushers. Many, including Sam Higbet, went from Rivertown. Sam wrote from California that if you wanted to find out what it was like "all a body had to do was to go sleep in the woodshed for three nights with the door open and swinging in the wind, eat nothing but pork cooked by yourself over a smoky fire in your yard, on rainy nights move over and sleep between the currant bushes and the fence, on the fourth day eat nothing but mule steak, and on the next, if you wuz still alive and hankered for it, broil up a nice piece of dog meat."

Levi said they could have the whole of California; he'd stick to his *Hoosier Girl* where he'd take in the gold after somebody else had most killed himself getting it. When on a single trip a steamboat could pan out anywhere from ten to twenty-thousand-dollar profit Levi figgered he'd do all right without digging all day with his tail in the water, wetter 'n' colder 'n an old hound dog's.

When the states involved in Alphonso Taft's railroad plans forbade the promoters to incur additional indebtedness, Levi let out a long breath. "Whew! That was a squeak. By the next rumpus I'll be strong enough to fight."

In the meantime the last spike had been driven in a bridge across the Ohio. The states of Virginia and Ohio had been joined up at Wheeling. At the dedication ceremonies Barnum's Tom

Thumb had driven across the bridge in a fairy equipage, a carriage drawn by Shetland ponies, the gift of Queen Victoria. Now up at Wheeling, at high water, river captains had to lower their chimneys, at times even lie by. "We can't get under the durn bridge. They got no right to do that to rivermen. We want no bridges. Helps keep this railroad mania alive. What's more it's dangerous to navigation. Jacob Strader! Boats named for him! He's not a true riverman."

Levi got through blustering about railroads and bridges when Cincinnati weathered the railroad threat and remained what nature meant her to be—a river town. But he'd no more than finished spluttering about the railroads when the whole country blew up right in his face.

California wanted to come in as a free state and there wasn't another one to bring in as a slave state to keep up the tit for tat. Everyone was at sixes and sevens, red-hot arguments flew all around Rivertown. Abolitionists and butternuts were pepperpots whose blood boiled. Some practical jokers fixed a hoax for the "soul hunters," the southerners who came to catch and claim slave property. Six straw men were thrown together and hid in a sort of tent made of cornstalks. The chief "soul hunter" was tipped off where the prey was hiding. As a result quite a few heads got punched. Down on Main Cross folks opened their mouths to voice their opinions but neither listened to the other. All the talk merely served to strengthen prejudices already formed.

One day Cory said to Molly, "I won't do it, you're none of the boss to me." When Molly tried to force her, Cory screamed, "Soul owner!"

So that was what the women who gathered at Hester's to sew for fugitive slaves called her!

Matt and Julee had been south for seven years. During this period Molly had worked her own ash-hopper the same as every other woman in Rivertown, but to these same ladies she was still a soul owner of slaves. What Molly didn't realize was that her new-found interest in self-beautification and glorification had lost her any ground she might have gained with the ladies of Rivertown and they delighted in picking on her on any pretext. There was only one thing on which everyone seemed to agree: you had to choose sides, be a hot-head one way or t'other.

Captain Cleve said, "They'll destroy the Union. They've tried

it before. Almost happened in '30. I remember every mail we expected to hear that the southern members had left the hall, Con-
gress had broken up. It happened again with Texas—and now!"

Levi ranted, "Blood and tobacco! Why don't they compromise!"

The gentlemen, Messrs. Clay, Calhoun, and Webster did. Just
in time in 1850 they got matters arranged. California came in a
free state; Texas was paid ten million dollars to accept suitable
boundaries and allowed to remain slave. The abolitionists damned
a more stringent fugitive-slave law; slavers cried the division of the
western territory was unfair to the South. But war was avoided
and Levi Blaisdell's blood vessels didn't burst. "Blood and tobacco! A war between the states would ruin river trade."

And Molly, too, was glad there was to be no war to disrupt, to
interfere with her new plan to cope with life. For once she knew
exactly what she wanted to do. Everything was going to be just
right. It was what Fate had meant her to do all the time. She was
going to be a credit to the family—the Fee family in Charleston.
Nothing would stop her. Levi wasn't the only one who could go
full steam ahead. She had at last found that hard central core of
her being. From now on she was going to suit herself—even it it
meant leaving Levi, for she doubted if he could follow her into the
new life she planned for herself.

Large with her third child, she brooded on how to begin being
a Charleston Fee in Rivertown, Indiana. What was the quickest
way to prove that she was different from these Hoosiers? She ex-
perimented with her voice. She laughed in various keys until she
found a high tinkling sound which pleased her. She'd be famous
for her high silvery laugh. It made her feel wonderful—so confident. Why, she hadn't felt so sure of herself since the days when
she play-partied Gaithe! Her new tinkling laugh sounded familiar
—like the little bell on Tuck's neck as the colt's legs carried Gaithe
to the West.

It was a prime year. Hawg! Hawg! Hawg!

People in Adams bragged they had packed close to a hundred
thousand hogs; they'd be proud for their town to be called Pork-
opolis if Cin didn't want the title. The Blaisdells, too, came in for
their share of hog prosperity. On the last day of November, 1850,
Molly had to stay inside the tightly closed house because of the
killing going on in the slaughter house across the yard in the Blais-

dell alley. That day prosperity could be smelled. Malodorous! Between 6 A.M. and 6 P.M. Levi Blaisdell caused to be killed, dressed and packed 827 hogs. The biggest pork day ever! While other folks were still "figgerin' on it" Levi had the pork onto his flatboats and was off to the South.

Levi was a hustler all right. Full of ideas, too. Grandiose. Maybe he *could* build a line of steamboats like the United States Mail, the Express or the Good Intent, maybe he *could* be his own forwarding and commission agent, not have to knuckle under to the opinion of others, maybe he *could* quit dressing pork, a stinking business, use the slaughter house for a warehouse, maybe he *could* build a commission house, his own wharf, maybe he *could* be king of the rivermen, maybe he *could* make lots and lots of money.

All this side of the gully Levi could use for his business; over on the other higher bank Molly planned to build a fine house. She'd heard of a combination carpenter and architect recently arrived from Baltimore who could execute a masterpiece of Greek Revival. There'd be a two-storied portico with Corinthian columns, tall engaged pilasters would flank the front door facing the river. There'd be front parlors and back parlors with matching marble fireplaces and costly tinkling chandeliers. She'd build a house which would outdo Papa himself.

She was through trying to please others, she'd had a lifetime of doing as other people wanted her to do. And did they love her for it? They did not! It only made them love her less. From now on she'd do exactly as she pleased. And she'd begin just as soon as she birthed the baby she carried.

Levi said: "You better hurry up and have that baby or you won't be ready for the *Hoosier Girl's* maiden trip. From what I hear up and down river I reckon they stand a good chance of getting Barnum to lay over at Adams with that foreign singer, her name slips my mind."

"Jenny Lind."

"Yeah, that's it. I got the notion it might be a good idea to cash in on the occasion as a send-off for my *Hoosier Girl*. Thought maybe I might take a crowd down to hear her sing, not that she amounts to anything, but it's a good excuse for an excursion. So if you want to come along you better tell your young-un to hop out of his nest."

Within the week Gramma Pilcher was sent for, castor oil having set up the contraction of the necessary muscles. By the time Gramma Pilcher had changed her apron, thrown a pair of scissors and some string into her pocket, grabbed her "umbrel" and teetered along the Blaisdell puncheon walk, the baby was already born. There was nothing for Gramma Pilcher to do but granny off and tidy up a bit.

Lucy Belle was a good baby right from the beginning. She could be picked up, put down, without even having her cradle rocked. No one paid much attention to her and hardly knew she was in the house. She was a solemn baby with great concentration and intent who took care of herself. Philip had been a joyous child, always wanting someone to play with him, while Cory—well Cory remained a peevish sickly child still claimed and largely cared for by Hester. Molly often said she hardly knew she had two children. This fitted in admirably with her plans for becoming a beautiful woman walking slowly through beautiful rooms, pausing now and then, a gracious princess before her people, permitting them to gaze upon her royal figure.

Yes, at long last, she was entirely free to jump off into the future.

"Hello! Who keeps house?"

Molly narrowed her eyes, to identify the tall, lean man standing at her open doorway. His eyes were incredibly blue against his bronze skin, gentle eyes but far-seeing, reflecting the big sky, the far high mountains.

"Gaithe!" she cried.

"Molly!" He caught both her hands and swung them.

They looked questions at each other trying to size up their feelings. Gaithe's eyes shifted before hers. He hurriedly asked the usual questions of a member of the family long away returned home.

A crowd gathered to hear him spin out the yarns of his experiences out west where he claimed they measured pork by the cord and held mass meetings by the acre. He made Hoosier brag piddlin' stuff. Folks were moving west as thick as the wedged flocks of pigeons which passed over the Ohio every year. Didn't make any difference whether they were dragged, floated or driven, just so they got west.

Yes, he'd looked all around and still thought Oregon was the country for him. Out there the winters were mild in spite of snow on mountain peaks. And timber! Compared to Oregon firs, Hoosier trees were nothin' but kindlin' wood. You ought to see a Kaliforny redwood tree. Sycamores? Naw!

And down in the valleys right under the snow peaks you didn't have to *make* hay; all you had to do was go out and take it, and pastures were good the year round. Why cabbages, turnips, and peas grew all winter. And wheat! Forty to fifty bushels to the acre. Yes siree, that was the country for him. He'd taken over as sweet a parcel of land as a body could want this side of heaven; he'd come east to look around a bit before goin' back for good. He let his eye shift around the room, lingering a moment on each face.

Molly felt her heart beating faster at a Gaithe grown to be a man. This was not the strip of a boy stumbling all over himself at the sight of the loveliness of his brother's bride stepping daintily across the gangplank of *The Rising Sun,* nor the youth with his sap rising when he clasped her, frightened by the unknown, nor the lad made bolder by his pride in his new power, nor the man newly arrived at his torment who had released his passion upon Salena. This was a man who had traveled far, having one adventure after another. He had won the strength to be a whole man. How like Levi he was—or like Levi when she had first known him before they had drifted apart.

Gaithe would understand her, appreciate her as Levi never had. Once again they would sit in the parlor with the black and gold japanned tables holding the silver coffee pot and fragile cups. Once again she'd lead Gaithe in the amenities of civilization, but this time with oh what a difference—Gaithe was now a man! Everyone had laughed when Gaithe told about a group of men coming upon a woman's sunbonnet lying abandoned on the trail and how they had formed a circle and done a dance around it. Yes, she would let Gaithe back in the bright sunlight of her femininity—and perhaps . . . She turned her bright eye upon him, but it was at Salena Cranch, now aged twenty-seven, Rivertown's old maid, that he was stealing glances.

Pooh! Salena lacked style. She never had learned to take advantage of, play up, her dark hair, her big dark eyes, her magnolia-textured skin. She remained dowdy and old fashioned in dull-brown, fitted basque and gathered skirt. Long ago Molly had given up trying to cipher out Salena, who had come to some kind of terms with herself about Gaithe. All these years Salena had spoken of him freely as though he were just across the river prospecting for a farm, and might be home any minute. Her serenity was uncommon, as if she might be "teched" and after all there was her doodledy father. Salena had been a fool not to have kept her style apace with her confidence. Oh yes, in spite of all she had been through, Molly knew she could cut circles around Salena in attracting Gaithe.

Then Levi's Hoosier challenge to Gaithe's western brag, "What about corn?" brought her attention back to the conversation.

"Corn doesn't do so good," said Gaithe.

"Then you can't raise hawgs."

Hawg! Hawg! Hawg!

Gaithe said, "We got plenty of everything else; don't need hawg."

"Thought you said hawg was measured by the cord?"

"Well if it was hawg country it would be. If we get tired of eatin' sheep and beef we'll have hawg shipped out to us."

"It'd rot 'fore it got around the Horn."

"Send it overland."

"Naw!"

"Yep!"

"How in tarnation?"

"Railroad."

Bang! Down came the front legs of the chairs of the rivermen angry at the infamy spoken by Gaithe.

"I came through Chicago on my way home. Gosh all hemlock, you just ought to stand at the corner of Lake and Dearborn. Puts Cin in the shade. You're goin' to see big shipping in and out of Chicago. We'll get our hawg in Oregon, don't you worry, and we'll get imports too, straight from New York. It's a better importing point than goin' roundabout to New Orleans."

The very mention of New Orleans brought up that same old question, "What about slavery?"

"They got no use for it out where I been. We're the ones that's goin' to rule this country, the western plains and the Northwest; we're the ones that's got the guts. We're the ones who won this country; we've put too much of our backbones into it; we won't give up one single scrap of it. Out there we don't roll in the wealth of the North grown fat on white immigrant labor, nor of the South on their black. Out there we're men who believe in men—democracy. Out there we know the worth of our kind of government. We're goin' to hold this country together, we're goin' to keep it a whole country, we're not goin' to see the East and the South tear it apart." Gaithe stretched himself very tall and threw out his chest, "Yep, it'll be an everlastin' great country once we get it all fenced."

"You've changed the least of anyone, Molly," Gaithe said.

Molly had bided her time in which to claim Gaithe. She was in no hurry because she hadn't been able to quite make up her mind as to just how far she would let the matter go. There was so much within her to be assuaged. Her mouth filled with bitterness at the memory of her hurts.

She tinkled her newly acquired laugh and said, "Oh Gaithe, thank you, it *is* sweet of you to say so but actually I have changed a great deal. I must *look* older." She was so brilliantly sure of herself, that she even dared to call attention to her age. She had more than made time stand still, she had forced it to turn back.

She had drunk quarts of motherwort tea to quiet her nerves, taken hundreds, thousands of Peter's Vegetable Pills. Every night, ready to drop, she forced her unwilling hands to smooth the creams on her dry skin, to brush one hundred strokes on her thin hair. She was the first to hasten to Lovell's down on Main Cross to get the newly arrived batch of *Godey's* and *Petersen's* Magazines. She was the first to speak brightly, have-you-seen-, did-you-read. Through all her activities there now ran a bright thread of sophistication which made her feel vivid. She paid particular attention to her attire, spent hours upon it, yet she was unable to triumph over what she wore; she was extremely conscious of it, posturing and preening to show it off.

"I didn't mean your looks, Molly. Sure you look older, but you've kept pert enough. I mean you talk and act like you did when you'd just come to Rivertown."

She tinkled her laugh, "Perhaps I have only just arrived. Oh Gaithe, will you ever forget that belling?"

She skillfully led the conversation into a pleasant reminiscence, carefully recalling only small gaieties, nothing unpleasant. Oh! It was good to laugh with Gaithe. She patted the place upon the sofa beside her and said, "Come, sit beside me." She pushed the black and gold table out of the way. "There, that's better."

254

But Gaithe wasn't in a play-partying mood. He became serious to the point of being solemn—and his mind was on Salena, not Molly.

"Oh, Molly," he asked earnestly, "how has Salena been? You know it was bad, plain ornery bad, Molly, what we did between us to Salena. She's been cheated for years, Molly. And so have I. God knows if I can ever make it up to her—or if she'll even let me try." He heaved a big sigh.

Molly drew herself up, her eyes bright with anger and unshed tears of humiliation because Gaithe wasn't even slightly interested in her, anymore. "Well, if you're so interested in how Salena is— go to her—ask her yourself!" And she stalked out of the room, leaving Gaithe alone and astonished.

It was degrading, it was fearful, it was horrible to have Gaithe blame her for what he'd done to Salena. It wasn't true. No one ever understood her—her actions the least teensy bit. Why, oh why, did she always lose everything she cared about.

As time passed, Levi wondered at the coldness between Molly and Gaithe. They had been such friends before his brother went out west. He made a mental note to ask his mother what was the matter with her younger son.

CHAPTER XXVII

L EVI WAS IN HIGH FETTLE, RESPLENDENT IN NEW BLUE BROADCLOTH, gold braid and gold-plated buttons; a steamboat captain ready to command with silver speaking trumpet. His entire fortune, the result of years of hard work, was beneath his feet. He was sole owner of *Hoosier Girl;* by his own efforts alone he had brought her into being. She looked saucy, did *Hoosier Girl* on this April day balmy as a cart of newly mown hay. Her decks, glittering in the bright sunshine, which was reflected from the brass cornets of the Rivertown Roarers, were a-crawl with Rivertowners and country folks, men, women and children. Above decks, in his glass coop, was "Gassy" Sanders, a close-fit pilot, who claimed he was qualified to run *Hoosier Girl* on a heavy dew.

"Gassy" refuted the popular conception of a river pilot as a taciturn man alone in his glass house, his eyes searching the broad reaches of the tawny spring river, his feet feeling the throb of the engines, his hands with a sixth sense seeking out the vagaries of the stream, his ears listening to the swish of the water tumbling from bucket to bucket on the paddle wheels. A romantic figure— the river pilot.

But not "Gassy" Sanders. He was as talkative as an old woman who opens her mouth and walks away and leaves it. Shooting a brown stream from his mouth into a fine new brass cuspidor, he leaned from a window and called down to Molly standing on the hurricane deck, "Howdy, Miz Blaisdell. See you got your best foot foremost an' your best side out."

She tried to discourage Gassy's familiarity with a cool look. However he just shifted his cud to the other cheek and said,

"You've no call to get your wind up. I only meant a compliment —you're rigged up in such fine harness. But it 'pears you're goin' for to git a sprinkle of cinders."

Below decks a hot engineer was sending out of *Hoosier Girl's* filigreed chimneys great plumes of smoke made by the dryest ash and the richest pine not to mention a noisome load of rancid bacon to get up a big head of steam sufficient to blow Levi's signature on his fine big steam whistle and have enough left over to propel the *Hoosier Girl* to mid-stream. Molly fled below in a hail of cinders.

The little gun on the forecastle boomed, the band blared, bells clanged, the whistle blasted, winches squeaked, capstans whirred, shouts deafened. Above all was heard Levi's roar through his trumpet, "Let's go!"

Molly was again full of vim. She had recovered quickly from the set-down she had had from Gaithe. Fiddlededee to Gaithe! Her solution to her own unrest was so easy; all she had to do was go—keep busy, be brilliant, scintillate. She practiced her new smile of gracious condescension as she hurried down the stairs.

"Howdy, Miz Blaisdell." Howdy! Howdy! Howdy!

It was a mixed crowd on board. In addition to the elite there were those who had been born on the knobs, raised on whiskey with a mite of branch water, pone and 'possum. Coatless and hatless the men stood six feet, six in their mocassins. These folks down off the knobs were so old fashioned that they thought native shrewdness better than "book larnin'," that they were as good as anyone else, and that everyone had a right to do as he durned pleased. To be sure there were class distinctions among them, the superior and the inferior; the former shaved once a week, the latter once in two weeks. But on this special occasion all boasted clean chins.

"Howdy, Miz Blaisdell. Got a tolerable boat ain't ye? Glad for ye." They were sincere warm-hearted people wishing her well with whole hearts; they were not paying homage to her new glamor, the new swing of her little stuck-out derrière.

Close, but a little to the rear of the knob men, were their women, thin, sallow, old fashioned in dress and bonnet. During her bartering trips into the interior, Molly had seen the farm homes of these women, the milk pans a-glitter in the sun, the churn and pails scrubbed white, the few rooms neat and orderly, the spinning wheel with the carded rolls upon its bench, long tresses and skeins hung on kitchen walls, beds made comfortable from field and flock, the table set with transparent honey, chicken, eggs, "put-up" products of vegetable and orchard.

Shy, the women smiled and nodded their heads to show that they joined their men in wishing Molly well. She inclined her head graciously toward them, swept forward, paused, bowed, swept forward again. One woman a mite less shy than the rest stepped forward to voice her own good wishes.

Then all of a sudden everything in Molly turned over; all the sweet music of being the grand lady turned sour at the sight of this farm woman, Mrs. Workum. For her contacts with Mrs. Workum had stirred in her the ability to appreciate briefly the rightness and stability of family love. Philip had bound her snug, safe, and happy to Levi. With love and a new-found loyalty, with a continual sense of warmth and well being she had lost her old fears and restlessness. For that brief time, like Mrs. Workum, she had known love, fortitude, hard work, and gaiety. She had had security of the kind that no danger or failure could destroy—or so she thought until she lost Philip. Her first baby had opened new depths within her where now all was dark and lonely.

At the sight of Mrs. Workum all the might-have-beens rushed in upon her. Without warning, her old wounds opened and bled. She was dragged down, down, down deep within herself. Her eyes stared unseeing until a backward movement of Mrs. Workum's drew her to the surface again. Then Molly's nose twitched at the smell of shoe blacking on coarse cowhide too stiff and stubborn to take the grease. Otherwise she was detached, removed, separate, and alone.

She must not allow herself to be swept into any tender response to Mrs. Workum. She must school herself to be hard. Never again would she expose herself to compassion, a fellow feeling for any-one else. Tears came to her eyes—tears for herself, tears for her might-have-beens. She had to struggle to steady herself to maintain her new public manner. She bowed to Mrs. Workum and murmured "Nice to see you," as she swept past.

Some one said, "Uppity! Captain's wife! Folks won't stand for her being so high and mighty."

She tightened her jaw against the passengers' steady gaze; she needed privacy to regain her composure. She turned into the captain's cabin where she found Captain Cleve already in possession. He said, "I'm a mite tuckered with so much goin' on. Knew my young-uns wouldn't mind if I took over in here to rest a spell."

Her impulse was to turn and flee. Instead she said, "Oh, no, of course not." But she couldn't abide the further threat to her newly found hardness in the old man's troubled eyes which followed her every turn in the cramped cabin. She paused and tapped her fingers nervously on a table.

Captain Cleve said, "Yes, I get tuckered since the rheumatiz took me by the hand and that last spell of ague laid me low. Don't reckon it means anything. Be as right as rain 'fore long, able to do a hop-waltz with the captain's lady."

"Yes, yes." She firmed her cheek against the old man's obvious bid for sympathy and comfort. Nobody ever gave her any, why should she offer it to him?

Captain Cleve said, "A fine crowd aboard."

A fine crowd indeed! Knob men wearing nose-cloths—sweat rags—cotton bandanas worn over one shoulder with the ends tied under the opposite arms. These handkerchieves were used to wipe off an overheated face or a thumb and finger after a mighty pinch and twist on a nose.

Captain Cleve said, "I was tellin' Levi the best way to keep a good patronage aboard is to be determined they do as *they* please. If he's got a preacher on board put on a serious countenance for Sunday mornin' and order the chairs set out in rows with Bibles and hymn books and take a front seat for the preachin'. Let the others play poker, euchre, brag-whist, and dance in the evenin'. In boat business you got to recognize that in all trival things the passenger is always right—operate on the jug-handle principle, all on one side—the passenger's side."

Well, she wouldn't stand for any such nonsense; the passengers would do as she bade them; the captain's wife would see to affairs in the salons.

Captain Cleve grew jocular, "Say, what's that you're wearin' in front of your face?"

"A brown veil!"

"No! You don't tell me! A veil! Durned if I didn't think it was the crispy fag end of a buckwheat cake baked to death."

"Well, it isn't!" What a thing to say about the dear little veil on her kiss-me-quick bonnet!

Captain Cleve sobered again and said, "Honey, what you so scared of?"

Molly fled.

In the dining salon at the captain's table Levi said, "Captain Cleve, sir, will you do the honors, set at the head of the table?"

"That's tolerable nice of you, my lad. Thank ye kindly but it's your place, laddie; you've earned it. Set up! Take the captain's chair. It's your'n."

Molly had been proud of the dining appointments of the *Hoosier Girl*, the plants and exotic decorations brought from Cin tastefully arranged around the cabin transforming it, she fondly thought, into spring verdue and bloom where neither Bacchus nor Ceres could want for a thing.

But now, when she saw the passengers like great flocks of vultures light, swiftly sweep the tables clean, rise with flapping wings, she loathed the whole business. Gulleted, without savoring, were hundreds of pounds of fish, hundreds of broiled quail, blue-wing teals, boiled dishes by the dozens, ham, corned beef, chickens and pork. Macaroni in forms or plain, potatoes, roasted, fried or stewed in cream, asparagus, peas, pie-plant sauce, jells and jams, radishes and onions. Of pastries and desserts as many as you please, of pies, puddings, charlottes, ice creams and cakes. An ample supply of port, sherry, madeira and claret—even champagne.

All drank ice water. Only a few tasted the wines; only one in twenty drank champagne. What need had old citizens, their cheeks dyed purple, of light stuff at table? "Hog wash!" They had made frequent visits to the more familiar brass foot rail polished to the nth degree, where they could gaze in comfort upon the pink and white plural chins of Sol Witmore, the bartender. He knew how to build up with his pudgy fingers a man-sized drink 'stead of a piddle in a glass you could snap 'tween thumb and finger. This was scarcely an atmosphere in which to be Mammy Fay's kind of lady. No, it wasn't easy being a queen on a steamboat.

Captain Cleve said, "Mighty important, the que-seen of a boat." Molly hardened the lines of her mouth and gazed with contempt upon the poor creatures who were unable to appreciate the refinements laid before them.

Thus it was with grievances aplenty that Molly arrived at Adams for Jenny Lind's concert.

The whole business was a dreadful bust.

Toots, bells, shouts sprang from the *Prairie Bird, Blue Wing* and *Fashion* in welcome of the *Hoosier Girl*, a sister boat newly arrived on the river. *Hoosier Girl* steamed up, rounded to, and tied up, by the greatest luck in the world, right next to the *Ben Franklin* which had fetched Jenny. A lot of good that did anyone. In spite of the throngs swarming up and down the public landing calling, whistling, demanding a glimpse of her, Jenny stuck in her stateroom. The only satisfaction anyone could get was to look upon the Rockaway fitted up expressly for Jenny to ride in. Folks had come from all over, from up-river and down-river, they had come not only on steamboats but in johnboats from Indian Kentuck, Mud Lick, Beer Creek and a half dozen other places, on horse back, in wagons, on foot they had come. The most exciting means of transportation were the steam cars. Folks from the state capital had sat on sofa seats upholstered in red-cut velvet, just big enough for two on either side of a long narrow aisle.

"I want to ride on a train," Molly said.

"And get snaked!" Levi said you got snaked when an iron hooping nailed to the sleepers busted loose and came through the floor, twisted itself on, amongst and through the passengers, spitting 'em like larks, 'til it got tired and went out the other end or through the roof. "Stay off cars, stick to steamboats."

"What if I want to go some place that can't be reached by water?"

"There is no such place," Levi said.

Molly could not forget that it was a pork house in which Jenny Lind sang, in spite of repetitious assurances that it had been gutted and arranged in the best possible manner. Beams had been removed and iron rods substituted, strong bands of carpenters, white washers, paperhangers, painters, laborers of all sorts had worked for days fitting it suitably for a concert. Choice seats were the settees but even the ordinary ones were covered with blue cotton goods manufactured expressly for the purpose and a good thing too Levi said, "So you won't splinter your bare back."

Levi, the fool, had had the temerity to criticize her rustling silk and brocade costume with the new bustle cascading with ruffles and flounces edged with embroidery and fringed. Levi said, "Aren't you kind of bare upstairs? 'Pears to me you might slip over that lowest edge of decorum."

"Oh! Mind your own brass buttons."

"Don't like to see you turn yourself into a perambulating bundle of dry goods. You've done something to yourself, Molly. I can't put my finger on any one thing, but you don't look like a she-woman. You've let yourself get too bony."

"Why wouldn't I be thin, bearing children, doing all my own work, helping you deck out your harlot steamboat."

"What in tarnation's name's got into you, Molly? What's happening to you—to us? I thought you'd got over your mopes."

Mopes! "Oh! Shut up!"

"Hush, Molly, don't let the passengers hear us. Come on, we'll be late if we don't go."

For weeks she had thought of being a queen on the *Hoosier Girl*, of sweeping down the aisle at Jenny Lind's concert, the envy and curiosity of everyone. But now she pressed her bare back against the rough blue cloth of the chair and looked about her— at too many red necks. They hemmed her in, bound her, held her a slave to their boorishness. It swept in upon her what she had done to herself. She had cut herself off from the culture and re-finements of her own way of life; she was alone, marooned with a bunch of red necks while in far-off places there was glamor, a Crystal Palace, recently opened by Victoria and her beloved Al-bert, where one could see the Kohinoor Diamond, carved ivory tusks, jades and porcelains from China, Persian rugs, the queen herself.

Molly thought bitterly, "And here I sit in a gutted pork house." This was no New Orleans Theater with elevated and commodious parquet, encircled by loges, grilles, tiers of boxes and galleries, supper rooms and ballrooms. There were scalding tears at the back of her eyes, but she would not let them fall. She had too much pride, and she did not want tears to spoil her new-found beauty, different, but beauty nonetheless in spite of what Levi said.

The trouble with Levi was that he'd never be any different. He might put on blue broadcloth and gold braid, shine his gold-plated buttons brighter than gold itself, but everything about him, like his new boots, talked so loud he gave himself away. He remained and would always remain what he had been that day he stood in his coarse homespuns on the levee in New Orleans—a flatboater, a river rat!

Just then Levi whispered coarsely, "Been figgering. Calculate this here place'd hold nigh onto twenty-five-hundred dressed hawgs and likely folks take up about the same amount of room. Reckon nobody's seen this much dressed hawg all at once. Worth a sight of money."

Queen!—of hawgs!

"I can't understand what in the name of pickles and human nature has got into you, Molly."

They were in the captain's cabin and something told Molly that she and Levi were going to have another of their fights. She felt her face go tense and haggard. This repeated quarreling and fighting took a relentless toll of one's looks. In time it would lie exposed for any and all to see. Levi was driving her to become a thin hard woman without love. He had no idea what an effort she had put forth to become the queen of his steamboat, how determined she had been to love her role. Did Levi thank her for it? He did not; he disapproved of everything she did.

He began criticizing her the very evening of Jenny Lind's concert. His refrain never varied: "I don't know what's got into you, Molly, I just can't make you out. Why'd you have to go and spoil folks' pleasure with your belittling remarks about Jenny? Folks were having a right good time talking things over 'til Miz High and Mighty had to elocute *her* piece."

"She was terrible. Divine my eye! Warbling! No looks!"

"She's a neat, respectable-looking girl, not uncommonly ugly. She's got a clear powerful voice, goes leaping from note to note. Don't make any difference to her how many lines, spaces in between, she can do as she fancies, has fun tricking with herself. But that's neither here nor there, the point is you had no business arguing with the passengers. You can't do it, Molly."

"Oh! For heaven's sake, Levi, let's not go all over that again, if you've told me once you've told me a dozen times to toady to the passengers."

"I don't want you to truckle to 'em. All you've got to do is to make 'em feel you're glad they're aboard, make them comfortable, 'stead of every time you sit down at table looking as if you had a stink under your nose. You behave as though the folks around you were to blame for it."

"They are!"

"For the last time I'm telling you, Molly, I won't have it. I've got to think of my *Hoosier Girl*. I can't afford to have you on board, sticking your nose in the air. When you come back from your visit to your kin, Quercus and Rutland, you're going to stay up the hill—I won't have you on board."

"What am I supposed to do up the hill, sit and wait for you?"

"Don't reckon I'll be coming, Molly. I don't have much pleasure up the hill. You've kinda drained me off over the years. Reckon we're through."

"Through!"

"Yeah! We've been through for a long time, hadn't you noticed? It ought to have meant something to you, our drifting apart. I've tried, Molly, but it's no good when the trying's all on one side."

"Well, I like that! All these years! The things I've put up with—gone through."

"Yeah! That's what I mean, Molly. You never think of anybody but yourself, you ought—."

A rising rage made her scream at him, "When have I ever done what I ought to do?"

"Reckon I could name the times on one hand, Molly, easily. There's something wrong with you. You never face the music; you always run away. Some day what you run away from is going to catch up with you; it always does. I used to think you'd grow up, quit being a young-un, face up to life, but I reckon you can't. So you just have yourself a good long stay down south."

"What are you tryin' to do, get rid of me?"

"I've been figgering this is a good time for you to have a nice long visit with your papa. I don't want any talk. Folks will think you're stayin' down south because I'm too busy getting started with my *Hoosier Girl*."

"She's a harlot!"

"Reckon you're right, Honey, right as rain. And by God I love her and I get more loving from her than I ever got from you. You're right, Molly, I've left you, I'm no longer faithful to you in my mind —I've lost my appetite for you. If I had any doubts I don't have any now—looking at you. You don't even have the grace to look worried. You don't even look scared of anything ahead."

CHAPTER XXVIII

"It won't be long now," said Gassy Sanders to Molly who watched from the glassed gazebo pilot house of the *Hoosier Girl.* She was looking for her first glimpse of Quercus Grove. "We're comin' right along, made good time through that last cut-off, made up the time we lost pumping up water in our boilers. Reckon you're gettin' almighty anxious."

"I'll be happy to see my kin."

"How long's it been?"

"More than thirteen years."

Gassy turned from the wheel to give her a closer scrutiny. He shot a stream of tobacco juice throught an open window of the pilot house onto the roof of the Texas and said, "You keep better'n most." He turned to Cory scrambling over the pilot house bench and asked, "Who you goin' to see, Honey?"

"Slavers!" shouted Cory.

"Cory!" Molly reached out in anger and gave Cory a hard smack.

"Slaver! Slaver! Black bloody slaver!" shouted Cory at Molly.

How *had* she ever produced this impossible child! Why had she brought her! She should have brought only Lucy Belle who lay asleep like a freshly nursed kitten in her cradle below. But Cory! I should have left her with Hester, Molly thought. But how would she have answered the question of the kin, "Cory? Where is she?" She couldn't tell them that Cory was more Hester's child than her own, that Levi's own mother hid escaping slaves in her cellar, fed them, clothed them, and passed them on

265

to the North. No, she certainly could not tell them that she had had bitter words with Hester over bringing Cory with her.

She and her mother-in-law had crowded one another in saying those things which each had kept suppressed, for too long a time perhaps. It was Hester, lacking Molly's younger resilience, who finally was goaded to the breaking point. "Your family are slavers, black-bloody slavers."

It was unfortunate that Cory had heard her. She was a miniature Hester now hurling words of hate at her mother.

But Gassy Sanders just winked a wicked eye at Cory and said: "You better watch out, where you're goin' them blacks are liable to rub you all over with goat butter if you don't do 'xactly as they say, and then you're no better than a doodlebug."

Cory said defiantly, "No they won't."

In a bright loud voice Gassy said to Molly, "That's our Quercus Grove chute comin' up on the right, Miz Blaisdell. I'll make my crossin' any minute now. Used to take my bearin' on a big lone oak tree at the point. It was swept away awhile back."

He must mean the oak tree where Molly had watched for Levi in those faraway days. And now it was gone. And now Levi was making good his wedding-day promise to ride her up to the front gate of Quercus Grove on his own steamboat. Life was certainly ironical!

Levi had said, "Sure, sure, I'm willing to give your kin a welcome on board, keep up the outward appearances for the time being so long as you understand how matters stand between us."

She had told him not to worry; she was just as through with him as he was with her. And furthermore she knew now that if she'd had any sense she'd have walked back onto *The Rising Sun* the day she first landed in Rivertown. Levi said he wished to God she had; things would have been a sight easier for him without her plaguing him all these years.

Since Molly had been away up north her correspondence with kin had been rare. There had been times when she hadn't had the means to send letters marked paid, nor later to purchase the required adhesive postage stamps. Once or twice a year Papa wrote still little notes which told her nothing; Uncle Philip less often, but giving invariably a full account of his family. The children had scattered, left their parents' roof, the girls to follow their husbands, and the boys to set their own ridgepoles. Cousin Buford, the eldest of Uncle Philip's boys, had brought home his bride, Miss Sidney Carroll, one of the Carrolls from up Greenville way, the year after Molly had left. They had produced a new batch of "kithin' kin." By now word must have gone round for the others to come home for a family reunion.

She'd never let on to them how matters had stood for her through the years, those days when she never saw a copper, those days of lean rations, the set-backs, the sorrows, the many, many bad times with Levi, nor this final break with him.

Now she'd pretend that all was well with her, wife to the captain of a steamboat, dressed in high style, able to queen it like a Charleston belle-picker with a little extra something of her own added. Quercus Grove eyes, big and little, would bug out at the excitement. Wagon loads of Rutlands would be down to meet her, the field hands in their Sunday clothes turning hand springs in anticipation of the barrel of whiskey Captain Levi would roll off the *Hoosier Girl* and set up on the river bank for them. And Julee! Oh! How good it would be to see Julee again! Oh! How wonderful to be waited upon again! To push Lucy Belle and Cory into trusted black hands! To sleep! And ah! to waken to the delight of being handed a tiny cup of strong black coffee!

Molly swept past the passengers crowding *Hoosier Girl's* lacy guard rails to take up her position at the top of the main companionway stairs where she would greet her kin and guide them to the main salon for refreshments. At her nod the band struck up "Home Sweet Home" and the little cannon on the forecastle was shot off.

This jubilation was rewarded by the appearance at the Quercus Grove landing of one carriage, one wagon, both empty save for their drivers, and a lone figure on horseback who dismounted and came aboard to be greeted by Captain Levi at the gangplank. Molly strained her eyes toward the plantation road but could see no clouds of dust set up by a procession.

"Here's your Cousin Buford, Molly," Levi said.

She hadn't recognized the boy with whom she used to race horses across far-flung fields. Cousin Buford was skinny as a rail; the cords of his neck stood out under his thin brown skin which was tinged with river-fever yellow. He looked pop-eyed and jaundiced, his hands fidgeted with shaking fingers. The thin, eager, jumpy boy had grown into a twitchy, old young man.

Cousin Buford told Molly that his parents sent their compliments to her, their returning kin and her husband, and they waited to welcome them beneath their roof, but they didn't feel quite up to making it down to the boat to meet her.

Levi said, "I'm downright sorry to hear that, Cousin Buford, because I planned to lay over a couple of hours to entertain the kin on board the *Hoosier Girl.*"

"Yes, Cousin Buford, let's send for the kin, the servants, the field hands. This is a celebration." Molly pretended she wanted them all to see *Hoosier Girl's* gleaming white fretwork, her lofty stacks crowned with gilded oak leaves, her bell with five-hundred silver dollars in its casting which sounded the sweetest, clearest note on two thousand miles of river.

Cousin Buford said, "Thank you, Cousin, perhaps another time."

Levi said, "In that case you better collect your young-uns, Molly, and get off. I'll be pushing along."

Uncle Philip and Aunt Lucinda had just plain given up, leaving the management of Quercus Grove to Buford and his railing wife. Everything was a sorrowful shock to Molly—the unclean pans in the cool house, the humpy cloth in the weaving shed, the lack of supplies in the store room, the increased number of bunks in the sick house, the leanness of the stock. "Why, Cousin Buford?" "The soil's gone, get poor crops. I want to sell out, but Father won't budge. He won't sell one slave, so we're overstocked. I put them out to slowpoke their way through a day. Not a one but is a master hand at inching down a row." But the greatest shock of all to Molly was Julee, a dark dull stain of her former self.

Julee said, "Lordy! Matt, Quercus, and me sure am glad you gits here 'fore it too late. You got to take us away from here."

So, after a short depressing visit, Molly gathered together her children and her slaves—now numbering eight (Quercus had acquired five little brothers and sisters since leaving Rivertown)—and went on to Rutland, stopping off in New Orleans to pick up her personal possessions deposited there for her by Levi before he sailed back north.

Molly approached this new phase of her life with determination; but in the heat of her compassion for Uncle Philip, and faced with the sorry state of affairs at Quercus Grove and her fear of what might become of Julee if left there, the hardness with which she had tried to armor herself began to melt. She would be a good daughter to her father in his declining years and an exemplary mistress of Rutland Hall. Unfortunately Papa had other ideas.

Nothing much had changed at Rutland Hall except that the little fly-sweep Ambus was now a handsome stalwart of seventeen years and waited on table instead of swinging above it. Horatio and Mammy Fay seemed not to have aged at all and Molly felt young and helpless again, gladly turning over to Mammy Fay the care and disciplining of her little girls. In a way the life was immensely comfortable and soothing, but with it all Molly felt tense and apprehensive.

In spite of her brave front, Papa immediately guessed the reason for her return. He understood that she had made a permanent break with her rough-neck husband. And in his old cold, unfeeling way he proceeded to order her life to suit himself. Within a few days of her arrival, Papa called Molly to the library and waved her to a stiff Chippendale side chair.

"Your arrival has been most opportune, my dear. I should not have grown weary of your delay. For I knew it was only a question of time—only a question of time—until you would give up your incongruous marriage."

Well! It was one thing to feel that way herself, but she didn't enjoy Papa glorying in her misfortune. Furthermore there was something vaguely alarming about Papa's calm acceptance of her return to the parental roof. She was soon to learn the reason for his philosophical attitude.

"For some time I have been formulating a plan," Papa told her. And then he proceeded to explain, with much historical background and embellishment, how that they would return to England—whence the Rutland family should never have departed—reassume the Stuart title which had been allowed to lapse generations ago, and fulfill the destiny which would have pleased Papa's dear Papa who had been buried beneath the epitaph *"Opposed to the Federal Constitution."*

That night Molly, her fingers tightly interlaced, faced the black oblong of her window to examine the images, dark and ugly, reflected there.

Papa had answered all her questions. He had thought everything out. Little Cory, for whom Papa had noticed Molly had little love, would be shipped back north to the Blaisdells. The baby, who could be molded into a lady, might go to Quercus Grove. It would be preferable if Molly entered her new life child-less—this would facilitate a new alliance. Mammy Fay would accompany them. The rest of the slaves would be sold. With the moneys received from their sale, and the sale of the livestock and the plantation, they could live in a suitable style once they got to England.

Molly thought of the luxury of the life Papa painted, even the glamor. And then she thought of the hardships of the life she had led for the past thirteen years. She remembered Levi's strong rough hands on her body, the ecstasy and completeness of their lovemaking, the joy and grief of little Philip's life and death, the reality of managing her log cabin house—these things would be totally incongruous in the paper-doll existence that Papa vizualized for her. Even Lucy Belle wouldn't fit. And Cory!

My God! she thought. I'm like Papa. I have done to Cory just what Papa did to me! No wonder Papa did not find it fantastic to urge her to leave her husband, abandon her children. Papa was only recognizing his own qualities in her.

So the next morning Molly told Papa she was going back to Rivertown.

Seldom had the present ever existed for Molly; it had been no more than an in-between time. She was always going back to what might have been or forward to what was going to be. Now, however, she was face to face with the bleak present. In the cold reality of here and now she was forced to make a decision. Neither choice held any warmth for her. She had to choose between the hopelessness of an incomplete life with Levi in Rivertown or the hopelessness of no life at all with Papa in England. She decided on Levi and Rivertown.

Molly had to wait several days in New Orleans for the *Hoosier Girl* to dock. When Matt burst into the hotel where they were staying to announce the boat's arrival, Molly was galvanized into action. In very short order their luggage was assembled and bag and baggage they departed for the levee.

"Julee, Matt, keep the children, stay with the luggage while I go tell Mr. Levi we're here. He'll send deckhands to help you all get aboard." Molly wondered how she would begin to ask Levi's forgiveness for all the mean things she had done to him over the years. That he would forgive her was inevitable—he always had.

She picked her way over the crowded levee toward the smoke-stacks of the *Hoosier Girl*. The gangplank was in place to provide a boardwalk from shore to boat; the marquee was unfurled and erected before the gangplank. Beneath the marquee on the levee planking the red carpet was laid. A high desk was placed on the carpet, and at the desk stood *Hoosier Girl's* highest-ranking officer—Levi—his back toward Molly. How easily he wore his blue broadcloth, his gold braid and buttons! Her heart stumbled, her steps slowed at the sight of her boatman. Her failures as Levi's wife crowded in on her. Realization of failures didn't do any good if it came too late. Everything good in her cried—let it not be too late!

"Oh Levi! My Levi!" she said softly to the upright back. A fine straight back had Levi.

He turned quickly. At the sight of her no welcome lit his face. The line of his jaw set with teeth clenched, an expression of deep-seated dislike settled upon his face. He did not speak.

Uncertainty spread through her, unraveling her new-found thread of confidence in meeting life. But she said quietly, "Levi, I'd like to go aboard, if I may, and when you can I'd like to talk with you about us."

"There's nothing to say. It's all been said."

"But things have changed. I've changed."

"Umph!"

"But I have, Levi, I have. I want to tell you about it."

"I don't want to even speak to you."

"Oh! Levi, you don't understand. I'm ready to stay up the hill—be a boatman's proper wife."

"You're not fit to be any decent man's wife. I know now the kind of woman you are."

"I know, Levi," she said humbly. "I've done nothing but make mistakes."

He gave a bitter laugh. "Mistake is too mild a word, Molly, when you truck with a man's honor."

Molly puckered her brow. "Honor? What do you mean?"

"Oh, Molly, stop acting so innocent. Ma's told me all about

271

you and Gaithe—what a fool I was—and poor Salena! Now I know what ailed her. No wonder she wouldn't go west with him! Well, thank God that's alright now. They're married and heading for Oregon—no thanks to you. There are plenty of ugly words for women like you. I'm ashamed I ever married you. Now take yourself off and go back to your Pa."

"Levi, what you're saying is outrageous—melodramatic. Your mother misunderstood my friendly interest in Gaithe. I'm going on board; we'll discuss this later. There are so many important things I want to tell you." She turned to the gangplank, but Levi got there first and barred her way.

"No you don't. You'll never set foot on my *Hoosier Girl* again, nor in my house."

"Levi, Levi, please! This is all a horrible mistake." She took a step forward to make him give way.

He shouted to the mate, "Haul in the gangplank. Cast off the lines."

The crew leaped to the captain's bidding.

Levi waited until the *Hoosier Girl* had a good three feet of water between her and the levee before he jumped aboard her.

Molly leaned far out over the ever-widening water. But the *Hoosier Girl* turned in the channel and stood up-river.

CHAPTER XXIX

Levi dealt molly a crushing blow that day in new orleans. He had torn her heart apart and shattered her feeble grasp on another new pattern for life. Her first reaction had been one of anguished bewilderment. Numbed, unable to eat, she had sat for days in her room at the hotel. "Plumb flatted out," Julee told Matt.

"Us oughts to do something," said Matt. "Mr. Levi's had hisself time to get back."

Molly roused herself and said, "Go again to the waterfront, Matt, ask questions. Don't come back until you get some word of the *Hoosier Girl.*"

Matt returned very disheartened, "Miss Molly, us talks to boatmen ups and downs the levee. Some say they seen dat little ole *Hoosier Girl* at Cairo, but she head up-river to St. Louis and St. Jo. They say Mr. Captain Levi take his boat out of the New Orleans trade. He go now 'tween Cin and St. Louis. He come no more down to New Orleans."

Julee whimpered, "How us gits home iffen Mr. Levi don' come?"

Molly waited in her chair and sent Matt time and time again to the waterfront. But it was always the same answer, "no *Hoosier Girl.*"

One day there came a knock at the door. It was the manager of the hotel, and when he had finished his polite conversation, Molly sat with a very flat purse in her lap.

"We must move," she said dully. "Matt, go to the waterfront and find us a cheaper hotel."

273

But when Julee saw Matt's choice of a bare, comfortless room destitute of carpet or curtains, she said, "Rottendy!"

"It doesn't matter," Molly said, "where or how we wait, just so he comes."

"Us hungry," Julee complained. But it wasn't easy for Molly to feed Cory, Lucy, Julee, Matt, Quercus, and all the little ninnies. "What you reckon Mammy Fay trick out to tempt you' papa's appytite for dinner?" Julee tormented her hungry self.

"Do you want to go back to Rutland?" Molly asked.

"Lordy Jesus, no! Us wants to go home to Rivertown an' run us a livery stable, like you promise."

Molly's plans for the future had included freeing her slaves, which she had already done, and the establishment of a profitable business in Rivertown. She and Matt knew horses, and with the interior developing as it was, a livery stable was almost a necessity in the area.

Julee went on, "Mister Captain Cleve take us if he knew."

Then all of a sudden Molly's bewilderment left her. The power of her heart and mind returned. She realized she must act, she must sit here no longer like a squash. She was Levi's wife, she didn't belong in a grubby hole on the New Orleans waterfront, she belonged in her own home in Rivertown.

"Matt!" she shouted. "Go out on the levee and watch for *The Rising Sun*. Watch sharp! We're *all* going home—to Rivertown."

It was incredible how high the grass and weeds had grown along the path, the front steps to the house. The pink of the conch shells scarcely showed through the grass; the gray of the piazza steps was scarcely visible behind the tall rank horse weeds. She walked steadily and straight through them and entered the dog-trot hall between the two log cabins.

There was a great deal to do to restore the condition of her house to a woman's order. But when she had finished straightening things out an enormous fear grew in her that Levi did not intend to return.

He wrote her: " . . . I've heard you've gone back to Rivertown. Reckon you've got the right to live there if you want to. I won't stop you. And I reckon it is lawful that I should send you the wherewithal; a man provides for his children and you can eat alongside of them. Ma has promised to keep an eye on the children's fetching up. But don't be fooled, Molly, just because I'm man enough to do my bounden duty. I'll do no more . . ."

It was heartbreaking to see the *Hoosier Girl* round to for her landing down at Rivertown's public wharf, hear her bells jangle, hear Levi roar orders through his captain's silver speaking trumpet, and yet give no sign that he knew she was up the hill waiting for him. He'd pull out and go down-river again. Once she put all her pride in her pocket and went down the hill, but Levi's rebuke was chilling. Only silence and a cold look of aversion.

The day the *Hoosier Girl* steamed up with one of the newly invented calliopes called a "Kal-e-ope," Molly rushed out onto the river bank. A "kal-e-ope" was perfect for Levi. It stood on the top deck and was played by old Fiddler Jim who used to fiddle for Levi on his flatboats. Jim wore muffs on his ears, heavy leather gloves on his hands. He stood in front of the keyboard with his body well pulled back and his face turned half away as if he was scared to death of the durn thing. He came down on the keys with his gloved fingers letting loose such clouds of live steam that it was a wonder he wasn't parboiled. Sharp piercing tones overpowered every other sound. Blares bounced off the top deck and fanfared across the water, rollicked all around Molly —a regular sockdolager kind of noise—commanding, compelling —a Levi kind of noise. Such a noise could mean but one thing— Levi was ready to forgive her.

She couldn't hurry fast enough down to the landing. But again she was rewarded with the same cold look of distaste and, "I told you if you didn't quit coming down to the boat I'd get out of the Cin trade. This does it—I'm switching to St. Louis–New Orleans right now."

A cold hand squeezed Molly's heart until she could scarcely keep from crying out with the pain.

Meanwhile Kansas bled.

There was a demand that the country west of Missouri and Iowa be organized into territories. Stephen A. Douglas, a senator from Illinois, had offered a bill which repealed the Missouri Compromise in that it left the decision as to slavery in the hands of the settlers themselves.

This made everyone go hog-wild, and the race was on to see which side could get the most folks into the territories to vote their way. The pro-slavery newspapers carried items calling upon the proprietors and captains of steamboats not to receive on board any passengers going to Kansas under the auspices of abolition societies. The editors of the anti-slavery papers shouted, "Infamous."

What Molly read was confusing except for the fact that Americans murdered Americans, aroused in their passions by one John Brown, titled Ossawattomie, who came as the liberator of the slaves.

Sides were being taken.

She herself couldn't choose. She couldn't join the passionate abolitionists, confident that God was with them. How did anyone know whom God favored? She couldn't join the passionate Southerners, frightened, but claiming their rights. If only the North would let slavery fall of itself, if only the South would let the North have its great industrial power, if both of them would let the thousands and thousands of people she had seen go past her door open up the immense West.

A letter came from Rutland Hall.

Papa wrote that if he had ever had any doubts as to the advisability of leaving America, this outrageous conduct of the abolitionists in the West would have swept them all away. So now he was putting into effect his plans for speedy withdrawal. He had gradually and quietly executed a considerable liquidation of his American holdings. He had taken advantage of the great burst of prosperity following the Compromise of 1850. By the time she received his letter he probably would have completed the sale of Rutland Hall and the slaves. Ambus, she would be pleased to know had brought more than anticipated, $2500.00.

"And you, my dear Mary, bone of my bone and flesh of my flesh, I do wish you would accompany me to the land of my sires. I am willing even to capitulate and permit you to bring your children, even the unpleasant one whose name slips my memory . . . This is your final opportunity to escape a country about to enter a black civil war which can only result in all being, 'BROWNED'. "

Gracious Papa had made a *bon mot*. Papa—jovial!

"Stop playing that dreadful game," she cried to her children. Cory had taught Lucy a game, *Uncle Tom and Little Eva*, which Hester had given her. It was played with pawns similar to checkers. Each side was a family made up of pawns to be separated, chased, and captured. Cory played Lucy's side of the game as well as her own so that Lucy never won. It was always Cory who screamed, "I won, I caught Eliza."

Molly wondered if Mrs. Stowe herself might not be surprised at the reception of her book. Mrs. Stowe made her Northern characters evil; she endowed the Southerners with nobility so that they would see the evils of their way of life and release the slaves from bondage. It worked out differently. The Northerners were the ones who should have been infuriated. Instead the book made every abolitionist, folks like Hester, see every Negro with a cut-off ear; every black back was a groaning Uncle Tom, every ninny a grinning Topsy. The abolitionists said, "You can't break up the Union for slavery." The butternuts said, "You can't break up the Union for abolition," and northern speakers swore by the sacred tomb of Washington, forgetting that he too had owned slaves, to keep the fires of American patriotism in their bosoms burning bright and fair. Even children had caught the fever.

Molly cried again, "Stop it, Cory, stop it, I say."

Hester came to her, "The whole of Rivertown is talking about you teaching your slaves to read and write with Cory."

"They're not slaves. They're free children of manumitted parents."

"You'd better stop it, Molly."

"The town's down on me if I have slaves. I sent them south, I'm still a soul owner. I free them, bring them to a free state but I'm still a slave owner. Even though I free them, I accept the responsibility of feeding them, clothing them. I give them money to spend.

"But when I start to teach the ninnies to read and write, the town tells me I can't do it. What is this freedom of the North that denies a ninny the right to learn more than just to make his mark? How is he to care for himself as a free man?"

"But you have to draw the line somewhere," Hester insisted. "The freed Negro's services should be limited to menial ones not requiring his letters."

"How can he own property and do business?"

"He can't do either. I am very pleased, Molly, that you have seen the light and freed your slaves. Your sleep must be refreshing without this guilt upon your soul. But you must not make the mistake of carrying your revelation of God's will to excess."

Good heavens! Molly thought. Anything I do is *always* misunderstood by Hester. Now she credits me with being an abolitionist!

Molly had started teaching the ninnies after Julee had come to her and said, "Matt, he say, now us chilluns are free they oughts to read an' write. Matt say I mus' teach 'em. He won't believe I done forgets how. He say I wants to pestigate him."

"Very well, Julee. You may send the children to join my lessons for Cory and Lucy Belle. See that they come clean. I'll not have a dirty ninny in my schoolroom."

It was Cory who scared Julee's ninnies until they all cried, even big Quercus, that they didn't want to read and write. Cory was a little she-devil who made the ninnies' black velvety eyes pop out of their heads at her lies of how Gran Hester Blaisdell had a great big dark cellar made especially to put black folks in who wanted the read-and-write freedom.

Julee said, "Matt, he say us thank you kin'ly Mistus Molly, us ninnies they waits a while to read an' write."

These past three years Molly had tried to show affection for Cory, and win her love, but the child remained in bondage to her own little self. Molly sorrowed for Cory and feared for her family's future. There was so much to see to and no one to help her with the responsibilities.

When she had returned to Rivertown she had expected little but hoped much. Now she was tired, worn out, and the situation had her whipped. The past three years were as three lifetimes of sorrow and pain.

Molly sought out Captain Cleve in his rocking chair on board *The Rising Sun.*

"What's to become of me?" she cried. "What should I do? Papa wants me to go to England with him, Levi has left me, he'll never come back. Half the time he doesn't even send me any money. Oh! I'm so lost. I haven't anything, not even a country. When I'm north I *feel* with the South, and when I'm south I *feel* with the North."

"I know, I know, my dear." Captain Cleve pulled his shawl closer about his shoulders. "There ought to be something an old man could say to help a younger person get along. Old age is the durnedest worst disease. Look at me, nothing but a bunch of wheezes and swollen limbs. Blast!" He hitched angrily in his chair and winced at the pain his body gave him in retaliation. In a calmer voice he continued, "There's only one thing I might say has helped me if I can find the right words to put it to you." He paused to find them. "When I can't change something I don't like, I try to figger out how I'm goin' to get along with the circumstance as it is. Then I feel more of a man. But if I dodge it, I feel meaner 'n tarnation. Gets to be a question with me how I can stand livin' with myself."

"Do you mean if we accept life we grow, and if we reject it we die?"

"That might be one way of puttin' it."

"Well—", Molly said, "I guess I'll just have to accept not knowing what's to become of me. I can't go to England with Papa. And I don't know what I'll do if the fighting starts between the North and the South."

"We're in for a peck of trouble. The real trouble's not slavery. That would right itself. No, the real trouble is who's got what and politics. Most troubles are. But folks can't or won't argue the real issues and try to figger a better way to use nature. Instead they make something into a cause and get properly riled up about it; they fasten their teeth into it and no power can make them let go. This country keeps on askin' itself to wade knee-deep in blood and by cracky this time it looks like maybe we would."

"Can't anything stop it?"

"Only one thing, cordin' to my way of thinking."

"And that—?"

"For folks to realize other folks got a right to their own opinions and to stick to their facts, stead of their feelin's."

"But slavery—is it right or wrong?"

"That's the feelin' side of the question. The *fact* is nobody's got the right to interfere with the slave-holdin' states, and they got no right to try to spread slavery. How are Julee and Matt gettin' along?"

"Not too well."

For some time Molly had been deeply concerned about Julee and her tribe, increased recently by two more ninnies, Bursus and Opie. Molly's household now consisted of twelve—not counting herself—ten of them black. It wasn't the proportion which bothered her, it was filling their stomachs through their ever-open mouths. They raised as much food as they could against the uncertainty of money sent by Levi. To date they hadn't suffered actual hunger but at times it was "mighty lean pickin's." What was worse was seeing Matt, Quercus who was almost sixteen, Ohio and Liney, thirteen and twelve, sinking into no-accounts with slovenly ways because they had no work important to them. She had seen how idleness had affected the slaves at Quercus Grove.

There were times when Molly fervently wished she would waken to find Julee's muchly enlarged cabin empty and the door left flapping and know that the wooly-headed nuisances had taken themselves off to follow the star which pointed north. But there was Julee always at the bin, "Us need more . . . . us blankets raggedy, us cold . . . us shoes wore out . . ." One day Matt in a discarded stovepipe hat of Levi's said, "Us works for our keeps."

Molly knew scolding words would have no effect on Matt. He was being badly treated, not given a chance. Caesar, Rutland's old coachman, had said of horses, "Bad tempers and bad habits come from bad usage." Matt was a good man turning into a no-account through no fault of his. Matt didn't earn his keep, he let Julee do it. Matt hadn't had to pay one penny to free himself and his children. Some slaves bought their own freedom. Maybe she had let him get his too easily. If he'd look around him he'd see how free white men worked. When challenged Matt said, "You promised us a livery stable. Us waits you start it."

So Molly told Captain Cleve of her plan to start a livery stable but said she hadn't been able to do it because she hadn't the means to buy the horses, their feed, the carriages. Now, however, the opportunity for such a business in Rivertown was greater than ever. The Ohio and Mississippi railroad went through Bluffton—only eight miles away and the county was building a pike to meet it.

"They are? Who's working?"

"They brought white men over from the Kentucky knobs for pikers. They don't dare hire slaves. I tried to get them to give Matt and Quercus work but they wouldn't do it. They said the white men wouldn't work with blacks." Molly sighed. "Well someone's going to start a livery service to Bluffton. I wish it was me."

"That'll cut in on way-point trade for the steamboats—a pike connectin' with the railroad."

Molly blamed herself for being so tactless. Way-point trade was the livelihood of old sick captains running antiquated steamboats like *The Rising Sun*. How could she have been so thoughtless as to rub in Captain Cleve's poor plight? She couldn't even say she was sorry; she just had to let her eyes speak for her.

Captain Cleve, twinging with pain, reached for her hand and patted it. "Never mind. Don't feel sorry, you've only helped me make up my mind. I've known right along I should sell this old tub of mine and come up the hill but I hated to come up just to die. You're in partnership for a livery stable, Miz Blaisdell—if—," he was as shy as a young man asking to be allowed to pay his respects, "—if you'll have me."

So Rivertown got a new business, signaled by a fine sign LIVERY and FEED and in very small letters C. Cleve—Prop. But everyone in Rivertown knew that it really belonged to Molly Blaisdell since Captain Cleve had given her the whole she-bang and a good thing too, " 'cos I know for a fact she ain't got the money even for grocery-store trade—and *him* eatin' good on his *Hoosier Girl* and pleasuring himself with female passengers. I've heard a-plenty.

"An' her a-slavin' away tryin' to keep her head above water and not lettin' on there's anything the matter. And sweet! Lord love us she'll go to no end of trouble to help a body out. Look how she's taken that old sick Captain Cleve right in. Yes, I know he's leavin' her everything but reckon it ain't enough to make up for what she's doin' for him. He's another mouth to feed—another chore to take care of. She's a good woman—Molly is. Even Hester Blaisdell admits maybe in the beginning she might have been mistook about Molly. Why Molly Blaisdell is just as *common* as any of us."

Molly now knew better then to ride down to the boat landing in one of the carriages with black Matt on the box and black Quercus up behind. A person like Miz Taft could do it in Cin, but Miz Blaisdell if she had business down the hill could walk there. So she sent Matt to haul other folks where they wanted to go, which suited other folks just fine.

Matt strutted like a new man and all the ninnies strutted like their father. Wasn't he now a moneyed man with everything set up proper in the lined book where Mistus Molly "in'ed and out'ed" his worth, Julee's and all "us chilluns?"

It took a lot of time, patience and effort on Molly's part. She put into practice some of Mammy Fay's plantation routines and added new ones. She was up early every morning to start the day. After breakfast she inspected the ninnies for the sick signs and cleanliness. She parcelled out work for each to do according to his ability. She measured and gave out the supplies, doing the bookkeeping so that Matt and Julee could know how many quarts of meal, how many pairs of shoes it took to provide for them and their children. The household under control, she then went to the stable.

Molly was meticulous in the supervision of the stable: every hoof was inspected for dirt, stone bruise, or loose shoe, every hair from mane to tail had to be curried and clean, each body free from harness scalds, stalls had to be properly shoveled out and fresh-strawed, rigs dusted and ready. When everything had been duly approved or corrected, she then gave Prince, stallion emeritus of the stable, a lump of sugar.

The stable ritual completed, she returned to the broad hall of the house. There she shivered while the hard chalk squeaked on the gray slates of Lucy and Cory in the front chairs, Julee's ninnies in the chairs behind. Matt now said to his children, "I lick hell outen you iffen you don't read and write the freedom way." Lessons finished she'd go see the needs of her patient, Captain Cleve.

The days became weeks, the weeks became months.

One day Levi appeared.

"To see Cappy," he said. "Heard he was heading for his last crossing."

Levi sat with Captain Cleve a short time. When he was leaving Molly tried to detain him. But he said, in that new chilling way he had toward her, "It's no use."

Captain Cleve soon grew worse and needed ever-increasing care. The past held his mind, "They're all gone. The old compromisers, Clay, Webster, Calhoun, they're all gone. The new ones—"

"Now, now, don't stir yourself up, you'll bring on an attack."

"Durn fools—if only they'd figger out how to use this country 'stead of fight—." He had so much more he wanted to say but now had to fight just to keep breath in his body.

Once after a long silence with eyes closed, when she thought he was asleep, he said, "What is truth? Too bad Pilate didn't wait to find out. Might have saved a sight of trouble."

The doctor came again and again to scar Captain Cleve's arm with his lancet to bleed him to syncope. Still fluids gathered in his body which had to be tapped and drawn off by the pailful. He was purged off with calomel until his salivated gums grew so painful he could scarcely stand the fluids Molly spooned into his mouth.

He complained, "Durn if I ain't taken enough calomel to load *The Risin' Sun* and been let of enough blood to float her. I'm beat, Molly. Have Matt set me in my chair, keep me under opium and let me go 'thout any more torment."

His eyes begged Molly not to leave him. Once when the room was filled with sunshine he said, "It's gettin' gloomy dark." She never knew when the filmed eyes quit seeing her, but as long as they opened and closed she sat where they might see her if they could. His fingers would press hers from time to time and once she heard his poor sore mouth say, "My little girl."

At times his hands moved back and forth across the top of his sheet as a boatman passes his hands on the lead line used in the dark to take soundings. Every little while his hands would stop as though he examined the signals at intervals as they went down. "Four Feet," he sang out at what he must have thought was a piece of flannel woven into the rope. His poor lips whispered with difficulty the sing-song chant of an old boatman sounding the depth of the water so that the Pilot far above him could put in for a safe crossing.

One day Molly had to bend close to hear his whispered, "Mark Four." The single leather strip with its one round hole signaling no bottom had gone down. After that he didn't speak again. The old boatman drifted into his last crossing.

She wept for the loss of her dearest friend but when she was done weeping there came to her a thankfulness that she had been privileged to be so close to this man of goodwill, kindly understanding, and gentleness. He had touched her at that inner core of her life where her loneliness lay.

She would try to make his charity and spirit her own.

CHAPTER XXX

Without warning in the early autumn of 1855 Hester was "tuk" with a stroke.

By evening of the day Hester was stricken, the Rivertown ladies were of the opinion that the stroke, while a heavy one, hadn't paralyzed anything vital. Miz Blaisdell might live on quite a spell and then again she might not. It was hard to tell—; they'd known folks, take Lizzie Freeman for instance.

At their evening consultation over Hester the ladies decided that a few days would likely tell, and any number of them were willing to put everything of their own aside and "set up" until they knew which way the wind would blow for Miz Blaisdell. She was a spare, strong woman which would stand her in good stead now she was struck down, and it wouldn't be any trouble to stand right alongside their friend and neighbor in need.

We-e-e-l, if Molly thought she could handle it alone—yes, sure there was Ira, but what's a puny man in the hour of trial—mebbe Miz Blaisdell, if she was to come to and know, might not like to have that black wench Julee putting her black hands on her—yes certainly if help wuz needed there wasn't one of them who wouldn't come running on the double, but goodness gracious they'd be scared out of their wits if they saw Matt's black face at their door. A body had to be mighty careful these days with the "soul hunters" chasing through town every whipstitch looking for runaway slaves.

At last she closed the door on them with a feeling of relief. It wasn't that she didn't appreciate their kind intent but she felt this was her job. Molly was glad that she, Julee and Matt had got there so promptly when Ira had sent for them. Ira said, "Seems like we ought to get her to bed. Don't see how—"

"Yes, sir," said Matt. Then in a second by some simple kind of movement he had Hester, piggy back. Her armpits hung on Matt's huge shoulders, his big, black paws held her crossed arms on his broad chest. He carried her up the steep narrow stairs and laid her upon her bed.

"Julee and I can manage, Pa. You and Matt wait within call."

Hester, the indestructible, now had to be cared for like the tiniest baby. Molly thought, I don't believe she would mind, now, that I am the one to look after her. Once she would have. She even seems to be a little fond of me—since Levi.

"Ma!" Molly said softly and stroked Hester's unconscious brow before starting to undress her. To Julee Molly said, "Take off her shoes and stockings." Molly's fingers hesitated a moment above the buttons on the front of the bodice where Hester's hands—now stilled—usually kept fumbling as for reassurance that all was well within. Molly sent a silent powerful thought toward Hester— please Ma, you don't mind any more that it's me, do you Ma?" Then with swift fingers she laid back Hester's bodice, the under-garments, the inner stays.

There within the folds of Hester's flaccid breasts lay a key.

It was a brass key, a strong key, capable of throwing a stout bolt, an important key, a key to guard valuables—a key to lock away and hide secrets. It hung from Hester's neck by a strange necklace of braided rawhide made in a curious way. The leather strands had been woven to a length which would reach around Hester's neck comfortably with a bit to spare. As one braids hair the ends of the rawhide had been brought together in one firm braid so that the necklace could not be slipped over her head. Further along the single braid had received the key, then the leather strands had been braided so cleverly and securely that it was hard to tell how the ends were fastened. Hester had risked no untying or loosening of the key. It could not be misplaced, lost or stolen without her knowledge. It was a key Hester would guard with her own life. This key was a part of her—a part of her mystery.

Julee said, "Us gots to cut this old halter thing off Mistus Hester. Us gets a knife."

285

"No Julee."

"Us must!"

The note of anxious insistence in Julee's voice made Molly look at her sharply. Julee quickly changed her expression. "Us only means dirty, old leather halter on a sick woman be in the way, maybe make Mistus Hester oh so-o-o sore."

"No, Julee. We have no right. When Mrs. Blaisdell comes to she'll want to know the key is there."

"What iffen she don' come to?"

"Mr. Blaisdell will know what to do."

"How long it take her come to?"

"I don't know, Julee. The ladies say the time varies."

"Us hopes to Jesus God she make it soon."

At last they got Hester's long spare body into a prim white bedgown. Its high neck covered Hester's secret.

Below stairs Molly was tempted to say to Ira, "What is this crazy device, like an albatross, your wife hangs around her neck?" She refrained. If Ira knew about the key then he would know what to do about it. If he didn't and she felt in her bones that he didn't, it was not her duty to tell him—at least not just yet.

Ira said, "Seems like the boys ought to know about their ma. 'Course Gaithe couldn't come clear from Oregon even if I could get word to him. Reckon I better just wait a spell and see how things turn out for Miz Blaisdell—then write Gaithe."

A silence hung in the room.

In it Molly's heart beat faster. A surge of gladness went through her. Surely if Levi came home to see his ma—surely—! Perhaps Hester, after all these years of antagonism to Molly, would be the means of bringing Levi back to her.

Ira said, scratching his chin, "Reckon I *could* get word to Levi." He sent a sharp questioning glance at Molly.

"Reckon," was all she could manage from her too-full heart.

"I wouldn't do it, Molly, less you want me to. T'aint right Levi should stay on the Mississippi—away from you. There's good enough trade on the Ohio. His ma's been right worried over you two. She used to say if Levi philandered it would be your fault but she says you've changed these last years and Levi's got no call to go on behaving the way he does. I keep tellin' her we mustn't meddle, you got to settle your differences yourselves. Nobody can know all the things between a man and a woman. But Miz Blaisdell would take comfort in knowin' things had been put straight between you and Levi."

"Send for him, Pa. Write out the message, Matt can carry it to Bluffton. Send it—*telegraph*. Send it to St. Louis, Cairo, Memphis, Vicksburg, New Orleans. Have Levi come home to see—his ma."

That evening Ira stood in front of the fireplace studying the embers left after warming up the evening meal neither he nor Molly had wanted but "you have to keep up your strength for what's ahead," the ladies had insisted.

Ira turned his worried, puckered face toward Molly. "I was just calc'latin' on Miz Blaisdell's fire. Reckon I ought to tuck a few coals to bed in her kettle for her. I can't remember a night all the years we been married not seein' her takin' care of her fire—makin' everything tidy for the night—a scrub to her hearth. Don't seem right—I plumb don't know what to do—ain't no sense to puttin' coals in kettle 'gainst mornin's need when all a body's got to do is put a friction match to a handful of dry shavings—'declare it's more'n I kin decide."

"I'll take care of it, Pa. You're too tired to decide anything. You go right up to the boys' room and go to bed. I'll see to things down here. Julee's watching Ma. She'll call me if she sees any change."

Molly was alone with Hester's fire.

Her first night in Rivertown as a bride she had been an unwilling witness to Hester's ritual with the fire. Then in her lonely hours of seeking for truth, she had come to realize that behind the facades of people like Papa, Mammy Fay, and Hester were deep passions which they never allowed others to see—that perhaps they hardly glimpsed themselves. Perhaps they too carried a burden in the deep, dark recesses of self which they longed to lay down as did she. No one could guess what Hester may have suffered nightly on this hearth. Only some age-old inner suffering could have bound Hester a slave to this fire upon her hearth. It was not her place to judge Hester for what she did through some compulsion beyond understanding, but she could perform with loving care the task which Hester was unable to do for herself.

Molly dropped to her knees. She drew Hester's black iron kettle close; she removed its perforated lid. With a shovel she selected the best, the most lively glowing coals, banked them carefully within the kettle, covered them with the lid and set the kettle to one side as she had seen Hester do time and time again. She

287

brought the necessary things and by the light of a stub of a candle she began to scrub Hester's white-ash floor boards.

The key, the key, she thought suddenly as she scrubbed the brush, it must be to the cellar where Hester hid runaway slaves. Why else had Julee been so excited about the key and tried to get it off Hester? A light burst upon incidents which had puzzled Molly for some time. Julee and Matt were a part of this underground-railroad business because Julee was always at the bins.

"Us got no grits for us supper."

"But surely Julee you can't have used all you have taken. Look at the book."

"Us don' care for freedom closeness. You forgets the book, Mistus Molly. Us totes what us needs—no more."

Molly's nose twitched in memory of dark nights when she smelled, wafted from Julee's cabin across the yard, the odor of hot fat frying. And Molly wondered how many had stolen their tired way across the cold river to stumble up her gully path into freedom land, how many runaway slaves had filled their aching empty bellies on Julee's hot cakes made with meal from Molly's own bins? Then she remembered at the livery-stable morning inspection how often she had seen her horses with drooped haunches, hanging heads, closed eyes, stumbling feet. Again and again it was a tired stable she inspected. Finally she realized that the mornings she found the horses tired were the same ones when her food bins were low.

"These horses have been out. Driven! Hard!"

"No'm, Mistus Molly, these horses they ain't been nowheres at all. You looks at you' book you don't see any mark like you told me to make. No ma'am, these horses ain't been no place at all 'cept right in us stable. No ma'am!"

How many runaways fed from her own bins had been carried on to the next "station" by her very own horses?

How many had been hidden in her own mother-in-law's cellar?

What if there were some hidden there now?

She took the stub of candle and found her way down the winding narrow stairs of Hester's cellar. It was a small cellar like any other Molly had seen in Rivertown. It held screened shelves swinging from the ceiling holding crocks of butters, "put-down" meats, its walls were lined with "put-up" cans of fruit and vegetables, bins holding the supplies of food for the coming winter.

It all looked innocent enough, but long ago Asa Cranch had said, "Don't reckon you could find it the clever way it's hid—." Why of course now she remembered that it was connected with the wood shed. Asa's words came back to Molly, ". . . folks in those buccaneer, bandit, Indian days allus had a way to get out if a body got hedged up."

Molly set her stub of candle on the upstairs table, took a shawl from its hook and found her way to the wood shed. She would have liked a lantern to light her way but she didn't dare; someone might see her. In the wood shed there was scarcely room for her to stand, so full was it of the coming winter's fuel. She would have to know exactly which sticks to move if she were to find the entrance to Hester's secret cellar. She took a stick of wood and rapped on the wood-shed door for attention and called, "Is anyone there?" There was no answer. "You must tell me if you are there. I must know if you have water. You are in no danger. Answer me, do you have water?" No answer came. She wondered how long a person, even a black one, could live without water. Molly decided she could wait for a time and then she'd have to do something. Did Ira know the secret door? Matt? Julee? Maybe Asa Cranch was the only one who knew how to find Hester's secret cellar and Asa was far away in Oregon with Salena and Gaithe.

Through the long lonely hours of watching beside Hester, Molly's mind moved in circles of one trouble after another.

Hester regained consciousness the day following the next and was able to swallow a little though she couldn't speak. She had a general paralysis. The ladies who brought calves'-foot jell and other delicacies said sometimes it happened that way and other times maybe only one side was "tuk." According to them, Miz Blaisdell had a little stroke but it managed to hit all over like, and any time they could be of any help just send somebody over.

Folks were staying kinda close to home these days on account of the fugitive-slave business. Made a body afraid to be out after dark and goodness gracious if a body got caught harboring one or helping one get away it cost three hundred dollars and a time in jail. But a body wanted to do her part to a neighbor in need and if Molly wanted help to just send word.

Hester could understand what was said to her but she couldn't answer except with her eyes.

That evening when Molly was bathing Hester's face she said

gently, "I know about the key, Ma. If anyone's in the cellar Pa better take the key and let him out."

Hester's eyes grew excited.

Molly said, "Doesn't Pa know about the cellar—the key?"

Hester's eyes said, "No."

"Ma! Is there anyone in there?"

Hester's eyes said, "No."

"Then don't worry about it, Ma. Nobody has seen the key but Julee. She won't tell. She knows I'd thrash her within an inch of her black life if she did."

An expression in Hester's eyes made Molly ask, "Does Julee know where the secret door is?"

Hester's eyes grew too excited. The ladies all said it was bad to allow such cases to get excited; it was apt to bring on a second stroke.

"Now, don't worry, Ma. You're getting better fast. Presently you'll be up taking care of things yourself. Pa got a message from Levi. He's coming to see you, Ma."

Hester's eyes brightened.

Molly said, "You'll stay a few days, Levi?"

"No. Got things to do."

"You'll come up to our house for the night?" He gave her such a cold look that she added feebly, "—for a little visit—," and still more feebly "—just to see how it looks."

Levi exploded, "Look, Ma's being sick doesn't change things between you and me. You can't take me in with your play-acting a daughter to Ma."

Levi! Levi! Her heart cried, What can I do to make you believe I've changed? But she said nothing.

Levi slammed out the door and soon there was heard the whistle of his *Hoosier Girl* and his "kal-e-ope" playing, *Dem Golden Slippers*. Once again Levi had steamed away.

One evening Molly was alone in the house with Hester, Ira having been sent off to enjoy a well-earned evening of fun at a lodge meeting. Hester had been readied for the night, sponged and powdered, moved to the other side of the big, double bed where the two feather ticks had been plumped to cool freshness. She'd had a last sip of water from the spout of a small china teapot and let her eyes thank her daughter-in-law for the ingenuity of her care.

Molly leaned over and laid her cheek against Hester's and said, "Goodnight, Ma. I have a few things to do downstairs before I come up to bed myself." She smiled down at Hester and said gently, "I have to put your fire to bed."

Hester's paralyzed mouth twitched slightly at one corner.

Molly on her knees before the embers was startled by a noise behind her and turned.

It was Julee, breathless, her eyes rolling like dice in a box, her face the color a Negro's becomes when drained of blood. "Us pulls the curtains," she whispered. She ran from window to window.

Molly got up from her knees, "What's the matter, Julee?"

"Us mustn't be seen. Us gots to have the key. Us gots no place to hide him. Us gots him outside. Us can't ride him out tonight. They already cross the river."

"Julee!" She couldn't bring a fugitive slave into Hester's house. And yet, Molly knew Julee could. "Mrs. Blaisdell can't have any excitement! it might kill her."

"Us knows." Julee's dark, velvety face crumpled. "But he one of ourn, Miss Molly."

"One of ours?"

Julee sobbed and nodded her head, "His poor back—he sold ter white trash—low-down white men what never before owned niggers, he boughten his slaves, no 'herited niggers. That kind git ter thinkin' too high of theirselves. All his niggers say they pure hates his guts. He gits mad like a hive of bees an' lets fly with his ole mule skinner. He lays on the lashes. The smart ones holler right off. But Ambus he too proud—"

Molly's ears grabbed the name from out of Julee's garbled hysterical chatter. Ambus was the cutest ninny who had ever swung in Rutland Hall's fly-sweeper swing and Papa had sold him for twenty-five hundred dollars. Molly felt her mouth go dry; from a tightened throat she said, "Is he *our* Ambus?"

"He ourn," sobbed Julee.

"His back, his poor back, Miss! Ambus he big proud Rutland nigger, most the finest. Ole white trash ties him to a tree. Ambus he not holler, even, he say, when the blood he felt runnin', he say he quiver, he shake, he puke in his own blood on de groun' but he mouth he never open in a holler. He say to hisself he a Rutland boy, he don't belon' dat white-trash man. He don't 'member when it ended but when he come to, he already rolled in a larded sheet. First chance he git he run off. Take a mighty long time 'fore he gits de chance. Matt he tell Ambus, 'you lucky boy, you make it. They kill you fer sure iffen they catch you.' Ambus, he say, he 'member all Matt tells him where us is at. Once he gits here he knows he safe 'cos he ourn. Yas'm he ourn, iffen he don't look it."

As indeed he didn't when Matt brought him before her.

Oh God!

For many a long, weary day his half-clothed body hadn't been filled with sow-belly and hoecake washed down with buttermilk, not to mention reward merrymakings of ham, chicken, and white-flour biscuits. He must have dragged his bare splayed feet the whole long way. His sore, cracked lips curled back on his white teeth, gave an ugly animal snarl to his black face. This couldn't be Ambus.

"Us made it, Miss. Us made it to you in freedom lan', Miss Mary Marie. Us belongs to you. Us a Rutland boy."

But he didn't belong to her. He had been Papa's property which Papa had sold to some man for hard money. By law that new white-trash owner had every right to find and claim his property. A person caught hiding a fugitive slave was fined three hundred dollars and thrown into prison. It was a risk she dare not take. But Ambus had risked, was risking, his very life by claiming his right to be a Rutland slave. Yet Papa had had no compunctions about selling a Rutland slave to a cruel master. Why should she have any about turning one back? The Papas of this world were the smart ones. They always came out the winner. What did it matter if a few pawns were lost in the game and went down in defeat?

There was no end to her burdens. She simply could not take on anything more—even little Ambus. Julee and Matt would have to take him out of here. It was up to them to do their own fugitive slave running.

"Waits 'til you see his back," Julee said. "Turn 'roun', Ambus. Up you' shirt tail."

At the sight of the red welts and ridges on Ambus' back, Molly had to put a hand on the table to steady herself. This could not be human flesh. She felt frightfully ill.

"Us gots to hide him, Mistus Molly. Us gots to get the key to the cellar."

With one part of her mind Molly rejected involvement in this illegal situation—with the other she was remembering Mammy Fay and her lectures on the Rutland responsibilities to Rutland slaves. Her thoughts were chaotic, her emotions raw. Papa had no *right* to sell Ambus—little Ambus.

Yes, she'd hide him! Cut the key from Hester. Use it. Hide Ambus. Free Ambus. She took a candle, held it high to light her way up the steep narrow stairs.

She felt a movement behind her, heard Matt's whisper, "Us got no time. The mens after Ambus, they here."

There was a loud rapping on the front door below.

"Get Ambus up the stairs, don't open the door," she said quietly. Ambus mounted swiftly in spite of his tired, splayed feet.

Molly knew at once that she had made a mistake; there was no safe hiding place in Hester's narrow upstairs.

Ambus' urgent whisper, "Lordy Jesus, not now, Lordy Jesus us *made* it. You broughts us all the way. Lordy Jesus hide us once more an' us never asks again. Help, Miss—help!"

The knocking below grew louder and shouts of, "Open up—," in coarse men's voices.

Molly opened the window in the narrow landing at the top of the stairs and put her head out, "What's wanting?" she cried.

"In the name of the law open up."

"What law?"

"Fugitive-slave law, ma'am. We got the right to search your house."

"We have sickness here." If only she could get time to cut the key free from Hester. She wasn't even certain that Matt and Julee knew how to get into the cellar. Asa Cranch had said it was cleverly hidden.

"Yeah!" The voice was nasty. "We heer'd that a-fore. There's nothing for it, ma'am; you better open up 'less you want us to break down your door. If you ain't got no fugitive you got no fear," the voice drawled, "but if you have—."

"You'll have to give me time to dress, I've retired."

"Oh! That don't bother us none, ma'am." They let out silly man-giggles as if they might have liquor inside their skins.

She slammed the window shut and hurried to Hester's bed, shading the candle so that the room was in shadow.

She leaned close to Hester and saw her eyes open and knew Hester needed no explanation.

Molly whispered, "It's Ambus, a Rutland slave. I've got to hide

293

him." Where, Hester, where? She knew Hester couldn't answer her so she didn't voice the question. Hester who had helped so many fugitives for so long would know what to do, but Hester could neither speak nor move.

Meanwhile the men below were pounding louder and louder. And they had the law on their side!

She looked frantically about Hester's bare room. It offered no hiding place for Ambus. One hand swept through Hester's dresses hanging in a closet, one peep under the bed, and Ambus would be a captive.

If Hester weren't in the bed she might try hiding him between the feather ticks—.

"Quick Ambus, between the ticks."

She fluffed the feathers to give him as much air as she could, enclosed the ticks with the bottom sheet and drew the bedclothes up loosely. She took one of Hester's paralyzed arms and laid it upon the counterpane beneath which Ambus lay. Even though she knew he was there, her eye couldn't detect Ambus' thin, starved body beside Hester's.

Then she picked up the candle, ran downstairs and unlocked the door.

Hester, who came from good, tough stock did not die from the shock of having black Ambus crawl into bed beside her. Indeed, she had improved to a surprising degree by the time Ambus sent the sign, a single bright feather in an envelope Molly had addressed to herself, telling of his safe arrival in Canada.

And Molly was able to move back to her own dog-trot house.

During the past several years on her own, Molly had grown up enough to make good use of the experiences of the past weeks. Finally she was free of the spiritual drags of her love-hate for Papa, her animosity toward Hester, her fear of Mammy Fay's black machinations. She was becoming mature and whole. She had tended Hester and nursed her back to a semblance of health; she had helped expiate her father's sins to his slaves by sending Ambus on his way to freedom.

With the country on its dreadful divided state, Molly had become integrated—acquired a perspective impossible to her former self-centered childishness. As with the larger errors of both the North and the South, she realized individuals were not totally

294

responsible for their peculiar personalities—they were the result of so much that was beyond their control.

Now she could forgive Hester's meanness, Papa's coldness—even her own selfishness. But she still had much to compensate for. Along the way she had picked up many obligations of her own which she had not fulfilled satisfactorily. She had failed Levi as a wife—no wonder he wanted none of her. She had failed Cory as a mother—no wonder Cory was ornery and mean. She had let down both husband and child. Gaithe! Salena! How many others?

Then she awoke one morning to a rooster's crow. She smelled the wood smoke rising from Julee's chimney; she heard Matt whistling softly on his way to the stable. A gentle breeze came from off the river. She raised herself high on her pillow. Truly it was beautiful, Levi's river, now that autumn's rains had covered the ugliness of summer's low water, washed over the piles of driftwood bleached gray in the sun, the stench of rotting fish on the hard-baked yellow sand, the exposed tree-roots crawling like snakes over the yellow, eroded banks.

Now the banks ran full, a wide ribbon wound around the hills. On the hills themselves, autumn had appeared slowly. Gradually had come a softening over the hills, colors as soft as those of spring, and old timers had said, "Not goin' be much color this year." But they had been wrong. Suddenly the hillsides were brilliant with the red blaze of hardwood trees, tulip trees with crowns of gold, hickories, and beeches yellow and brown, oaks, wine-red. The morning sun came over a Kentucky hill and shot its first beam through an old-rose dogwood tree fairly taking Molly's breath away. Then she heard the weird sad note of a boatman's horn from off the water. She bounded out of bed and ran to a window. Levi! Levi!

Her mind had played her a trick; Levi was no longer a flatboater; he was a steamboater on the Mississippi. But there really was the sound of a boatman's horn. And soon a flatboat swung into view. At its sweep was one of the few old "ripple-kickers" left on the Ohio. She watched until the flatboat floated from her sight.

Levi! Levi! We're wasting time. Come back, Levi, come back, she cried.

CHAPTER XXXI

In the spring of '56 Molly with the help of Ira decided to branch out with her livery business. Ira had done well building stout wagons to carry folks on their way west.

"Yes *ma'am,* 'low I could build an omnibus capable of hauling folks in safety to the cars at Bluffton."

In a way Molly felt like a traitor to Levi, the riverman, when she pushed her own business by taking advantage of the "iron horse." But she had felt the pinch of tight money this past winter and she had so many mouths depending upon what she earned from the livery. She needed to buy so many shoes, so many dresses, pants and shirts, so many woolens, so many covers in the cold winter. And Levi had grown so careless, so irregular about sending any money in spite of reported good trade on the Mississippi in contrast to the Ohio. Therefore Ira encouraged her to take advantage of the "iron horse."

An item in a Cin paper told the story. "There does not appear that same activity on our wharf that was wont to gladden our eyes in the days gone by. Merchants and manufacturers look to speedy shipments and prefer rail to water. Travellers do not generally care for expense and want the quickest route, preferring the jolting car to the elegantly fitted-out steamer." Cin was no longer strictly a river city. Last year, '55, she had reported that she was exporting about as much east as she was south, most of it going by rail. And this spring, '56 saw not a packet of the famous Union Line on the Ohio. Along with many others, it had joined the call of the West.

To compete with the railroads, the boats went all out to empha-
size the luxuriousness of their mode of travel. But the live-freight
—ladies "in hoops again," that monstrosity of fashion, and gentlemen in stiff, starch-standing collars and narrow bow ties, hair
moderately long, curled and parted at the side, side whiskers or
beard all around—did not make up above deck for the lack of dead
freight below.

To Molly's eyes, the new omnibus couldn't possibly have looked
any finer. On a sturdy wagon bed Ira had built seats running
lengthwise; for overhead protection he had mounted ribs and
canvas like a Conestoga wagon. At the rear he put a small narrow
door with little steps which could be unfolded for passengers'
descent. Up front was a high box for Matt complete with whip-
stock and whip, brake bar and lever.

Ira said, "Do you think it should have a mite more red on its
wheel spokes?"

"No," said Molly, "it's perfect."

Matt said, "Looks same-likewise de bandwagon. Us glories in
its ambiguity. Us hitch up now."

The bus was pulled by descendants of Prince, a fine pair of
sturdy matched bays. Molly fondled their soft noses and they
in turn craned their necks toward her pocket for their reward of a
lump of sugar. "Git-up," said Matt, lifting the reins. The horses
leaned into their harness with good spirit. Behind them in the
roadway's spring mud they left deep fresh tracks of Rivertown's
first omnibus off to meet the "cars" in Bluffton.

Now, while Molly's bus rolled to meet the train, a boat might not
pass her house for two hours. There had been a time when she
could hardly lift her eyes without seeing one. La Belle Rivière
was a strumpet, the hussy's very origins were a part of the riverman's defeat. She sprang from rapid streams, rugged hills and
poor soil, while her competitor, the Upper Mississippi, came
gently, 'twas said, through rich soil and level lands. The railroad
shied away from this rugged country and swift streams, preferring the old trails west where the huge Conestogas had found the
easiest going. For this reason St. Louis and Chicago were becoming more important than Cincinnati and Pittsburg.

These changes reached far back onto the rugged knobs where
men worked their fields, slanted between sky and river, with old-
fashioned scythe and grain cradle instead of mowing machine

and reaper; where they threw a bag of grain across a mule's back and rode to the grist mill. Less and less came down off the knobs to the boat landings for shipment. No more in autumn did long lines of wagons wait for unloading, no longer did River-towners have to seek safety, behind fences, up galleries' high steps, within doors, from droves of hogs being driven for slaughter.

"Why?" Molly asked, already knowing the answer. Northern enterprise. The mouth of the Mississippi had been rolled back to New York, Philadelphia, and Baltimore. The pull out of the Ohio's valley was no longer to New Orleans by water but by railroad to northern ports.

But surely the South still needed what the North had and the North still needed things from the South. The North said, "Pooh-pooh!" Northerners felt so high and mighty because they had economic sufficiency. "The South's got to do what we say." The South said, "Pooh-pooh!" Southerners could teach the North its place in one short brilliant campaign—of war. Sides for sectional conflict grew ever sharper.

In far-away Washington, the highest court of the land argued the case of a Negro, Dred Scott, suing for his rights as a free man. The old Kansas wound of the abolitionists had broken open again, stirring up the whole fester of slavery and bringing fugitism again to a high pitch.

Molly thought sadly of her need for Levi—especially with Cory who was still a difficult child. Oh, Levi, Levi, we do need you! But now with trade on the Ohio not so good he had no reason at all to come home to them.

She told herself sternly that she mustn't allow herself to get depressed; there was a great deal to see to. But first she'd freshen herself, take a sponge bath, put on a clean dress, and go out on the cooling board where she could relax from her routine pressures and enjoy her inner freedom. Much was uncertain—yes—but now she knew she could rely on herself. She was free to grow.

She stood before her wash stand in her chemise and tipped the Queen's ware pitcher to fill the wash bowl. She laid the cool sponge to her eyes and it felt good.

Someone came with heavy footfalls up the front steps, opened the front door, and stood in the dog-trot hall.

"Who's there? What's wanting?" she called.

The heavy footsteps came to her door; a hand lifted the latch, swung open the door.

She stood staring at Levi—her husband. How old and tired he looked! Something dreadful must be the matter with him the way he slumped against the door jamb.

"Molly!"

"Yes Levi," she said. His manner over the last few years held her off, kept her from running to him, clasping him to her.

He continued to stare at her.

"Levi! What's happened? What's wrong? Why do you stare so?"

"I want to look at you, Molly."

She became conscious of her appearance, an old rail of a woman caught in her shimmy tail, her breasts sagging, her hair every which-way, her face stiff with soap. She felt at a disadvantage before Levi's staring eyes; her body was too old to be seen in the bright harsh light of day. "I'll dress," she said.

"No, Molly," he said. "Just stand there the way you are. I want to see you just as you are."

She stood uncertainly and had to fight to keep fear from mounting. To stand so before Levi took more courage than anything she'd ever faced up to. Oh! dear God don't let him see me as I *look*, let him see me as I *am*.

Levi went on: "He said you'd lost your looks, that I had taken your girlhood, misused you, forced you to hardships, made you miserable, unhappy, worn you out. Did I ruin your life, Molly, like he said?"

"Who said all this?"

"Your father."

"Papa! You've been to Rutland Hall?"

"No, he's staying in New Orleans. He had someone watch for the *Hoosier Girl* and came down to see me. Molly, you never told me he wanted you to go to England with him."

"Since I wasn't going, it wasn't necessary for you to know." To hide her emotion she turned to the wash bowl, rinsed the soap from her face and dried it.

"He's giving you another chance, Molly. He's waiting for you in New Orleans. You'd better go. Business is not so good, even on the Mississippi. I've been taking reverses with this Kansas trouble. I can't give you the things you want, and I reckon you and me mebbe kinda overcrowd each other. You ought to go with your pa. He can give you the kind of life you were used to—the kind you want. I can't."

She stood quietly and spoke gently without bitterness, "No Levi, I'll never go with Papa. If you feel that you and I can't manage together," she let a smile play on her lips, "you're free to go. I'll not bind you in any way. I can take care of myself and the children. You're free, Levi, free to be yourself."

"Molly!" Her name wrenched from his throat like a groan.

"Oh!" she gasped as her eyes looked within his where she had never looked before, and she saw now how much he still loved her.

So finally—all the tight heart-squeezing fears were past. Against his blue broadcloth and gold-plated buttons she whispered, "It's too good to be true—it's better than I deserve. Oh! Levi, my Levi, what if I had gone?"

"Your pa made it clear to me that I was selfish—thought only of myself. I want you to have a fair chance to start over again. After the way I've been acting I couldn't very well expect you to believe that I want you—need you—the way a fish does water."

Here was no youth who was the leaping trout of the waters, no bodacious ripstaver young man who boasted of being half-horse, half-alligator—this was a gentle, understanding man who loved her enough to free her.

And now it was the second Sunday of April, 1861. In March Hester had taken her place beside her little daughter, the first Cory, in the family burial plot. Molly missed her and grieved for her own Cory, to whom Hester had been so close.

There came a rap at Molly's door—Julee, with her morning coffee.

Julee had no comprehension of how difficult it was to buy coffee to put in a cup. When Molly told Julee to omit her "open-you eye coffee," Julee had replied, "Un-nnh!"

"But it's pure silly of me to let you bring me coffee in bed."

"Us bring, us got the right, us milk sisters."

Molly laughed, "You know, Julee, I used to be jealous of you because I thought you had a prettier whorl to your belly button than I. Mammy Fay tied yours while some dirty old doctor man tied mine. Aren't young-uns funny the ideas they get?"

"For God sure!"

Molly and Julee were quiet.

Then Julee said, "How you reckon you' papa and Mammy Fay make out in that faraway England place? Reckon they cat and dog it there same as they did here?"

Molly said, "Probably. They've got the habit. And by now they've both forgotten why they hate each other. But they really need each other. Papa holds Mammy Fay and Mammy Fay holds Papa."

"Reckon so." Julee sighed. "Us gots us own pestigation worriments."

"What's the matter now, Julee?"

"Us don't want to speak, but Matt say iffen us don', he's goin' to."

"What is it, Julee?"

"It's this-a-way, Mistus Molly. Matt, the chilluns, everybody got that old Mr. Itchy Foot. Matt say now us don' fugitate no more, on account of Mistus Hester she gone and us not got her big cellar, us don' got no purpose to stay, us be better off to go somewhere's away from the river. Dat ole river, hit slave on one side an' free on other. The paterollers they scare us niggers. Matt he been studyin' on the signs an' he say hit's gettin' close to the time us makes tracks out-a here on account of hit ain't no place to fetch up the free chilluns. They get kotched an' took back acrost that ole river mos' any night. Matt say there's goin' be a war among the white folks."

"Where would Matt go, what would he do?"

"He gits the word from Ambus, again. Ambus say Canady not satisfy him. He come away to Boston. Ambus say he makin' out pretty good with white folks in Boston. He send word does Matt come, he job him in biggedy liv'ry stable, no little old rottendy one like ourn here. But Mistus Molly," Julee screwed her face tighter into the worriment wrinkles, "I swear a-fore the sweet lovin' Jesus God, I won't run away from you. Who take care of you, does I go? Mistus Molly you got to do somethin' about Matt, what the Lordy God cain I do?"

"All right, Julee. We'll plan something. In the meantime why don't you take them all fishing and have a fish fry? There won't be a soul in Rivertown who'll want to hire a rig on graveyard-cleaning day."

"Thank ye kin'ly, Mistus Molly. You think on what to do while

301

us go fish-fryin'. Iffen you don', Matt, the chilluns, every last one of 'em,—they run away—gone like shelled corn. They pestigate us mornin', noon, and night."

After breakfast Molly told Julee to hurry with her work and get gone. She, Cory, and Lucy would fix their own picnic basket to take to the cemetery.

Every spring Rivertowners set aside a Sunday, after church, for graveyard cleaning. Families, men, women, and children, who had their dead in Cedar Hedge (everyone had someone), went out to spring clean for their loved ones. They took the necessary tools and cleaned off the debris of winter, cleared the poison ivy out of the periwinkle, cut grass, propped up tombstones and planted flowers. It was an all-day affair but not given over to unhappy memories. Folks called cheerily back and forth across the lots, came to borrow a hoe, stayed to lean on it and pass the time of day. Current-day gossip vied with lively stories about the departed, and many a courtship began at a graveyard cleaning. No, it was not a day of sorrowing.

Lucy said, "I wish Pa was here so's we'd be a whole family."

Levi had returned the *Hoosier Girl* to the Cincinnati–New Orleans trade only to have the river turn against him; navigation was often closed. For two hundred days out of the three hundred and sixty-five the Ohio hadn't been able to float even a fully loaded flatboat. River conditions had been much as they were back in '38, Molly's first year in Rivertown—dried up half the time, frozen the other half. Only now Rivertowners were hauled to the cars at Bluffton in Molly's omnibus while the *Hoosier Girl* sought business on the deeper Mississippi where competition was keen and not very profitable.

Then in '57 came another trade revulsion which just about finished Levi and his steamboat. The only way he remained afloat at all was by sticking to the Ohio where he carried both passengers and freight at low rates and in small quantities. It was a humiliating, sorrowful day for Levi when he had to watch for any chance hail on a lonely shore and push the *Hoosier Girl's* proud nose into a hole in the willows for a coop of chickens. Finally he was forced to tie up for three months. His cheeks sagged with despair, his eyes told her how downcast he was from the failure of his *Hoosier Girl*, who in spite of all his efforts to keep her shining, gleaming, began to look like an out-dated, broken-down, dirty old tub of a steamboat.

Molly cried, "Let's give her a fresh coat of paint." And they did, even when Julee complained, "Us gots no grits for supper."

At last Levi said he was going to Cin to take another chance; things looked a little better again. He was there more than two weeks getting enough cargo to head South. When he landed but briefly to tell Molly goodbye he said, "Got four hundred tons of freight and a hundred and forty-six passengers. Look at them, Molly. A hundred and twenty-four of 'em are ridin' deck, only twenty-two's got staterooms. I can't leave you a cent. Reckon you'll have to make out, somehow."

"Reckon. Don't worry, Levi. I'll manage."

Levi wrote that business wasn't much better on the Mississippi, he was still moseying in and out of the willows but he'd heard things were a mite better up at St. Jo and by God he'd get the *Hoosier Girl* there if he had to feed her boilers with her own guard rails.

But from St. Jo he wrote that he hadn't got a paying load the whole way and that business was as flat there as on the Ohio. He was going to try to get the *Hoosier Girl* down to St. Louis where he'd look for a load for the South. He'd seen lean times on the rivers before but never had he heard rivermen belly ache so much over it. By this time he felt so low he all but dragged his tail on the cracks in the wharf's planking and from the amount of activity on any one of them it'd be better to plow 'em up and plant them in 'taters.' To a man, the boatmen wanted to sell out their boats. The only reason they didn't was because there were no takers. Levi said he wouldn't sell the *Hoosier Girl*, but if business were brisk it would be easier to sell her for $30,000.00 than for $10,000.00 right now, and he hoped Molly and the children were getting along all right. He wished he could put in words what it meant to him to know she was pulling a strong oar for him back home.

Business had picked up some but nothing like it used to be; or maybe business was good again, but the way of doing it had shifted. The steamboats had done away with the flatboat business, and now the railroads were doing away with the steamboats, and by and by something else would push the railroads out. Molly hoped the steamboats would last Levi's time. They would, she thought, if the North and South didn't each overcrowd the other with their passions. There were strong wills on both sides—hot heads. Would they be willing to recognize that changed conditions in the country already had forces at work which would automatically solve the problem of slavery? Would they be willing to wait for these forces to act gradually or must they hasten them by violence?

Lucy laughed and said, "Ma you've gone wool-gathering again."

"So I have. My gracious, we haven't even put the eggs on to boil."

Just then Cory came into the kitchen and looked into the baskets, "Ma, you know I don't like deviled eggs; they rile up on me. I don't feel so good. I don't feel like going to Cedar Hedge."

Molly looked at Cory, *her* daughter, a big fat lump of a girl. She'd tried hard to right things for her and she'd keep on trying but it looked as though she was too late. With impartiality, Molly had dressed Lucy and Cory alike, but she thought she had made a mistake when she had fixed their differences forever in a daguerreotype. Lucy was dainty and darling with her lace-ruffled pantaloons peaking from beneath her full skirts. But Cory! Cory took one look at her likeness and sobbed, "I hate myself." If only Cory wouldn't eat so much. "You don't even want me to have *anything* to eat. You'd like me to starve!"

Now Molly said kindly, "Oh you'd better come along." One of Cory's troubles was wanting to be wanted; she held off in order to be pled with, scolding, anything to get attention.

"I want to go," sang Lucy, placed, rooted to the whole of Rivertown. "Everybody goes to clean their own. We'll do Gam for Gramp."

Ira, free at last, had picked up his westerly journey which Hester had interrupted by refusing to carry her pot of fire beyond Rivertown. Molly remembered now what he had said:

"I'm jest goin' to light out and go. Reckon I'll end up with Gaithe and Salena but first I want to see all the track my wagon wheels have made. I aim to know what I mean when I say, 'these here United State of Ameriky.' I want to know what I'm talkin' about."

But now Cory was jangling again for attention. "I don't want to clean a lot of old graves."

"I do," sang Lucy, "Ma, will the periwinkles be in bloom?"

"Oh yes!" Molly said, trying to keep her delight in Lucy from showing.

"I love periwinkles—they're so blue."

The very color of her eyes, Molly thought fondly. To Cory she said, "You'll feel better, dear, if you come with us."

"I don' wanna."

"Not even for Gam? She'd like it if *you* especially came to tidy the place where *she* sleeps. You meant a lot to her, Cory, and there is that other Cory for whom you are named."

"She wanted her, she didn't want me. Gam wanted me to be that other Cory. I hate the graveyard, I hate Rivertown, I hate this old log house—. Why can't we have a nice house like other folks?"

With some difficulty Molly had convinced Levi, or so she hoped, that she no longer cared a tinker's damn if she didn't have a fine house across the gully on the higher bluff. She had urged him to go ahead and sell the land. They were plenty comfortable in their clapboarded log-cabin houses with the wide dog-trot hall between, not to mention the added wings.

"But Molly, I want you to have a fine house."

"Oh fiddle-de-dee, Levi. You're a boatman and I'm your wife. We'll roll with the river, my Levi."

She would never, never try to force him away from what was as natural to him as the breath he drew. She was a trifle tardy with her efforts, but a riverman she'd help him to be.

"I love a log house," said Lucy, who always loved everything and everybody.

"I hate you most of all," shouted Cory.

Molly's heart cried, Cory, Cory! Aloud she said, "That will do, Cory."

Lucy came close to Molly and leaned against her. She rubbed her cheek over Molly's hand. "We'll have fun, won't we, Ma? Ma, will you let me do little Philip for my very own?" Lucy pulled away from Molly in order to look at her. "What's the matter, Ma? What made you jump?"

"I thought I heard a boat. Run see."

She hadn't but she must have a few moments alone to compose herself. She had laid the terrible burden of unwantedness upon Cory because of Philip. Too late she tried to love her but Cory was so hard to love. Up to now she had failed but she would have to

305

keep on trying. For she herself certainly knew how hard it was to be an unwanted child!

"Ma! Ma!" Lucy came running. "You did hear a boat. It's the *Hoosier Girl*. Pa'll be here for the graveyard picnic."

Instead of putting in at the Public Landing, the *Hoosier Girl* steamed up to the Blaisdell gully where Gassy Sanders pushed her nose in close to the pink and white rifts of spring bloom. Molly ran out onto the river bank to see what ailed Levi. She hadn't heard him make such a to-do with the *Hoosier Girl* since the early days. Fiddler Jim was lost in a cloud of steam while he blared the "kal-e-ope," the whistle was blowing, the bell made of silver dollars jangled its sweet sound. And not a single passenger at a guard rail for the landing! Where were the passengers? What *was* Levi up too? *Where* was Levi, the captain of the craft?

The *Hoosier Girl* was so close in on the high spring fresh that with a good running jump Molly could have landed on her hurricane deck. She said hello to Gassy Sanders in his pilot house almost level with her. Her eyes searched every deck for the fine figure of the blue-broadclothed, gold-buttoned captain of this palatial craft, empty of passengers. A deck hand in homespuns lounged in the shadow of the doorway to the Texas. She nearly jumped out of her skin when he raised the captain's silver speaking trumpet and spoke right into her ear, "Sweet as Punkin and cute as a pair of little red shoes." It was Levi!

Here was the Levi she had been afraid she might have lost. He was her Levi, completely whole again, a bodacious riverman full of brag and bluster. He again wore his homespuns as only Levi could wear them so that you thought of the man within them and not of what he had on outside. He was the same Levi she had fallen in love with that day on the New Orleans levee. Levi! My Levi!

"Come aboard, Molly." He spoke again into her ear with his trumpet. "I've got a present for you." He tipped the silver tube toward the main deck. "Lay her a gangplank," he bellowed in a true Levi bull roar.

The bride of the river went aboard.

At once she recognized the smell of horse, the urine-soaked straw. She heard stomping and neighing. "Levi, what are you doing loading the *Hoosier Girl* with horses? Oh, our lovely *Hoosier Girl*, she stinks just like a stable and so do you."

306

Levi grinned, "Reckon I do. Been kinda busy shoveling out."

"Levi! You didn't—! Why what will the passengers—where are they anyway? This is a mighty funny kind of a steamboat."

"No passengers, Molly. I'm home to tie-up."

Oh no! He shouldn't have to go through another tie-up. Really, Levi had taken enough of a beating. Why, if he didn't have a good season this summer he'd be back on a worse snag than he was in '57. Levi was no longer a young man to be buoyed by the hopes of a better tomorrow. She knew bad days lay ahead for him; she only hoped she would find the way to help him off the bars when he got stuck. "I thought business was better," she said aloud.

"A little, Molly, but what there was has been knocked clean to hell by this Sumter business. There's not a thing moving on either river."

"They won't fight. They'll have more sense. They'll find some way."

"Sure, they'll fight, Molly. They *want* to fight. The first gun's already popped off."

Molly gasped.

"You don't have free trade and free navigation after a six pounder shoots across the *A. O. Taylor*'s bow down at Memphis. Between the goldurned cotton planter and the goldurned abolitionist they've managed to kill river trade deader'n a door nail."

Poor Levi!

Levi said, "I've got worse news for you, Molly."

"Bad news?"

"Yes, they've fired on Sumter. The war's started, Molly. North! South! They've overcrowded each other."

"Oh Levi! How dreadful!"

Levi said, "I didn't know how *you'd* take it, Molly."

"Take it! Why Levi Blaisdell! South! North! West! No one part is important. But put altogether we're a great country. Fools! Fools!"

Through a window of *Hoosier Girl* she could see the great rifts of pink and white bloom filling the gully beside her house and then she remembered Aunt Debbie, the old pioneer with her sunbonnet, on *The Rising Sun* chattering of the trees of betrayal and the trees of the Cross blooming side by side as a reminder.

"Bully for you, Molly. I feel that way myself. Got to learn to roll with the changes when they come. 'Pears to me you and I are all set for whatever comes, eh Punkin?"

"Yes Levi, that's right, no matter what comes."

" 'Course river trade is already dead on the Ohio, no matter what happens. You see that for yourself, Molly. It's the same all up and down river, just the same as you see from your own windows," Levi said.

She had known it for a long time, but she hadn't thought Levi did.

"Toward the end Cap Cleve thought the river was about done for. The railroads will not only take our business but set our rates and regulations too. Cappy said when it happened a man should recognize it, and not try to roll with something that had quit rolling. I've quit, Molly."

"But Levi, you're a riverman."

"I'm a trader too, Molly. Hardly seen money this whole trip. Been swapping up and down the Mississippi. Figure I can't lose on horses no matter which way the wind blows; men will either ride 'em to kill each other or to settle up the country west. Either way horses ought to be good for trade."

"So that's your present, a boatful of horses?"

"Naw! You come take a look."

He was a beautiful colt.

"I figgered Prince was getting kind of old for a good horsewoman like you. The fellow I swapped this one off of said he was a good race horse. I knew you wouldn't want just *any* horse after Prince. How does he look, Molly? Is he all right?"

She could have wept at the anxiety in Levi's voice that perhaps he hadn't judged well enough for her. "He's beautiful, my Levi."

In the dusk of the lower deck he bent his long strong body toward her, his arms folded her closely to him. "Say that again."

"My Levi, my Levi."

"It's been a long time, Molly."

They were quiet, each holding the other close.

"Come along, we'd better get up the hill. It's graveyard-cleaning day. I'm so glad you got here but you'll have to take a bath," she said, leading the way up the path.

"Me? Take a bath? Why?"

"Because you stink of horses, my fine Captain Blaisdell."

Levi grinned and threw his arm around her waist, pulling her close. "We'll see who has the bath, Half-Pint." They both laughed in memory of the bath Levi had given her when she had wailed at "this wooden country." Oh it was good to see him bodacious again.

He said, "Got to get Matt and the boys to see to unloading these critters."

"I let them go on a fish fry."

"Christamighty, Molly! What a way to do business! Close up shop!"

"I thought nobody would hire a rig on graveyard day."

"How d'you get so smart you can figger what the other fellow's going to do? Here I need Matt worse than tarnation and you've got him off on a fish fry. Gosh all hemlock! It's high time you had a man come up the hill to tend to this livery business." Oh, Levi would take care of Matt's restlessness.

Juba this and juba that. All of her went pat, pat in a happy rhythm—all of her except that which told her she had failed with Cory. This, too, she would have to learn to accept.

Her whole body swayed freely in the wilderness of her time; she swayed westward to the far reaches of the country; she swayed southward to the red heart of the land; and she swayed outward to that future, not yet known, where a new world waited.

"Gee whillikers! Takes your breath."

"What Levi?"

"The gully full of pink and white bloom. Makes a body feel good to see it again."

She saw Levi now with a fresh eye. There was something indestructible about him. He knew how to roll with life. Levi had always been free, always able to accept things; his time with its blunders and setbacks, the very injuries it dealt him. He was vitality itself. She realized now that it was this quality in Levi which had first attracted her to him, held her, and would hold her to the end.

A new vitality filled her now too. There wasn't enough water in the whole of the Ohio and the Mississippi to drown her spirit; the hills weren't steep enough to use up all her strength. She turned to Levi and answered his smile with one of her own. Free in the warm, bright, steady air, she turned toward him. Her love for him was so great that she could love him and have love to spare— enough for the whole world. And she felt she was fashioned in some extraordinary way. She was the first, the only woman, to stand up-right beside her man.

So she put her Molly hand in Levi's and walked up the gully path to the old dog-trot house, now a new home secure against all dangers and failures, newly furnished with understanding love.